I0736979

Fragrant
HARBOUR

R.R. Lycette

Published in Australia by Sid Harta Books & Print Pty Ltd,
ABN: 34632585293
23 Stirling Crescent, Glen Waverley, Victoria 3150 Australia
Telephone: +61 3 9560 9920, Facsimile: +61 3 9545 1742
E-mail: author@sidharta.com.au

First published in Australia 2022
This edition published 2022
Copyright © Estate of Ray Richard Lycette 2022
Cover design, typesetting: WorkingType (www.workingtype.com.au)

The right of Ray Richard Lycette to be identified as the
Author of the Work has been asserted in accordance with the
Copyright, Designs and Patents Act 1988.

All rights reserved. No part of this publication may be reproduced, stored in a retrieval
system, or transmitted, in any form or by any means without the prior written permission
of the publisher, nor be otherwise circulated in any form of binding or cover other than
that in which it is published and without a similar condition being imposed on the
subsequent purchaser.

This book is a work of fiction. Any similarities to that of people living or dead are purely
coincidental.

Ray Richard Lycette
Fragrant Harbour
ISBN: 978-1-925707-97-7
pp414

About the Author

Ray Richard Lycette was born in Levin, New Zealand, in 1929. His father, Ernest, was an English coalminer who enlisted as a private in the British Army in the First World War and left as a captain. Following emigration to New Zealand Ernest worked as a council overseer. 

Ray worked hard, became dux of his college and was awarded a medical scholarship. He met and married Gillian while they were both students. After graduating, he became a pathologist and worked in Hawkes Bay for twelve years before moving to Hong Kong in 1973 with Gill and their youngest daughter, Elizabeth, while their three older children remained in New Zealand.

In Hong Kong he worked in the Queen Elizabeth Hospital and the Kowloon city morgue, where he conducted post-mortems on swimmers escaping from China and anyone who died in suspicious circumstances in the city. Ray said all the events described in *Fragrant Harbour* were possible; he witnessed many of them, including the stock market bubble, and used written accounts from refugees to describe Wa Hing's rescue of his mistress.

Ray described Hong Kong in the seventies as a colony where four and a half million people lived in a social and economic system similar to England a hundred years earlier. He visited China during the Cultural Revolution and remained fascinated by Chinese history and politics all his life.

He and Gill witnessed great change in Hong Kong during the eighties, particularly during Governor MacLehose's term. They lived in Hong Kong until 1986, making friends with many Chinese and Europeans from all levels of society. They then migrated to Australia where Ray worked as a locum pathologist for Sullivan and Nicolaides Pathology, one of the country's largest and most respected pathology services, until his retirement in 2002.

Ray died in 2012.

Fragrant Harbour has been edited by his daughter, Margaret Atkin, and his widow, Gillian Lycette.

Also by RR Lycette

Red Dragon in a Green Circle, set in Hong Kong, the United States and China, continues the story of Woo Sing following a Russian invasion.

www.lycettebooks.com

To Ray's friends in Hong Kong

Chapter 1
Dangerous crossing

Woo Sing's arms felt heavy, their rhythmic movement independent of any conscious action on her part. Her earlier willpower had long ago lapsed into nothingness. Several times she was aware of choking, or swallowing seawater. Occasionally she vomited a searing combination of salt and bile. She clung to the hope that Wa Hing was the small black blur in her immediate line of vision. Ahead of him loomed the dark mass of a headland, towering and threatening, never appearing to get closer.

They had entered the water at dusk, Ah Hon following her. Wa Hing had gone first, a few strokes ahead in the vastness of the dark sea. They had shared the last of the stale rice cakes in silence, trying to crush their fear. The distance felt even greater with each fleeting glance in the fading light. Woo Sing wondered if any of them would see the dawn. Many had set out on this swim yet few ever wrote home. Nobody knew whether the sea or the city had swallowed them.

They knew the disgrace that would follow if they allowed

their fear to persuade them to return to the commune. They would be shackled to the lowest jobs forever. The resigned face of Woo Sing's aunt appeared as in a dream. There was no sympathy in her look, only misery, for now she would have to bear such added shame.

A ripple of water hit Woo Sing, draining her remaining breath. A loud ringing sounded inside her head; numbly, deliriously, she realised death was near. Strands of sea plants wrapped around her legs, gently restraining her, slowly pulling her downwards. Blackness closed in, the ringing slowed. Gratefully, she opened her mouth and the water rushed in.

A tight band clamped round her chest. Like a fish on a string, she was jerked up and into the light. Wa Hing stood waist deep in water and dragged her to the beach. They landed on a strip of sand studded with sharp stones and fell down, shocked and exhausted.

A dull pain in her cheek woke her. A stone had abraded her skin as she slept. The sun was already drying the seaweed caught in Wa Hing's hair and a soft breeze playfully piled sand in his ear.

Aching and cramped, Woo Sing struggled to stand. Too stiff to bend down, she nudged Wa Hing's thigh with her foot. He grunted and sat up, coughing up a frothy bloodstained mass. He shook the seaweed from his hair, smiled, and stood as though rising from a good night's sleep.

'Welcome to Hong Kong,' he said, laughing and pulling some of the largest pieces of seaweed from her clothes. High jagged rocks crowded the beach, hiding them from anyone higher on the hillside. Wa Hing found a small hollow where they rested in the shade under dense and windblown shrubs, glad to be alive in this new and exciting land.

Wa Hing suddenly remembered. 'Ah Hon,' he said, scrambling over the rocks.

Woo Sing expected Ah Hon had landed close by. He was a better swimmer than her and had been the last to enter the water close behind them.

Wa Hing returned and shook his head. 'We are on a long strip of rocky coast. Ah Hon could have landed anywhere.'

'We had better meet as arranged at his uncle's house,' said Woo Sing. She struggled to speak, her throat felt as if the flesh had been torn out and only a long, cool drink would ease the pain. They waded around the boulders and clambered over rocks. They rounded a headland into a cool sea breeze, a welcome relief from the heat.

Ah Hon was stretched out on the sand, lying on his side, his back towards them, one arm pillowing his head.

He could have looked for us instead of relaxing on the beach, Woo Sing thought. Perhaps his talk of protecting her had no more value than the commune chief's promises about better wages. Angry but relieved, Woo Sing fell on her knees and roughly shook him.

'Why did you not look for us?'

The body rolled stiffly over, brown eyes already greyish and opaque. Sea lice were beginning to nest in their corners and the cheerful mouth was drawn into a slight sneer. The face, which had once expressed so much, said nothing, and they shrank back in horror. It was a nightmare never to be truly understood or forgotten. It numbed Woo Sing into a calmness that surprised Wa Hing.

She would have married Ah Hon if they had remained in the commune. She supposed she had loved him. "Love" was a word rarely used by her friends, and she didn't know what it meant. But Ah Hon had been the happiest part of her first eighteen years and now he was dead.

Wa Hing dragged her away. 'We cannot bury him, we must escape, others will find him.'

She calmly closed Ah Hon's eyes, forcing them hard against stiffening muscles. She knew this was the last time she would touch him. They walked on, slowly and deliberately, without a backward glance.

They crossed a mass of broken rocks and on to the next small beach. As Wa Hing jumped down onto gritty sand, he startled a thickset middle-aged man, his back turned towards them. Wa Hing sensed trouble as soon as the man faced them.

'I know you are swimmers deserting the greatest cause in the world and I shall see that you are punished,' said the man.

Woo Sing and Wa Hing feared they had swum in a circle and landed back on the coast of mainland China. He told them he believed in Chairman Mao and would dearly love to live in China but his family wanted to stay in Hong Kong. He realised they were exhausted and broken.

'I get one hundred dollars for each swimmer,' he said as Woo Sing and Wa Hing stopped walking. They realised China was truly behind them. To allow themselves to be quietly led back to the mainland, like two runaway water buffaloes, would be crazy. In Woo Sing's mind this would betray all that Ah Hon had died for.

Wa Hing judged the power of his tired and stiff limbs against the age of the man. Although the man was older, his was the more powerful build. Perhaps they could get him at a disadvantage as he climbed over a rock. He tried to indicate this to Woo Sing but she seemed oblivious to her surroundings. She had caught sight of a chunk of wood, about four feet long and two inches thick, directly ahead of them. Only a few paces away, then two paces. Trembling and sweating with fear and anger, Woo Sing sprang forward, seized the timber and, wielding it shoulder-high like a great sword, struck Chairman Mao's admirer across the throat.

The man was lifting his arms to protect himself as the blow fell. A look of surprise flashed across his face as he flopped down, dead before he hit the sand.

Woo Sing let the wood fall from her hand and Wa Hing flung it into the sea. They walked on without a word being said. She had seen others die during the Cultural Revolution but she had never killed, not even a small animal. Neither her action nor Ah Hon's death bothered her. All she could think about was her burning throat and the drink needed to cool it.

Wa Hing's voice broke into her misery. 'We must tidy ourselves, avoid any villages, and get into the city. Then we can find Ah Hon's uncle and be safe.'

A scattering of houses appeared in the distance, built close to the sea with hills rising behind them. They climbed slopes covered with a slippery and dusty grass and detoured around a wide bay. As they trekked down the last hill towards a sealed road, Wa Hing found a trickle of brownish water. They joyfully sucked up as much as they could. The bay narrowed to reveal a mainland town on the other side.

'Don't look at it,' said Wa Hing as they walked on downhill.

The road was busy, mainly with trucks like those on the mainland, but there were also brightly coloured buses that tooted as they passed. On either side were fishponds and well-cultivated vegetable fields, a few solid-looking houses scattered through them. Behind were more hills with a covering of low trees and grass.

The scene was peaceful but the effects of the swim and three days with little food had exhausted them. *This is torture in heaven*, thought Wa Hing, but he said nothing as he looked at Woo Sing staggering by his side. It was now well past noon and the heat blasted from the tarred road as they plodded on.

A bus stopped to let down a passenger, but when Wa Hing showed the driver the few coins he had, he was told, 'No good in Hong Kong.'

The driver lit a cigarette and put the bus into gear, hesitating as he glanced at the exhausted Woo Sing. An elderly man seated behind the driver leaned forward to give them some coins and the driver, exhaling, nodded and said, 'You can get in.'

Wa Hing found a seat at the back and Woo Sing sat up the front half facing the other passengers. A girl stared contemptuously at her. Woo Sing, enjoying sitting and getting to the city without effort, discounted her contempt and sleepily returned her inspection.

The girl, about her own age, displayed her attractive slender legs without shame, even though the youths sitting next to her were looking at them. Woo Sing noted the fine texture and elegance of the girl's stockings. The cloth of her skirt was of a style and pattern she also found pleasing and she understood the girl's contempt as she thought of her own clothes.

Yet, surely no matter how beautiful the clothes were, no decent woman would dress like that. She must be one of the huge army of prostitutes said to be part of capitalist society.

The skirt matched a blouse that clearly outlined the girl's small but graceful breasts. Colourful earrings provided a final bright touch.

Woo Sing imagined herself in such an outfit. *But I would lengthen the skirt to cover my rather thick thighs, muscular from work in the paddy.* Sleepily admiring the girl's blouse, she unconsciously let her hands rise to her own breasts. The girl noticed and smiled slightly.

Woo Sing felt humiliated as the question of clothing had not occurred to her. She thought most people would wear blue suits as they did at home. Confused and angry, she fell asleep despite the lurching, bumping bus.

When she woke, the countryside had changed, with smaller, less well-tended crops, and houses like in Canton. She wondered if Hong Kong was merely a fabulous city imagined by the peasants in her province.

A few of the passengers were watching her, noting a tall

girl of about eighteen years, slender with a round but finely proportioned face. Coarse clothing failed to completely conceal an elegant figure. Long jet-black hair, roughly plaited, heightened the pallor of her face. Obviously a refugee and close to collapse, but of little interest. They had their own problems. Woo Sing wondered if there were informers among them. She was unaware there was nothing to be frightened of, that none of them was any keener than her to confront a government official.

No one considered helping her and their interest soon faded as several began discussing the price of rice.

Despite her sore throat and aching limbs, Woo Sing turned her head to look at the road ahead for her first glimpse of the city. It was more than she had imagined. Incredible buildings of massive size and great height were jammed together like vast beehives. Concrete towers, slim and shaft-like, appeared to be stuck onto the hillsides like bamboo on a cliff face. The stark look of the huge buildings was broken by festoons of drying clothes hung out by residents of tenements closer by.

The bus bumped past a slender bridge on tall piers. She saw only a few workers, not the huge crowds of men and women who would surround such a project at home. Woo Sing wondered why and then caught sight of a huge crane and gigantic tractor with a vast shovel at its front.

The thrill of seeing the skyscrapers evaporated as they entered the crowded city. The heat, smoke and noise did not encourage one to look any higher than the face of the person opposite. A giant plane flew barely above the rooftops, the shockwave from its engines tearing at the air even in the bus, and yet nobody noticed.

The bus turned sharply off the main road, entered a shaded narrow lane and stopped in front of some rickety stores covered with vegetables and fruit. On one side of the road were filthy three-storey buildings with a wide balcony circling each floor. Litter discarded by thousands of tenants covered the ground around the buildings.

Wa Hing was deep asleep, his head slumped forward, his body thumping into that of his neighbour with each swing and turn of the bus.

Wa Hing's neighbour took his revenge with a sharp dig of his elbow into Wa Hing's chest. He awoke with a cry of pain before realising what had happened. He smiled at the scowling passenger and half crouching, picked his way forward through the baskets and boxes in the aisle.

The driver gestured for them to get out and as Wa Hing stepped down, said in a not unfriendly manner, 'Mong Kok.' With that brief introduction, they had arrived unnoticed in the city of their dreams.

*

A blind beggar squatted between two food stalls. Through a mist of fatigue and hunger, and because she could walk no further, Woo Sing stopped to stare. Wa Hing, a few paces ahead, stepped back to throw some of his useless mainland coins into the old man's plastic feeding cup.

'Do you know Ming Tak Street, uncle?' Wa Hing asked, interrupting the flow of thanks.

'A taximan will know,' the beggar replied.

Wa Hing supposed that a taxi was some sort of government car. That was the last thing he needed.

'Is there any work about here?' he asked.

The old man turned his head towards Wa Hing who wondered for a moment if the beggar was really blind. Puzzled by the question, the old man turned his head directly to the source of the voice to catch every nuance and guess the character of the questioner. Wa Hing waited silently. For all he knew, the beggar might hate refugees and be able to recognise them by their accent.

'There was a fire here a few nights ago and you could get a job cleaning the rubbish,' the old man replied, feeling the coins suspiciously.

Wa Hing dragged Woo Sing away. She had briefly fallen asleep where she was waiting. She could barely walk so he half carried her as he shuffled around a corner to a derelict and burnt mass of timbers and twisted iron. He gently lowered her into a sitting position, with her back against a broad pillar. She promptly fell into a deep sleep.

A cluster of workmen squatted at the rear of the site, obviously waiting for someone. They watched Wa Hing closely as he walked towards them. *They are even more suspicious of me than at home*, he thought sourly.

'I want a job,' he said, trying hard to smile.

Nobody appeared to have heard until a boy about his

own age waved his hand towards a passageway leading off the exposed site. Wa Hing walked along the damp passage, with its acrid smell of wet, burnt wood, wondering if he was going into a trap.

A hand roughly grasped his shoulder. He turned in the semi-darkness to see a short, thickset man wearing a soldier's yellow helmet above a disagreeable face.

'I'm looking for work,' Wa Hing said.

'Come outside,' the man grunted. When they reached daylight, he said, 'Show me your hands.'

Apparently satisfied with the inspection, he said, 'One dollar an hour, start now.'

Some of the workers were listening, but none gave any sign they had heard the offer that Wa Hing accepted. He was certain this was the first time he was being exploited by a capitalist rather than a communist.

'Can I have some tea for myself and my girl?'

After some hesitation, the boss pointed to a battered urn.

Wa Hing filled two large mugs and quickly topped up a small bowl with cold rice from a metal pot. Woo Sing had slumped at an angle against the beam and her face was already partly blackened with char. She woke long enough to drink and eat, wondering vaguely, but not caring, how Wa Hing had found food so quickly. *Perhaps he had stolen it. No matter.* With the sounds of the demolition in her ears, she again fell asleep, head cradled in her arms, half sitting and half lying against jagged and blackened timbers.

Wa Hing was wearier than he could ever remember being.

Even the long harvest days at home had not been so bad and one could always discreetly doze through party meetings.

The swim had taken most of his strength, but the sleep in the bus, the rice and the tea had helped refresh him. Now a strange exhilaration gave him the strength to carry the greasy, blackened timbers.

All his life he had worked hard, not always willingly, but always hard, and he had not swum to Hong Kong to work hard again for someone else. He would soon remedy that. His workmates carried on at a methodical and steady pace, about the same as that in the commune, and he managed to keep up with them despite his exhaustion.

The air was thick with water vapour, dust, and the fumes of the endless line of cars, buses and trucks ceaselessly passing the site. A light breeze that squeezed between the buildings served only to stir the contaminants into a more potent and smelly mixture. By late afternoon, the heat had become intense.

A nearby steam hammer was pounding forty-four-foot steel strips into the ground. The sound of each rhythmic blow physically jarred Wa Hing's body as the reluctant steel was driven into the granite. The glue-like stinking air, the heat and the noise were fast tiring him, but as he saw his work-mates were also slowing down, he kept going. Carefully, and he hoped secretly, he did a little less than his fellows, selecting the lighter pieces and walking a fraction slower.

The light was fading when the boss stopped work for the day and Wa Hing received six dollars with great glee. It was about a month's wages at home; surely they could live for a few days on it.

'Come back tomorrow and see if there is any work,' the boss said before walking away to pay the others.

Wa Hing asked for the remainder of the rice, now cold and sprinkled in soot. 'Okay,' the boss replied, a little surprised as Wa Hing scooped it into his dirty shirt and carried it in triumph to the sleeping Woo Sing.

Woo Sing woke slowly, her limbs still stiff and cramped.

'Woo Sing, be quick,' snapped Wa Hing, and still half-asleep she staggered with him to the pavement.

The city had an energy that alarmed Wa Hing. The pavements were crowded, and people walked quickly with clear purpose. Despite the crowds, there were few collisions of bodies for their pace was uniform. There seemed an unspoken agreement that for the split second that a person covered a piece of ground, it was theirs to own.

Woo Sing noticed most people looked clean and well-dressed. Ashamed of her battered state, she wished for night to fall quickly.

In a long narrow alley off the main street, they found a pile of broken fruit boxes. In a nearby stall the owner crushed juice from cane. Wa Hing bought two glasses and, together with the cold rice, they felt they had enough. The cool, sweet drink soothed the ache in her throat and Woo Sing again began to doze.

'I never thought my first day in the city would be mainly spent asleep,' she told Wa Hing. He smiled for he could see her strength and humour were returning.

He asked Woo Sing to wait before disappearing into the crowd. He found the beggar and gave him a few coins, saying, 'This is a good coin this time, uncle. Thanks.'

The old man recognised his voice and began to curse him, but then felt the coins and thanked him profusely, leaving Wa Hing to wonder if he had been too generous.

When he returned, he woke the sleeping Woo Sing to shift her further into the alley. He found a small gap between empty stalls. Piling some packing on the ground and broken cases in front to hide them, they crept into their bedroom and settled down to sleep. The traffic had slowed and although the air was like a slimy blanket, they were in the city and content. As Woo Sing fell asleep, a mangy dog with several large scabs over its ribs sniffed at her filthy trousers but soon moved on.

Chapter 2

First impressions

Shortly after dawn, Wa Hing was watching and listening for early hawkers. Woo Sing still slept, but stirred noisily when someone knocked over a box at the entrance to the alley. Not daring to whisper, Wa Hing gently covered her mouth and shook her arm. She woke, rigid with fear, and struggled to free his grip until she recognised him.

A group of men entered the alley, moving quietly and talking in low tones. Wa Hing briefly saw a chopper reflected in the first rays of daylight. Sweating with fear, Woo Sing watched Wa Hing move into the alley in time to see the last man silhouetted against the dawn light before he turned off the path.

'We must go now,' whispered Wa Hing.

Woo Sing replied plaintively, 'Wa Hing, I have to ...'

'Do it in the straw,' he said, walking away into the alley. Woo Sing was glad that their corner was still dark.

Afterwards, she joined him and he said gently, 'Never mind, Woo Sing. Today will be a lot better.'

It was painful to resume walking with all the bruises and strains of the previous day, but there was no choice. There were already people on the streets, absorbed in their own business.

They turned a corner and a cool salty breeze chased away the humid air. Wa Hing led them through streets and alleys, always keeping the breeze in their faces.

'Today we will find the sea,' he said, and Woo Sing wondered why, for yesterday they had fled from it.

They passed a wharf with a few lighters and fishing boats. The streets were frighteningly similar—like an endless nightmare. Woo Sing slowed, but Wa Hing walked on. The terrifying thought of losing him made her increase her pace again, painful though it was.

'Don't lose me, Wa Hing,' she said, panicking.

He pointed to a nearby food stall. There were dumplings and bean curd; neither looked warm but would be good enough with hot tea. They made their purchases and sat on the heavy planking that bordered the wharf, watching as the rising sun picked out the outlines of a great building across the harbour. As she gazed across, Woo Sing forgot her bruises and wondered at this city of miraculous wealth. Surely if there was enough money to build this place, there would be enough for all who lived in it.

She began to laugh and Wa Hing joined her as she put down her bowl of bean curd and danced along the wharf. As Wa Hing clapped, she noticed the storekeeper watching, astonished but amused. She was filthy, shabby and smelt terrible, but she did not care for she was alive and had arrived.

As they returned the bowls, the food seller grinned. 'I enjoyed your dance. I swam across ten years ago and I too felt like that.'

Wa Hing began to deny it, but the food seller said as they walked away, 'Do not fear me. Good luck.' When Wa Hing returned to ask where Ming Tak Street was, the food seller pointed at a red, battered car.

The car was the owner's house and livelihood and he was still asleep when they rapped on the window. He was annoyed at being woken and grumbled about working late.

'How much to Ming Tak Street?' asked Wa Hing.

'Five dollars,' the owner replied, looking at his two clients and judging how much money they had.

'Three,' countered Wa Hing, and they settled on four, which was all they had left.

The deal made, the owner leapt from the car with such vigour that Woo Sing and Wa Hing stepped back in alarm. Ignoring them, the man raced into a public lavatory and returned in the time most men would take to undo their clothes.

'A powerful bladder,' chuckled Wa Hing, but Woo Sing ignored him. He was known for making inappropriate comments and had been criticised several times at youth meetings for them.

The car owner waved aside the food seller's suggestion of breakfast and pushed his two customers into the back seat. They jolted off in what Woo Sing quickly realised was a far from luxurious vehicle with the springs in the seat penetrating the more delicate parts of her anatomy. Wa Hing was seemingly unaware of this, and as they hit a big bump, she wondered if he had an iron bum. She blushed at this indelicate thought, wondering if he had influenced her. Rough as he was, she now trusted him.

A small plastic horse, suspended by a string, dangled in the middle of the windscreen. She thought it must be a lucky charm. Only much later did she learn that it was a receipt for protection money paid to the triads. If the driver displayed this week's plastic toy, he was safe. After passing through several narrow streets, the car entered a four-lane highway.

The tops of the buildings were lit by dawn's rays, with the lower parts still in semi-darkness but sufficient for Woo Sing to see incredible displays of clothes and furniture and luxury items. She wished the car would go slower.

'What shall we tell the old man about Ah Hon?' Wa Hing asked grimly, breaking the silence.

Shock and disgust overcame her as she realised that she had forgotten about him. His death still seemed so unbelievable that she had not grieved.

'We better tell him the truth,' she replied.

'He may not allow us to stay with him,' warned Wa Hing, and she knew how serious that could be.

'I think we should tell him that Ah Hon felt weak before he entered the water and said he would come later,' suggested Woo Sing.

'Why didn't we stay with him, then?' asked Wa Hing.

'Ah Hon insisted we swim on,' was the reply. It was a lie, but she could not think of anything better, and she imagined Ah Hon would have approved if he had known.

The car entered a large housing estate with greyish-brown, four-storey buildings packed close together. The outside balconies were laden with washing and pot plants. The general effect was congestion and squalor, and yet the people on the crowded balconies and streets did not look downcast.

Block twenty-five was identical to block twenty-six and block twenty-four, but they hoped that in twenty-five they would find a home. The stairs to the fourth floor were narrow and dirty but neither Woo Sing nor Wa Hing were surprised. They knew what a struggle it was at home to keep a building's exterior clean.

We did not come here for clean corridors, thought Woo Sing.

The people who passed them did so on the opposite side of the stairs, watching them carefully and suspiciously.

'It will be all right when we are known here,' whispered Wa Hing, sensing her disquiet.

The doors were shut, and door ten—with its rusting grille—was the least inviting door Woo Sing had ever seen.

Wa Hing knocked several times, and eventually the grille opened. 'Who are you and what is your business?' a quiet and melodious voice asked.

'We have a message from Ah Hon for his great uncle, Tong Pooi,' replied Wa Hing cheerfully.

'We are his friends,' Woo Sing added desperately, breaking the silence that followed Wa Hing's words.

She felt sick at the lies, but they had to find somewhere to stay to lessen the risk of being questioned by the police. The city had already shown it was not likely to look after newcomers.

They heard at least two chains rattle and the clatter of a heavy bolt before Tong Pooi quickly opened the door. As they entered, the old man pushed Woo Sing forward so he could close the door. Only when it had again been bolted did he turn towards them.

Tong Pooi was old, much older than either of them had expected. But despite his shabby black clothes, he had the quiet and ancient dignity of a scholar. The cut of his clothing in the old style gave him an air of authority, mixed with shyness and delicacy of manners. Above his very thin tall and erect body was a large, narrow face sporting a traditional wispy beard, completely white. His deep-set eyes revealed nothing. After a brief welcome, he waited, and it was obvious that his patience would outrun theirs.

They were in a tiny cubicle, about four by six feet, with a small bed and table taking up most of the space. The table carried an ink block, brushes and sheets of paper. They remembered how Ah Hon had told them that his uncle was a letter writer.

Wa Hing briefly described their journey from the commune to the water's edge, their tiredness and hunger, and how Ah Hon had felt too weak to swim but had insisted they go on.

'We argued and nearly decided to return to the commune,'

said Wa Hing, noting the anxiety in the old man's face. 'Ah Hon insisted that one person could hide for a day or two, but three could not, and we would put him in danger by staying.' He had decided that his guilt over one lie might as well cover many.

Woo Sing said nothing, but sensed she was being carefully inspected. Tong Pooi studied her face, not Wa Hing's, waiting to see her reaction. She hoped she looked truthful.

Tong Pooi was silent. Woo Sing and Wa Hing waited, unable to conceal their feelings much longer.

'Thank you for the message,' he finally replied. 'I shall see him in a few days.' Noting their anxiety, he bowed towards the bed and stool. 'Please sit in my humble home.'

Moving with a rapidity surprising for his age, he produced a Thermos of tea and a small plastic container of very stale buns and a scattering of dead cockroaches.

Selecting the bun furthest from the cockroaches, Woo Sing took the initiative. He was less likely to refuse her than Wa Hing.

'We have also come for help, kind uncle,' she said, trying to remember the ancient way of polite conversation. 'We have no money and no place to sleep, but I did not realise that your house was so beautifully proportioned for one person.' She felt pleased with this last phrase. Ah Hon, too, had thought Tong Pooi's home would have several rooms, but it was obvious that three could not sleep there. Woo Sing felt nauseated at the thought of another night in the street.

'I cannot help you find work as my money is barely enough

for myself. But Woo Sing can stay here and sleep on the floor for tonight. Wa Hing can sleep in the little cupboard on the balcony where an addict sometimes sleeps, but I have not seen him lately. Tonight, I will bring home enough food for all of us.'

After his longest speech in many years, Tong Pooi picked up his black brush and papers and guided Wa Hing to the door. Before leaving, he briefly spoke to someone in another cubicle.

The door closed and a young, slender woman came out from behind the edge of the cubicle, carefully latched the door and disappeared as silently as she had appeared. Woo Sing peeped over the wall of the cubicle, which stopped eighteen inches below the ceiling. The room was about fifteen by twenty-five feet, with rough planks and packing cases dividing it into crannies, each packed with mysterious bundles of ancient and battered cloth. There were a few panels of bright paint which, rather than cheering the space, enhanced the grimness.

A long row of bunks reached to the top of the cubicle wall, and on each was stacked the residents' possessions. Small folding tables were stacked neatly against the partitions or filled the last space on the bunk. Most residents had purchased several large plastic buckets for water. There were numerous small stools and an occasional chair for a wealthier resident. The floor, or what could be seen of it, was clean. Despite the crowding and apparent confusion, the room was cleaner than the corridor outside. Wide windows, some with glass but all with bars, allowed a breeze to chase endlessly around the thousands of nooks in the room. Woo Sing was staring gloomily at the ceiling when she sensed a nearby presence. She turned to find a young woman smiling at her. 'I am Seung Mei. Tong Pooi asked me to show you the washroom.'

Woo Sing had forgotten how dirty she was and felt ashamed.

The bathroom was large, with three concrete tubs and several ancient showers. The water was cold, so there was no risk of scalding. The walls were damp and mouldy, and the floor was cracked and slippery. Close to one wall was the only lavatory. Judging by their casualties on the floor, even the cockroaches were having a hard time surviving. The door had been partly wrenched off its hinges.

Woo Sing washed herself and her clothes quickly, aware of the glances of tenants coming down the stairs opposite. Wrapping herself in Seung Mei's large towel, she glanced along the corridor and, finding it empty, ran back to the room.

She heard coughing as a tenant came down the stairs and knocked frantically on the door to be let in. Seung Mei was horrified. 'Don't ever do that again. It is inviting trouble. Put your wet clothes on and walk back to the room.'

Woo Sing was too embarrassed to reply. Seeing this, the other woman produced a flask of tea and some attractively clean cups.

'Where can I find work?' Woo Sing asked anxiously.

'That is not easy,' was Seung Mei's guarded reply. 'My husband works in a plastic factory. He is on night shift and the pay is quite good. About twenty dollars a day.'

'That sounds fine. Is the work difficult?'

'Not difficult, but dangerous. The machines have no safety guards.'

'Then the workers should hold a meeting and complain. That is not difficult,' said Woo Sing condescendingly.

'The workers would lose their jobs and more would fill their places,' countered Seung Mei.

'Then they should ask the State,' responded Woo Sing.

'The State has a lot of laws already, but when the inspector comes, he takes his money at the door and makes a good report,' said Seung Mei.

'Then they should inform on him,' replied Woo Sing.

'That would be disastrous, for they would never get another job,' said Seung Mei, horrified.

Woo Sing had no reply.

Seung Mei changed the subject. 'We swam out several years ago, and even with two children we have saved enough for a sewing machine,' she said proudly.

Woo Sing's clothes were hardly dry when a small boy knocked at the door and asked for her in a strange and almost unintelligible dialect. Woo Sing was surprised, especially when the child told her shrilly that Tong Pooi had sent him to take her to work.

After hungrily taking another cake from the tin, she followed the child down the street until they came to a small open space where several roads converged. Among heavy traffic, hawkers' stalls, pedestrians, and litter, Tong Pooi had claimed a small recess off a footpath, a remnant from an architectural miscalculation. He had squeezed in a small table and two stools and had set up his business.

Tong Pooi had a client who was getting excited, and Woo Sing waited while the old man wrote it all down, gracefully but with great speed. Noticing her, he stopped the man by lifting his brush. 'A stall assistant is sick. I have found you a job,' he said, quickly pointing to a middle-aged man attending a clothing store.

Her job was to sell cigarettes from a shop that consisted of several shelves propped against a wall and at present boarded up. She was given small change and told to bring any larger notes to the owner. 'I don't think you will get many big notes,' he said rather sadly.

The money units were simple and she decided that if she gave too little change, the customers would tell her. She stood blankly in front of the shop watching an incessant flow of non-smoking pedestrians passing by. When a labourer stopped and bought a packet, she thanked him so enthusiastically that he was surprised and kept glancing back as he walked away. Business improved slightly but she was surprised by how few customers there were. *Perhaps people don't smoke as much here as at home*, she thought.

As the dreary hours slipped towards nightfall, she caught herself thinking of the cool evening walk back from the paddy, with the prospect of a warm meal and a cheerful family. It was no use being homesick. *The choice has been made,* she told herself firmly. She glanced back at Tong Pooi, waiting for a client, and wondered if he ever thought of home.

She received five dollars for the day's work and tried to tempt the owner with an offer of three more hours of work for a dollar. He hesitated, but decided he would watch the stall now. Tong Pooi worked until ten or later, so she leant against the wall close to his stall and slept.

They returned to the block late at night. As they entered under the dimly lit stairs, she sensed that it was an ideal place for an ambush and so walked close to the wall. *If we are attacked, he will need to escape and I may have to fight*, she thought, feeling lonely and frightened.

The doors of the balcony cupboard were slightly ajar and Woo Sing pulled them open. Wa Hing was asleep, but the dim light was enough to expose deep cuts and bruises on his face. He looked almost dead, and she felt she was again witnessing a nightmare, like the horror of finding Ah Hon's dead body.

Her presence was enough to wake Wa Hing. 'I am not too badly injured, but my face is very sore,' he said. 'When I went to the building site, the workers accused me of taking too little wages. They attacked me with bamboo poles and chased me away. I spent our last money on a car home,' he finished bitterly.

'No matter, Wa Hing. I have a little more,' she said, trying to sound unconcerned.

'Why did Seung Mei not let you in?' asked Tong Pooi angrily.

'They were frightened that I had been fighting with the police,' Wa Hing replied wearily.

They took him to Tong Pooi's cubicle and Woo Sing washed the cuts with a rag of doubtful cleanliness. It was the only one available, although Tong Pooi offered his one clean shirt.

Woo Sing repeated the dreaded journey down the stairs and found a stall still open where she bought cooked rice and dumplings. Wa Hing ate greedily, wincing as the food passed his swollen lips. He had not eaten all day. 'I have a lot to learn,' he said as he set down the empty bowl.

'My money will keep us going for another day, and perhaps tomorrow I will find work again,' Woo Sing said.

Wa Hing nodded and tried to grin but was stopped by the pain in his torn facial muscles. Somehow, they managed to find three places to sleep and, despite the coughing of old men, the creak of furniture and the whimpering of children, the sticky night obliterated the day.

In the morning, Woo Sing opened her eyes to contemplate the dusty legs of the camp bed and thought with pity of Tong Pooi owning nothing more than a little folding table, the folding bed and three stools, and perhaps his writing block after all his years in the city.

'Why must Ah Hing get up so early, Ah Pooi?' Woo Sing asked. Despite only knowing Tong Pooi a short while, she felt comfortable referring to him in the informal tense.

'I'm taking him to a government hospital,' the old man replied, as though talking to a child.

'Thank you,' she replied, 'but isn't it early for treatment?'

'He is going to earn money,' Tong Pooi said, as if there were no other reason for going to a Western hospital.

'I will try to join the queue and then sell my place to some-one who is really desperate or very impatient,' said Wa Hing, with as little lip movement as possible.

'He may get up to ten dollars,' Tong Pooi said proudly, pleased he had thought of the idea. It had been a long time since one of his old friends had made a small living that way.

At dawn, the two left for the hospital and Woo Sing mar-velled at the vigour of the fragile old man. He had adopted them in the last few hours and she knew they had found a trusted friend.

Woo Sing consumed some tea from the Thermos and a small bowl of rice. On hearing Seung Mei's voice, she went to her cubicle and asked again about work.

'Sometimes you can find a few hours' work by walking about and asking, but be careful of the triads,' she warned.

Woo Sing walked slowly along the streets, which were already becoming crowded with a very smug section of Hong Kong society, the people with jobs and an income.

Stopping in a small recess, she found a drink stall and spent a few cents on a cool drink. Her throat was still raw from the sea, but now she noticed it less often. She began to ask the owner about jobs, but stopped when she saw an old man chipping plaster from bricks across the street.

He was squatting outside a rough wood and iron stall with an open front. Inside was debris from numerous building sites, bricks and small pieces of corrugated iron. The junk looked to have held together squatters' shacks, hawkers' stalls, carri-ers' carts and addicts' dens as they made their way from poor to poorer in the city.

Woo Sing walked across the street, forgetting about the minibuses. She received a blast from one as it skidded to a stop twenty inches from her. She walked on, ignoring the driver's comments about her eyesight and intelligence.

'For eight dollars, I will clean bricks all day,' she said, stopping by the ramshackle stall.

The arthritic workman stopped and inspected her. *He is looking at my arms to see if I have worked before*, she thought. He waved his hand towards the back of the shop as he slowly rose from his tiny stool. 'Take off your shirt,' he said.

Woo Sing hesitated. *They want to see my muscles*, she thought. She hesitated. She needed a job and was wearing a brassiere, so she slipped off her shirt. The man quickly pushed her tattered brassiere upwards and began feeling her nipples.

His hands were so calloused Woo Sing doubted he could have felt much. For a second, she was too surprised and shocked to respond. Then she pushed his hands away and pulled her brassiere back over her breasts. Red-faced and angry, sweating and trembling with embarrassment, she struggled to replace her shirt. Once it was in place, she ran from the shop. But at the entrance she remembered Seung Mei's words about work and Wa Hing's face. She looked at the stool for a few moments before sitting on it and began chipping bricks.

Noise from traffic on either side of the double row of jerry-built stalls drowned out the sound of her work. It was very hot and the traffic dense and slow. With her stall set close to a corner, Woo Sing felt an unwelcome blast of diesel fumes blown at her as each vehicle stopped and restarted.

After noon, she stopped and walked across to the drink seller, who sold her a drink and offered her a small bowl of rice, which she ate greedily. Only later did she discover how generous he had been as a free bowl of rice was a rare gift in Hong Kong.

Towards nightfall, after a hot, dusty and exhausting day, she set the chisel down with her blistered hands and went in to claim her money. The day's work had produced a large heap of clean bricks, which the old man carefully stacked with their best sides facing outwards. He was seated at the back of the shop when she entered, and although he looked rather tired, his eyes twinkled when he looked at her.

'Since I have seen your top half, I would like to see your bottom half to complete the picture,' he said. 'I will give you two extra dollars.'

Without a word, Woo Sing seized a large and very sharp chopper from a nearby bench. She drove it hard into a supporting post, which split with an impressive sound.

The old man promptly began counting out money and with trembling hands held it well in front of him. Woo Sing noticed in his haste he had added the two extra dollars. She snatched it all and left the shop for the long walk home. She had trouble finding Ming Tak Street but once there was cheered to find a jubilant Wa Hing.

'I was third in line and after the first two went in I became worried I would have to go in next,' he said. 'But I changed places with the fourth man, and soon after a man arrived with a sick baby and begged for a place. I was worried for a while, for the man I'd swapped with who now stood before me was also very tempted, but he too had a sick baby. I asked for fifteen dollars, but the man said he needed two dollars for the fee and a dollar for medicine, so I brought it down to ten.'

Woo Sing listened, forgetting her tiredness, so excited was Wa Hing at his first business deal.

'A man several places back offered eight and the patient looked at me, but I said nothing and held out both hands for ten.'

They counted their money while Tong Pooi looked on in amazement. They had almost twenty dollars between them and a great feeling of security and confidence replaced their fears of the morning.

Thrilled at earning such a huge amount in one day, Wa Hing asked about her job.

'I spent the day cleaning bricks,' she said, trying to forget the scaly hands on her nipples.

'I think we owe you five dollars, Tong Pooi,' Wa Hing said, giving him the money, which was received with dignified gratitude.

'I suggest we eat out at a stall, this evening,' the old man said, looking at Woo Sing's dusty clothes.

'First I will wash, Ah Pooi,' she said.

As she borrowed soap and a towel from Seung Mei, she thought, *This city is filthier than the pigsty at home.*

The washroom door swung back to the wall. She eventually

gave up trying to jam it shut with wet paper. As the cold water washed away the brick dust, she noticed an iron bar, an inch thick and two feet long, obviously meant to hold the door shut.

She bent to pick it up and, on looking up, she stared disbelievingly at two boys standing by the door, admiring her. The older, who was about sixteen, opened his shirt to show a knife strapped to his chest. He moved towards her.

She had dropped the bar to cover her groin with her hands, but now snatched it up and started swinging it blindly, screaming. The bar struck the boy, who doubled up and, gasping, moved to the door. The younger boy had already run off. As her attacker moved to the stairs, she pushed him hard. The screams of pain he had been trying to utter finally came out as his head hit the stairs. Rolling, screaming and bumping his head on each step, he disappeared around a corner. His screams continued for a minute or so, accompanied by running feet and slamming iron doors. When they stopped, there was a sudden stillness as everyone in the huge and crowded building waited, hoping they would not see anything.

Woo Sing slipped back inside the washroom and held the door shut as Wa Hing ran down the corridor. She did not want him to see her naked. 'I am all right, Ah Hing. Some boys were peeping, but they have gone,' she said.

Knowing that few locals knew Mandarin, he switched to that language. 'Is that true?'

'Yes. There is nobody here but me,' she replied. Then she added, 'Would you please wait by the door?'

As the cold water again relaxed her, she idly wondered what her old combat instructors would think of her. *How strange that I was taught to fight against Western Dogs when they invaded China, but instead my first fights were against a grasping Chinese man and a silly Chinese boy in this capitalist city.*

By the time she and Wa Hing walked back to their room the sounds of the building had returned to normal levels.

With his face now less painful, Wa Hing was cheered by the prospect of a good meal. Tomorrow he would return to the hospital, hopefully for another successful day.

Tong Pooi was pleased that he had received his first unearned five dollars in many years. *Despite their modern and immodest ways, these young people are kind and helpful. Soon Ah Hon will arrive and then I will be content.*

Woo Sing was too tired to be happy, yet the relief of surviving another day was enough for her to anticipate the meal with some pleasure.

Tong Pooi knew a stall with a few chairs, so customers could sit and eat rather than stand. They enjoyed the food and listened to Tong Pooi talk about what his village had been like when he was a child.

'Our village has always been reasonably prosperous,' he said thoughtfully.

'They would still let you be a scholar, Ah Pooi,' said Woo Sing.

'But I would have had to learn their rotten new script,' he said with a ferocity that astonished the others.

The evening was milder and less humid than most during

the Hong Kong summer, and although there was distant lightning, the sky was otherwise clear. The stink of the day had gone with most of the traffic, and in the sweeter air, Woo Sing caught the fragrance of a flower stall. She closed her eyes and imagined herself walking along a village path back home. The path had a few trees and wildflowers where she had played as a small child.

A minibus hooted noisily and her dream vanished. They walked slowly, stopping to inspect a few stalls selling clothes and shoes, and a vast range of plastic ware.

'Plastic is the real rice of Hong Kong,' said Tong Pooi rather sadly.

'How's that?' asked Woo Sing, surprised.

'It feeds many mouths,' he said, somewhat mysteriously.

Unwilling to talk further about plastic, which bored him, Tong Pooi announced that he would tell them about the English.

'They are a strange race,' he began. 'Much given to the love of dogs and horses and even cats. These they value much higher than the men of any other race but their own. They live on the island, rule the colony, and send a great deal of money back to their home.'

'Why do we Chinese allow it?' asked Woo Sing.

'Many do very well out of it,' said Tong Pooi. 'Not many who have fled from the mainland want to return. If you want to succeed, you must learn to speak English fluently. Then you will understand them and use their superior airs and hypocrisy to your own advantage.'

'Do you know English, Ah Pooi?' asked Wa Hing.

'No, Wa Hing, and perhaps that is why I have never become rich,' said Tong Pooi quietly.

This information alarmed and impressed the young couple.

'The English do not often come to my street,' the old man said, trying to justify his failure.

Then we shall seek them out, thought Woo Sing, but she remained silent.

'They shout if they are annoyed with you and demonstrate their coarse manners,' he

continued.

'Then what do you do?' asked Woo Sing.

'Stay silent and smile. Many of my friends say you can get good deals from them if you are patient,' replied Tong Pooi.

'Do they take money?' asked Wa Hing, thinking that this could be a way around the language problem, for he disliked studying.

Tong Pooi was silent for a while, but finally he answered, remembering what his friends had told him. 'No. They do not take money directly. They have Chinese middlemen who collect it, including the police.'

'What about this language?' asked Woo Sing, not interested in the money.

'It is very hard, I am told,' said Tong Pooi. 'There are many small joining words that don't mean much to us, but they think these words are very important. It is said to be a very precise language. My friends say that many English talk with such precision that their words seem cold.'

'If it is so precise, it must have many tones,' said Wa Hing, unable to conceal his dismay.

'It is said there are hardly any,' Tong Pooi replied, adding, 'But I don't know anything else.'

He thought little about the English and disliked talking about them at any length. Like the traffic and the scramble for money, they were one of the many problems of the city. But Woo Sing was not put off so easily.

'Are they warlords, then?' she asked, remembering her commune history.

Tong Pooi was mildly irritated by her persistence, although he was used to it, particularly in female clients.

'In a way,' he said. 'They ask the advice of a few rich citizens that they have chosen to advise them and so they declare that they have consulted the people. Like warlords, they are powerful, but their justice is better. They don't shoot people now but if one of their own is caught, they find old and strange rules to excuse them. Our people laugh because we are not fooled, and it is a double laugh because the English think we respect their justice.'

'But they have built buildings for the poor,' noted Wa Hing, puzzled.

'The city would have been ungovernable if there had been too many in squatters' shacks, replied Tong Pooi. 'When people have a cheap house, they do not make such a fuss.'

He stopped, his tone indicating that these were his last words about the English.

They remained silent for the last part of their journey home, while the two young people still thought of the English. This was something they had not thought of in the village, and obviously further information was needed.

The room was cool. Apart from a few whimpers from sleeping children and the noise of the fan, it was also quiet. As Wa Hing and Woo Sing drifted into sleep, they decided that tomorrow they would seek out the English and make a preliminary study of these dangerous and powerful people.

Chapter 3
Tailing tourists

When Wa Hing returned from his hospital "job", Woo Sing was ready to go in search of the English.

'Twenty dollars this time,' he said gleefully. This meant neither of them had to feel guilty about sparing a day to look for the English, or *gweilos*, as they were called by the Cantonese. Tong Pooi had written some instructions, but they were in the old script and difficult to follow.

It was humid and the sun dazzled them as sunlight bounced off the glass of the grand harbour buildings.

'Capitalism may be evil, but look at their buildings,' said Woo Sing.

According to Ah Pooi's instructions, they were close to the Star Ferry, a service that criss-crossed the busy harbour. They were making their way there when around a corner lumbered the two of the largest people Woo Sing had ever seen. Both were elderly and tall. Their bodies shook as they walked with fat that was not firm but hanging. Woo Sing and Wa Hing slowed to a stop as they watched them approach. Woo Sing heard Wa Hing draw in his breath at the sight of the old lady, whose short and scanty dress displayed large areas of pink flesh. On her thick arms were many bangles, and on her podgy hands numerous rings. Despite a pink and kindly face, the woman's eyes seemed rather hard. The man's huge, bright shirt hung loosely over his chest and formed a small skirt over his belly. Slung across his chest were two cameras, while colourful shorts and sandals completed his outfit.

After they had passed, Woo Sing said, 'They are very fat.'

'But not stupid,' said Wa Hing, for the man looked aggressive and shrewd despite his bulk. He wondered if these were the English.

'Many warlords were fat,' said Woo Sing. Wa Hing said nothing, but shook his head. This would be more complicated than he had thought.

They boarded the ferry, spending a precious fifty cents as advised by Tong Pooi, who had told them to take the top deck where the foreigners were. It cost them an extra thirty cents, so they carefully but discreetly inspected the many *gweilos* they had paid to see.

A tall and slender girl walked past them, her long *gweilo* nose spoiling an otherwise attractive face. Wa Hing shifted restlessly in his seat. The girl's large, rounded breasts could be seen under a thin black blouse; her buttocks and thighs were closely outlined by her white trousers. It was possible to see her underclothes.

Woo Sing wondered if Wa Hing desired the woman. Her thoughts were interrupted in the crush as people raced to leave the ferry. Wa Hing grabbed her arm and they joined the crush, following the girl in the black blouse. Looking down to avoid stumbling on the wooden planking, Woo Sing noted that Wa Hing was excited, and indecently so. She found herself blushing furiously as she walked alongside him.

The young woman noticed Wa Hing's interest in her and stopped on a broad paved expanse at the foot of a flight of steps. She moved her body at him in a way that Woo Sing had not seen before. She looked knowingly at Wa Hing, smiled contemptuously, and slowly walked away.

Wa Hing forgot his lust in a rage of humiliation, and Woo Sing saw him trembling slightly. *I will make the gweilo woman pay dearly*, he thought, unsure of how that could be done. Woo Sing felt sorry for him and thought of taking his hand, but she was unused to this situation. Instead, still blushing furiously, she gently tugged at his shirt and led him towards the area where Tong Pooi said they would find the English,

It was a little after noon, and although the streets between the tall buildings were wide, the footpaths were narrow and there was a river of people, mainly *gweilos*, tall and thin, the men silent and wearing business suits. Woo Sing let go of Wa Hing's shirt but continued to watch him carefully; in the crush of people it would be too easy to lose him.

No one looked like a modern warlord. Dispirited, they found a small park and sat down.

'Wa Hing, there are so many people that one can't look at any one of them,' complained Woo Sing, and so they decided to return. They disembarked from the ferry, this time at the twenty-cent exit, and felt disappointed with the day's progress.

'Maybe the old man let his imagination run away with him,' said Wa Hing in a weary tone.

'Never mind, here we are back with the fat camera *gweilos*,' said Woo Sing. 'Look at those, Wa Hing,' she added, as a compact group of short people rushed past intently, following a man who was waving a small green flag.

'I think they are Japanese,' Wa Hing said as he watched the flock change shape, funnelled through the roils of people.

The stairs at home were a final drag after their day on the pavements. They knew that it was impossible to seek out the *gweilos* directly. Perhaps if they found work, that would bring the English to them, for they still believed Tong Pooi's words about how the English were the key.

Woo Sing slept late until woken by someone crying. She heard Seung Mei passing and called her in.

'I thought I heard someone crying. Is one of the children sick?'

'The family in the cubicle next to us will have to leave,' she replied. 'Chen Tien Wa has lost her job. She has been sick for a few days now. Her husband only finds casual work since he has chest trouble. They and their three children will have to move to a shack, as the rent here will be too high now.'

Woo Sing's sympathy was quickly overridden by the thought of a newly open job. 'Can you tell me the name of the factory, Seung Mei?'

'I don't know. Ask them yourself,' Seung Mei said.

Woo Sing went around to the other cubicle to find Chen Tien Wa.

'I'm sorry you've lost your job,' she started, 'but I'm looking for one. Can you tell me the name of the factory?'

The woman ignored her. Woo Sing felt angry. She wanted the job badly and the job surely no longer mattered to this surly, unresponsive woman. Her anger faded when she thought, *But I do not matter to her either.*

She sat by the woman's side and considered. Wa Hing is right; Hong Kong exists on deals.

'If you tell me the name of the factory and I get the job,' she said slowly, thinking as she went, 'I shall give you half of my first month's pay.'

Chen Tien Wa looked carefully at Woo Sing, trying to determine whether this was a real offer. Finally, she said, 'The Golden Plastic factory. But your clothes are too rough.'

Seung Mei had been standing by listening. 'Woo Sing, we are almost the same size. I will lend you some clothes.'

The two women frantically sorted through the few suitable clothes for Woo Sing to try on. After a final inspection, she was soon on her way in a loose blouse and black trousers, neither too clingy nor too shapeless. With her hair pulled neatly back from her forehead into a plait, she gave an impression of intelligence, cleanliness and efficiency. The shoes were rather tight, but better than her battered sandals. They were the most elegant clothes she had worn, and her new poise and confidence elated her. *Whatever happens today*, she thought, *when I have a little spare money, I will buy some pretty clothes.*

Not many, and I will choose them very carefully, but I will buy them for myself.

The factory was on the third floor of a large industrial building. An iron door opened into a single room containing several noisy machines and about thirty people. A sickly smell like rotten fruit penetrated the room.

The workers didn't look up as she passed. They were on piece-work rates. Most of the space not already occupied by workers and machines was filled with sacking and covered bales. Woo Sing stopped in front of a young man in a tiny, partly glassed-in office at the back of the room.

'I have come for a job and I will work hard,' she said, deciding that a direct approach was best.

The man's reply was in a slightly different dialect, perhaps Hakka, so she desperately rearranged a few of the words and guessed at others. The reply, she thought, was that he had already arranged a replacement for Chen Tien Wa.

He explained that there was a vacancy, but it had been promised, although the worker had not yet arrived. Woo Sing thought he sounded annoyed about that. Another deal could be made, and she had little else to lose.

'I will work here until lunchtime for nothing, and if the new worker does not arrive by then, the job is mine. How is that?'

The boss looked doubtful, nobody worked for nothing, but she smiled at him.

'All right,' he said. 'Wages are four hundred dollars a month, no bonuses, six days a week. If you're late twice you're dismissed.'

She followed him to a long narrow bench where four women stood along one side. They were picking out spoilt plastic flowers and counting and packing the rest. She took the empty place and, without any sign from the women or the boss, began to work. The flower stems were rough and easily tangled, while the flowerheads pulled off easily, making the work irritating and tedious. The women worked swiftly and silently as the boss spent his time carefully watching them.

It's better than weeding or planting rice, and much better paid, Woo Sing thought.

After an hour or so, she began to feel her mind dividing into two thought centres, one for sorting, discarding, counting and packaging, and the other thinking about Wa Hing, Tong Pooi and the woman who had lost her job. By noon, her fingers were aching and raw, and she half hoped that the expected worker would arrive.

The boss slowly approached, inspecting workers on the way, and said, 'The job is yours.' After a short pause, he added, 'For as long as you work hard, but not a second longer.'

She nodded her assent. The joy of having a job anaesthetised her stiff and burning fingers, and she was elated.

She was annoyed with herself to find she had forgotten to bring money for lunch. The women sat close to the bench and ate from a pan of rice brought by a messenger. A container of tea completed the meal. Woo Sing sensed the older women's resentment. Perhaps the last worker had been their friend, or perhaps a younger woman would quicken the pace. She went to the lavatory and drank from a tap, which dispensed warm water with a faint taste of the chemical that could be smelt everywhere in this place.

Woo Sing went out to the balcony. Several men were resting on strewn bales. They looked at her sleepily, but with curiosity, and a few smiled.

'You may have this,' said one of the older men, pointing to a little rice left in the bottom of a large pan.

'Thank you, comrade,' said Woo Sing with a smile. Then, dismayed, she noticed the man scowling.

'We do not use that word here,' he said.

'I'm sorry, I did not know.'

'No matter,' said the old man, regaining his composure. He poured her some tea from a flask.

'Tomorrow I will remember to bring money for lunch,' she said after thanking them. The men all laughed loudly.

'Little sister,' one said, 'you must learn to look after yourself here, for no one else will.'

'Perhaps the boss will,' said one, grinning, but several others frowned.

'He better not,' the older man muttered.

Woo Sing didn't understand this, but was relieved that the men, at least, were friendlier than they had been in the commune.

A bell rang and the workers went quickly back to their stations. The women occasionally spoke to each other as the afternoon dragged on, and the attention of the boss became less persistent. They spoke in low voices in the dialect of the Chui Chow people, not one Woo Sing knew well so she understood little of what they were saying.

The day finished and she signed the book, the boss carefully marking it from midday onwards. Without glancing at her co-workers, she left the factory into a street packed with workers. Without a breeze, the noise, heat and people pressed on her until she became indifferent to everything. At home, she found Wa Hing already returned, chopping some liver. Tong Pooi would not return until later.

'Not too fresh, but very cheap,' Wa Sing said cheerfully, but his nose was wrinkled.

'Soup, is it?' asked Woo Sing, noticing the bundles of fresh green vegetables on the chopping board. She washed while he cooked, and the delicious smell of the soup spread through their tiny quarters. They left a third of it for Tong Pooi, who, with his connoisseur's nose, she thought might detect the state of the liver. Wa Hing declared it didn't matter.

Tomorrow she would have to return the clothes, but she was too tired to buy her own tonight. Wa Hing volunteered and he left for the market, taking her borrowed clothes with him. As she settled down to sleep on her tiny couch, Woo Sing thought of the time when she would have money to choose the clothes she wanted; clothes that would fit perfectly. With this comforting thought, accompanied by the lingering smell of plastic, she fell asleep.

The ex-factory worker and her family had already left when Woo Sing awoke. Therewas a note indicating that the woman would return at the end of the month for her promised compensation. Wa Hing had carefully laid out work clothes and gloves, as he'd seen that her hands were swollen and red.

Wa Hing had not yet found a job, and the hospital had only paid five dollars yesterday. Although they still had some dollars left, there was not enough to last until Woo Sing received her first wages. Their mutual anxiety was overcome by Wa Hing's optimism. 'Today, I am sure a job is waiting for me,' he said.

Woo Sing laughed. Taking three dollars and a handful of cooked rice wrapped in paper, she left for the factory.

Tong Pooi had asked all his clients to tell him of any new jobs. His clients were mostly old and poor, but they had great affection for the gentle old man who charged so little yet wrote so precisely and beautifully.

Few knew how much he longed for someone from his own clan to join him. He was becoming apprehensive about Ah Hon's absence, and the reluctance of the two young people to mention him. *The truth delayed is often the truth twisted*, he thought, *but there is nothing I can do. They were good company and so far had shared whatever they had earned.*

He could easily have returned to China, as he had come to Hong Kong long before the communist victory. However, he could not bear to see the ways of his old household destroyed forever.

He often tempered the phrases of his clients and softened their demands or threats to take the sharpness off the worst of their letters. Many of his clients were astonished by the favourable replies to their requests. They did not guess that their rough emotions had been transmuted into letters that would have been suitable for an emperor.

Occasionally, a young man would ask him to write a love letter, but he always referred them to a younger scribe. He felt he could not compose such letters because he thought them false.

Because of Woo Sing's success, Wa Hing was desperate to find work. He admired and liked Woo Sing and would have accepted her body if she'd offered it, but he would never ask. There was something secretive, powerful and violent about her character, which he both feared and felt drawn to. But right now, money was more important than desire. Her success made him want to find his own.

He walked briskly past the construction sites he had visited before and into a district where the crowds were denser and the buildings only a few storeys high. Their age showed in their crumbling masonry and the wooden beams propped against the bulging brick walls. Looking at them as he rested in an open marketplace, Wa Hing thought they resembled the workers in the commune; if several gave up, all would come tumbling down.

In the commune, he had been accused of being too cheerful for a good communist. His replies in meetings were labelled as 'too optimistic about the behaviour of his fellow men'. His comrades had not minded his lack of dedication, as it meant the leader was constantly criticising Wa Hing and had left the rest of them alone. The berating had enlivened the frequent meetings, which otherwise tended to be dull and repetitive. Wa Hing's undoing had not come from his professional role as a scapegoat, but because of that strange woman, Woo Wai San.

A dedicated party member, Woo Wai San was married, and her husband had been away for two years organising a tractor unit in a distant commune. Normally, he would have had his usual share of holidays, but he had forgone them to ensure there was no slackening in his vigorous development programme.

Woo Wai San had spoken little at meetings, but all respected her dedication. She had a child of three years, and she supervised a nursery school.

A thunderstorm, which had broken out after a long and gruelling meeting, had brought them together. Wa Hing had boldly offered to walk with her to the stream at the end of the village. The bridge was being rebuilt and the swollen stream with its stepping stones could be hazardous. To his amazement, they had only gone a few steps in the darkness when he had felt her arm about his waist.

'I am sick of the meetings, sick of the village, and as my husband won't come back to me, you will do,' she said. 'At least I can trust you for this.' Her voice sounded strained and angry.

Wa Hing had yearned for such an experience but, like most young men, he knew how severe the penalties could be, depending on who was involved. They'd walked in silence, and he was astonished to find himself complying. He entered her small, old house, dreary even by their village's standards.

There was a single large room and a much smaller back

room. Within the large room, an old woman and Woo Wai San's child were asleep, lying as close as they could to a small glowing fire in a wall chimney. There were some chickens in a bamboo coop, also close to the fire. They had prepared themselves to an accompaniment of thunder, the old crone snoring, the child whimpering and the chickens cheeping.

Woo Wai San had undressed in the semi-darkness, and Wa Hing had watched as she crouched and spread her legs wide, placing something inside her body.

'To stop a baby,' she'd whispered.

The tremendous risk they were taking made him feel momentarily sick. But the sight of her body, incompletely lit by the sheet lightning, drove the thought from his mind. They clumsily clutched at each other, groping and stumbling, before tumbling to the floor. He'd followed her instructions, and although the first time was not what he had imagined, they were both satisfied.

It had been difficult to meet secretly, and only rarely did they do so. Woo Wai San had roused great appetites within his body, and their lust for each other was unabated by fear.

When Wa Hing was one day transferred to the hardest work team in the commune, he knew they had been discovered.

That night, at an ominously quiet meeting, the leader spoke. 'Some absent comrades, who have become quite powerful while away, will be returning home soon.'

Wa Hing had never thought seriously of the swim to Hong Kong, but now it became an urgent reality.

When he emerged from his reverie, the noise of the traffic and the pounding of a pile-driver brought him back to his need for work. At least he was alone, and free to do as he wished now. But that also meant that no one cared what happened to him.

His face was troubling him. It remained painful and the wounds were slow to heal. He was tired of the pain and upset when people looked at him. He also wondered if the wounds were making prospective employers suspicious, and several had asked him how he'd received his injuries.

The first time he told the truth, the boss shouted, 'Get out, troublemaker.' After that, he told everyone that he had been robbed and beaten up. This was generally more acceptable, although the word triad was mentioned several times.

He aimlessly walked into a narrow lane filled with packing cases and straw. At the other end, three men were struggling to lift a heavy piece of furniture onto an ancient truck. The training of the commune came reflexively; without hesitation he noted the exact point on the object that would apply lift. Stepping between the two men, he lifted strongly upwards and slightly outwards.

The huge upholstered chair moved so rapidly that the man receiving it had trouble stopping it from toppling on to him.

The three men were elderly, matching their truck in age and decrepitude. The man on the truck spat noisily over the side, the saliva streaking on the already filthy wall.

'Thank you, thank you,' they muttered collectively, surprised, for freely given help was remarkably uncommon.

'If you come with us and help unload, I will give you five dollars,' said the man on the back of the truck.

'I can do that,' replied Wa Hing, both pleased and surprised for he had not thought of money when he was lifting.

That was one commune reflex that had paid off, he thought, as he climbed onto the truck and helped tie the heavy chair down. As soon as the truck engine started, he knew it was missing a cylinder.

'The engine needs fixing,' he said to his nearest workmate.

'Why? It is still going,' was the reply.

'But it sounds bad,' he protested.

'It has always sounded like that. It's a good engine.'

The truck crawled, stuttering and jerking through the traffic, and began slowly to climb a long hill. Soon a line of cars and trucks dragged behind them, the driver and his workmates quite indifferent to the effect they caused. The workers gazed placidly back at the lengthening collection of vehicles, although some drivers risked overtaking them. At the slightest opportunity, a car or minibus would roar past, the anxiety of the driver showing in his tense face.

At the summit, the truck pulled to one side and the following traffic rushed downhill like water spilling from a dam. The descent was fast and exhilarating and Wa Hing admired the skill of their driver, especially when he swerved around the tighter bends. Only later did he come to realise how essential was that skill, for there were almost no brakes.

Outside a large house, with much shouting, grunting and spitting, the three elderly carriers began unloading the chair.

Wa Hing, on the ground, took most of the weight until the others had clambered down. Taking a leg each, they stumbled slowly to a large door where they were received by a young female servant. In a very arrogant manner, she led them briskly to a large storeroom.

'Unpack it,' she ordered.

The old men stared at her, or at parts of her, and chuckled. Disconcerted and annoyed, she left the room.

The house was grand and as Wa Hing glanced out of the storeroom, he saw it was filled with fine old furniture. The chair itself was of a great age, but damaged and worn in many places. While the carriers finished their work, Wa Hing opened another door and peered into the next room. It, too, was filled with rich hanging scrolls and ornate furniture.

The servant girl returned and looked suspiciously at him, but the boss man said, 'The boy is okay. He is a new immigrant.'

The servant girl looked amused and superior. Wa Hing felt he would like to humiliate her but did not know how. Despite her contempt, he marvelled at the riches of the house, a richness like that of an ancient emperor's court. He left reluctantly, but as he followed the men to their truck, he kept stopping and glancing back.

The house was set among trees, apart from the other smaller dwellings. Numerous noisy dogs were kennelled in the lesser houses, while the larger house held none. Wa Hing thought it strange that the poor owned dogs and the rich did not. It was only much later that he realised the noisy dogs were a warning for those who dared to enter.

The truck was slowly driven back to a small village, where the three carriers announced they would have a meal. They did not invite Wa Hing so he asked if he could look at the engine while waiting for them. Reluctant permission was given; the owners could not resist the temptation of a cheap repair.

Wa Hing quickly found a blocked injector valve. With the rusted tools available, he cleared the valve and readjusted the timing. He also cleaned the filter, which was full of accumulated filth and rust. Anxiously, he started the motor, which at first refused to turn over. After he had cleared an airlock in the injector line, it roared into action with such vigour that one of the men ran from the restaurant. Pausing, he gazed in a puzzled way at the truck, as if reassuring himself that it was indeed theirs. He turned slowly and re-entered, leaving Wa Hing to finish tightening an accelerator cable.

Wa Hing noted the wiring to the lights had long since rusted away, as had various other parts not completely essential to the working of the vehicle. He was pleased with his efforts. *Maybe my self-taught skill with engines might be the key to a better job in the city.*

At last, the three carriers returned, looking pleased with themselves. Their pleasure was doubled by the repair of the engine. During the return journey, one of the carriers asked many questions of Wa Hing. His interrogator was surprisingly astute, and despite Wa Hing's reluctance to answer, the man found out much of his history; why he had left and where he had come from.

On their return to the alley, he was told there could be a job for him in about two weeks and he should return then. Wa Hing said he could not wait that long, as he required immediate work.

'Although you do not think it, I could spend at least two weeks repairing and repainting the truck,' he said.

'Wait here,' said the boss man, Ah Hung.

Wa Hing watched him enter a small office and speak on a telephone.

He was surprised that such a small firm could afford a telephone. Nobody he had ever known had even faintly dreamt of owning a telephone.

The other two men sat quietly, not bothering to talk, waiting in the coolest part of the hot and confined alley.

Ah Hung returned and said, 'I can give you fifteen dollars a day for three weeks to repair the truck. You must make it mechanically sound, and all the rotten timbers must be replaced, but nothing must be done to the paintwork.'

While he was puzzled about the paintwork instruction, it did not concern him in the slightest, so he replied, 'I accept, of course.'

It was probably a very low salary, but he did not care, because it was more than enough for them to live on.

Ah Hung added, 'Apart from the repair work, your duties will include helping to deliver furniture and other goods. You can start tomorrow, and for today's work you can take five dollars.'

Wa Hing noted the address of the office and almost gave Tong Pooi's address to the boss, but some instinct restrained him. The secretiveness of those who lived in the city was beginning to make him cautious and suspicious of all.

Wa Hing arrived at the flat first, bringing with him their meal for the day contained in several newspaper parcels tied with coarse flax. As well as fresh vegetables and chicken guts, he bought three oranges to celebrate his new job.

Woo Sing had left the cubicle untidy. Her habits were already changing. She had previously been ruthlessly tidy, discarding everything that did not have a place. Now a casualness was creeping into her regime. As he tidied the cubicle, he realised with amusement that he, who had constantly been reprimanded for his untidiness, was now becoming the tidy one.

His thoughts turned back to his home. While he tried to stop thinking of his parents, he found himself thinking of Woo Wai San, and wondered if she ever thought of him.

Her husband must be home now. Many comrades would enjoy hinting at her behaviour and making solicitous inquiries about her husband's tractor project. Wa Hing had always thought her husband had about as much soul as the tractors he professed to love. If he found out she had been unfaithful, Woo Wai San would pay an old-fashioned penalty. The village would say nothing, the party would say nothing, and, in a few days, she would go silently about her job bruised, subdued and disgraced, both inside the party and out of it.

Wa Hing viciously chopped the vegetables into tiny

fragments. He felt a dangerous anger at the thought, imagining how he would defend her if he could. But these were vague, dreamy thoughts that soon vanished when Woo Sing returned.

Woo Sing was very tired but strangely cheerful, and even a little excited. The women at work had remained cool, but as she now had food with her, she was indifferent to them.

She went to the other end of the passage to wash carefully, closing the door and fixing the iron bar in a place she could easily grab it. Tong Pooi could have told her that the two youths had not been seen since their bathroom escapade, and that her actions were secretly appreciated by the harassed women on all floors of that vast building.

When she returned, they ate their meal with Tong Pooi, crouched in the cubicle and talking quietly. Tong Pooi listened intently, but said almost nothing. Nothing of the mainland was mentioned, as neither Wa Hing nor Woo Sing wished to remind the old man of Ah Hon, of whom he no longer spoke. He felt that the two young people, excited about their new life and successes, had lost interest in the fate of their companion. He wondered if they were concealing something of importance, but decided they were too open in nature for such a thing.

If they had good news, they would soon tell it. Ah Hon must have been caught and was probably serving the usual six months gaol sentence. He was sorry for the boy, but he was young and robust, and after he returned to the commune, he would no doubt attempt again to come to Hong Kong.

Tong Pooi would wait. He had waited for many years to see the child, who was now a man. Another year or so would not matter. Many things about him had changed, yet he felt no older now than when he had first heard of the boy's birth. In the meantime, Ah Hon's two friends would provide company and interest.

Wa Hing was no scholar like Ah Hon was alleged to be, and Tong Pooi felt no obligation to teach him those characters and ideas that set the scholar apart from other men. He would wait. He believed that in the end, time would deliver Ah Hon to him, or deliver him to time, and his yearning would be gone. To see this last member of his line was the only expectation he had allowed himself, and he was not going to destroy that now.

Tong Pooi was wrong in his estimation of the couple. Wa Hing thought little of Ah Hon, but when he did, it was with guilt. He knew he should have escorted Ah Hon more closely through the water, knowing that Ah Hon was not as good a swimmer as he was. Instead, the surge of freedom and excitement had driven him into the water ahead of the others. It was only when nearing the free shore that he had recollected his companions.

He had swum to the shore, climbed a rock and immediately seen Woo Sing floundering slowly in a wide circle. He had easily reached her and pulled her ashore. Once the water was cleared from her mouth, he could have climbed the rocks and searched for Ah Hon, but he had forgotten. This forgetfulness made him very uneasy.

Wa Hing and Ah Hon had had many differences in the commune. Ah Hon had always been more accepted than Wa Hing, which he felt was unjust. Ah Hon was more deeply antagonistic towards their society, but had better concealed his feelings. Despite this, they had been good friends, driven together by their unacceptable background of being the grandchildren of landlord farmers. Both knew their prospects were poor, and that the old village hatreds continued.

It was Ah Hon's quiet initiative that had got them to Hong Kong. Wa Hing often thought that if only he had glanced around before jumping from the rock to rescue Woo Sing, he would probably have seen Ah Hon and rescued him. He never told Woo Sing of this, fearing her words and her anger.

Woo Sing also thought of Ah Hon, remembering his smile and his laugh, and the feeling of easy pleasure when he was nearby. She was sorry he had paid such a fearsome price, but despite the problems of each day, she could now sense the future. For generations, her family had left its mark on their little village. Every clan or family in the district had experienced the harshness of the Woo clan. They had lived in a landlord's tower and, when communism came, Woo Sing's family paid the inevitable price, ordained by the actions of countless ancestors.

Woo Sing, a tiny and frail child, had been permitted to live because it was thought she would perish during the two years of semi-starvation that the remnants of the family endured.

A softening of official attitudes had quietly brought the family back into village life, but it was many years before Woo

Sing realised she was different. At first it was puzzling, for no matter how she tried and excelled at school, the warmth of official approval was withheld. As this realisation hardened from puzzlement and suspicion to certainty, she learned to conceal her abilities, even in school examinations. Although she knew the work, she was careful to write an average reply. At the end of school, her fate was certain to be resettlement in a distant part of China, where a different, but perhaps less prolonged, antagonism would exist. The fragments of the family would be further broken.

As she had entered the water with Ah Hon, his optimism had restored a little of the confidence in their journey. The choice had been clear, swim or die, and they had not faltered in their resolve.

When the meal was over, each put their bowl and chopsticks away in a personal niche in that packed cubicle. Likewise, their thoughts were quietly and carefully filed away, like some child's secret to be forgotten often, and as often rediscovered.

'There is a cubicle next door that is empty,' came Seung Mei's voice. They looked up to see her in the doorway. 'The rent is quite reasonable.'

'I'm sure Woo Sing will be very pleased to move there,' said Tong Pooi, relieved.

Woo Sing was a little fearful as she said, 'Of course, how lucky I am.'

She transferred her few belongings to the cubicle. Although tiny, it seemed huge and empty compared with her previous quarters. She realised she was breaking away from Wa Hing and Tong Pooi. The nest-like atmosphere of closeness they had built would soon fade. The long journey on her own had now begun.

61

Chapter 4
Gaining acceptance

Each morning, Woo Sing rose early and walked to the factory, thus saving the cost of a bus ride. She had been ignored, then insulted, and now finally accepted by her women workmates, who nevertheless still passed comments about her shapeless clothes.

'It looks like you have just come out of one of the women's prisons,' said the woman who worked nearest to her.

'Perhaps you are right,' Woo Sing replied carelessly, and for a day or two none of the women spoke to her at all.

The packing had become routine, without conscious effort. Indeed, a few times at night she woke to find her hands making vague packing movements beneath the bedclothes.

Two of the youngest boys in the factory were always staring at her and grinning to each other. One lunchtime, she quietly moved behind some bales to listen to their chatter.

'What do you think of her breasts?' asked one in a serious manner. 'Do you think they would flop with her clothes off?'

'Hard to say,' replied his companion thoughtfully.

'What do you think of her legs, then?'

'Can't see them through the trousers, but they're probably all right.'

'I wonder what she is like between her legs,' the first said wistfully. He was clearly the more curious one of the pair.

'The same as all the others.'

Woo Sing did not stay to hear any more. Blushing, angry and quite sick, she slipped away. She was so angry that she could hardly eat her lunch. For a few moments she considered walking over to give them a good hiding. But her job was worth more than that.

That evening, as she showered, she examined herself and decided she would try to meet with the approval of her two admirers. However, for them, the subject would remain theoretical. She wondered about wearing a dress to work, but all the other women wore trousers.

A couple of days later, she sat with the boys at lunch.

'I suppose you have many girlfriends,' she stated innocently, staring directly into the eyes of the more amorous one.

He stuttered, glanced at his companion and blushed red with awkwardness and embarrassment. He muttered, 'Not many.'

'I don't have much to do after work myself,' Woo Sing said daringly.

'I have to go straight home,' he blurted, and his companion sniggered.

'Oh, how boring,' replied Woo Sing and she walked off, pleased.

On the last Saturday of the month, the factory staff were not on routine duties. Instead, the manager rushed about, shouting and directing them to clean the room. They packed large amounts of rubbish into bags and baskets, carried them downstairs, and stacked them against a wall. Bales of material were moved away from windows and doors, and many were lowered into waiting trucks. By evening, the factory was unrecognisable, clean and spacious. Several protective guards were brought out and placed around the more dangerous machines. Some of the workers protested, as the guards slowed down production for those on piece rates.

'Oh, shut up,' said the boss. 'You know why they are here. They won't be here long, and you know that, too.'

Woo Sing asked no one about the changes and wondered if the factory had been sold. *It is no use worrying*, she thought. *I will wait for next week.*

On Monday morning, a middle-aged Chinese man and an elderly European man arrived and walked about the factory. They measured the access to the windows and balcony, and opened several of the cans of chemicals neatly stacked along the wall. The supervisor followed the men about, but as the conversation was in English, Woo Sing did not understand it. A fierce argument developed between the three men, and finally she asked one of the women who spoke a little English to explain what was happening.

'They are government men who say that the factory is not properly protected from fire,' she replied.

The men reached a deadlock and went into the tiny office

only to emerge shortly afterwards, looking satisfied. The Chinese inspector said loudly in Cantonese, 'I am satisfied that the factory is safe, and the laws and regulations are being followed.'

Most of the workers went on with their work. To Woo-Sing, some seemed amused, others irritated. Some enjoyed what they referred to as a 'tea ceremony', but there were those who found it frustrating because it caused them to lose time and money. Whatever their view, all agreed this annual bribe to the fire department was necessary. It was well-known that owners who resisted payment had their factories closed, and it was rumoured that some even burned when the fire brigades took longer than usual to arrive.

The month passed and when Woo Sing received her pay, the boss said, 'Discuss your pay with nobody. You can return next week as a permanent worker.'

She started to thank him, but was quickly pushed out of the line by the worker behind her.

It seemed like a lot of money. Even if she had promised half to the previous worker, it remained the largest sum of money she had ever had. With Wa Hing also working, she felt confident that they were now financially stable. She could now think about finding that colourful blouse she wanted. As the boys in the factory liked her figure, she would display it a little more.

Men here sometimes looked at her in a way she had never noticed at home. At first, she had been deeply offended, but lately she had become more used to it, and now felt a strange mixture of annoyance and pleasure. Their life was different in ways that she couldn't discuss with her two male companions. She was constantly aware of the difference between men and women, and she starkly felt the resulting tension. She had never imagined that Chinese, living so close together and separated by four miles of water and barbed wire, could be so different.

She arrived home to find Chen Tien Wa waiting for her in Tong Pooi's cubicle. The woman was nervous and ready to fight for her money, which she probably did not expect to get. Seung Mei was sitting with her, watchful and tense, prepared to stay as her witness if needed.

Woo Sing was hurt by their mistrust but had come to learn this was common in Hong Kong.

'I have the money, come and have tea with me,' she said quietly, smiling.

Chen Tien Wa almost collapsed with relief, and as they reached the cubicle, Woo Sing was surprised when she hugged her tightly. She let the woman hold her for a few moments and then, gently freeing herself, said, 'I hope we can be friends.'

She said this sincerely, for she was missing female company. Seung Mei was busy with her sewing and children, and although she was pleasant, Woo Sing felt she couldn't gossip with her.

She counted the money for Chen Tien Wa so that her anxiety could be finally relieved.

Woo Sing said, 'I think I will spend a little money on some clothes.'

Chen Tien Wa said, 'The Kowloon city market is the best place, even the *gweilo* women go there.'

'What style would you like?' asked Seung Mei.

'Style?' asked Woo Sing, puzzled. At home, the concern had been for the strength of the stitching and the cloth to resist the many washes it would receive during its long life. Clothing was rationed and even if one made one's own, there was only one way of making a blouse as far as she knew.

'Oh, the usual style, of course,' said Woo Sing, hoping she sounded confident.

The two women laughed and asked, 'What is that?'

Woo Sing remained silent, a little disconcerted.

'Tomorrow, come with me,' said Chen Tien Wa. 'I know one or two store owners and I might be able to get you five per cent off.'

'If they are very cheap, I shall get several new things,' said Woo Sing, her excitement rising.

'No, no, only a blouse and trousers,' said Seung Mei quietly.

Chen Tien Wa and Seung Mei realised Woo Sing could look beautiful and indeed she was attractive even now. Athletic and strong as she was, she would be no match for the local triads, who were always on the search for girls for the brothels of Wanchai and Tsim Sha Shui. Without conferring, both women knew it would be safest for Woo Sing not to flaunt her beauty.

Seung Mei left to prepare the family meal and in the brief silence that followed, Chen Tien Wa looked intently at Woo Sing as she quietly packed the teacups onto a small shelf.

'Can you help me, Woo Sing?' she asked.

'Of course,' replied Woo Sing, almost adding, *Chairman Mao says we must learn to trust and help each other.* She stopped short, though, realising that such comments sometimes incited anger in those around her here.

Chen Tien Wa said, 'My husband is sick with TB and only works a little. He often stays at home and helps me assemble plastic things. I did not tell him about the money because I think he takes heroin for his cough and chest pains. If I take home such a sum, he will find it and probably not believe me when I tell him how I got it. Also, he will use it for heroin, even though he is a good man and loves me and his children. I will take a little home. and come once a week for a little more. Is that all right?'

Woo Sing was so surprised that at first she didn't believe she'd heard correctly. Memories of lectures and photographs about the pre-revolution drug days came rushing back. She knew that Westerners had forced drugs on China—at first for profit, but later to chain and break its people. Some of the stories were so horrifying that she had not believed them. Still, the English were a treacherous race and she had begun to hate them for the suffering they had caused.

Woo Sing was silent, and Chen Tien Wa waited patiently. Then, becoming alarmed at Woo Sing's silence, she said, 'No matter, I will go.'

Immediately, Woo Sing jumped up and said, 'I am not angry with you but with the English who do this to us.'

'But it is the Chinese, not the English, who smuggle in the

drugs,' said Chen Tien Wa gently.

Woo Sing was confused. Not believing Chen Tien Wa, she dismissed the issue as too difficult to cope with.

'I have more time than you. Tell me how to find your hut and once a week I will bring the money.'

Chen Tien Wa wrote down the way to her hut and left, more cheerful and confident than she had been for many weeks. There was now a little more money for another few weeks and she felt that Woo Sing would not let her down.

Woo Sing was exhausted. Her exultation at buying some new clothes, and her rage at the English, led to her aimlessly shifting small objects about the cubicle to distract herself. Wa Hing knocked and cheerfully asked to enter. He slowly pushed aside the faded cloth, which doubled as a door. Woo Sing was so pleased to see him that he received a smile he had only seen Ah Hon receive before.

He sat next to her and listened in silence while she talked herself out of her fury with the English and their drugs. She said nothing of Chen Tien Wa.

Wa Hing said nothing but already knew, as Tong Pooi had told him—indeed had warned him—that the Chui Chow controlled the drugs in Hong Kong. *The stupid English with their noble ideas of justice strove to break the trade, but their laws were such that the Chui Chow could easily beat them. With a combination of bribery and clever lawyers, few drug peddlers and no drug bosses ever went to gaol.*

It was no use telling Woo Sing this now. She already had enough on her mind. One had to accept Hong Kong as a new world and make the best of one's opportunities, for it was only money that mattered.

Wa Hing had brought a parcel with him. From it he produced a large fish, its eyes still bright with freshness. With a flourish, he also produced a variety of vegetables and herbs, and Woo Sing was soon restored by the sight of good food.

They prepared the meal together. Everything was chopped particularly fine, the sauces prepared with extra care, and everything left uncooked until the last possible moment. They set the small folding table in the most elegant style that the spartan cubicle would permit.

Tong Pooi arrived with a few more vegetables and could not be persuaded to set them aside until the next day, when they would no longer be fresh. These were quickly prepared and added to the dishes. Honour satisfied, the old man sat quietly, but could not completely contain his excitement for the meal.

Wa Hing had arranged for the fish to be baked in the oven of one of the more affluent tenants from where he brought the browned fish to the centre of their tiny table. It was the best meal Tong Pooi had eaten in years.

Wa Hing had frequently been given the most menial kitchen jobs in addition to other work at the commune, and so had learned a little about cooking. Eventually he had made friends with the best cook in the village restaurant. The man was easily flattered and Wa Hing had charmed his best recipes from him. The crisp vegetables and slices of fish were delicately chosen, eaten and savoured.

Plain rice followed by a clear, delicate soup, finished the meal. Woo Sing declared it their crowning success in Hong Kong so far.

Wa Hing smiled broadly, pleased because he knew she did not usually give such sweeping compliments. Woo Sing had noticed the scars on his face were very prominent, especially when he smiled. Shocked, she understood that he had paid a terrible, permanent price for his early attempt at getting a job.

However, the pleasure of the meal quickly drove the thought away. Tong Pooi had eaten nobly and elegantly, holding his chopsticks in the ancient and correct way, which neither of the other two could manage. He felt deliciously drugged from the fullness in his stomach and, gently excusing himself, made for his bed.

Wa Hing found a small and secret place for Woo Sing to keep her money while she cleared away the remnants of the meal. In the six weeks they had been in the city, a rough but comforting domesticity had developed to replace the uncertain and hazardous atmosphere of the first few days. Woo Sing felt that her cubicle was now part of her world. It was her little haven away from the work and strangeness that occupied her days.

*

A week passed without much to distract the three from their long daily routines. Wa Hing usually slept late on Sundays, as did Woo Sing, who was learning to sleep despite the incessant rattle and clatter of the tiles as neighbours gathered for week-end games of mah-jong.

On the weekends, Wa Hing went for long walks to learn the geography of the streets. He learned where one could park a truck without attracting a fine, and which small streets could avoid the long lines of cars that often block the roads for hours. He began to draw a small map on paper that he'd begged from Tong Pooi. Gradually an ever-widening circle of the city around their home became known and mapped territory. He was not sure why he was putting so much effort into this, but like his study of the restaurant cook and the commune mechanic, he felt that this knowledge would one day be of immense value.

He was now able to guide Woo Sing to the squatter area where Chen Tein Wa had settled. He left Woo Sing at the entrance to a narrow alley, as he had no desire to listen to the talk of the two women. He was afraid the children would stare at him and discuss the scars on his face and so preferred to wander about outside. The scars were still painful and occasionally discharged blood and pus.

Woo Sing picked her way carefully along the narrow alley, hemmed in by a broken concrete path and a smelly trickle of drainage water. The path, barely able to fit one person, was interspersed with mounds of dog's muck and spattered with the spittle of numerous wayfarers. A mangy cat struggled along the path ahead of her. The doors of the shacks were mostly shut, but Woo Sing peeped through those few that were open and found the interiors neat and clean, the rough furniture arranged carefully. One even contained a television set, before which sat an old woman assembling plastic flowers.

Chen Tien Wa and her family occupied the last shack in the alley, which ended against a muddy cliff face. The house consisted of a single room, about ten feet by six. The children slept in bunks arranged along one wall, and the couple in a makeshift bed against another. It looked as if the bed became a table during the day with the addition of a few rough planks. The walls were made of thick packing wood, with any gaps stuffed with waste cotton or paper. One wall had a small area of bright orange paint, where a previous tenant had attempted to brighten the gloom. The effect only enhanced the darkness and damp.

The bed/table was functioning in the latter role when Woo Sing arrived. The family was seated around it, assembling a crude plastic picture frame. A small boy of about eight years, carrying an immense bag of plastic materials, followed Woo Sing into the room. Woo Sing helped the child deposit his load and, with a brief thanks, he jumped out of the room, slamming the door and causing the whole house to vibrate.

The family stared at her. The only sound was the laboured breathing of Chen Tien Wa's husband. He began a fit of deep coughing, his pale face sweating with the exertion of gaining his breath. Chen Tien Wa looked surprised to see Woo Sing and then welcomed her. She regretted not having brought sweets for the children; next time she would remember.

The children watched, detached and clinical, as their father struggled and gasped. Finally, he cleared his windpipe, spitting a large amount of green slime into a part-filled bowl by his side. The children watched silently until he recovered and then turned to their own work. Woo Sing tried to listen to Chen Tien Wa chatting about their room and its advantages, but she repeatedly turned to study the man. His bright eyes watched her in turn, all the while picking up and assembling plastic pieces.

After a few moments the tension faded and Chen Tien Wa made tea. Woo Sing accepted a cup with barely concealed reluctance, relieved to note that the man had his own mug. She briefly told Chen Tien Wa about her week, not mentioning their glorious meal. The family was not interested; they were too focused on their task. Woo Sing sat at one end of the table and, noting the simple construction, began assembling pieces.

'I get a little bored on Sundays so perhaps I can give you a free hand for an hour or so,' she said.

For the first time she saw the children smile and again regretted not bringing sweets.

To Woo Sing's relief she learned that the husband, Chai Dung, came from a village not far from her own so they spent the afternoon chatting and laughing about the happier side of village life. The room was intensely hot and the ventilation poor. When Woo Sing removed her jacket Chen Tien Wa apologised, 'Most huts have a fan but we have not got one yet. But after our next payment, I think I will try to buy a small one.' She dropped her voice. 'The triad man came a few days after we arrived and offered me some cheap electricity stolen from a factory across the road. I told him we were too poor and he became very angry. He shouted at me that those who use oil lamps sometimes find their houses burnt down but this never happened to those who paid for electricity.'

Woo Sing could think of nothing to say.

'I quieted the man down,' continued Chen Tien Wa, 'and promised to buy my kerosene through him. It means we will pay a little more but at least we won't have a fire.'

Woo Sing knew that there was nothing else to do, for even Tong Pooi paid the triads his small contribution. She had heard him telling Wa Hing how, in his early days in Hong Kong, he had refused. A day later they had returned, upset his table, smashed his ink block and pushed him against the wall. She guessed that even her factory boss paid the triads, although she would never dare ask anyone in the factory about it.

Chai Dung slowed his rate of assembly and spoke very slowly to save his breath. 'We once lived in Java in a small village. It was like paradise but we didn't know it then. I went from Canton as a young boy and lived with my uncle who owned a village shop. We were not rich but we were richer than the Javanese who owed the old man a great deal of money. Ah! It was a beautiful place.'

He stopped work for a while to allow his memories to take him away from this little shack, back to the village on the edge of the Javanese rice fields.

'Ah Dung had been visiting me when the rebellion broke out,' added Chen Tien Wa. 'The old man and his family were murdered and Ah Dung and I were lucky to get out to Jakarta.'

'What did you do then?' asked Woo Sing, not surprised, for she had heard this kind of story before.

'A rich relative managed to buy our way back to China,' replied Chen Tien Wa.

'Someday we will get back to Java,' said Chai Dung. 'I am sure the Indonesian government will one day want us back. We have to become Indonesians but what does that matter as long as we can go home?'

Neither Woo Sing nor Chen Tien Wa said anything but both knew Hong Kong was likely to be the grave site for all of them, and definitely for Chai Dung.

Woo Sing finally felt that her fingers could not move. The huge pile of plastic components had been transformed into a smaller pile of cheap picture frames and, in the process, the children had fallen asleep. Their heads, shoulders and arms were sprawled across the table among the remaining components. They had earned enough for at least three days' food, and even at their age, they knew the importance of that.

Chen Tien Wa walked down the little path with Woo Sing, who gave her the money and left. Woo Sing walked quickly home as she did not wish to be caught in a strange neighbourhood late at night. She had no money at all and knew that if she was stopped by thieves, they would be angry and probably slash her, to remind her to have money next time. She already knew of this quaint Hong Kong custom that forced even the poor to carry a few dollars for the robbers.

*

Back home Wa Hing had kept some of the rice warm. As Woo Sing ate, she looked at a large piece of paper he had spread on the folding table. About half of it was covered with a plan of the streets, each street showing several code marks that Wa Hing had devised to indicate important features.

Another sheet consisted of the streets around his workplace. It was his secret ambition to one day join the two maps. Tong Pooi took a great interest in the drawings, which he secretly felt were in poor style. Furthermore, he could not understand some of the simplified characters of the Mao era, and this annoyed him.

Wa Hing had been teaching him the simplified characters. Tong Pooi felt that a scholar should know them, as he might be asked to write a letter in the new style. The characters lacked grace, Tong Pooi said; he believed there was little opportunity for enhancing them in a scholarly way. *This was one thing that should have remained unchanged*, he thought. *This is the ultimate destruction of my homeland.*

With Wa Hing intent over his map and the old man grumbling to himself as he practised the new characters, Woo Sing felt alone, tired and dreary. As sleep closed in, she thought about how the women at work were becoming slightly more friendly. *Perhaps tomorrow I will try to listen to the boys and their optimistic plans for my body.*

The night was hot and humid, and although she fell asleep quickly, she woke early. Feeling fresh after a quick shower, she arrived early at the factory and was surprised to see the boss already there. He was usually in a good mood but today he scowled at Woo Sing and disappeared to the back of the factory.

At lunch, the two boys sat on a bench and hardly noticed her. Annoyed, she walked past them, mimicking the manner some young women used in the street, but she was clumsy and the boys giggled. She retired, red-faced and furious with herself.

She was thinking about new blouses and shoes, and the afternoon was peacefully progressing when a sudden warm gust of acrid smoke made her cough. She took little notice. Such fumes often came from other factories in the building. But within a minute, the fumes were much thicker, and cries cut above the sound of the machinery and the traffic outside.

A fire alarm began ringing and she heard a great deal of shouting in the street below. There was a brief hesitation before a mass rush began towards the factory's narrow entrance.

Fumes poured in through an elevator hatch and Woo Sing saw she had no chance of reaching the door. She asked the nearest women to help her push a bale of material against the hatch. The five women struggled with the bale, while the men fighting for the entrance shouted encouragement but did not return to help. The bale sealed the opening and the fumes lessened, although everybody was still coughing and gasping. After several minutes, Woo Sing saw that the last few were going through the door and she crawled along the floor under the layer of smoke.

The factory door led to a landing on to which two

stairways opened. A river of stumbling, shouting, terrified people poured down each stairway, getting mixed up on the landing and surging down the stairs. Thick smoke billowed above them, then momentarily cleared, and she realised a layer of hot air and gas was forming in the upper part of the stairway.

Pressed against the wall, she stretched her hand up as far as she could, as she had been taught, and felt for the gases. She judged that as they had not yet formed and the fire was well above her, it was better to wait until most people had fled. The noise was like a great river of sound, with individual screams occasionally rising above the general roar. The smell of fear, sweat and desperation mingled with the smoke.

Already she could see a body on the landing. Crouched low by the door, Woo Sing waited. A young girl stumbled, screamed for help and fell. Anchoring one arm about a door pillar, Woo Sing reached into the lashing mass of legs. The girl saw her, put out her arm, and their hands and wrists locked. Woo Sing pulled the girl towards her into the doorway.

They were making good progress when the girl screamed as a heavy foot crushed her ribs on the left side. Woo Sing heard them crack, even above the noise of the fire and the shouts of the workers.

The girl's grip weakened and another foot crushed her other side. With her grip slackening and a final agonised look at Woo Sing, her terrified eyes went blank.

It was useless to hold on so she let go of the body, soon to be swept away by the remorseless horde. The torrent stopped as rapidly as it had formed and the noise quieted into the crackling of fire above.

Woo Sing picked her way down the stairs, carefully stepping around crushed, bloodstained corpses. An old man wearily dragged himself downwards, putting his weight against the stair railings as one leg was obviously broken. Woo Sing was bending to help him when a fireman in a mask tugged at her arm and gestured for her to walk. He picked up the old man and she quietly followed.

The heat was becoming intense, and several firemen passed her on their way to the burning floor. Close to the ground floor, the air was sweeter, and as Woo Sing stopped for a second to glance around, she noticed a crumpled and quivering bundle in the doorway. A child, she thought, still alive but overlooked by the firemen. She quickly dragged the whimpering bundle into an upright position. To her surprise, the body did not straighten and she found herself staring into the terrified face of a tiny hunchback woman who appeared to have suffered little injury. Clutching her arm and half carrying her, Woo Sing made her way to the main door and the open air.

The street was crammed with a confused and totally haphazard tangle of stalled and jammed cars, fire engines, hoses and people. A couple who seemed to be the last to escape from the building were led across the street by a policeman and pushed into the crowd. Trapped there, they watched as hoses were unravelled in what seemed to Woo Sing a very unhurried manner. Nor was there any rapid effort to turn on the water, even though the top three layers of the building were engulfed in flames. The fire on the factory floor was bursting from the windows and licking its way along the wall above.

'Probably not enough yet,' a bystander said with a grin. To him, the fire was simply an exciting and interesting event in an otherwise routine day.

Woo Sing was puzzled. 'What do you mean?' she asked.

The man lowered his voice. 'Everybody knows you have to pay the firemen to turn the hoses on, and you have to pay them to turn the hoses off, otherwise they will drench the goods on the other floors of the building.'

'I do not believe it,' said Woo Sing.

'Well, then ask the firemen,' said her informant, laughing.

Woo Sing saw one of the factory boys and realised that a crushed body she'd seen had been his friend, the theoretical lover. Sickened and exhausted, she began to cry. The hunch-back woman, continuing to hold her hand, led her gently through the crowd and away from the congested street.

Chapter 5
Aftermath

They walked into a more salubrious area, silent, each centred on her own thoughts. Woo Sing noticed that people were staring at them and realised they were covered in grime and soot. The hunchback woman stopped a taxi that drove them to an apartment in an even better part of town. At the top of a flight of stairs, Woo Sing was shown into a spacious and comfortable apartment. Exhausted, she lay on an elegant couch, forgetting about her rough and soiled clothes, desperate to block all memory of the events of the last few hours.

The hunchback woman had the sharp features, bright eyes and slightly sly look of those who use their wits to ensure that their handicap does not impede their way through life. She returned with her elderly mother, who was an elegant woman, and the two of them looked down at the semi-conscious girl with her blackened and tear-stained face. They roused her and led her to a bathroom, where they helped her to wash in cool water.

Woo Sing said nothing, but stood quietly, letting the water

wash the dirt and the worst of her fears away. Once more she faced an uncertain future. For now, she had no job, but at least she was better off than the young factory boy and the old man she'd seen. She knew that friends or relatives would weep as the occasion demanded, but only for a little while, for this city ignored tears and pressed forward with more urgent demands than grief.

Ng San Fong watched Woo Sing as she washed herself. Even though she owed her life to her, she could not help feeling jealous of the woman in front of her with her straight limbs and erect spine. It was an old emotion she had consciously conquered, but now roused by this exceptional figure. She fetched some of her mother's old clothes, which fitted Woo Sing reasonably well. They smiled at Woo Sing's coarse and simple underclothing, with its careful patches and mending.

Certainly she was a Chinese immigrant, probably an illegal one, and most definitely poor, thought Ng San Fong. *Young immigrants have a local reputation for being lazy and prone to crime, but this one is obviously different, and perhaps we could help her in some way.*

They discussed this in English, with Woo Sing listening but obviously not understanding. Woo Sing thanked them for their help and promised she would return the borrowed clothes the next day when she had washed and repaired her own.

'Please have some tea and stay to meet my father,' the hunchback woman said in a commanding tone.

'I must return home before it is too late,' Woo Sing replied. 'The others will hear of the fire and worry about me.'

'Then I will take you in our car.'

The car was the most luxurious Woo Sing had seen, with the driver in a separate compartment. During the journey, the hunchback woman said, 'I do not work in that building. I am a designer of plastic goods and often visit that factory. My name is Ng San Fong but you may call me Ah San. I would like to be your friend, as you saved my life, and I think that being a friend is the best coinage with which to pay this big debt.'

Woo Sing felt sick and exhausted. She hardly heard the woman's chatter, but she nodded. She wished that the car would sprout wings and fly its way over the traffic.

Tong Pooi was already home, his old face pale with anxiety. Wa Hing had not yet returned and would probably be very late, as he was working hard to finish the truck. Ng San Fong spoke briefly to the old man, who trembled violently while she gave details of the fire. He made Woo Sing lie on his bed, and after begging Seung Mei to make some clear soup, he sat quietly by her. Ng San Fong had not been in such a room before. As she studied the scene, the last few dregs of jealousy drained away and she became determined to befriend this girl. She left with a big smile, after making sure Tong Pooi had her address.

Woo Sing turned and twisted restlessly on the bed, her imagination recreating fragments of the most wretched afternoon of her life. As resolutely as she tried to drive the visions from her head, just as resolutely they returned. She was not afraid of death, nor was she a stranger to it. She remembered how she had killed a man on the beach, or at least thought she had, for they had never examined him. Each time she closed her eyes, she found herself staring into the eyes of the dying girl on the stairway floor. Tong Pooi, desperate to calm her, rushed into the other cubicle.

'Ah Mei, please go to the herbalist at the corner of the street and tell him to send a sleeping draught.'

As Seung Mei tidied herself to go out, the old man rushed back to his cubicle and found some money. The herbalist on the corner had a sound reputation for the effectiveness of his medicine, but Tong Pooi would have been furious if he had found out why. The herbalist mixed the most potent sedatives of Western medicine with bland Chinese herbs.

Woo Sing drank the mixture with relief, and shortly afterwards began to feel relaxed and sleepy. The terrible sensations of the day slowly receded and she fell asleep on Tong Pooi's bed.

She woke next morning to find Wa Hing sleeping on the floor by the bed. He had arrived home very late and when he heard the story from Seung Mei had decided to sleep on the floor in case Woo Sing woke in terror or became ill from the effects of the fire. Tong Pooi had slept in her cubicle.

She stayed late in bed for she felt there was no point in going to work. She never wished to see that factory again. She washed and patched her clothes and tried to wash the elegant clothes that she had been lent. That evening, Tong

Pooi and Wa Hing secretly watched her, but she seemed quite composed and, still tired, fell asleep.

When Ng San Fong called next morning, they went downstairs to the luxurious car. It was surrounded by small boys eagerly trying to touch the glistening paintwork without receiving a push from the chauffeur, circling the car like a frantic bird protecting its nest.

The car left amid the cheers and shouts of the children, while the red-faced driver stared straight ahead and muttered darkly to himself. Ng San Fong shut the partition window, and the two women giggled most of the way to Ng San Fong's house, where dinner was being prepared.

The meal was superb, but not in the same way as the magnificent one Woo Sing had had with Tong Pooi and Wa Hing. Ah San's parents were grateful and flattering, and repeatedly commented on Woo Sing's bravery in saving their daughter. They asked several times about how Woo Sing had come to Hong Kong, and how long she had been there, but she gave vague replies, unaware these were almost as revealing as a straight answer, for her two questioners were very shrewd.

Ng San Fong's father was a kindly and friendly man, much older than his wife. He offered to employ Woo Sing in one of his factories, but she politely declined.

'I have seen factory life and want no more of it. I have been told that the English have the key to success in Hong Kong and I would like a job where I can study them and learn their language.'

The old man laughed so much that the wicker chair in

which he was sitting swayed and creaked alarmingly.

'It is certainly very helpful to know the language, but not vital,' he said. 'It is a hard language to learn, very precise, and it has many fine shades of meaning. However, I have many English friends and I will ask around about if there is a simple household job for you.'

Woo Sing was pleased and assured her host, 'I will not do anything to cause you loss of face.' The old man roared with laughter and told her to be patient.

'I am meeting an old friend, Sir William Williams, tomorrow, and I will see if there's anything in his household,' he chuckled.

*

Chen Tien Wa was assembling the usual pieces when Woo Sing entered. The children were playing at the end of the filthy pathway. If they noticed the rubbish, it had little effect on their boisterous play. Their happiness was even greater when Woo Sing gave them a small bag of sweets.

Woo Sing told her sad story briefly.

'You will still get your money,' she added hastily. 'I will be able to pay you each week. I will soon have a job again, perhaps it will be an even better one.'

Chai Dung had been away all day, and Chen Tien Wa gloomily suspected he was working for a drug vendor. As the heroin greatly eased his cough and breathing, she did not feel bitter about him having it, just worried. He had been a good husband when in full health, and even now, despite his gaunt and drooping flesh, she still loved him.

His coughing and breathing tormented the children and herself at night, and on the rare times when he attempted to embrace her, she had to consciously force herself not to withdraw from him. It sickened her to indulge in a tragic mockery of the pleasure they had once enjoyed. She briefly and hesitatingly tried to tell Woo Sing of these feelings, but the girl, although listening carefully and sympathetically, obviously did not understand.

'You are still a child, Woo Sing, but soon the city will change you,' she said. She hoped the process would not be too harsh.

They began to talk of other things, exchanging information about cheap food stalls or where second-grade vegetables could be bought, information of great use to householders.

Chai Dung arrived, looking cheerful. 'Very nice to see you, Ah Sing,' he said. He sat at one end of the table and began to sleepily put together the plastic pieces, but soon lay across the bed and fell asleep. Despite his shallow breathing and the slight rattle of the repulsive secretions in his windpipe, he slept easily. The two women continued to chatter in low tones. The murmur of their voices and the clatter of the pieces became, to Chai Dung, the Java wind. The women noticed him stir and smile, and were pleased.

Chen Tien Wa urgently pressed Woo Sing not to get involved with the English.

'They are harsh masters,' she said bitterly.

'And have you worked for them, then?' enquired Woo Sing, knowing that Chen Tien Wa had not.

'Of course not, and I never shall,' was her reply.

'I have heard that the English are better masters than the Chinese, who demand more and pay less, and one does not have to suffer the nagging of the old grandmothers and amahs.'

'I don't believe it,' said Chen Tien Wa crossly, although secretly she had heard these complaints. She tried another tack. 'What is wrong with being Chinese?' she asked.

'I am not against them,' Woo Sing replied. 'I am proud to be Chinese but I wish to be successful in Hong Kong. Tong Pooi keeps telling me that the English are the key.'

'He does not like them any more than I do,' said Chen Tien Wa.

'But he is more realistic,' said Woo Sing patiently.

'What do you do expect to learn, apart from the language?' asked Chen Tien Wa.

Woo Sing was confused, and finally said, 'I do not know.'

It was getting dark in the hut, and after Woo Sing gave Chen Tien Wa some money, she picked her way down the revolting path towards home.

Wa Hing was intent over his map, trying fretfully to fit a new area on to the paper, which was beginning to look most confusing. To pass a little time, Woo Sing sat with him and quickly realised that he had not paid much attention to map reading in his geography or defence classes.

'You have no idea of scale, Wa Hing,' she said, for the map

was full of detail, but the larger sections were distorted. 'You must keep the proportions of the street distances the same on the map as they are in the town. You have made Ming Tak Street as long as Ching Tak Street, but Ching Tak Street must be three times as long.'

Wa Hing replied, annoyed. 'It does not matter, as all the marks are there.'

'But you will never join the parts of the map properly,' said Woo Sing.

It was a great disappointment, but after thinking for a while, he decided on a strategy. 'The only way to measure is to count the flagstones on the pavement. I will have to start my map again, but this time it will be a true one.'

He did not want to tell Woo Sing that he hoped to be made a driver and needed to convince employers of his value. Woo Sing could see little point in the map, for he could buy one, but she could see it had gripped his imagination, and for that she was grateful. Both had now an objective: Wa Hing to learn the structure of the city and Woo Sing to study its masters, the English.

Of the three, only Tong Pooi would continue to live his life in the truly Chinese way, quietly blending into the pattern of the city and avoiding all conflict. Even his yearning to see Ah Hon was subdued; the silence of the other two had forced him to stop thinking of what might have happened.

Ng San Fong called again. Woo Sing was becoming used to her bossy manner.

'You must pack your clothes. My father has found you a

junior amah's job at the home of Sir William Williams,' she announced grandly.

'Who is he?' asked Woo Sing.

'Oh, a friend of my father,' replied Ng San Fong casually. 'He is a very important businessman.'

She did not tell Woo Sing what she suspected, and what her father would never confirm, that Sir William was a link between many of the Chinese businessmen and those government officials whom they wished to consult secretly. *In any case, such matters would not concern a junior amah in his large household.*

Woo Sing felt afraid, and said, 'I cannot leave without saying goodbye to Ah Pooi and Ah Hing.'

'Leave them a message and pack your things,' said Ng San Fong crossly, having expected more gratitude.

'Bye bye, Ah Mei,' Woo Sing shouted, as she stuffed her few pieces of clothing into a plastic bag.

*

The Williams' mansion was a long way from Kowloon, and particularly from Wong Tai Sin, where Tong Pooi lived. It was two-thirds up the road to the Peak on Hong Kong Island. The Williams family had been established there for more than a hundred years. Not only did the family look down on the town, but they also looked into it, as there were few secrets, commercial or state, to which they did not have access.

Once more they rode in the chauffeured car and Woo Sing

enjoyed staring coolly at the jolted and overheated travellers in the minibuses they overtook.

After a little hesitation, Ng San Fong said, 'Lady Williams is strange even for a *gweilo*. She was born in Hong Kong, but she does not like Chinese, and you must at all times try to keep out of her sight.'

'Are there any English servants?' asked Woo Sing.

'I don't think they would work for her for long. We Chinese can stand her ways better, and we can make ourselves almost invisible, but they cannot,' said Ng San Fong. Then she said to the driver, 'You must park in the street away from the house. If someone notices a junior amah arriving by car it would be very awkward.'

As they got out, the chauffeur pulled Woo Sing to one side. 'If you get into trouble, the best policy is to look stupid or keep smiling,' he whispered. 'It makes them feel better even when they are very angry. I know, for I worked for one once.'

They waited in a small room just inside the rear gate. After a short time, the housekeeper, a Scotswoman of early middle-age, entered. To Woo Sing's surprise, she spoke fluent Cantonese. She seemed kind and after a few minutes, Woo Sing was quite at ease.

The three-storey house was built in a grand style, with a wide veranda on three sides, on to which many rooms opened. There were numerous large doors and archways. Below the veranda lay the city, a thousand feet below, its endless noise barely audible. In the summer, a cool breeze often blew through the rooms, and in the words of one of the Williams ancestors, took the heat out of the air.

Woo Sing found her duties simple to learn, and although the hours were long, she was still fresh and energetic at the end of each day. This was by far the easiest work she had ever been blessed with. On rare occasions, she caught a glimpse of Lady Williams, a tall, thin woman, straight-backed and grey-haired.

Two large Afghan hounds dominated the domestic scene and much of the servants' lives. Woo Sing was instructed to walk the hounds around the various paths and roads, a chore she much enjoyed, as it removed her from the confining and slightly tense atmosphere of the house. The housekeeper, Miss Campbell, had fitted her out in the regular amah's uniform: a white tunic of loose and ill-defined shape that hung over loose black trousers.

This uniform, although apparently careless in shape, had been carefully designed generations before. Much thought had been given to it by previous wives and mistresses. It had the profound effect of reducing the prettiest girl to a dowdy servant, of no attraction to the men of the house. It could be said that few of the great couturiers had ever designed a costume so precisely fitted for its function.

On the first day, after Woo Sing had taken the dogs for their walk, Miss Campbell had given her a word of warning. 'Hold the dogs on a tight leash for if anything happens to them, I cannot stop you from being dismissed. Lady Williams is very fond of dogs and is the president of a local society to protect them.'

Woo Sing laughed. 'A society to protect dogs? That's hard to believe.'

'Yes, but you must know that you are not allowed to eat dog meat in Hong Kong.'

'No,' replied Woo Sing, not interested, for she did not like dog meat anyway. She said nothing more, but decided these English were truly, wonderfully mad.

Miss Campbell was a distant relative from an impoverished branch of the Williams' family and had been favoured with the task of keeping the local servants at a decent distance from their employers. She achieved this with discretion and kindness, which drew approval from both sides of the domestic frontier.

Had Sir William Williams been more perceptive, he could have used her talents much more profitably in one of his great enterprises. Perhaps he did know this, and had decided that a peaceful household was more important. A tall man of rather childish good looks, he remained aloof, dealing with those below him either coldly or facetiously, as the mood took him. Miss Campbell had served him faithfully, even though he had scarcely noticed her for many years. She knew he found it easier to impress young, inexperienced girls than mature women.

She too had been rapidly taken advantage of in a strange land, in a new situation where her great prospects were not easily discarded. Fortunately, she had not become pregnant and when he had tired of her and taken up a new secretary, she had found it difficult to appear sufficiently distressed to pander to his vanity. Although he was a poor copy from the impressive Williams' mould, she felt that his son, Kim, had somehow inherited those former, finer qualities. Perhaps that was because she had reared the child herself.

Woo Sing, though not fond of the dogs, was most efficient with them, and they became her special task. One day, there was to be a Ladies and Dogs afternoon in the grounds of one of the great Taipan's houses. That day, her full attention from early morning, was given to the grooming of the dogs. After lunch she took them to the front of the house and waited for her mistress. The limousine arrived, and with much gentle pushing and wheedling, the dogs were placed on the back seat with their mistress.

'Charles, I do not like a Chinese girl riding in front with you,' Lady Williams said sharply. 'Please place her in the luggage container.'

'My lady, the luggage container is already full,' replied the cautious driver.

'Then empty it,' Lady Williams said, irritated.

'My lady, the luggage container is airtight, and the girl would suffocate in a few minutes. She would be dead by the time we arrived at the gardens.'

Woo Sing did not understand, but obviously she had annoyed the great lady, for perhaps the dogs were not properly groomed. However, Charles grabbed her arm and firmly placed her beside him in the front seat, and Lady Williams, slightly pink in the face, said nothing further as Charles drove away.

It was a bad day for Charles. Shortly after reaching the lowest streets, he encountered roadworks and a long diversion, which took the party through the back streets of Sai Ying Pun. Lady Williams had not seen this area before and as the car slowly drove past the stalls, squalid shop fronts, and broken pavements, she saw to her horror a series of mangy and dirty dogs, most with their ribs clearly displayed.

She stopped the car and almost got out and brought some of the dogs back with her. Restraining this impulse, she decided more official aid was required and announced she would speak with the governor that afternoon. A small child was affectionately patting one of the more repulsive specimens. Lady Williams felt he was being too rough and noted how early in life Cantonese cruelty to dogs began.

They finally arrived. Although they had been delayed it was still early and some time before the other guests would arrive. Lady Williams' friend and hostess, Lady Alice, greeted her effusively and commented on the beauty of the dogs.

'My dear, the dog amah does not match them in grooming,' Lady Alice said bluntly.

Lady Williams looked at Woo Sing carefully for the first time. 'Her clothes are the same as they always wear, Alice.'

'Quite so, dear Angela,' replied Alice. 'But the girl's hair does not match the uniform and so detracts from the appearance of the dogs.'

Lady Williams knew her friend's secret passion was the grooming of hair.

'Indeed, you're right,' she replied. 'Perhaps you could

quickly take her away and look for scissors and a comb.'

Woo Sing was busy restraining the dogs, which were both deeply interested in Lady Alice's poodle. The two women approached her and Lady Alice tilted her head slightly upwards and looked very carefully at her. Woo Sing recoiled, as the woman was obviously intending to cut her hair.

Lady Williams said sharply, 'Stand still, girl.'

After hesitating, Woo Sing decided against running away and stood quite still. Carefully noting the shape of the girl's face and finding it surprisingly beautiful, Lady Alice accepted the challenge.

In ten minutes or so, Woo Sing received a hairstyle she initially resented but later accepted and kept after realising how it enhanced her face. Both women stepped back, immensely pleased at their work. Lady Alice had styled her most imaginative hair cut in years. She would dearly have loved to have it photographed, but knowing her taciturn friend, decided it was unwise to ask.

Woo Sing had adopted a careful lack of expression that she had learned to use during criticism sessions in the commune. Certainly, some things one learned at home were very useful here. The dogs pulled her away from the two women and she allowed them to take her around the small but exquisitely cultivated gardens and lawns. Guests arrived and the minor affair of the servant's haircut was soon forgotten by the two women.

Lady Williams, with the technical skill of one accustomed to many a social skirmish, cut off the retreat of the governor.

She drove him steadily backwards with the relentless energy of a Panzer division at full stride. Finally, the governor settled down to listen attentively, or apparently so, although he was really enjoying the sight of a pretty amah struggling with two Afghans on a leash.

'Mange,' said Lady Williams. 'Sai Ying Pun is full of mange. It is a desperate situation, Governor, and must be dealt with very quickly.'

The governor started back slightly. *The confounded woman has somehow gotten into a slum area and now wants me to rebuild it for improved dog health.*

A kind but forceful man, he had great affection for the Chinese and little for Lady Williams, but her voice was far more powerful than the combined voices of the squatters and slum-dwellers. He said vaguely, 'I think a committee would be the answer.'

'Indeed, that is an excellent idea,' replied Lady Williams.

'Thank you, quite so,' muttered the governor, considering a mental list of those civil servants whom he particularly disliked, who might be asked to serve as committee members.

As they made their way back to the main crowd, he said, 'I shall give the matter my immediate and undivided attention, Lady Williams.' Then, with a beaming smile, he escaped into the middle of the melee of guests, dogs, amahs and servants. The governor really did not like dogs, and this annual event was one of the unstated reasons why, in his annual secret report to the Colonial Office, he steadfastly maintained that Hong Kong was still a hardship post for senior civil servants.

As the day ended, even the Afghans were exhausted. They had taken Woo Sing on endless marches about the garden, had burnt the stems of numerous tender bushes with their frequent urination and, finally, in a moment of glory, had taken a few threads out of the governor's white trousers.

Miss Campbell was surprised to see Woo Sing return with a different hairstyle, but she kept her counsel until the dogs, family and staff were fed. Upon finally entering Woo Sing's tiny room, she found the girl staring into a small mirror, trying to assess the damage.

'Come with me, Woo Sing,' she said, and led her through a back passage to her room. There, in front of a large mirror, she sat Woo Sing down.

'You need not tell me who cut your hair. It does look very nice and if you want to improve it further, I will cut it a little bit more for you.'

Woo Sing twisted her head into those universal poses by which women either admire or criticise themselves in mirror. Miss Campbell waited patiently, and finally Woo Sing asked, 'What shall I do?'

'I would let it grow a little and then keep it that way. It makes you look very attractive. You know, many important women in the colony have consulted that strange lady about the best hairstyle for them, so you are really very lucky.'

Woo Sing was still not convinced, but she was very tired and decided to leave the matter.

'Thank you very much, Miss Campbell,' she replied. 'I would very much like to learn English so I can deal with this kind of situation. I am at a great disadvantage without it.'

'I will lend you a small book,' Mis Campbell said. 'And when you get your first pay, you should buy a cheap radio. Every evening on the radio, there is an English lesson.'

*

Tong Pooi and Wa Hing were pleased to see Woo Sing when she returned for a visit; they had missed her more than they wished to say. Wa Hing's employers were very satisfied with his work and he was now permanently employed as a driver.

'A driver, Woo Sing,' he said proudly.

'Don't you need to have some sort of document?'

'Oh, you mean a driving licence?' replied Wa Hing. 'That is not a problem. My boss bought one for me. I did not even have to go down to the office. As for sitting a test, that would take months. Even if you did sit the test, you still have to give the examiner his 'tea money'. So why not buy a licence straight away?'

'That seems very reasonable,' said Woo Sing.

Tong Pooi started to say something, but Wa Hing interrupted him and said, 'Look at my new map of the streets, and all to a rough scale. My boss says even now I know more about the streets close to the factory than men who have worked for him for years.'

Tong Pooi patiently waited for the flow of words to end. 'Please write to me, Woo Sing, if you cannot come to see us. I will write to you a little each week.'

Woo Sing realised, in a vague way, that the old man was desperate not to break the new link with his two friends. She could not resist teasing him. 'I might write in English, Tong Pooi, and then you would need a scribe.'

The old man smiled and said, 'When your first letter written in English arrives, I will learn English, too.'

The excited look on Woo Sing's face made him feel he had spoken rashly, for he did not want to learn that troublesome language.

The hours of freedom were soon gone and after paying a brief visit to Chen Tien Wa and slyly slipping her some money, Woo Sing was escorted back to the Williams' mansion by a very curious Wa Hing.

Chapter 6
Language lessons

The Williams' household ran by the clock inside Lady Williams' brain. For weeks at a stretch, the clock would run smoothly, coinciding with the time kept by other residents of Hong Kong. During these periods of calm, the household worked methodically, but with a serenity marred by the knowledge of turmoil ahead.

Woo Sing began work during a calm period. As the weeks passed and the strangeness of her surroundings faded, she rejoiced in the good food, the light work and the progress of her English. Miss Campbell had seen many Chinese try to learn the language and even though she believed that many had a gift for learning they failed to make progress.

Woo Sing turned her energy to mastering the language and at first found the construction of the few characters of the alphabet childishly simple. Once she grasped the concept of building letters into words, she made rapid progress. The building of words into sentences was a greater challenge. To her, the sentence construction lacked the order and logic of

Cantonese and Mandarin. It took her many weeks to understand words of one or two letters made such a difference to the meaning.

Meanwhile, the precision of Lady Williams' English periodically failed when she became disturbed and her instructions became increasingly vague. The staff knew their survival in these times depended on following Miss Campbell's instructions with infinite care. These episodes appeared to be spontaneous, and many of the staff believed that they were related to the movements of the moon or the wind. Others felt that an unhappy, restless spirit was the cause. Miss Campbell knew that this spirit arrived when Sir William was again bolstering his inadequate ego and excessive conceit by pursuing a new secretary or office girl. Lady Williams wondered why she sometimes felt feverish; only Miss Campbell understood the cause.

Woo Sing's early morning job was to groom the dogs and take them to her mistress's bedroom. Once there, she knocked twice and let the dogs through the door, without showing herself and, most importantly, her Chinese face.

The huge animals sat by the end of the bed while Lady Williams fed them titbits from her breakfast. After the meal, the dogs were released into the passage, where Woo Sing waited out of sight to catch them.

Today, Woo Sing knocked twice, opened the door slightly, let the dogs go, and stepped away. She had barely turned away from the door when it was flung open and Lady Williams, in a transparent gown, stood before her. The gown concealed nothing and the startled girl shrank back from the gaunt and sagging body.

'Who told you to let the dogs into my room? You Cantonese witch!' shouted Lady Williams.

Some of the meaning came through and Woo Sing opened her mouth to reply, but the shock was so great that no sound came out. Miss Campbell found her—a totally rigid Woo Sing, mouth open, confronted by the statuesque Lady Williams.

Miss Campbell said quietly, 'Lady Williams, this girl will be dismissed.' She grabbed hold of the dogs and gave them to Woo Sing, who quickly hurried away.

Lady Williams had asked for the old transparent gown the day before and Miss Campbell was annoyed with herself, because sometimes this kind of thing was the first sign of trouble, and she had missed it.

During their brief spell of freedom, the dogs had eaten all the breakfast and the cook had to begin the long and elaborate preparations again. Lady Williams allowed herself to be escorted back to bed, given the morning paper, and offered a long drink of gin. She became very fond of this during her 'feverish' times.

Woo Sing stood in the kitchen, bitterly reflecting on her life's endless cycle of hope and disaster when Miss Campbell entered.

'Stay out of sight for two days,' she said. 'Take the dogs for long walks, morning and afternoon. The dogs will not be needed. In two days, the mistress will have forgotten all about it.'

The cook, who had been cursing in Shanghainese, stopped to advise Woo Sing, 'Follow those orders and you will be all right.'

He resumed cooking and cursing, knowing full well that the breakfast would probably be returned without a bite taken, along with orders for his dismissal.

Chauffeur Charles also dreaded these times for he was frequently called late at night to drive to her ladyship's friends' houses, only to have the instructions cancelled at the last minute. Or worse, he would be directed to bang loudly on locked gates to wake those within.

Charles still occasionally suffered a recurring nightmare concerning an incident in one of the more confused and crowded parts of the city. On a late-night drive, Lady Williams had once stopped the car and attempted to take a dog from a child who was escorting the mangy animal on an urgent midnight journey. Within five minutes, the car was surrounded by shouting, cursing and spitting residents, beating their fists on the panelling.

Unable to believe that anyone would want the dog, they had thought that an attempt was being made to steal the child. Lady Williams had remained outside the car, treating the mob like a pack of badly trained foxhounds needing a cuff or two. Charles, who was not the faintest bit concerned about her ladyship's safety, had locked the car doors and waited.

An alert resident phoned the police with the car number and a clear cryptic message went to cars in the area: Lady Williams in Mong Kok. The police pacified the mob by explaining that the woman loved dogs and that she was harmless, mad and English. The people had retired into their crowded and overheated rooms while a trembling Charles drove a totally unsubdued Lady Williams home to her bedroom.

Woo Sing required more practice with her English and asked Miss Campbell to recommend a cheap class. She introduced her to Police Inspector Campbell, a nephew who had recently called on Miss Campbell to ask for practise in Cantonese. He was a young man of cheerful character, with looks that could charitably be described as manly or rugged, rather than handsome. Any emotions aroused in him through conversing with an attractive Chinese girl were quickly dispersed by Woo Sing's intense concentration and speed of reply.

He quickly improved his Cantonese as she was not only a good pupil but a demanding and persistent teacher.

The weeks passed into months, and apart from her visits to her friends, Woo Sing's days were fully engaged with obligations to Lady Williams and her dogs, Inspector Campbell and his lessons, and the quiet instructions of Miss Campbell.

Her debt to Chien Tin Wa had long been repaid but she continued to leave a little money and give the children sweets. Chien Tin Wa noted this and protested, but Woo Sing continued regardless. The two women had therefore kept up the pretence, although both knew that it could not last forever.

Chai Dung was steadily becoming more emaciated. Chien Tin Wa would pause during her assembly work and note how his features were already drawn into an impassive death mask, with only his heaving chest indicating he was still alive. Once, when his cough became very severe, she looked for the heroin dealer and begged a packet. The price was beyond her means and the alternative was obvious. The deal was carried out in a dingy backyard where she patiently waited while the man enjoyed himself. Afterwards, she hurried home, disgusted and sickened by her behaviour, but pleased with the heroin.

Inspector Campbell made several attempts to question Woo Sing on her previous life, particularly in China, but he was met with a polite but determined evasiveness. Eventually he realised that whatever Woo Sing's views were on China, she was not going to criticise her native land to a stranger.

*

The Williams' household received the visit of Kim Williams, heir and young master, with remarkably little fuss or outward sign of affection. The atmosphere was set by both parents, who, after accidently creating the solitary child, had decided that the most obvious solution to the problem was to ignore it. A rather shy boy, he accepted the indifference of his parents without much anguish, for an amah had supplied maternal affection and Miss Campbell had guided his early development until the boarding school had imposed its own regime.

Despite his mother detesting all things Chinese, he had learned Cantonese as a child, and when out of her hearing, he spoke to the servants in their own language. His interest in the Chinese culture was one he found increasingly difficult to conceal from his parents. They had decided it was a passing phase.

The morning was exceptionally clear, and although the city was already showing the first traces of thin smog on the Peak, the spring day was much as it had been when the first fishermen had entered the harbour.

Miss Campbell spoke rather tersely to Woo Sing. 'Master Kim will take the dogs this morning. You may walk a small way behind.'

Kim disliked dogs, but it was a convenient way of escaping the house and of convincing his mother that he liked her pets.

'They are her real children,' he had once observed to Miss Campbell, and she'd marvelled at his lack of bitterness.

It had also enabled him to escape from his father, for on his previous holiday, Sir Williams, in a rare mood of fatherly concern, had directed one of his old mistresses to take the boy out of himself.

Her attempts to teach the boy had been so direct and aggressive, and his responses so unsatisfactory, that after a detailed report from her, Sir William had shrugged his shoulders and decided to leave such things alone.

Kim had not realised that the dog amah was to accompany him. For a while he was puzzled, wondering why an attractive young girl was following a few steps behind. Eventually he understood who she was, and passed the dogs to her. He told her, in Cantonese, to be very careful.

'Of course, I shall be careful,' she replied in a broad Scottish accent.

He was stunned and stopped for a moment. He leaned up against a railing and roared with laughter.

She turned quickly and the dogs dragged her forward. He walked a little way behind her, noting her easy grace and quickened to catch up and inspect her more closely.

She was pretty and, being Chinese, it could be assumed she would not be coy or make sly advances. So he decided he would walk the dogs each morning.

He said, rather shyly, 'You were not here when I was home last time.'

Woo Sing replied, 'No, Master, I have only been here a few months.'

'You must have been born in Hong Kong for you know English quite well. Or rather, Scottish,' he said, laughing.

'No, Master, I have only been in Hong Kong a few months,' Woo Sing replied.

'Then where did you come from?'

Woo Sing was trapped and could think of no convenient lie.

'I came from Macao,' she replied, inspired at last.

Kim replied, 'I don't care how you came here, or whether you have a permit or not. I would never tell anyone. But if you did come from China, I would really like you to tell me about it because I am very interested.'

Woo Sing stopped and turned towards him. 'Is that a promise, Master?'

'Of course,' he replied.

Woo Sing inspected him closely for a few seconds, then

said, 'I did come over the border a few months ago, but I am an unimportant person and know nothing of the government of my country.'

'I do not want to know of the plans of your government. I want to know how ordinary people live and what they think about.'

'I can tell you how I lived and what I thought about, but everyone in the commune has different ways of doing things and different thoughts, and mostly they keep them to themselves.'

Kim looked at her with disbelief. 'We are all of us different, you know. Just as different as you all are,' she said,

Kim stared at her for a few moments, and said, 'Of course, of course, I never thought of it in any other way.'

Little more was said as both preferred not to talk and they returned home, each to their own place in the household.

The dogs enjoyed their new companion as they associated him with longer walks over new and more exciting ground. Miss Campbell noted the new arrangement and discreetly rearranged Woo Sing's duties so that she and Kim were able to spend most of the glorious October mornings walking around the island. Even on that crowded bit of rock, as Kim discovered on his solitary walks during past holidays, there were places of seclusion and beauty to be found.

Woo Sing felt the world of the resettlement block and Tong Pooi fading into remoteness, much further than the few miles across the harbour. She had missed an occasional weekend, but had always written to Tong Pooi and had begged Wa

Hing to visit Chen Tien Wa.

There were few visible signs of autumn around Fragrant Harbour, but the clinging air and stifling heat of summer had disappeared, with a new vitality flooding the city and its people. Kim began to lead the dogs and observers noted this with amusement. The young couple would have been shocked if they had known how many noticed them, but fortunately these people kept their observations to themselves. From those Chinese they met, Woo Sing sensed some antagonism at her companionship with a European, but she cared little for their opinion.

Usually they walked, but on one pleasant morning Kim tied the dogs to a massive post, ignoring their barks of protest as he and Woo Sing sat on a bench beneath a shady tree.

'Do you like it better here than there?' Kim asked casually.

'Better than where?' asked Woo Sing.

'Why, mainland China, of course,' replied Kim, understanding that he would need to be tactful. Woo Sing was silent for a while.

'I like it here better, because it is more exciting, and although it is very cruel, one can make progress.'

'You did not make progress in mainland China?' asked Kim.

'There was nowhere for me to progress to as I belonged to the wrong family. Perhaps, if I had stayed, my children would have outlived the hatred. But a man can live for sixty or seventy years and if he passes on his hatred to his son, that makes over a hundred years of hatred. I could not wait that long,' she said.

'I thought you were allowed to repent.'

'But I never did anything wrong to repent of,' she replied angrily. 'It was my parents and their parents, and their parents, who did the wrong things. In my home, things are very slow to change and even if they do change, after a little while things always seem to come back to where they started.'

'You hate the communists, then,' said Kim, feeling he could be a little bolder.

'Of course not,' replied Woo Sing. 'They have done a lot for my homeland, and seeing this place, I think what they are doing is right. I did not realise it when I was there, and perhaps it is right that I should pay the penalty for what my ancestors did. I still love Chairman Mao. He is not responsible for every bad commune leader or corrupt official.'

Kim said quietly, 'It is the culmination of the passions of a people that make its history. A leader like Mao senses those passions and directs their energies.'

'What does 'culmination' mean?'

'The adding together of things.'

Woo Sing said quietly, 'If one could add up all the passions of my people, they could build a paradise. Even Chairman Mao has not done that.'

'Make a paradise, or destroy the earth?' replied Kim.

'Chairman Mao understands us,' Woo Sing argued. 'He knows that we Chinese have a passion to succeed in whatever we want to do, and we have a contradictory passion to avoid changing anything at the same time. That is the thing I find so strange here. People are always trying to change things.'

'You mean that the local people are trying to change things? But you say they hate change.'

Woo Sing was confused. 'Well, I think they are very progressive,' she said defensively.

Kim felt he was not getting the information he really wanted. 'How do you love Chairman Mao?' he asked.

'Like you love anybody,' Woo Sing said.

'But it must be different,' said Kim. 'A long time ago in Europe it was the same. Men went off on crusades to fight for God and thousands of women locked themselves away, saying they loved only God.'

Woo Sing said tartly, 'But we did not lock ourselves away. We worked hard.'

'Merely a matter of detail. You loved some person you would never even see.'

'Like I love my father, then,' said Woo Sing angrily. 'I do not wish to talk about it anymore.'

She got up, untied the dogs, and started to walk along the path. Kim caught up with her.

'I am sorry, Woo Sing,' he said. 'I am a tactless Westerner, but I am really interested in your country and I wish it well. It would be much easier to wish it well, though, if I could only understand it better.'

Woo Sing stopped. She looked deep into his earnest *gweilo* face, and believed him.

'I'll tell you a bit more from time to time but do not ask me those sorts of questions again.'

They wandered along a narrow path that twisted about the

side of the Peak and came to a small outcrop of rock. Again, they rested. There was little space, so they sat close together, idly commenting on the features of the city.'

'You see, my people can build great things,' said Woo Sing proudly.

Kim remained silent, not wishing to provoke another argument by saying that, for the first fifty years, it was English ideas and Chinese hands that had built Hong Kong.

Instead, he spoke tactfully. 'Yes. My father tells me that since the war, your people have done a great deal for the city.' Indeed, the sea, the city, and the hills together gave the illusion of one of the nobler works of man.

Woo Sing's interest in the city's history was lost as she became aware of Kim's body close to hers. She could see that the feeling was mutual for he was no longer sitting in an easy manner. The sensation was not so much pleasant as urgent and charged and she had no wish to shift herself away. She had felt such emotions before as a younger girl and had experimented with stroking and touching her body a few times. Later, a more powerful feeling had sometimes arisen in the presence of Ah Hon and she realised that for several weeks she had forgotten about him, not once remembered that cheerful face and strong will, which had sustained her through the most miserable years of her girlhood.

She began to cry, and Kim, at first embarrassed, placed his arm about her. 'I am very sorry if I have upset you.'

'No, you have not upset me,' she said. 'It is something that I will never tell anyone else about.'

She felt his hands on her breasts and her nipples became firm to his rather bumbling touch. She turned to him, pushing his hand away. She noted how his face had that peculiar expression of excitement and expectation she had sometimes seen in Wa Hing. She was frightened and stood up.

'I am a Chinese girl, not a Western girl, and you cannot touch me.'

As they walked back, Kim looked so distressed that she let him hold her hand along the secluded parts of the path. But she remained silent, for she was thinking of Ah Hon and Kim.

Despite her angry denial, she was happy to hold his hand. With such confused emotions, she felt quite ill and exhausted by the time they arrived at the house.

Kim was alarmed by the intense disturbance he had aroused in the girl. *Obviously she was not prone to superficial or passing passions*, he thought.

'I have only a few days left before I must return to school. Please let me walk with you,' he said before they parted.

Woo Sing was silent but realised they could not be seen standing and talking for too long. 'I would be very sad if you do not come,' she said.

He left her and returned to his bedroom, elated. There was nothing wrong with him at all as the tightness in his trousers amply proved. It had been his father's frightful old whore who had turned him off before. Now he knew that he was a man and a vague idea began forming in his mind.

Woo Sing kept herself busy for the remainder of the day,

helping in the kitchen and doing the extra duties of the wash amah, who was ill. Several times, she walked along the balcony with the clothes basket in her hands, apparently on her errands but really trying to get a glimpse of Kim. That night, although tired out, she struggled to sleep, her mind busy practising conversations for their walk the next morning. The conversations seemed to always finish with them holding hands and sitting close beside each other, and her excitement made her restless. She turned from one side of the bed to the other.

She tried thinking of Tong Pooi, Chen Tien Wa and her old friends, but they were part of another world and she would certainly not see them until the next morning. It was so stupid; Kim was a long-nosed *gweilo* boy, not particularly good-looking and certainly not manly like Wa Hing. Yet he made her feel special in a way that Ah Hon had only managed a few times at home. He would be gone in a few days and by the time he returned, she would have either left the house or learned to manage her own feelings. With that in mind, she fell into an exhausted sleep.

The autumn was passing with each day seeming clearer, cooler and more refreshing than the one before. Their walks became longer and much slower, developing into moments of apparently accidental touching and brushings of their bodies.

Frequently, they seemed to accidentally arrive at their secret outcrop, with its confined sitting space. He had begun to kiss her, and while she no longer protested, her Chinese purity made her restrain his hands, for that was simply going too far.

'You are not very emotional,' he said rather impatiently as she reflexively pushed his hands away.

She was unsure what to say. 'It is your Western impatience that is emotional,' she replied.

She got up and looked out over the city as Kim lay by her side. He asked quietly, 'What do you really know of emotion?'

'The things I feel now are something like, but not the same as, what I felt at home.'

'But you have never said that you had a male friend at home.'

'Oh! It was not a man,' replied Woo Sing. 'It was the team.'

'The team?'

'Yes. Sometimes when there was a special construction problem to be solved, usually with a lot of work to be done, we would march to it. We would shout and sing and follow the red bannermen, watching the banners flying in front of us. And we would work for hours, slowly, continuously, like the waves of the sea forever moving. And when we marched home, we were very tired, but we would still sing and shout, and I would see the red banner ahead of me. Many times, there was such passion in me for our team and the red banner, I would have followed it over a cliff.'

She turned, looking down at him. Smiling, she asked, 'Do you understand?'

He was not interested, for he was looking up at her, half twisted and set against the sunlight and the blue sky. 'No, I do not understand. That is your passion, but perhaps I have one of my own.'

'All Western men are the same,' teased Woo Sing. 'They

think only of girls. In a commune not far from ours, there was written across the door of the doctor's clinic, 'Making love is a mental illness and a waste of time'.'

'Really? Is it true?' asked Kim, sitting up.

'Of course! Why should I tell you a lie?'

'And did you believe it?' he asked quickly.

'When I read it, I did not understand what it meant,' replied Woo Sing.

'But you know now,' said Kim, trying to suppress a grin.

Woo Sing was silent. These Westerners had a way of trapping one in an argument, so that either one looked foolish or had to admit something. It was a technique she had seen before at home, but it was not practiced with such skill there.

'Perhaps I do,' she said, offended.

'I am sorry,' replied Kim. 'It was a stupid question.'

'Tomorrow, you leave,' said Woo Sing. 'But I will often come up here and think of what we have talked about.'

'Woo Sing, could you do me a simple favour?'

'I'm not sure.'

'It is nothing serious,' said Kim. 'I would like to take you to a restaurant this evening for a meal. It would be a Western meal and a change for you. We can go secretly.'

'How could we do that?' asked Woo Sing, realising by the way he had framed the question that she had given her consent. *This wretched English language was very tricky but there seemed no harm in going for a meal, especially a Western meal, which would be something new to tell Tong Pooi about.*

'Charles will arrange it,' said Kim. 'He is very good at

getting people in and out of the house without them being seen.'

'What would Miss Campbell say?'

'We will go after you finish work,' replied Kim.

'But I have no proper clothes to go to a restaurant,' said Woo Sing, with some relief in her voice.

Kim thought for a few moments. 'I know a girl I can get some clothes from. She is about the same size as you and Charles will bring them to your quarters.'

'What if I am discovered? I do not wish to lose my job.'

'Of course not. If that happens, I will speak to Miss Campbell and I'm sure everything will be all right.'

'I will wait for Charles in my room, then,' replied Woo Sing. They parted ways.

Kim was pleased that he had promised to accompany his father to the board meeting that afternoon for it would fill in a few hours before the evening meal with Woo Sing. They entered the imposing building that housed the offices of the Williams' company.

One hundred and twenty years before, the first company building had been a shaky patchwork of bamboo framing and some light wooden planks. That building was small, but the owner had been tough and energetic and had understood the Chinese businessmen. As the colony prospered, so the Williams' firm continued to move from one building to another. But as the buildings rose in height and grandeur, so did the members of the family decrease in their grace and performance. This was carefully noted by the jovial board members to whom Sir William took obvious pride in introducing Kim, who was aware he was being closely scrutinised as the next controller of a considerable financial empire. The same board members noted a rather uninterested, distracted youth, with few of the necessary business graces. Several made a mental note that perhaps the Williams' empire might be ready for penetration in a few years' time.

The board was discussing the amount to be paid to an informer for some promised secret information about a competitor.

'Fifty thousand is a great deal to pay for someone's new marketing plan,' Sir William said crossly. 'These people are getting too greedy. A few years ago, we would have had a competitor's complete account for a little over five thousand dollars.'

'I believe someone once paid twenty thousand dollars for ours,' said an elderly board member rather coldly.

Sir William flushed and looked very angry. He was aware that it had been one of his private secretaries who had made the deal, and that the accounts had been removed from his bedroom. In fact, they had not been removed—his secretary had entertained him in bed while her husband frantically photographed the documents beneath the bed. *She had been a wretched girl.*

He also had to pay a considerable amount for photographs taken by the husband. This was to avoid them being supplied to the markets in the seedier parts of town.

They had become a prosperous and happy couple and now

owned a successful restaurant, nicknamed by those in the know as The Golden Bedroom.

When the meeting finally ended, Kim departed with relief.

Meanwhile, Charles knocked lightly on Woo Sing's door and pushed a large parcel into her hands. 'Put these on quickly. I shall come back in about ten minutes.'

There were shoes, stockings, a long flowing dress and a delicately made jacket. There was also an ornate brooch, which she decided after some thought must be designed to be put in the hair. The gown was beautiful, a little loose in parts but nonetheless the most glorious clothing she had ever worn, and certainly better than anything she'd dreamt of buying in the market. The front was very low cut, but it did not matter, as her brassiere covered the bare flesh. Charles returned, knocked on the door, and without waiting for Woo Sing to reply, entered. He stared at her for a moment or two.

'It is very suitable. You are quite beautiful, Woo Sing. If you know what you are doing, you will get a long way in this colony, and even become quite rich from this household. If you listen to me, that is, you could do very well for yourself.'

'I will be most grateful for your advice, but we had better not delay, for the master is waiting.'

Charles could not resist a grimace. After all these years, it made him wince to hear some half-grown boy referred to as the master, and then he caught sight of Woo Sing's front and roared with laughter.

'You cannot go out like that with those ragged old underclothes showing,' he said, and Woo Sing blushed.

'I have not got anything suitable for this dress; it will have to do.'

Charles sat on the chair and roared with laughter. 'Woo Sing, you certainly need taking in hand. I think I can help you a great deal.' He grinned and stood. 'First you will have to take off that battered bit of modesty.'

'I certainly will not.'

'Then you will embarrass the master,' he explained. 'You will look foolish in the restaurant. In any case, all the Western women wear such clothes and no one will notice you unless you go as you are.'

'Leave the room then, please,' said Woo Sing. Charles departed with a grin. She joined him a few minutes later, blushing furiously as he inspected the now revealing garment.

'I think the young master will now find that very satisfactory.'

He also decided he would pay more attention to Woo Sing after he had taken the young master out to Kai Tak airport and disposed of him for the next few months.

Kim stared at her for a few moments as she walked down the path ahead of Charles. The third family car was waiting. As Charles opened the rear door Woo Sing stepped back to allow Kim to enter, but he gently pushed her forward. 'In the West, the lady always enters the car first.'

Woo Sing gave them both a small bow and climbed in as gracefully as she could manage.

The restaurant was towards the top of a gigantic building and provided a dramatic view of the lights of the harbour.

Woo Sing was pleased when they entered, for no one seemed to take any notice of them and she noticed many of the woman, some of them Chinese, wore similar dresses to hers. As she was preparing to sit down, Kim walked behind her and gently pushed her chair forward. Taken by surprise, she sat down with rather a thump.

She noticed one of the Chinese women at a nearby table smirking at her, so she returned the stare. When the woman turned away, Woo Sing felt she had won a small victory. Her pleasure was cut short when she glanced at the table and saw the huge array of knives and forks.

'Can I have chopsticks?' she whispered to Kim.

'Do as I do and no one will notice,' he replied.

Woo Sing had often seen the cook grilling the large pieces of steak that Sir William was so fond of and had always found the smell delicious. When Kim asked her what she would like, she said, 'I would like a large piece of steak, the same as your father eats.'

Kim laughed and said, 'And so it shall be, and we shall wash it down with champagne.'

'Is that wine? For I do not like wine, it is bitter.'

'This wine is not bitter, it is sweet.'

'Once, when I was ill as a child,' she said, 'I had to drink a small glass of snake bile wine each evening and it was so bitter that the taste stayed in my mouth all night.'

'Why did you drink that?'

'At the time, I was feeling very tired, and my mother thought that the wriggling of the snake trapped in the wine would make me more energetic.'

Kim had learned by now not to laugh too loudly at Woo Sing's theories and said, 'This wine is not bitter and although it sometimes makes you wriggle, it is very nice to drink.'

Woo Sing carefully followed Kim's way of eating, and as he kept filling her glass with the sweet wine, she started to care less about what others thought of her dress and her style of eating. The lights of the city became dazzling and fascinating and the strange Western music with its throbbing rhythm made her feel very happy.

Towards the end of the evening, when she had to relieve herself, Kim leant forward to whisper, 'There will be no Chinese name on the door, only a picture of a woman. That is your door.'

She entered the gleaming room, full of white tiles, numerous basins and large mirrors. It was the first time she had used a Western toilet. As she sat slumped back, half asleep and dizzy, she thought that if this was the Western life, she liked it very much. She had already come a long way from Ming Tak Street and with the help of that kind Charles she could probably go a long way further. She returned to Kim and after drinking more champagne, which she decided made one thirstier than before, they decided to leave. She felt dizzy, with happiness she supposed, and took Kim's offered arm without the slightest trace of embarrassment.

Charles once more opened the car door with a flourish. Full of food and overfull of wine, she sank back into the soft upholstery.

Kim had said little towards the end of their glorious evening, but she supposed that he, too, was tired and slightly dizzy with the wine. As the lights of the city flashed past and she felt herself slipping into a pleasant sleep, she felt his hands on her breasts. But now she was too tired to bother pushing him away. In any case, it was a pleasant feeling, and she thought, *Perhaps we Chinese are too strict about such matters.* For it was such a pleasant feeling, and there seemed little harm in it. Kim was kind and generous, and Charles had promised to look after her. The lights were even more dazzling, and as she turned to Kim—who seemed close and ready to kiss her—she giggled, 'If you are not quick, I will soon be asleep.' The lights of the city receded as the car climbed the Peak, and as she drifted further into sleep, she vaguely felt his hands on her thighs.

*

Now and again, Miss Campbell allowed herself the luxury of lying in bed a little later than usual, secure in the knowledge that the household servants would follow her careful instructions to the word. She had devised these instructions over many years and they had gradually been perfected to accommodate the eternal Cantonese aspiration to never accept a decision for which one may later be held responsible.

Most possible domestic situations had been covered and with alternative solutions. Although nothing was ever written down, all the servants concerned knew the correct drill.

She was therefore considerably annoyed to be gently shaken awake by one of the senior amahs.

'Missy. Ah Sing is not in her room, what shall I do with the dogs?' asked the woman.

It had been an oversight in the tight planning, for it was the dog amah's job to take the dogs to the mistress's door and there were no back-up instructions.

Miss Campbell sighed wearily. 'Ah Gin, take the dogs to the door yourself and when Woo Sing returns, send her to me immediately.'

The woman disappeared and Miss Campbell, her late sleep ruined, lay in bed composing a short speech for Woo Sing about how she had lately become somewhat too familiar with Kim. It was now no use allowing her to develop any hopes of a position better than dog amah for it would disrupt the delicate balance of face within the servant household. She was quite pleased that Kim had left on the early morning plane for she could now discipline Woo Sing, who was a pleasant and spirited girl, but whom she suspected had rather grand ideas. She bathed, dressed and prepared for the inspection of duties. On her way, she decided to enter Kim's room to list the details of what would need tidying and rearrangement.

The room was at the end of a long balcony. Woo Sing lay spreadeagled on the bed, still asleep and covered by a single sheet covering her. The scene filled Miss Campbell with rage. She tore away the covering sheet and slapped the girl several times to wake her. In a fury, she noticed that the girl had bled into the sheet, a detail that would have to be concealed from gossiping servants.

Woo Sing woke with a pounding headache and a sensation in her body much the same as when she had landed on the coast. Unbelievably, she was naked and it was Miss Campbell who was slapping her.

It must be a nightmare, she thought. Then her mind began to function and as Miss Campbell's hand once more descended, she remembered the previous evening with its termination of desire, pleasure, struggle and pain, mixed into a confusion of feelings and sensations. She held away Miss Campbell's hand and pulled the sheet over to partly cover her body. She fell back exhausted, tears running across her cheeks.

This was the ultimate disgrace; she had been cheated, robbed and abased. The only positive was that her family would never know. She sat up, cold sweat forming on her forehead, and began swallowing. Miss Campbell quickly held up a large antique bowl into which Woo Sing vomited copiously. Between her tears and vomiting, Woo Sing cried to her rough nurse, 'He has destroyed me and I trusted him.'

Miss Campbell calmed down. The memory of her own experience with the senior Williams smothered her fury. She roughly dressed Woo Sing and used her knowledge of the servants' movements to get the girl back to her own room without being observed. By the time they reached it, Miss Campbell's sympathy had been restored. She noted with alarm that although the vomiting had ceased, the girl seemed to be passing into a state of shock, and not making a sound.

This was a bad sign. She quickly fetched the most senior amah, an intelligent woman able to be trusted and relied upon as entirely discreet.

Ah Heung, alarmed at the girl's condition, whispered to Miss Campbell, 'Please, Missy, you stay until I come back with some herbs. I know the right medicine for this.'

Within a few minutes, she returned with a bowl of hot brownish fluid with a penetrating smell. The two women made Woo Sing drink at least half a pint. After a few moments she vomited most of it up, but they made her drink more. Soon she became drowsy and fell into a deep sleep.

'There is a sheet in the young master's room. Destroy it!' Miss Campbell ordered Ah Heung,

Ah Heung looked at Miss Campbell. They knew each other intimately and Miss Campbell suspected the amah knew of her own problems with Sir William. She also knew Ah Heung had once been a young amah in an old-fashioned Chinese household. There were few things that each did not understand of the other, but both women knew of Woo Sing's feelings. All this passed in the meeting of eyes, for little was said.

'I shall do it immediately, Missy,' Ah Heung said and hurried away.

Miss Campbell visited the kitchen and gave her Shanghainese colleague instructions for lunch. Next, she turned to Ah Wah, a young amah who was watching curiously. 'There are at least two big blotches on the dining room table. You must polish it immediately. It's your job to keep it spotless.'

The girl blanched and rushed off to find rags and polish.

Miss Campbell knew the table was without the slightest blemish. By now she was thinking more clearly, and she realised that Woo Sing was more a victim than an accomplice.

Kim, the lonely little boy she had tried to make into a decent man, had betrayed her. This situation had shattered her normal hard-headed Scotswoman's self-control. She rarely had time for childish emotions but now she flung herself on her bed and wept.

Next day, Woo Sing appeared much better and Ah Heung coaxed her into having two bowls of plain rice. Ah Heung felt that the worst was over as she watched Woo Sing scoop the rice into her mouth with typical peasant lack of delicacy. In mid-afternoon, Woo Sing had another visitor, Charles.

'I hope that you are much better now,' said Charles.

Woo Sing looked at him guardedly, but he was an important person in the household, so she replied, 'Yes, sir, I am feeling a little bit better.'

Charles felt it was now or never and there was little to lose. 'Woo Sing, you are a pretty girl, but you know now that you have no use to any man for a wife. You can stay on as an amah or lead a better life with me to look after you.'

Woo Sing simply shook her head, stirring Charles to attack more vigorously. 'Woo Sing, you know you are dirt in your own people's eyes. Even your own family would not want to know you now. Once you have had one man, the rest come easily, and after a while you will even like it. I have an important friend who looks after girls with your problem. You can become very rich working for him—and for me, of course.'

Charles had been so determined that he had not heard Ah Heung enter quietly. She pulled him from the room. Outside, she faced him, saying, 'Mister driver, the girl looks a good proposition, but I think she may bring you endless trouble. Take my advice and leave her alone.'

Charles knew Ah Heung was an honest woman but also knew her brother was a triad. He had seen one man chopped to death and had no desire to see those long, sharp, shiny blades descending in the last moments of his life. He shrugged and walked off. *The old cow will probably pass her over to her brother*, he thought. *But I would rather be a live chauffeur than a dead pimp.* And so his plans for Woo Sing were abandoned.

Ah Heung returned to the room, and Miss Campbell followed her.

Ah Heung sat on the bed close to Woo Sing, and said, 'Ah Sing, this has happened to many amahs before. It has happened to all of us. We survive.'

Miss Campbell sat on the other side of Woo Sing. Putting her arm around the girl, she said, 'Yes, it has happened to all of us, Woo Sing. All of us.'

Woo Sing looked at her strange *gweilo* face. It was one she knew she could really trust. The three women sat quietly for a few moments before Miss Campbell got briskly to her feet and looked sternly at Woo Sing. 'Tomorrow you will resume your duties and no more shall be said of this.' Woo Sing nodded.

After Miss Campbell had left, Ah Heung spoke quietly. 'Ah Sing, I have bought you something to put inside so that you will heal quite quickly. The herbalist said to put a little on twice a day and soon all will be mended. Never tell a man what happened. Although they pretend, most men are too stupid to ever know.'

By the next day, an orderly routine was once more established and any trace of Kim's visit had vanished. Lady Williams vaguely noticed that the photos of her son were missing from their usual places in her bedroom and drawing room. She was irritated, and intended to ask Miss Campbell. But the drawing room photo was soon replaced by a glorious shot of her Afghans and she forgot about it.

Sir William also noticed some changes in the drawing room but could not work out what they were. His mind wandered to his secretary, who was rather simple but great fun, for she had many tricks. He had been dismayed to find that an old prostitute had taught her for the colossal sum of five hundred dollars, but his dismay was soon lost in pleasure.

The dogs sensed the change in their morning handler as Woo Sing was much sterner than before and their walks much shorter.

Lady Williams, ever sensitive to the Afghans' condition, remarked, 'The dogs have lost their bloom, Miss Campbell.'

'I shall see to it immediately, my lady,' said Miss Campbell, and soon found the cause.

'You must walk the dogs at least two miles each day,' Woo Sing was told firmly. 'And you must brush them much more thoroughly than you have been doing these last few days. I do not expect to have to tell you again about this.'

Woo Sing accepted the sharp words without comment and within a few days, dogs and mistress were once more exploring the roads and paths of the higher levels of the island.

Inspector Campbell said to his aunt after one of his Cantonese lessons, 'Woo Sing is very cold and distant. I am very sorry if I have offended her. It was quite unintentional.'

'It is no fault of yours,' his aunt replied. 'It is nothing. I am sure she will once again become friendly, but never try to be anything but a willing pupil.'

He felt sick and angry as he left the house, for he knew of Sir Williams' reputation. Inspector Campbell had grown to like Woo Sing a great deal. Although reluctant to admit it, she had begun to occupy a considerable part of his thoughts. The language lesson was the highlight of his week, but there was nothing he could do but accept the advice of his aunt and wait.

No more gweilos, Woo Sing thought as she walked the dogs. *One day, I will get my revenge, but that is a long time away.* She knew it was not only *gweilos* who raped women. Many of the Wanchai bar girls had been raped and forced from their families. At least she was lucky enough to have met this disaster at the hands of a stupid *gweilo*, rather than the triads. She wondered whether Wa Hing was any better than Kim, but she still felt she could trust him. She even wondered if a younger Tong Pooi had ever treated a woman shamefully. The idea seemed laughable, but the thought occurred several times and she never resolved it.

She realised, too, that Kim had grossly displeased Miss

Campbell for she overheard her say to Ah Heung, 'He has hurt me as much as he hurt her.' Hearing that, she knew she had a friend she could trust.

Woo Sing did not know how deeply Mary Campbell had been hurt, and that against the advice of many voices within her, she had written to Kim the day after the episode.

Dear Kim,

Yesterday morning I removed a shocked and shamed girl from your room. Her anguish has been hard for me to watch and harder for her to bear. For whatever the stirrings of womanhood in her that encouraged your behaviour, there is no doubt that she is a naive girl. Both of us vastly overestimated your capacity for trust and human decency. I have somehow failed, in the early years of your upbringing, to really understand your true character, and perhaps to change it. Of course, you will laugh at me as very old-fashioned. Whether you ever change such an opinion will depend on the degree of justice that life hands out to you for such despicable actions.

Your ex-Nanny Campbell

Confused by doubt, grief, rage and disappointment, she finally mailed the letter, not expecting a reply. Nor did she ever receive one.

Chapter 7
Decision Time

Towards the end of Woo Sing's schooling, a cyclical change had occurred in China's education policy. For a brief time, there were family planning classes that left the children stunned, and even a little excited, about the forthright discussions on birth control and the disastrous results of excessive or unanticipated sexual activity. The expectation was that the girls would seek more information when they married. The classes had hardly begun when the policy changed and the time allotted for family planning was given over to political debate.

Recalling those lessons, Woo Sing felt it may have been a chemical urge of sexual desire that had prompted her to accept Kim's invitation. Her mind had been preoccupied with meeting and talking with him, casually touching him, and enjoying the strange sensation of it.

They had freely wandered into a close relationship. Some of it was her own fault, but most of the blame was his.

In the commune, her day was planned around the party. In Hong Kong, the last few months had revolved around one man, and a rather shy and timid one at that. It was pointless to compare Kim with Wa Hing, they were so different. As for Ah Hon, she could not bear to think of him; if thoughts of him persisted she distracted herself with English lessons.

She was generally rather casual about her menstruation. That was especially so during the Cultural Revolution and when they'd been hard at work gathering the harvest. Even now, when she realised that exasperating time had not occurred, she supposed it was the effect of the herbal medicine and thought no more about it.

It was Ah Heung who made the discovery. The early roundness of Woo Sing's stomach was apparent when she caught sight of her standing in profile against the light.

She took Woo Sing into her room. 'You don't look very well. Are you having one of those bad days?'

Woo Sing was not sure what Ah Heung meant. 'Oh, no, I feel very well.'

'Lie on the bed,' said Ah Heung and placed her hands on Woo Sing's stomach.

'Wait until I return.'

She came back accompanied by Miss Campbell who, in her blunt Western way, asked Woo Sing when she had her last period.

Woo Sing was shocked. It was a gross impertinence to discuss such matters. She said nothing.

'Answer, Missy,' ordered Ah Heung.

'Not for quite a long time.'

'Then you are expecting a baby,' said Miss Campbell. She

made no effort to cloak her anger.

Woo Sing at first said nothing, then, 'No.'

Ah Heung shook her head. 'Yes. How many times were you with the young master?'

'Only once.'

'This house must have very bad Feng Shu,' murmured the old amah.

Mary Campbell tried to contain her fury. She did not know why she was so angry, or who she was angry at. 'Stop that nonsense, Ah Heung,' she said.

Ah Heung looked offended.

'I am sorry, Ah Heung. I don't know what to say. You will have to get rid of the child, Woo Sing, otherwise you cannot stay here.'

'Yes, I think that is the best way,' said the distraught girl. 'But how will I arrange it?'

'I'll find out.'

Ah Heung had a practical idea. 'Missy, Woo Sing could always have the child and then sell it,' said Ah Heung. 'If the child looks European, we can sell it as a European baby, and if it looks Chinese, we shall sell it as Chinese. In either case, we could get a good price.'

'If she does, she will have to let the baby grow in her elsewhere. She cannot stay here.'

'Quite so,' murmured Ah Heung. Some of the part-*gweilo* children were valuable to their mothers, if the *gweilo* father could be made to pay for the child's education and upkeep. Even if they could not persuade the young master that it was his child, they could still sell the child for a fair sum.

'You will have to make up your own mind,' said Mary Campbell as she left to get on with her duties.

Woo Sing struggled to think how she would tell Wa Hing and Tong Pooi what had happened.

'I shall do as Miss Campbell says,' she told Ah Heung.

'It is very dangerous,' said the old amah, 'When I was young, one of my friends had this same trouble and they carried her body out the back stairs in the middle of the night and threw it in the harbour.'

'I think I should do as Miss Campbell says,' repeated Woo Sing.

She was not sure why she was so insistent on doing as she had been told, but since she had come into the house, she felt she had lost her confidence and self-reliance. To feel that one was a pawn or a lesser person was not new, for she had experienced it in the commune. Here, the feeling was more powerful, and she did not understand why. She had been warned about the English by many people and had not believed them. Their methods of dominance were different from those that she had expected. Tong Pooi was right—they were best avoided.

Mary Campbell retired to her room in a bitter mood. *There had been nothing but trouble since Woo Sing arrived in the house. Although little of it had been the girl's fault. Perhaps I was too harsh in insisting that the child be destroyed.*

She knew that would be done by some old amah or unregistered practitioner. The girl might die, as well as the baby, and she was not a bad person.

She was annoyed with herself; she had fallen into the familiar *gweilo* trap of thinking of her Chinese friends as not as human as herself. Once, when she confided this to an old Cantonese friend, he had replied, 'Perhaps it is because there are so many of us that it's hard to imagine that we are all our unique selves. You know, we Cantonese do not think much of the Shanghainese.'

Mary Campbell had felt somewhat comforted but still she knew she could not command another woman to destroy her baby, no matter how inconvenient it would be for the household's routine. The more she thought of it, the more dangerous her advice seemed. Several times she walked to the door, then turned away, not wanting to become involved in a matter she knew must be solved by a Chinese solution. She thought of her old friend, Jeng Gei, and her little house at Pak Tin. She would visit Jeng Gei and talk the matter over with her. First, she would see Woo Sing.

The girl was quietly polishing the dogs' collars when Miss Campbell entered. Woo Sing looked at her with mixed fear and affection as the woman sat next to her.

'Woo Sing, forgive me. I was wrong to order you to do anything with your child. It is your choice alone and I will help you, whatever you decide. I have an old Cantonese friend who I think will look after you. If she agrees, I will take you there in a few days' time.'

*

The young doctor was obviously busy and very friendly until the problem was stated. Brusquely, he asked for the urine sample that Miss Campbell had told Woo Sing to take with her.

'Pay at the door before you go and come back for the result.'

An elderly nurse told her the outcome. 'What an immoral girl you are,' she said. 'No doubt you enjoyed many customers so what do you expect? The doctor will not help you but you can go to a government clinic where they will arrange for your delivery.'

The nurse paused. 'However, if you want some other solution, I have a friend, and it will cost you at least a thousand dollars.'

Woo Sing ignored the abuse and thanked the woman politely; she might need her help in future. The test revealed nothing new and she wondered why Miss Campbell insisted it be done. She had noticed before that *gweilo*s seemed to want the same answer twice. She knew she could get a much cheaper operation, but even if it were only three hundred dollars, she still did not have the money. And she dare not ask Wa Hing or Tong Pooi.

She would have to have the child, and everyone would despise her. But if she sold it the new parents need not know how it had been conceived, and perhaps they would be wealthy and look after it well. She could not earn enough to support herself and the child, so would not be able to pay for the child to be taken care of in a nursery.

She asked Miss Campbell to tell her more about Pak Tin and Jeng Gei.

'It is a peaceful place, very isolated and quiet,' said Miss Campbell. 'You can have the child, as Jeng Gei needs an assistant. She is kind, but not rich, so there will be little money left from your wages. Everything is possible after you have had the baby. You can sell it, or if times are better, you can pay a baby nursery to care for it.'

Woo Sing decided she would live in Pak Tin and think about the child later. She wanted to leave this house. Apart from Miss Campbell, it had become a hateful place. But first—and she felt sick at the thought—she must muster the courage to tell Wa Hing and, even more painfully, Tong Pooi.

Her hand was forced when Wa Hing and Tong Pooi arrived on the day she was due to leave for Pak Tin. Tong Pooi had not received a letter for some time and he was alarmed and suspicious about the treacherous English.

It came as no surprise when they listened to Woo Sing tell her story. She spared them nothing except the powerful memory of the struggle, pain and pleasure of the final act. Woo Sing knew she was permanently cheapened in their eyes by carrying and bearing a part-English child.

She thought Wa Hing would maybe understand, but Tong Pooi was older and she knew the familiar Hong Kong word, 'defiled', would be uppermost in his mind. Without their support, she really would be alone, so she waited quietly once she had finished her story.

Wa Hing broke the strained silence. 'I will kill the Englishman when he returns,' he said. 'Slowly. I will chop off his head, so he feels the pain and the blood running down.'

Tong Pooi did not know what to say. With the caution of old age, he put his arm around Woo Sing's shoulders and remained silent.

They sat silently for a while, Wa Hing torn between rage and despair, for his affection for Woo Sing was now defined. He could love her, but the knowledge that she did not love him was bitter. To have even half given herself to the Englishman was unbelievable. Surely the English had some strange power to diminish the Chinese; Woo Sing had left them to be mistress of her own fate, and now returned as the discarded night's pleasure of an English schoolboy.

Tong Pooi, for all his suspicion of the English, suspected both participants were the victims of an absence of any family control. Such a situation would have been impossible in his youth, although he did recall hearing about several cases of rape, or ill-usage, of servant girls by masters of the household. Perhaps such matters had not really changed. He felt sick and disappointed. The young people had brought him great pleasure, and had in part eased his pain at the non-arrival of Ah Hon, whom he now suspected had been caught and imprisoned as punishment for an attempted escape.

His thoughts drifted to the young baby.

'You must have the child,' he stated. Woo Sing and Wa Hing looked at him, surprised. 'You could sell the child for about five hundred dollars instead of paying one thousand dollars to destroy it,' he mumbled. 'Also, it is too dangerous. I have known a number of women clients who have disappeared forever, and a bad operation was probably why.'

Listening to Tong Pooi, Woo Sing realised she had trapped herself by giving her savings to Chen Tien Wa. She would have to borrow at thirty per cent interest, or bear the child. Wa Hing had saved two hundred and Tong Pooi was so poor that his savings would amount to perhaps a few hundred dollars. They were kind and forgiving men, but did not really understand. She decided to ask Chen Tien Wa for advice.

Wa Hing came with her and spent his time talking to Chai Dung while the two women sat assembling another huge mound of plastic components.

'I need an operation, Ah Wa,' said Woo Sing.

'I told you to keep away from the English,' Chen Tien Wa could not resist replying. 'They are no better than the triads, and more dangerous because you cannot understand them.'

Woo Sing saw the look on her face and bent her head, pretending to have trouble fitting together two parts. But Chen Tien Wa's dark expression face was only partly due to Woo Sing's news. She had suffered the heroin peddler's attention a number of times and her self-loathing eventually had given way to an acceptance of the humiliation as the price for her husband to die quietly and peacefully. If she became pregnant, she would have to attend to it herself and risk the consequences. But the peddler was old and feeble, and hopefully sterile.

Only on one occasion, and much to her disgust, had she had an orgasm. Usually, she patiently waited for the old man to delude himself that he had given her satisfaction. With these thoughts, she could hardly concentrate on Woo Sing's problems.

Woo Sing had hoped the older woman would have some acceptable secret answer. Of course, there were none. There were no answers when one was really poor. Chen Tien Wa had learnt that long ago.

'Let us consult the spirit of Amah Rock in the morning,' she said.

Woo Sing was amazed and almost offended at what seemed a childish answer. She knew Chen Tien Wa was not a communist and still believed in the old ways, but surely no answer could be found by consulting a stone on a hilltop. It was the sort of silly rubbish that Chairman Mao had been right to condemn and abolish. But, to please Chen Tien Wa, she agreed.

*

The stone steps were already warm, although the sun had hardly risen. There was a freshness in the air and a light breeze carried the fragrance of incense down towards her. Woo Sing knew the legend of the faithful amah with her child on her back. She had waited so devotedly for the return of her fisherman husband that the gods, in their pity, had turned her to stone. Within the rock, her spirit survived unchanged.

Numerous incense sticks and offerings were jammed into crevices in the rock and about its base. A number of women were already there, their faces expressionless, their thoughts turned inward. Woo Sing thought that their journey was for her benefit and was surprised when Chen Tien Wa approached the rock with closed eyes and pressed her body against the stone. Woo Sing walked away as Chen Tien Wa whispered into a crevice, not wishing to hear her friend's confidence.

'Spirit of the rock, do not give me a child,' whispered Chen Tien Wa.

She listened quietly but heard no answer, and so she spoke once more. 'You must believe it is not for myself but for my husband, and only once have I responded with pleasure, and it is hard to always be cold.'

The sun was now strong and the incense heavy in the air. As Chen Tien Wa pressed close to the stone, she thought she felt a slight vibration, as though the rock answered.

Woo Sing could not bring herself to talk to a stone, but pressed against the rock and felt the early roundness of her abdomen firm against the granite. Perhaps there was some message to be heard, for thousands of sensible women came here. Perhaps the patient amah of the rock, too, had thought to abandon her child, as day after day had dragged at the weary muscles of her shoulders while she endlessly searched the sea before her.

Woo Sing knew shame was irreversible; no matter what she did now, she could never redeem her purity in the minds of her Chinese friends. If she destroyed the child, it seemed she would also lose the respect of Tong Pooi, Miss Campbell and Ah Heung.

Had she destroyed the child as soon as she was aware of its existence, she would have felt only satisfaction, but now it was beginning to claim her body. The rock felt cool, but even with her ear pressed against the stone, she could only hear the beating of her heart. Woo Sing became aware of the heat and incense in the air as the sun's rays now struck directly at the rock. The amah spirit had not spoken to her, or if it had, she had not heard. But she felt calm and contained. She noticed the features of the women about her; intense, concentrated and yet reposed.

Chen Tien Wa waited, pale but composed. For a brief while her sunlit face softened into that of a faded but gentle beauty. The two women turned and walked slowly down the steps. By the time they reached the path leading to the road, Woo Sing knew she would keep the child and rear it herself. She had seen so much of death, had even killed a man herself, and perhaps fate had decreed this as her atonement.

Without a word, the women turned to look up at the rock, now fully lit by sunshine. Whether the gods had turned a woman and child to stone, or whether the granite shape had been a freakish accident of nature, it had brought centuries of troubled women to the shrine and had endowed the site with an air of serenity. Here, away from family and the city, a woman could confront herself, secure in the knowledge that the stone would keep her secrets.

*

Tong Pooi was waiting, anxiety playing on his face.

'I will keep the child and, if you wish it, as he grows, you shall teach him,' Woo Sing said.

'Of course, of course,' the old scholar mumbled, turning away to hide his tears of relief.

'I will write to you Ah Pooi as soon as I am settled, and perhaps Ah Hing will bring you to see me now and again.'

She faced Ah Hing. 'Please do not desert me now even though I may disgust you, and when your time of trouble comes, I promise to help.'

Wa Hing smiled and kissed her for the first time. He picked up a tiny box hidden behind a plank in the table. Without a glance at its contents, he placed it in her pocket. Woo Sing bowed her head and briefly clasped his hands in hers. Silently she picked up a few belongings and left. As she walked down the stairs, she thought about how the city had changed them. She had been diminished, but Wa Hing—the cheerful, lazy and irresponsible Wa Hing—had become a man.

The two men sat quietly after she had left.

Tong Pooi said, 'She is not a true Woo. Despite her skill as a fighter, she is thoughtful and truly kind, and the Woo clan were not that. When I was a child, I remember a large earthen mound not far from our village. It was a deserted place, said to have many restless spirits roaming nearby. None of the Woos ever visited there. A long time before, a powerful Woo clansman had died and left instructions for his burial. Even that long ago, his instructions were regarded as barbarous. Within the grave were placed eight young women, one for each decade of his life. The grave was covered, except for several wide bamboo poles that took air to the tomb. The women were instructed to keep the lamps burning, for the old man hated the darkness. For three days, the tormented relatives heard the cries of the young women. Then came silence, the bamboo poles were withdrawn and the grave was covered. That is the sort of the people the Woos were. Even though their neighbours despised them, they remained a powerful and rich family until the Japanese invasion. Even then, they were better placed than most. The family broke up in the fifties, and it is the innocent descendants like Woo Sing who have to bear the burden of their reputation.'

Wa Hing was interested in Tong Pooi's story for his own clan had reason to remember the Woos. But as far as he was concerned, it was only a story of long ago. He had never known anything but communist rule until he had come to Hong Kong and knew that the party had exploited the rage of the peasants to destroy the old families.

Tong Pooi cooked vegetables and chicken bones. The two men ate the rich broth in silence. Tong Pooi was pleased but anxious for Woo Sing; Wa Hing was also anxious but bitter too. How he would love to slowly break that Englishman's neck, or beat him with the end of a long pole until all his ribs were broken.

His thoughts wandered to Woo Sing, and then to a girl he had met two days before. As he left the office with his pay, a co-worker pulled him by the arm and said, 'Come, come.' They had gone to the back of the truck, where the old man pulled aside the canvas to reveal a young girl sitting quietly inside.

'Only fifty dollars,' the old man said. 'She is clean. I know, for she is the daughter of a friend of mine.' When Wa Hing hesitated, the girl drew up her frock and spread wide her legs, showing that her skimpy dress was her only garment.

Wa Hing had dragged himself over the tailboard of the truck and taken her. She was very young and small, but that was no concern of his for she was getting paid for her services.

She lay gasping and whimpering until he finished. As he drew back on his knees to do up his clothing, he turned to three old men who were grinning and enjoying the spectacle. There was nothing to be said, so he had paid and left.

'Very good, very good, you are very good,' he heard the old man say to the whimpering girl.

He had enjoyed the girl but the pleasure was nothing like that of his acts with Woo Wai San. Back there, in the old cottage, with the firelight flickering on the crests and hollows of her body, his excitement had been more intense, more significant.

Increasingly his memory of their passion had returned and with Woo Sing a painful burden in his mind, he decided he would return to Canton and bring Woo Wai San back to the city. It would require thought and planning and he would have to practise swimming again. To be caught would mean death.

*

Miss Campbell drove carefully along the potholed road. Waterlogged paddy fields stretched out beside it. The road branched at Lau Fan Shan and became even narrower as it wound about the low coastal hills. Across the bay were more hills, sparsely covered with trees and wind-battered shrubs. When the tide retreated, it revealed mile upon mile of deep mud. This was not the route they had taken to Hong Kong and Woo Sing was glad, for the mud looked terrifying.

'Deep Bay should be called Death Bay, not only for those who have died, but for the survivors,' Miss Campbell said. 'For many, it is the beginning of the death of their hopes for a better life.'

'I do not regret coming,' Woo Sing replied. 'I am disgraced, but not beaten, and someday I will master this city. Life is hard at home because it is always the same, but here it is hard because it is unpredictable. But not everyone is as lucky as I am to have a few true friends.'

'Woo Sing, I'm very pleased you have decided not to destroy the child and I hope you will allow me to help you look after the baby. It would help me feel less useless.'

'But you are not useless, Miss Campbell, you manage a large household.'

'If it were my own family, it would be satisfying, but where I am now, it is useless.'

The women lapsed into silence until reaching Jeng Gei's restaurant, a basic shop with an outside café located near a village school. It was the only commercial venture for miles.

Jeng Gei was well past middle-age and somewhat stout, yet there were few wrinkles in her pleasant, round face. She presented as calm and gentle, but Woo Sing was soon to learn she was a hard businesswoman. She showed Woo Sing her room along a narrow passage; it was even tinier than the one she had left, but clean.

'You can have all the food you can eat and twenty dollars a week,' said Jeng Gei.

'That is very generous,' said Woo Sing.

The hours were long but the work came in broken shifts dependent on the release of a torrent of children from the school. The area was prosperous and most children were obviously well-fed and healthy, but this did not deter their appetites for something sweet or spicy.

The shop had regular trade during the day, but when school was out it was flooded by a mass of struggling children, all clamouring for Woo Sing's attention. The rich bought with reckless abandon, secure in the knowledge that tomorrow would provide. The poor bought more judiciously, weighing taste, cost and size.

Woo Sing served everyone quickly and calmly, working systematically back and forth along the counter. Jeng Gei noted her competence.

Woo Sing was amused by the various ways the children advanced towards the counter. There was much polite, if firm, slipping around shoulders or squeezing between bodies. It reminded her of eels in a basket, all trying to get through one small hole in its side. Even so, she never saw a fight, or even an exchange of angry words.

A few customers came for meals, particularly on weekends. For these, Jeng Gei prepared a few simple dishes, mainly of fresh fish or shellfish, which the sea provided in abundance.

She reminded Woo Sing of the old peasant women of her village, tough but friendly, sometimes prone to fits of cackling laughter, and less often, to muttered curses. Jeng Gei lived alone and never mentioned a husband, family, or even the smallest fragment of a past life. Yet she had a genial nature and obviously regarded Woo Sing's problems as no real disaster. Jeng Gei was firm with her young customers, but in a maternal way, and Woo Sing soon realised she derived much pleasure from their presence in the shop.

Tong Pooi received regular letters from Woo Sing, mainly recounting the minor incidents of her calm sequence of days. Always the writer of letters, he had received few in return in his lifetime and the pleasure he found in those from Woo Sing gave him a new measure of his value in the community. He began to devote an even greater care to his craft, and his letters became less scholarly and more intimate and personal.

'Ah Pooi, you are a very modern letter writer,' one client declared.

He felt like replying that perhaps he had returned to an ancient style, where men and women wrote simply to tell each other of themselves without seeking to create an impression or false affection.

In his weekly replies, Tong Pooi told Woo Sing about the affairs of his street and the activities of Wa Hing, who was now keeping more irregular hours. His firm had increased its delivery of furniture so much that night work was required. Wa Hing had lately lost some of his cheerful nature and spent many hours studying maps. Tong Pooi was pleased that the boy had remained with him and attributed an underlying tension he sensed in Wa Hing to the absence of Woo Sing. Tong Pooi had long ago ceased to speculate over the relationships of others, but realised some strong bond existed between his two friends.

Miss Campbell made frequent visits to Pak Tin, but neither she nor Woo Sing discussed the problem which had brought the girl to the restaurant. Woo Sing enjoyed these visits, which were usually on the weekends when the children were away. They would have tea or a bowl of soup at one of the tables overlooking the bay.

One afternoon, Miss Campbell asked Woo Sing if she would mind if her nephew, Inspector Campbell, called at the restaurant to continue with his Cantonese lessons.

Jeng Gei was happy with the arrangement, for if any triads came to her restaurant, it would be useful to have a European police inspector occasionally dine there. Woo Sing was not so sure; he seemed a pleasant man, and their relationship was strictly professional, but he was a *gweilo* and she was resentful of them.

'You must not allow things to stop you learning the language, and he is grateful for your lessons in Cantonese. I would be pleased if you would allow him to come,' said Miss Campbell.

Woo Sing nodded. There seemed little harm in it and it would please Miss Campbell.

Jeng Gei said, 'I would like the inspector to come in ordinary clothes because in uniform he might drive other customers away, but the triads might know of him.'

Woo Sing's pregnancy was now obvious and she felt deeply ashamed as she waited for the inspector at the end of the path to the shop. He walked slowly, carrying a large parcel, stopping now and again to admire the view.

'Thank you for letting me visit you,' he said. 'I need the lessons and I hope you will keep me as a friend, for I have bought some English books for you.'

Woo Sing led the way to a private table at the rear of the building. Here, in the clear sunshine with the winter light reflecting off the waves in the bay, she once again lost herself in the mysteries of English. It seemed both logical and illogical, and yet she was beginning to see that it had the precision and beauty of an intricate jade carving. She energetically resumed the studies her circumstances had forced her to abandon.

Jeng Gei was keen to learn a few simple words. The two women practised as they made the vast number of sweets they daily needed to fill the bottomless stomachs of the children. 'Friendly sharks,' Jeng Gei had once called them.

One day, Woo Sing overheard two of her most innocent-looking customers discussing her condition in a very straightforward way. Gazing at her and smiling, they spoke in a form of English that Woo Sing recognised as much poorer than her own. No doubt they were using English to conceal their discussion from her.

'Do you think she is married?' asked one.

'A *gweilo* sometimes comes. Perhaps she is married or

perhaps she is his girlfriend,' said the second.

'Perhaps she is a bad girl who likes making babies.'

'She is very beautiful, but her belly is so big. When do you think the baby will be born? I wonder if it will be as pretty as her.'

Their harmless comments so angered Woo Sing that she looked directly at them and said in English, 'You know that Chinese gentlemen do not discuss a woman in her presence.'

Two pairs of eyes opened wide with amazement and fear flashed across their startled faces. The boys raced off and Woo Sing's anger eased.

Jeng Gei came from the back of the shop to see what all the noise was about. She found Woo Sing roaring with laughter although unable to tell her what had happened. Jeng Gei returned to the back of the shop happy that she had heard her young assistant laughing for the first time. It was some days before the two embarrassed boys returned, but Woo Sing served them in her usual gentle manner.

Inspector Campbell became a constant visitor. Although he was always friendly and courteous, Woo Sing thought him shy and perhaps lacking emotion. They developed an easy companionship in their studies, with half of each session devoted to English and half to Cantonese. Miss Campbell, whose broad accent had been reduced by her long residence in Hong Kong, noted with amusement that Woo Sing's English had a strong Scottish flavour.

Inspector Campbell did not discuss Woo Sing with his aunt, but he felt he was becoming increasingly attracted to her in a way that had little to do with Cantonese lessons. Her pregnancy had softened her beauty and she was different from the vivacious and carefree young girl he had first met. He felt she was probably more intelligent than he, and certainly her gift for languages was greater.

It was hopeless to reach any closer and he knew that any foolish move would sever forever a slowly growing friendship. The child soon to be born was never mentioned, but he had been long enough in Hong Kong to know the degree of disgrace and shame felt by a young Chinese woman in Woo Sing's circumstances. The language lessons gave his week a focus to look forward to, and afterwards to savour, and he was determined that whenever Woo Sing required help, he would give it, discreetly and at whatever cost to himself.

The calm of the restaurant, with its many hours of happy activity, almost obliterated the sense of time and Woo Sing felt relaxed and secure living and working there. The days were still cool, but it would soon be spring, and then the clammy heat of summer would descend.

One day, Wa Hing arrived quite unexpectedly, and although Woo Sing was delighted to see him, it was strange that he had not brought Tong Pooi.

'Is Ah Pooi well?'

'Yes, he is very well and sends his best wishes.'

Woo Sing noticed Wa Hing was tired and more serious than she had ever known him, but his body seemed broader and more powerful than she had remembered.

'It will soon be summer,' said Woo Sing, trying to find

something to say to relieve her friend's tense and watchful state. He nodded but did not reply.

Woo Sing asked, 'Big brother, what is wrong?'

As he replied, he seemed to become his cheerful self again. 'I have decided to return to China and rescue Woo Wai San. I have been practising swimming and studying some maps I managed to buy in a shop. I have told no one else and only you shall know.'

Woo Sing was hit by the same wave of fear she had felt when they'd first entered the water. 'Failure will be death,' was all she could reply, battling to control her emotions.

I must be calm, she thought, *for it is only the baby that counts now*. They were silent for a long time, both occupied with their thoughts.

'You never told me that you loved Woo Wai San,' said Woo Sing.

'It was a very dangerous friendship,' said Wa Hing. 'Anyone who knew of it would also have been in trouble. 'It was a secret and you know to have a secret at home is so rare that it is a great pleasure. But it is also to be shared with no one, for harbouring secrets is dangerous.'

'How can you be sure Ah San will come back with you?'

He looked uneasy. 'I can't, but if I don't go, I will never know, and I must know.'

Woo Sing had never heard him speak so seriously. 'If you desire her that much, then you must go,' she whispered. 'But I shall miss you very much, for while I know you are in the city, I never feel really alone.'

'You have Tong Pooi,' he said gently.

'He is old.'

'You have this Miss Campbell, then,' said Wa Hing.

'She is a *gweilo*,' said Woo Sing quietly.

'But she sounds a very good one, and surely one can trust some of them. They cannot all be bad.'

'I do trust her and think I will trust her nephew, too. But it is hard to ask a *gweilo* for anything.'

'Why?'

'It is the way they look at you when you ask for something,' said Woo Sing, feeling she had lost her point. The baby must have felt annoyed too because it began kicking vigorously inside her. 'I love you as a brother, Ah Hing.' She looked hard at his scarred serious face and reached across the table to touch his hand.

They were silent for a while. Woo Sing remembered Woo Wai San but with little feeling. She had always seemed so pure and dedicated to the party and it was extraordinary to learn of her secret life.

Wa Hing interrupted her thoughts. 'I have not told Tong Pooi. I have not told him because it would upset him so much. I will tell him that I'm going to work in the New Territories for a while. If I'm not back in a few weeks you can tell him the story. I will send you a letter before I go. The water is too cold now but I cannot leave it too long for later it will be too warm.'

He did not have to explain; the warm water would bring the sharks and he saw Woo Sing shudder. She knew it was no use trying to stop Wa Hing. He had clearly made up his mind.

'How can I help you?' she asked.

'If I do not come back, think of me for no one else ever will, and never abandon Ah Pooi.'

'I promise, big brother,' she said quietly.

'Little sister, I must go now,' he said, turning away from her and walking back down the path.

She sat at the table, watching his easy gait. The restaurant seemed such a tiny spot in a huge world, empty of friends and full of fear. Jeng Gei came to the table and noticed her distress.

She sat close. 'Whatever the trouble is, Ha Sing, there are only two things that matter now, you and the child. All else must wait or stand by itself.'

'You are a good woman, Jeng Gei,' smiled Woo Sing.

'Nonsense, I am just your boss,' said Jeng Gei sharply.

Woo Sing did not believe her, unaware that Jeng Gei had loved and lost so much before. As they walked to the back of the shop, Woo Sing moved close to her friend and regained her sense of calm. She picked up a knife to resume work and thought, *To be Chinese and a woman is surely to know a great deal about life.*

Chapter 8
Desperate return

Wa Hing had always feared water in any amount larger than would fill a bucket. His mother believed it was because her husband and most of the others in their village had drowned when a retreating army had blown the flood-gates apart. It mattered little whether it was a prenatal effect or stemmed from his mother's frequent recounting of that horror. Wa Hing hated water.

As a child he had despised the men who had opened the river on to the land on that lovely summer's day and snuffed out the life of the village with no more thought than of pinching out a candle before sleep. He had dreamed of revenge as terrible as his young mind could grasp and later had sought information about the army and who might have led it. Nobody knew much about it and those who did said little. He had become obsessed with this army, about which no one knew anything. Eventually an old family friend had taken him aside and begged him to forget the incident.

'The past that living men remembered is so bad that to

think on it is to dwell on sorrow all one's days,' the friend had said. 'The past cannot be changed and only you can make the future.'

'How can I make the future if I do not understand the past?'

'That is a question from a clever young man, but when you are old, you will forgive a lot of the past.'

The argument had lapsed but he did stop thinking about the army.

Not long afterwards he had surprised his family by enrolling in the commune's swimming lessons. There he had mastered his fear of sinking and learned to control the movement of his limbs.

The long swim across the inlet to the border control area at Sha Tau Kok had greatly tested him. His breathing had failed him many times and often he had to tread water until his breath returned. If he tackled that swim again he would have to get his breathing right. He knew no one who was a swimmer and it was useless to ask Tong Pooi.

While on one of his furniture delivery rounds, Wa Hing had noticed lessons advertised at a government swimming pool and decided to sign up. Most of the pupils were young children and he was often mistaken for an instructor. At first, the children had teased him but said very little when they saw his muscular limbs.

A *gweilo* instructor solved his breathing problem, teaching him to breathe slowly and regularly, allowing his head to sink beneath the water and blow out the air. They had not taught this in the commune and it was only after much effort and some sly jeering from his fellow pupils that he had finally mastered it.

This was the first time Wa Hing had met a *gweilo* and the instructor's concern and pleasant nature made learning much easier. He spoke broken Cantonese, but that was enough to encourage Wa Hing. He soon found his breathing difficulties had ended. He thanked the instructor profusely but he did not attend any more classes. Instead, he found a secluded beach and, at every opportunity, swam back and forth across the mouth of the bay. The water was cool and the sea sometimes rough, but he continued his regular workouts despite the unwritten local law about the danger of swimming after October. His body was now relaxed and buoyant in the water and he felt confident about tackling the swim to the mainland.

Wa Hing needed to retrace their original route as closely as possible and, after much searching, located their landing point on a map of the coast. He secretly studied the shore through an old pair of cheap binoculars until he finally identified the long ridge sweeping down to the sea.

He spent a few of his free days at a village close to the end of the bay, making out he was fishing from the wharf. In reality, he was learning the ebb and flow of the tides from the old fishermen who mended nets there. He bought a pocket compass and committed much of the map to memory; to be captured with it in his possession would mean death as a spy. He could easily dispose of the compass but a map would be more difficult.

Wa Hing knew Woo Wai San might have left the village, or not wish to return with him. Perhaps she had suffered a change of heart and would denounce him as a traitor. If she did return with him, the journey back would be more dangerous than before as active pursuit was a strong possibility.

Wa Hing took two days to steel himself before asking Lai Gwok Yuen, the short-tempered boss of the furniture factory, for two weeks' leave.

'There is something I have to do, boss, and it will take two weeks.'

'You had better tell me.'

Wa Hing had feared this response and, much as he loved his job, he was prepared to sacrifice it if necessary.

'It is nothing to do with this business, boss. It is a personal matter I have to settle, nothing illegal. If it's successful I will tell you all about it. If not, then I will be dead.'

'If it's even remotely linked with this business, you will be dead anyway,' said Lai Gwok Yuen. 'And even if you are not dead, we know where you live and where your girl lives. The old man and the girl will pay the price for you.'

Wa Hing insisted it had nothing to do with their work. 'If I am caught, no one here will ever know. It will not be in Hong Kong, boss.'

'Okay, but you must tell me when you come back.'

It is a risk, and perhaps I should have him killed on the way home, thought Lai Gwok Yuen. *On the other hand, he's a good driver and I think he is telling the truth. In any case, he knows nothing.*

April brought the early warm days and Wa Hing visited Woo Sing, now very large with her child.

'I've seen you studying the local maps so could you draw me an outline of the coast where we landed?' Woo Sing asked.

She produced paper and a pencil and Wa Hing sketched his idea of the spot. He suspected she wanted to find the place where they had left Ah Hon.

Woo Sing's speech and manner seemed so calm and loving that he wondered whether she really cared for his safety. Woo Wai San was so different, yet he was very fond of Woo Sing too. He had never allowed himself to compare the two women as it did not seem the right thing to do.

Jeng Gei brought tea and sat down with them. Together they watched a line of battered old junks thread a careful path through the mud banks. Woo Sing realised this might be the last time she saw Wa Hing and struggled to find what to say.

'Chairman Mao was right, Wa Hing,' she said. 'Life is full of contradictions. We did not understand this in the commune because life there is ordered. But here, life is all choice and often we choose the wrong way. I hope your choice is right and it will be only a few days before we see you return.'

'We shall be thinking of you,' Jeng Gei said quietly, and left them alone.

After sitting together in the sun for a while, Wa Hing stood and walked away, saying not a word. Jeng Gei looked down from her shop at the seated figure of Woo Sing and the receding figure of Wa Hing. She smiled at the thought of Woo Sing's talk about choices, as life had given her few choices. It had mainly been a series of disasters to be faced the best way possible. These days she thought of neither past nor future but gleaned and hoarded the tiny pleasures of each day. She had lost two men and two families and knew that to gain a child, however fathered, was far easier to bear than to lose one.

Wa Hing slowly descended the narrow path. The warm sun and the still-dry air caressed his body. A light breeze blew off the sea and the sweet charm of the day made him feel all his troubles existed in some other world and at some other time. He savoured the sensations of the spring day and for a brief moment thought about abandoning his plan, of walking back to Woo Sing and asking to stay. He knew she would agree but let the thought pass and continued to walk on. The tides would be right in three days' time. The weather had settled into a spring calm and he felt that his body and will were poised to go.

*

Over the next few days, Wa Hing revealed to Tong Pooi his intention to be away for a few days. The old man was anxious but resigned himself to his companion's absence. Tong Pooi never questioned Wa Hing about his activities nor did he comment when Wa Hing returned home very late, silent and exhausted.

Wa Hing found the company of the old man relaxing, particularly when Tong Pooi told him the traditional stories of their province. Both would return to a faraway and fanciful

164

China where treacherous magic foxes masqueraded as women, where magic herbs really possessed the powers now hopefully ascribed to them, and where the greatest scholar in the land was always rewarded and honoured.

Tong Pooi guessed Wa Hing was planning a serious project but did not enquire. He had long suspected that Ah Hon had met with disaster and wondered if Wa Hing was attempting to rescue him.

Tong Pooi produced the dry beef strips and dry rice cakes Wa Hing had requested and watched anxiously as they were carefully wrapped in thick plastic and carefully sealed with tape. Wa Hing had bought short blue trousers and a red vest that Tong Pooi well knew was not the sort of clothing worn in Hong Kong.

Wa Hing had also carefully sharpened a long-bladed knife and added a small leather strap to his belt to hold the knife in place. He seemed very confident and cheerful, and the old man went to bed less anxious than before.

Next morning, when he took a bowl of rice to Wa Hing's room, he found it tidy and empty. This worrying sight provoked him into visiting a temple for the first time in ages. As he watched the smoke curl from the burning incense sticks, Tong Pooi felt the fear of impending horror.

*

Wa Hing entered the water early that evening after lathering his body with thick oil as described in his swimming book.

It was well known that more men than women drowned on the swim from China and Wa Hing wondered if that was because the female body contained more fat and therefore lost less heat. If the water was too cold, an agonising cramp was the final earthly sensation of many who tried the journey.

The water was cool, but he had no fear of it, so he waded out as far as possible to conserve his strength. The oil created a pattern on the water and Wa Hing smiled as he wondered if it would help the sharks swallow his flesh more easily.

He swam slowly and lazily, resting and floating every few minutes. The headland, his target, had disappeared from view, but the hills behind were a guide. The compass was watertight and in a handy pocket, but he had doubts about reading it at sea even though the moon was due to rise later. Swimming in this direction carried greater risk because he had to land in a specific point on the coast to escape capture. Unexpected help came when he was given a bearing by flashes from a searchlight on the China side. He knew the light was on a headland about two miles west of his objective. To swim towards the light was safe at such a distance.

The water remained reasonably warm and, although slightly tired, he made excellent progress in the first four hours. A few strokes later he felt a powerful current sweeping him westwards from his bearings. He responded by increasing the rate and power of his strokes. Determined not to panic, he fought his way slowly back to the correct course. The moon had risen and its light fell on a shape low in the water. Wa Hing felt tremors of fear, thinking it was a shark.

Relief followed when a second look revealed it was a swimmer, moving rapidly with the current in the opposite direction.

Wa Hing swam to the man's side, catching him by his shoulders.

'Welcome, brother,' he shouted.

Then, beneath the moon's light, he saw the body was already bloated. The face and bulging eyes had been transformed into the features of the rotting dead. Wa Hing vomited as a wave washed over the body, flinging his vomit back into his face. Sickened and winded, he swam rapidly away, concentrating on beating the current and driving the wretchedness from his mind.

The tide's powerful flow ran in a very narrow band and within an hour he had swum through it. His limbs had lost their strength and the coast was still a fair distance away. Time was now a factor so Wa Hing decided to let the current carry him towards the searchlight and the headland. From there he would swim back along the coast, aided by a counter-current.

The moon was high and the sea phosphorescent. Crests of small waves formed a magical circle of interweaving patterns and ever-changing designs around his body. He allowed the current to pull him landwards, at times swimming to ensure he would not be carried into the beam of the searchlight.

A steady swim in the two hours before dawn brought his target headland into view. Dawn was breaking and the light was turned off as the coast became clearer. The time had passed when swimmers would enter the water. He drifted close enough to the headland to hear waves breaking on the shore.

Stumbling and falling, rising and crawling, an exhausted Wa Hing made the last few yards out of the surf. The swim had taken much longer than he had calculated. There was not enough time to climb the ridge and descend into the tall scrub and brush of the higher valleys.

He clawed his way fifty feet up a narrow cleft in the rock face. There the cliff turned sharply, obscuring him from the beach and offering a flat area where he could sit and rest in comfort. A trickle of water flowed down a nearby boulder face; at last he could have a drink.

The sky was rapidly lightening. Dark and mysterious shapes about him were revealed as ordinary rocks and crags. Wa Hing had a good view of the curve of the bay. In the rising light he saw two guards patrolling the beach, enjoying the cool sea breeze on a fine spring morning. To his horror, Wa Hing realised he had failed to cross the beach on the stony patches. His footprints were not only clearly marked in the sand but led directly to the rock-cliff.

The speed of the incoming tide could well decide his fate, especially if the soldiers remained distracted by their enjoyment of such a delightful day. He resolved to use his knife if it came to it.

The two men were only about two hundred yards away with the tide yet to completely erase his footprints. Waves washed up to the final few marks, but never over them. Wa Hing watched anxiously, willing the larger ones to save his life. His view of the beach was restricted to a small area sighted through a crack in the rockface. If he could see the soldiers, they could see him. He waited, listening carefully for any exclamations or change in tone of the men's voices.

Everything went silent. Even the waves made no sound. The soldiers' talk was so low that he could no longer hear it. They had obviously seen the prints and followed them to the base of the cliff. The boots of a climbing soldier scratched noisily against the rocks and Wa Hing slid his knife from its crude sheath. If he could kill the climbing man with one blow and grab his gun, he might yet be able to shoot it out with the soldier on the beach. The guard was so close now Wa Hing could hear his laboured breathing as the cleft became steeper and demanded more effort. The man would be out of breath and easy to kill but he must get the gun before the body fell.

The soldier paused and shouted back to his comrade. Something like, 'Too many cigarettes for rock climbing.'

The man on the beach laughed and replied, 'I'm quite happy sitting on the sand.' He had probably put his gun down, raising Wa Hin's hopes of having surprise on his side. He must remember to aim very low when shooting so far beneath him. He had once done very well in the commune shooting competitions by using that tactic.

The guard moved forward. A hand appeared around the rock face seeking purchase on a cornice. There was a long scratching sound as the guard's foot slipped. The man cursed. Another pull of his arm and his head and shoulders would come into view.

Wa Hing felt sick. His body trembled. He braced himself to strike. The guard's foot slipped again and the man growled to his companion that it was too steep to climb much further. The beach soldier shouted back that they had missed breakfast.

'It is due to that idiot cook falling in love with the village girl and forgetting to set his alarm clock. That's why I can't climb—lack of a proper breakfast. My stomach's rumbling.'

Wa Hing remained poised to strike. The climber muttered something and began his descent.

Wa Hing thought the lovesick cook had probably saved the lives of the three of them. He trembled violently, leaving his body drenched in a cleansing, relieving sweat.

The guard reached the beach, unamused by his colleague's jokes about climbing Mount Everest before breakfast. They moved along the beach and Wa Hing sat back and sweated some more. He waited a few minutes before moving to look out from behind his rock. At the last second, he pulled back, realising the danger; the guards could probably scan the rocks from a distance.

The water seeping from the rock collected slowly in a clay hollow at its base and the sun was high before there was enough for Wa Hing to drink. A small rice cake completed his meal. He had to be careful with food now that the journey had taken an extra day. The rocks absorbed the sun's rays making his hideaway so hot that he felt he was being slowly roasted like a chicken on a spit.

He woke stiff and cramped but pleased that the sun had

passed behind the ridge to the west. It was now chilly and there was enough water to quench his thirst. He celebrated the success of his first twenty-four hours by eating two rice cakes.

With the coming of dusk, he moved stiffly from the cleft and made his way slowly along the beach, keeping close to the base of the hill. The ridge loomed above him and he took a while to locate its spine and begin a rapid ascent. He wanted to be well out of sight of the beach when the moon rose. A narrow, broken path led him between larger boulders and up to the crest. By moonrise, he was into the higher scrub and tall, coarse grasses.

The ridge was clearly visible. The sky over the distant city was bright with reflected light. Wa Hing used his compass to check his bearings were as he expected. He wondered if Woo Sing was thinking of him and decided she was. After resting on the summit and taking a drink from a stream, he began the long night's journey to a distant hill where he planned to hide and sleep like all creatures who fear the day.

Dawn was beginning when he found a hiding place close to the peak in one of the long tongues of dense undergrowth spreading up from the valleys. He took careful note of the main features, quenched his thirst with a trickle of water and fell asleep, not waking again until well past noon.

The next stage of his journey would be the most difficult. During the day, groups of workers could be out collecting firewood. Here there was also less cover. But it was near the village where he knew many hiding places from his childhood.

Towards dawn, and after a thankfully uneventful night's walking, he found a resting place among a tangled mass of bushes at the base of an ancient quarry. It was clearly a place not visited by the local farmers. There was also plenty of water and wild winter rice.

Voices, sounding casual and unexcited, woke him just before noon. A commune team was working a fallow area immediately beneath his hiding place. They were breaking the heavy dried clods of soil with iron hoes.

To be a renegade has its compensations, thought Wa Hing, as he watched the implements bouncing off the hardest lumps. Secure in his hiding place, he watched the group's ceaseless activity—a stark reminder that his future in the commune would have been dominated by iron hoes and hard sods of red soil.

At a shout from the leader, the workers dropped their tools and moved to a patch of soft grass, green from the seepage of the quarry. Here, close to Wa Hing, they rested in the warm spring sunshine, talking quietly about complex commune politics. Several dozed off after a bowl or two of plain rice and a pot of hot clear tea.

Wa Hing knew the feeling of emptiness and exhaustion. An hour's sleep would refresh them enough to work until the hour before dusk. Two of the fitter men brought out a chess set. Wa Hung could see the board quite clearly and as a keen player began to take an interest in their moves.

One was obviously an inexperienced player and Wa Hing had to force himself to refrain from calling out advice. As he leaned forward to obtain a better view, a branch beneath his elbows cracked sharply. The chess players looked up in surprise. Wa Hing remained perfectly still, trying not even to blink.

'A rotten branch in the sun,' said the better player and they resumed their game with an intensity that took away all thoughts of the approaching afternoon.

Wa Hing took no more interest in the game but concentrated on staying still while trying to shift his weight off the branch. He felt it flexing with the slightest movement and spent the remainder of the meal break waiting in an agony of stillness for the men to resume their struggle against the soil.

He slithered back into the denser foliage. The spring sun played over his body and he soon fell asleep.

The breeze that woke him had a sharp sting to it. The workers had long gone and Wa Hing scoffed down rice cakes and scraps he found in the workers' rice pot, carelessly thrown into the grass. He could now move quickly along the path bordering fields and villages.

The pattern of house lights became familiar. Strange new emotions made him realise he was nearing home.

He could not visit his family as some of them might inform the party of his presence. He longed to speak to his mother but the risk was too great. Briefly, he wondered if he should surrender to the commune leader and start life anew. Life there was not so bad. No one repeatedly faced the prospect of having no money, whereas in Hong Kong having money in one's pocket seemed as important as blood in one's veins.

He could stand being punished because he knew after a few months of repentance he would be accepted back.

He decided he must be more exhausted than he thought to allow himself to consider such a move. It would betray Woo Sing and Tong Pooi, and the throb of the city that had entered his soul. The noise, the crowds, the attractive girls, and the opportunity to be rich was too much to be thrown away in a moment of tiredness.

His old hiding place was exactly as he had remembered it, a broken hilltop overlooking the village covered in stunted and twisted pine trees. The area was forbidden to the children because several deep ancient pits were hidden in the dense undergrowth. Wa Hing had often broken the ban as a child and knew where the pits were.

He saw the village clearly in the rising sun. The same trucks arrived from the commune town and the same workers loaded the same produce onto them. It had been Wa Hing's ambition to be a driver of one of those trucks, a much sought-after job available only to very reliable party members. Smoke rising from chimneys suggested most of the villagers were now awake. Then he noted with alarm there was no smoke coming from the isolated cottage where he had met Woo Wai San.

He convinced himself it was too soon to lose hope so he retired to his primitive bed, comforted by knowing how the day would unfold in the village.

It was still warm and bright when he awoke. He fed on rice cakes from his precious store and risked drinking the brownish and bitter fluid in one of the pits. He lay down and peered carefully over the crest of the hill at the village below. A single row of eighteen brick houses faced a wide dirt road. Opposite was a large grain store. Wa Hing could scarcely believe what he saw. *Can it be true? Is that really Woo Wai San pushing a cart of precariously balanced rice sacks?*

The sight of her straining figure stirred memories of their love-making. It confirmed the wisdom of making his perilous journey. As most of the workers were in the fields, he puzzled over the significance of her duties in the village. She was probably in disgrace with the party or her family for no one was helping her with her heavily laden cart. She disappeared from view behind the grain store where she would have to deposit the bags and sign various registers. It was unusual to be storing rice at this time of year and Wa Hing wondered why.

A truck dropped a work team at the end of the street. The men, all of whom Wa Hing recognised, walked wearily towards their homes. Wa Hing knew that feeling but also knew most of the men would be pleased with their day. This was the way it had always been and probably always would.

Wa Hing watched the slow flow of the workers along the dirt street. He knew nearly as much about them as he did about himself. He could easily imagine the conversations they were having. Their women would not return until later from working in the commune's factory.

He had to judge the time carefully. He and Woo Wai San needed to be long gone by dawn. The light began to soften, the shadows in the valleys deepening.

A light shining in Woo Wai San's house tempted him to walk straight down to it. Instead, aware of the risk, he made his way slowly down the hill and crossed the road by walking along a stream and under a rough road bridge. This brought him to a low belt of bamboo about thirty yards from the house. It was now dark and the waning moon would not appear for several more hours.

Nausea overcame him and the sound of his racing pulse echoed loudly in his ears. To reach the house unseen was easy—he had managed it many times before. There was a small side room off the main room where all the residents slept for warmth.

Trembling, he stood up against the side of the house. Hearing no sound, he bent his head to peer through the back window. A lamp lit the room and as far as he could tell it was empty.

There was no murmur of conversation. No hint of Woo Wei San's husband's usual monologue about the party, his tractors and the failings of comrades with less steel and fire in their makeup. Maybe he was asleep or not due home until late. Nor could Wa Hing hear the old woman's constant grumbling.

He caught an agonisingly brief glimpse of Woo Wei San as she dashed past the open doorway. There was little time to lose. The next few minutes could be his last minutes of freedom for ever. All his scheming had focussed on reaching the house. Now he had arrived, he had no clear plan for the next few steps.

He considered knocking on the door and quickly dealing with the men. But bloodshed or violence might make her unwilling to escape; and if she did come, pursuit would be relentless.

Outside the front door he saw a bamboo crate containing at least a dozen ducks. He cut a thick stem of bamboo from a nearby thicket and poked it at the ducks. The burst of furious quacking that followed sounded like an alarm sure to bring the village running.

Nothing happened. Wa Hing resumed the prodding. Again, the ducks quacked in annoyance but no one came. After a third prodding, with the ducks flapping around the cage, the door opened. A figure appeared holding a lantern up high so he could not see who was behind it. The person, a woman, stepped forward with the lantern now low in front of her. Wa Hing gasped. It was Woo Wai San. She walked hesitantly towards the cage.

Wa Hing moved quickly towards her. 'Ah San! It is I, Wa Hing.'

Woo Wai San missed his words and was aware only of a shadowy figure. She moved quickly back to the door. Again, he called, this time loudly, while setting himself to fight the husband if he came to the door.

Woo Wai San held the light high and recognised him. 'Ah Hing, Ah Hing, Ah Hing,' she chanted, her excitement almost out of control.

'Come in, quickly,' she urged. 'I never expected to see you again. There's no one else here.' Ah Hing's gamble had returned better winnings than ever expected. She ushered him inside and bolted the door.

'My husband is away, the old woman is dead, and my baby is left with my mother-in-law. I have been in disgrace since you left.'

The room was warm. Wa Hing embraced her and the great urge that had brought him all those bitter miles took charge. They made love fiercely, the act over almost before they had time to savour it. A brief period of reflective silence followed before Wa Hing said in a low voice, 'I came here to take you back with me. There is a better life in the city for both of us.'

Woo Wai San said nothing for some time as he waited in fear for her reply. 'I have thought of running away but I have not the courage nor the knowledge. I am not sure if I want to go. There is little here for me but if I am caught it would be very bad for us both because I am a party member.'

Wa Hing said nothing, but dressed quickly and filled a bowl from the large pot simmering by the fire. He tipped a helping of cold cooked rice resting on the food bench into the soup gobbled it all up with all the gusto of a starving man. He devoured the meal with as much gusto as he had just used on his lover.

'Your face is scarred, Ah Hing,' said Woo Wai San. It felt as though she had hit him and a new rage against his violent workmates flared in his heart.

'I had an accident. It will soon heal and disappear. It was no fault of the city,' he lied.

'If I wait for a while and then declare that I strayed from

the true path, I will be reinstated in the party,' said Woo Wai San. 'I still like living here and I can get my baby back later on. If I leave, I shall never see the child again.'

'Your child will belong to the village as much as to you. You know it will go to the creche and you will see it for a while in the evening, or perhaps only on rest days. In Hong Kong you can have another child with you all the time. I can earn enough for both of us.'

'I need more time to think about it,' she said. 'Stay here for a day and then I will return with you the next night, or you can return alone.'

Wa Hing refilled his bowl with the delicious soup, which seemed better than anything he had eaten in Hong Kong. Between gulps, he presented his ultimatum. 'The decision must be made in the next hour. I am sorry, Ah San, but that is the way it must be.'

He had decided Woo Wai San was too unstable for him to risk the chance of her betraying him to the party to regain favour. He desired her, but did not trust her, as perhaps he would Woo Sing. He consumed a third bowl of soup and packed what food he could find into his shoulder-bag. Woo Wai San saw he was determined to go and knew she must decide quickly. She walked restlessly about the hut, looking at each portion of the dark interior.

'If only you had written to me and given me a little more time,' she complained.

'That would have been too dangerous,' he said.

She stopped by the fire and cast her eyes over the room. 'I

like it here,' she said. 'This isn't such a bad little house.'

'The city has many sights, and many things are available there that you cannot even imagine here. You will never go far in the party, but in Hong Kong if you are lucky and work hard you can become rich.'

'I never thought of that,' said Woo Wai San.

She had come to learn that what she wanted most of all were men. They were not readily available in the commune, but might well be in Hong Kong. She glanced at Wa Hing and decided that he would do for a while.

This lust had only begun after she'd borne her child. Before that, like others in the village, she had enjoyed her husband but there were so many other things to do that one was often very tired.

She loved her country, its fields and hills. Had enjoyed seeing it change and grow. And was proud of her own small efforts to make things better. She had no dispute with the intentions of the party although all the talk became boring at times. If she had not had this desire for men, she would never want to leave China.

If her husband had been home more often, they could have lived a secret life of pleasure, of which even the party could not completely disapprove. *Many other women must feel this way,* she thought. *Perhaps it runs in the family.* Her mother had abandoned her and fled with another man a long time ago. Her grandparents, who had brought her up, never mentioned the episode, but Woo Wai San felt that she was beginning to understand.

The party changed the people and the landscape, but the landscape changed much faster than the people. Perhaps the girl-child she was now abandoning would one day complete the cycle, or perhaps the party would remake her into their preferred mould. She hoped so. She gathered her few simple clothes, glancing occasionally at Wa Hing, waiting tensely and watching her closely. She did not love him and neither did she feel he really loved her. But they were two of a kind with their feelings driving them against the tide of Chinese behaviour and custom.

The village street was deep in shadow. Clouds darkened the rising moon. But a light shone in Woo Sing's old home and Wa Hing would have dearly loved to tell her family that she was safe.

Chapter 9
Snakes and sharks

A light rain was falling when they left, and Wa Hing was unsure if it would be a help or a hindrance. They would leave more tracks, but in the unlikely event of dogs being used, the rain would wash their scents away. He turned to look back on his beloved home, appearing irregularly through the drifting rain and knew he would never see it again.

Wa Hing decided they would use the paths and road until two hours before dawn. He could not travel so fast now and walking was easier on the road.

They would hide and sleep during the first day in an ancient overgrown cemetery. An acrimonious argument among three communes over the ownership and use of the cemetery had caused it to be abandoned and it made a good sanctuary. Even the party had not been able to resolve the bitter differences among the older people. It was therefore decided the next generation would settle the dispute.

They had been walking steadily for several hours when Woo Wai San said, 'I would like to rest.'

Wa Hing grunted. He gave her a rice cake from his bag but said nothing, nor did he slacken his pace. An hour later they turned onto an overgrown path to climb a broken, rocky ridge. Graves were scattered among the bent pines that looked as old as the tombs themselves.

On the steeper and more overgrown part of the hillside they found an ancient grave that had been unearthed, perhaps to gather bones for a ceremony. Wa Hing removed rotting pine needles and branches from the entrance and they crawled into the narrow chamber. It was a tight fit so although soaked from the rain they remained warm.

Wa Hing decided that come daylight it would be almost impossible for anyone to find them if they kept close to the shelter. He crawled out of the chamber and disguised all traces of their presence. They ate a portion of cold rice and drank sparingly of the water. After a very brief kiss they fell asleep.

Next morning, they sat quietly, letting the sun warm and dry them. The long walk, the cramped sleep, and the danger of their pursuit stilled their passion of the previous night. They sat contentedly and talked of the events in the commune during the past few months. They bathed in a clear stream running close by and dried off in the sun, eating rice and strips of dried beef.

The following days were tiring, but without problems. Wa Hing calculated that the extra food from Woo Wai San would enable them to last several extra days and so decided to take the journey in easy stages. It would be better for Woo Wai San if she did not arrive at the coast too exhausted.

On the last day traversing this terrain, Woo Wai San left him to attend to her own needs but returned surprisingly quickly.

'There was a movement not far away in the undergrowth, just above us,' she said.

'Quick,' replied Wa Hing, packing his satchel and handing it to Woo Wai San. He held his knife in one hand and a fist-sized stone in the other and motioned for her to move to the left of the clearing so that he could hear the crackling of branches to the right.

They crouched and waited. Wa Hing tensed as the tell-tale sound moved across the top of the clearing. Perhaps it was a solitary soldier from a search team that had split up. If Wa Hing could silence him, they could slip away, although after such a move, relentless pursuit would be inevitable.

Wa Hing moved carefully to track the path of the noise. A brown back appeared on the path below him. He jumped on a hard and fast downward trajectory. He locked his arm about the man's neck, stifling any cry and prepared to strike upwards under the breastbone and to the heart.

As they crashed heavily to the ground, Wa Hing's knife became briefly tangled in a stray branch, delaying his thrust long enough to see his opponent was a mere youth. He turned his blade down at the last second, digging it deeply into the ground. The boy did not struggle, realising that remaining still was his only chance of survival.

'Do not cry out or I will kill you before the sound travels ten yards,' said Wa Hing.

He released his grip and slowly extended his elbow. The youth released a deep sigh as air rushed into his starved lungs. Wa Hing let him stand; he was so slender and fine-boned that he would not be any match.

'Are you alone? Who are you?' The young man nodded. Wa Hing and Woo Wai San realised he was merely a student as they helped him remove sticks and leaves from his clothing.

Woo Wai San smiled and offered water and a rice cake. 'Take these.'

As he ate, the youth talked. 'My name is Lei Yuk Sin and I want to get to Hong Kong. I have been travelling two days with little food and saw you leaving the ridge at dawn. I knew you must also be going to Hong Kong and so spent the day looking for you. I am so frightened on my own.'

The three of them sat on the grass at the edge of the clearing while Wa Hing thought what to do. If they took the boy they might attract more attention, but if they were chased, they could split off from him and hope the soldiers would follow the boy. If they refused his request to join them, he could well get caught and possibly inform on them, putting them in greater danger. Wa Hing would either have to kill the boy or take him with them.

Woo Wai San was also at risk so it was only fair to ask her opinion. He took her aside. 'We will have to take him with us or I'll have to kill him. We can't let him roam on his own now that he has seen us.'

'Our life together cannot be clouded by the murder of a boy. He is Cantonese and one of us, let him come.'

'You are welcome to join us if you do as I order,' Wa Hing told the boy.

Lei Yuk Sin agreed and they began the long climb back to the main ridge. Wa Hing took in his bearings before night finally wrapped its protective cloak around them. The sky was overcast and the ridge-top path barely traceable. It frequently led them to the edges of ravines. A huge rock-face appeared abruptly out of the blackness. Only after several weary hours spent crisscrossing the crest did they descend to a long, sweeping, broad-backed ridge and a more defined path. It wound through low, dense foliage, twisting around craggy, jagged boulders and rocky outcrops. Progress speeded up. All three were satisfied with the night's journey.

The path rose again and the vegetation thinned into tall, tangled grass. Wa Hing halted abruptly as a loud hiss warned him of a snake almost directly ahead.

'Stop. You two make a circle about four yards to one side and then tread more noisily through the grass to give it time to move away.'

He did not want to leave the path as it would be difficult to find again in the darkness.

He heard Lei Yuk Sin call out, 'We're lost, we're stopping on a small mound we've found.'

'Move forward but keep the sound of my voice on your left,' directed Wa Hing. 'You must keep going forward. Hold hands so that you don't lose each other.'

'We don't know which way is forward,' Woo Wai San replied, anxiety in her voice. 'We will have to come back towards your voice. We're safer on the path than in the grass.'

Wa Hing took a tentative step or two along the track, hardly visible, even when he leaned forward. The snake gave a loud hiss. Wa Hing stepped back several paces. He remembered watching a school friend die from the bite of a snake they had disturbed when playing one day. Wa Hing had opened the bite with a sharp stick and although they immediately turned towards home, within an hour the bitten ankle was swollen, a mass of blood had collected beneath the skin. A bloody diarrhoea had so weakened his friend, that older youths had had to carry the dying child home.

A cry from Woo Wai San brought his attention back to the present peril. 'We have gone back to the mound because a snake hissed between us and your voice.'

Lei Yuk Sin gave a loud shout to scare the snake. His cry echoed around the hilltops.

'Be quiet,' Wa Hing commanded. 'Sound will carry a long way and might attract the soldiers.'

'I'd rather a few years carrying dung to the fields than a snake bite,' Woo Wai San said.

Their little team was breaking up in terror. Every move brought a hiss or a rustle. Wa Hing groped among the bushes to find a branch about three feet long and reasonably straight. He poked it ahead of him, creeping towards the sound of his companions who were whispering each other's name to quell their fear.

A loud and definite hiss erupted close to Wa Hing. Then he heard what he suspected was large snake moving away, probably a cobra. A person stopped breathing a few hours after a cobra bite. No fuss, no messy bleedings, just death. He eased forward, almost falling over the squatting bodies of his friends.

'There's nothing to do but wait until dawn,' he said. 'You might as well sleep.' He sat down patiently to wait out the night.

The others were still sleeping when the first traces of dawn showed in a clear sky, promising a fine, warm day. Wa Hing would have preferred misty rain to conceal their journey.

Woo Wai San had sprawled across the sleeping body of the young boy as if to protect and warm him, for he was lightly clad for the mountains. Wa Hing woke them for a quick meal. Both were stiff, cold and grumpy from their restless sleep and the rice cakes were eaten in silence. They made an early start in case they had to keep moving for a few hours.

As the sun lifted above a ridgetop, they saw a column of ten soldiers. His companions made as if to run, but Wa Hing held them back, sat them down and urged silence. If they ran the soldiers would quickly spot them.

The light was bright and clear. They watched the soldiers advancing rapidly along the ridge. Wa Hing noticed that each watched the man in front, leaving it to the lead man to keep his eyes on the path. He was probably as scared of snakes as they were.

The soldiers were barely fifty yards away when they next

appeared. Wa Hing realised they must have moved further from the path than he'd thought. A soldier glanced towards them and back to the backside of the man in front. Another man looked more steadily in their direction. Surely the patrol was playing with them, waiting for them to break and run so that they could be shot for resisting arrest. A third man glanced over and stopped to shade his eyes. Wa Hing realised then that the sun was behind them.

A following trooper collided with the soldier still gazing at them, knocking him forward and into rough bushes at the side of the path. Wa Hing resisted the impulse to laugh as the man angrily turned on his inattentive colleague. He watched the troop move over a small crest. They waited ten more minutes until the receding soldiers approached a corner. They would now be out of view until the soldiers gained higher ground.

They gathered their few belongings and, as the soldiers disappeared, moved rapidly off the ridge into a steep valley. A few minutes later they entered dense undergrowth. They stopped in a sunny clearing, shocked, relieved and exhausted. The snakes were entirely forgotten.

After a wash in a stream, a drink and a rice cake, they prepared to wait out the day. Wa Hing fell asleep almost immediately, the long vigil alongside his sleeping friends having proved more tiring than a night of walking.

'Wake me an hour before dusk so that I can map out a route through less rugged country,' Wa Hing told them before he slept.

Woo Wai San and Lei Yuk Sin also fell asleep but woke in the late morning fully refreshed, impatient at the prospect of the long day ahead. So many hours to fill. Woo Wai San found the lengthy need for silence oppressive. She craved conversation and nudged Lei Yuk Sin.

'Why do you want to go to Hong Kong?'

'For the same reason as you.'

'Do you know anything about it?'

'I know it will be very different.'

'Wa Hing told me it is rich but very dangerous,' said Woo Wai San. 'Many of the people do not care for immigrants from China and are hard on us.'

'How can that be? They are all Chinese comrades, apart from a few English warlords.'

'I think you should forget the word *comrades*,' said Woo Wai San.

For a while they lay quietly in the grassy hollow, gathering their thoughts, until Lei Yuk Sin resumed the conversation.

'China has no real use for me and I have no use for China,' he said. 'I have worked very hard at school ever since I can remember. I enrolled in all the programmes for young people that I was asked to join yet when the time came for me to really learn the subject I loved, I was sent into the fields to work, something requiring no brain at all.' He stabbed savagely at the grass with a dry twig.

'I am sorry to hear that,' Woo Wai San said. 'I was never very good at school and perhaps the party thought you despised those who work with their bodies, so decided to teach you a lesson. I don't think you have learned it.'

'Why did you leave, then?'

Woo Wai San felt herself blushing. 'I am leaving for personal reasons that do not concern the way I worked. Nor do I hate China. I am proud of the commune, but for other reasons I don't fit in.'

Lei Yuk Sin was puzzled but decided not to annoy her with further questions. He suspected she had saved his life. Once they were in Hong Kong, he would thank her and repay her somehow.

'I could not even earn enough work points to live,' he complained. 'The work was so heavy and we were given the hardest and dreariest of jobs. The girls were worse off than the men for the peasant women were harder than peasant men, who would joke with us now and again. To think we left Shanghai in such high spirits. We really believed the peasants would welcome us and that we would find new ways to do things, mechanical ways, mathematical ways, ways from the school at Shanghai. I love mathematics and during our journey to Canton I dreamed that I would be able to use my skill for community economics and the estimating of crops and production. But they hate us and despise us because we know more of the world than they do. We know more characters and can read things that are not meant for them.'

Once again Woo Wai San's companion had made her feel guilty. What he said was partly true, for she had teased and bullied two girls transferred to them from Tien Tsim.

The girls had had more spirit than Lei Yuk Sin and soon sarcastically coped with the put-downs of Woo Wai San and her friends. Within months, the two girls had proved their ability to work and suggested effective solutions. The work team came to accept them, at first reluctantly, but later wholeheartedly.

'China was once ruled by brains without hands,' Woo Wai San said. 'And what a mess they made of it.'

'Now they're trying to use hands without brains,' replied Lei Yuk Sin.

'Not so. You are saying most people in China are stupid because they never went to a senior school. That is a ridiculous thing to say.'

Her anger silenced Lei Yuk Sin. He delved into his thoughts a long while before braving further discussion. 'I am sorry. It is only because I'm no good with my hands but good with my head. I also wanted to help China, and am prepared to work very hard, but only in the way I know best.'

'Let us not quarrel,' replied a mollified Woo Wai San. 'We may never see our land again, so let us enjoy the day. I know how bitter you feel, and we have long years ahead of us. Maybe we will change and learn, and China will too, and perhaps one day we will be allowed to return and help in new ways.'

'When I get to Hong Kong, I shall work hard, become rich, and then study at the university,' said Lei Yuk Sin.

'I do not really know what Hong Kong will be like,' said Woo Wai San. 'I always thought of it as a magic city. Wa Hing has not had time to tell me much, but he did say that it was better than here, with many things to do and buy.'

'Do you think we could stay together for a few days after we arrive so that I can learn from Wa Hing?'

'Of course, but say nothing now. I will try to speak with him when we land on the beach.'

They dozed in the sun. Looking at the dreaming face of Lee Yuk Sin, Woo Wai San realised she had already become fond of the clever, shy scholar. She wondered how many city children did not measure up to the tough life and hard ways of the peasants. There was no gentle answer for even she knew that they were required in the countryside to be 'the yeast and the bread', and those who fell by the wayside perished or picked themselves up as best they could.

He was brave to try to make the journey alone, without the slightest knowledge of the city. She did not desire him, but she liked him and hoped Wa Hing would let him stay for a while. They could look after Lei Yuk Sim until he found his own way. She suspected that Wa Hing liked the city because it was easy for someone of his cheerful ruthlessness to succeed, but the gentle Lee Yuk Sin might soon be crushed.

Wa Hing woke while the others were still asleep. Leaving his satchel as a sign that he would return, he climbed to the crest of the high ridge and inspected the landscape. He was worried that the shouting of the night before had attracted the soldiers, and that they might return along the path they had used in the morning. It was very unlikely that they could avoid being seen at such close range again.

He was studying a tall, distinctive rock on a ridge parallel to theirs when he realised that he had seen it before, but from another angle. Their route became clear. They needed to drop down into the valley and climb the opposite ridge. Then they would be in familiar territory. Excited and pleased, he returned to find an anxious Lei Yuk Sin sitting alone. The student had woken to find them both gone and took a while to realised their satchels were still there. Woo Wai San was away for some time, Wa Hing becoming increasingly impatient until she eventually returned.

He briefed them. 'If we leave the cover of this valley now, we can reach the river by dusk and climb the ridge on the other side. From there, I know the route to the coast.' He packed his satchel, and the others, greatly relieved, followed.

They reached the ridgetop in the early morning and, after a brief rest, trekked along a broad rocky crest with the barest covering of grass. This eased Woo Wai San's fears; she was terrified of snakes and didn't think she could bear to see another one.

Wa Hing turned his mind to Hong Kong. He was anxious to return to Woo Sing. He must also tell Woo Wai San about Woo Sing and Tong Pooi, and about what had happened to Ah Hon. Tong Pooi would be certain to ask about him and Woo Wai San would have to give a suitable answer. He would leave the explanations until they landed on the beach.

He needed also to gently push Lei Yuk Sin away. The city would terrify him and he suspected the youth would ask to stay with them. He already had enough people relying on him.

As they walked along the ridge, the sky to the south was bright with the lights of the city, still many miles away. His companions gasped with wonder when he pointed out the glowing night sky.

'The city must be very grand to display itself in the sky at such a distance,' said Lei Yuk Sin.

They woke in late afternoon and rested in the sun. Each was occupied with thoughts of the coming night. The zone into which they were heading was patrolled by military detachments. It had been rumoured the patrol used fierce dogs that the soldiers did not always pace with. Instead, they set them loose and thus failed to arrive in time to restrain them from attacking runaways. Prisons were said to house several badly scarred inmates.

*

Their food was getting stale but hunger gave it flavour. Several times during the night they heard distant voices or the barking of dogs. For one scary moment, they crouched in a group of rocks as a search party discovered and chased another group on a nearby ridge. A long high-pitched scream ended in the sound of a body crashing through branches. Silence followed. They guessed a dog had chased a woman over a cliff. Shortly after the lights of torches flashed on the adjacent ridge, they clearly heard soldiers haranguing a man, shouting at him with a mixture of abuse and questions. The replies were inaudible, but one of the soldiers shouted 'sister' in an unbelieving way. They sounded angry, perhaps not so much at their captive but at what being a member of the Peoples Liberation Army compelled them to do. Nobody liked killing their young countrymen, even if they were traitors.

The sounds and lights died away as soldiers and captives moved off the ridge. Silently, the three companions moved forward, tense and frightened, but determined to reach the coast. Two hours later they looked down on the sea, dimly lit by the waning moon. The lights on the far side shone bright and welcoming. Wa Hing selected their hiding place with great care. Each knew today there would be no talking, only stillness and silence.

'The sea looks so calm,' said Lei Yuk Sin, but Wa Hing could only think about how it had killed Ah Hon and could well kill them too.

The sun was setting as they ate the rest of their now very stale food. Energy would have to come from determination. They rested but did not sleep well. Lei Yuk Sin had several inflatable bags in his pack and he agreed to share these with a grateful Woo Wai San.

'You are a true comrade, Ah Sin.'

Wa Hing flinched when he heard the word 'comrade'. Ah Sin seemed genuine and Wa Hing decided he would leave any decision about the boy until they were safely on the beach. He had grown to like his quiet determination and admired his passion to learn. Wa Hing had never had these passions but admired them in others, including Woo Sing. Lei Yuk Sin and Woo Sing might become good friends and he thought about how he must introduce them.

There was no need to land in darkness, so Wa Hing waited until dusk before leading them off the ridge. Once down on at shore level, they hid behind rocks until it was safe to move across the beach.

The water was warm, although Wa Hing noticed Woo Wai San shivering as she entered. They would swim close together to help each other and keep their spirits up. He recalled how Woo Sing would have drowned a few yards from shore if he had not been close by. He suspected that if they had all stayed together Ah Hon would still be alive.

The other two struck out swiftly but Wa Hing cautioned them to slow down. 'There is a long way to go and you will be tired soon enough. Swim slowly and calmly. We will swim out to the centre and let the tide carry us to Hong Kong.'

Wary of the darkness, he stayed close by. After hours of swimming and resting, they arrived at the point mid-stream where Wa Hing had previously fought the current. This time it was nowhere near as strong. All of a sudden, a light flashed over the water a few hundred yards away. A patrol boat had begun a systematic search of the area.

'Not a sound,' warned Wa Hing. His heart rate soared. The familiar sick feeling rose in his stomach. They stopped and waited; there was no way they could swim fast enough to get away. They would be discovered within minutes. The searching lights flickered on the surface of the choppy sea. *If only we could reflect the light*, thought Wa Hing.

Lei Yuk Sin whispered, 'Let's cut up my plastic float and put our heads beneath it to reflect the light. They will think it is the waves.'

Wa Hing slipped out his knife. He cut the float free, splitting it into two sections. Lei Yuk Sin and Woo Wai San shared the larger piece and he spread the smaller one over as much of his head as possible. The boat was now nearly on them and moving quickly. They heard the thump of its propeller and turned their faces away.

The water shone bright around them and Woo Wai San was close to shrieking with fear. She felt Lei Yuk Sin trembling as he grasped her waist. Wa Hing tried to sink low in the water but the light had passed them by before he could make any movement.

Two minutes of agonised apprehension followed. *Have I lost them?* To shout for them could bring the boat back. For a few despairing moments he was alone in the blackness, more worried than he had been at any other stage of their journey. If he lost them now, he doubted they would have the strength to swim on alone. He would have taken his mistress and a harmless youth to their deaths.

He caught sight of them as he was about to risk calling out. They were riding the crest of a small wave, illuminated by the lights on the shore. For an instant, the two heads were silhouetted against the sky. It was all he needed. With a few powerful strokes he was by their side. Both were scared witless. The sobbing Woo Wai San released Lei Yuk Sin to embrace Wa Hing.

'There is nothing to stop us now,' he said. 'We will swim on.'

Woo Wai San looked surprised. She shook the water from her hair, laughed and began to swim. Her laughter restored their spirits and the tedious process of swimming and resting resumed.

In the breaking dawn, Wa Hing saw they were making good progress. They were far from China's shore and in a position where the current would help them. The mistake they had made last time was swimming to shore instead of letting the sea carry them. They had exhausted themselves and Ah Hon had paid the price for their miscalculation and impatience. He estimated that this way they would land in two to three hours. The day was fine and they would soon be drying in the sun.

The other two had seen the shore and were excited and cheerful but Wa Hing cautioned, 'We still have some hours in the water ahead of us so let's not tire ourselves now. Keep going as we have been doing.'

'I am feeling tired and need to rest,' said Lei Yuk Sin.

'I feel fine,' said Woo Wai San. 'Have your other float back for a while as I'm okay treading water.

They fixed the floats to the boy. 'When I have studied and become rich, I shall repay you,' he said. 'It might be many years but I shall remember.'

They drifted on, saying little but watching the steadily approaching shore.

A scream of sheer terror echoed across the waves. 'My arm! My arm!'

It was Lei Yuk Sin.

Wa Hing turned to look back, chilled by the horror of what

he saw. The frantic boy was waving a torn stump. Blood was spurting out, staining the water a deep crimson.

'Swim on,' Wa Hing shouted to Woo Wai San, but she appeared unable to move. He seized her arm. Swimming and struggling, he dragged her away from the bloodstained water. Sharks would go into a frenzy if they detected blood. They would bite anything near, even each other.

A few strokes on she had recovered enough to say, 'I will swim now.'

Lei Yuk Sin screamed, 'Don't leave me.'

Wa Hing hesitated, glanced at Woo Wai San, then swam back into the widening circle of blood. He saw no sharks but had learned from the fisherman that they were not particularly big fish, just very vicious.

When he reached Lei Yuk Sin, the youth's ashen face and staring eyes told him death was inevitable. Regardless, he undid his belt and tightened it about the bleeding stump.

'Make as few movements as possible and I will pull you out.'

The half-conscious Lei Yuk Sin faintly uttered his thanks. Wa Hing pulled him a few yards.

The boy screamed again. 'They're biting my legs!'

Blood once more stained the water.

Wa Hing felt something brush his leg and let the boy go.

'Don't leave me, I don't want to die,' he screamed. But Wa Hing swam on. He knew he was unable to save him.

He caught up to Woo Wai San and they swam on in a silence broken only by the cries of the dying boy. They soon ceased.

Chapter 10
New beginnings

By the third day, the worst of the bleeding had stopped. An exhausted Woo Sing was visited by Miss Campbell, who tried to conceal her anger at Woo Sing for choosing to give birth in the tiny room at the back of the restaurant. The labour had been no more than three hours and Jeng Gei had delivered the child without trouble. It was the bleeding afterwards that had sapped Woo Sing's strength.

Neither Jeng Gei nor Woo Sing could understand this. Two months before the birth, Jeng Gei had brewed up a mixture of sweet vinegar, pigs' feet, hard-boiled eggs and ginger. Towards the time of birth, she had added pigeon droppings, as these were said to be beneficial. She had boiled this concoction each day for Woo Sing to drink half a cup of the thick brown liquid.

Yet still she bled. The ginger supposedly helped to drive the air from the womb after the baby had emerged and Jeng Gei decided that she had not fried the ginger for long enough.

For the first two days, Woo Sing's thighs and buttocks

remained wet with blood. The room smelled of stale blood and sweat, even though Jeng Gei kept the room and bed-clothes clean.

Woo Sing had visited the hospital twice during her pregnancy, and because the doctors and nurses seemed so uninterested, she decided to let Jeng Gei look after her. Even some expensive herbs from the local Chinese pharmacist had failed to stop the continuous trickle of blood between her thighs. She was too exhausted to worry about the child crying in Jeng Gei's room and had held him only briefly.

At the birth, Jeng Gei had gasped, 'Very big,' at her first sight of the head. Although she had delivered babies before, she was afraid of easing out such a large head and body. However, the baby had come out easily, propelled by a large blood clot. He was large even for a boy, and to the women's relief, he looked Chinese.

In desperation, Jeng Gei sent a brief message to Miss Campbell, 'Woo Sing not well, bleeding.' The housekeeper arrived a few hours later with Inspector Campbell who immediately drove back to a telephone at Lau Fan Shan and convinced a medical friend to come to Pak Tin that evening.

Miss Campbell noted the fear in her nephew's face and thought how susceptible European men were to beautiful Chinese girls. When Doctor Brown arrived, he quickly took in the situation but wondered about the circumstances of the girl's pregnancy and his friend's involvement.

'This is Western medicine, based on science, and I know exactly how it works,' he said quietly to Woo Sing.

When Miss Campbell translated this, she grasped from the look on Jeng Gei's face what she thought of the treatment. An injection stopped the bleeding and the doctor gave Woo Sing some pills with clear instructions about taking them.

He took Inspector Campbell aside and they looked carefully at the baby.

'The child looks mainly European,' said the inspector.

'Yes, and appears to be in excellent health,' replied the doctor. 'The mother is very beautiful.'

'Someone else thought so, too,' said Campbell bitterly, revealing his affection and blamelessness in the affair.

Jeng Gei owned several tiny, but beautiful, jade carvings, which she pressed into Doctor Brown's hand.

'There is no need,' he said.

'Your medicine is better than my medicine,' said Jeng Gei humbly.

The doctor had been long enough in Hong Kong to qualify this. 'Only sometimes.'

They returned to Woo Sing's room to say goodbye. She smiled at them. Because of these trustworthy *gweilos* she was safe.

She was tired but soon would be better. As she drifted off to sleep, she thought about Wa Hing and wondered if he had found Woo Wai San.

*

As they let the sun dry their sodden clothes, they said little to each other; grateful to be out of the water. Woo Wai San was in shock. The frightful screams she had swum away from were no passing nightmare but a reality that she would have to live with for a long time. Although Wa Hing regretted Lei Yuk Sin's tragic end, his main worry was how to tell his companion about Ah Hon's death and Woo Sing's pregnancy.

He made a tentative start as they walked along the beach. 'I am sorry, Woo Wai San, but there is something I must tell you.' He paused, summoning his willpower. 'Ah Hon did not arrive safely. We found he had drowned only a little way from here.'

She sank abruptly to the sand, her head in her hands, sobbing and unable to stem the tears. 'This is a terrible place, Wa Hing. Why did you bring me here? Why? Tell me now.'

'You had to know so that you can avoid the subject with Tong Pooi. If he asks, you must say that you have not heard from Ah Hon since he left.'

'What does Woo Sing think of deceiving an old man? Or perhaps she is dead, too! Ah Hing, tell me about her.'

'Later,' Wa Hing replied. He felt the situation slipping out of his control.

'Tell me now.'

'Woo Sing is alive and well but she has her own problems.'

'I am not walking any further until you tell me the truth.'

Her words angered Wa Hing. *Why did I risk my life for this woman? If the sharks had bitten off parts of me when I first swam over, I would never have had to worry about her again.*

'She was raped by an Englishman and is expecting a baby.'

Woo Wei San could not believe what she was hearing. Much as she disliked Woo Sing, she couldn't imagine the disgrace she would be suffering.

'What a hell of a place you have brought me to, Ah Hing. Two dead and a girl defiled and now stuck with a bastard. What is this place? How could anyone want to live here?'

'It is free,' he replied.

*

Tong Pooi had great difficulty concealing his tears of joy and relief upon seeing the young people again. They were exhausted and very subdued. The girl was very different from Woo Sing, much more demonstrative. She had hugged him affectionately when they met. 'It is good to see you, uncle. I'm sure we will be good friends.'

Tong Pooi, surprised, murmured, 'Welcome.'

Perhaps this public affection was communist teaching. It pleased him while also feeling annoyed at the destruction of traditional manners. He confirmed Wa Hing would share his cubicle and the girl could stay in Woo Sing's tiny space. There was no mention of Ah Hon and the old man again returned to waiting.

'I think Ah San will need to stay home for a few days, Ah Pooi,' said Wa Hing, pleasantly but firmly.

'Of course, of course, just like Ah Sing.'

Next day, Wa Hing went off to work and Woo Wai San was left to rest and sleep. But when Tong Pooi returned the following day, he noticed Woo Wai San had bought modern clothes, which he felt she did not know how to wear.

Several times he was shocked, yet fascinated, to see a long length of inner thigh exposed when she sat down. It disturbed him; how could he tell her to sit more appropriately? He felt it unfair that he had to sit in his own room and gaze only at the ceiling.

He began gently. 'I have noticed Ah San, it is fashionable in Hong Kong for young ladies to sit side-on in their chairs, or to sit … er … cross-legged. I think you should do the same otherwise people might suspect that you are an unsophisticated person from the country.'

Woo Wai San was surprised by Tong Pooi's fashion knowledge and was pleased to receive his advice.

She crossed her legs, exposing the lower edge of her pants and an expanse of leg and buttock.

'Would this do, Ah Pooi?'

The old man blushed. 'No, there must be some other way, perhaps you had better ask Ah Mei.'

Woo Wai San, changing her position. 'What about this?'

'That is better,' the old man replied, desperately wishing he had never started the conversation. 'However, if you do not cross your legs but sit with them close together and pull the skirt edge down that may be best.'

Woo Wai San stood up, pulling her skirt first up and then down before sitting again. 'Like this then, Ah Pooi?'

Tong Pooi felt the sweat on his forehead as he gazed steadily towards the back wall of the cubicle.

'You are not looking, Ah Pooi,' said Woo Wai San crossly.

He looked briefly. 'I think that might be better but you really must ask Ah Mei.'

'Very well, Ah Pooi, thank you for telling me.'

He nodded and decided he would never again tackle modern fashion.

*

Woo Sing began to feel much stronger, and despite Jeng Gei's hints about changing back to Chinese medicine, she continued to take the Western doctor's pills. Her bleeding stopped and she began to suckle the child. They thought that her milk might have dried up in the days after the birth, but she endured the child's biting on her empty nipples until her milk began to flow.

She was feeding the baby when Ng San Fong arrived. Ng San Fong had never seen another woman's breasts and felt that old devil of jealousy surface as she compared them to her own. She hoped her feelings did not show.

'I did not know for some months, Ah Sing. My father said to let you settle down. I did not come or write in case my presence influenced the shape of the baby.'

Woo Sing laughed, grateful for her friend's concern. 'Surely you don't believe all that nonsense. I am pleased you have come. You are clever and perhaps can think of a name for the child.'

'Will you keep him or sell him?'

Woo Sing hesitated. 'I think I will keep him, Although I hate his father, I think I might love the child.'

Ng San Fong excused herself for a moment. She returned with a large parcel of baby clothes. The two women sorted through them together, holding them against the child. Ng San Fong felt a deep stirring of emotion. A vague plan began to form but she said nothing.

*

Wa Hing settled back into driving the furniture truck. His companions were curious about his break. *Unnecessarily curious*, he thought.

Finally, his boss tackled him, 'We like to know what our employees do when they leave us for nearly two weeks. I could have found another driver, but didn't, because you are strong and reliable. I may not be able to let you have the job for much longer, though, because my boss needs to know what his employees are doing at all times.'

Wa Hing decided to keep the pact made with his boss before he left because it was clear he would not drop the matter. In the secrecy of the office, he said, 'I swam from Kwan Tung a bit over a year ago and during the last two weeks I swam back to bring a girl to Hong Kong.'

Lai Gwok Yuen stared at Wa Hing. 'That must have been incredibly dangerous. Tell me about it. I've never heard of such a thing before. There are sharks and patrols and sea currents and dogs, and searchlights ... I don't believe it.'

'I can bring the girl.'

Lai Gwok Yuen thought it over. 'No, just tell me about it and I will decide about the girl after.'

Wa Hing described his journey, omitting little except the most personal matters about Woo Wai San. When he began to describe the death of Lei Yuk Sin, Lai Gwok Yuen stopped him, 'I have a son of that age, I don't want to hear any more. I am satisfied. You will probably keep your job and maybe we can even offer you a better one. I shall let you know tomorrow.'

Wa Hing returned home, puzzled and concerned. He liked his job and it paid enough to support Woo Wai San as well.

He received a message from Ng San Fong that Woo Sing had given birth to a boy and both were well. He and Woo Wai San planned to visit her the next Sunday with Tong Pooi. He hoped the meeting between the two women would at least be polite, if not friendly.

Woo Wai San did not seem enthusiastic about the city and he suspected she had lost her feelings for him as well. Perhaps she missed her child or maybe was still exhausted from the journey. Several times she stopped him from slipping into her bed, making different excuses. She didn't appear to feel the urgent desire she once had.

Woo Wai San felt no joy at her arrival, although she had come to love the gentle Tong Pooi. He gave them space in his cubicle, gave them what food he could spare and he never asked her about her past. Wa Hing, however, had become a stranger, although she admired his cheerfulness, his courage and his optimism. She could see why he liked this city, but it was different for her. She felt the ever-present mass of people were forming walls, slowly crushing her. There was no place here without noise. If she woke at night, the noises in the block reminded her of her insignificance in this vast beehive. She remembered the silence of the village at night; a cool, desirable balm. It had been a pleasure to be lost in that silence.

The beggars disgusted her with their blindness, sores and soiled stumps of limbs. She began to realise that many of the phrases she had mouthed at party meetings had meaning. She had learned the sentences used to condemn the capitalists and their exploitations. It had meant nothing then; now she understood it but it was too late.

If only her body would drive her to Wa Hing and other men she could manage, but desire had left her. A few times she thought of leaving and swimming back, but the prospect of that endless sheet of water and its waiting sharks halted her.

Tong Pooi was looking forward to visiting Woo Sing, although he was worried about the features of the child. However, he knew many Eurasians did well in Hong Kong, skimming the best of both worlds. He felt very modern for he knew the disdain of many of his friends towards half-caste children.

Wa Hing, too, was desperate to see her. He was worried that she would change towards him and wondered what Woo Wai San would say.

*

They sweated in the sticky heat of summer as the bus bounced along the rough road to Pak Tin. Woo Wai San noted Woo Sing's eyes were glistening with tears when they arrived and she embraced Wa Hing and Tong Pooi.

She turned to Woo Wai San. 'Welcome to Hong Kong, Ah San. It is difficult and dangerous to live here. I will try to help you to avoid my mistakes. You must ask me what you want to know.'

Woo Wai San held out her hands. 'Ah Sing, we were not friends back home. I am sorry for the past and sorry for the insults. From now on I want to be your friend. Surely we can help each other.'

Woo Sing replied briskly, 'Of course.' She turned to the others, 'Let us take tea. There are no customers and Jeng Gei is anxious to meet you.'

She had not mentioned the child, and Tong Pooi fretted that something disastrous had happened. He sat awkwardly, cooled by a sea breeze. There was much to discover from each other but no one knew where to start. When Jeng Gei brought out the still unnamed child, Woo Wai San rushed from her seat and took him from her. 'He is beautiful, Ah Sing, and so large.'

Tong Pooi knocked over Woo Wai San's vacant chair in his keenness to see the child. A small Chinese face stared impassively back at him. He was elated.

'Wonderful, wonderful,' he shouted.

All turned to stare at him and he stepped back a few paces. Woo Sing sat with eyes lowered and face flushed, hands trembling.

'Little sister, the worst is over for all of us,' said Wa Hing. 'From now on, things will be better.'

Woo Sing smiled up at Woo Wai San, affectionately cradling the child.

'Thank you, big brother. Let us take tea.'

Woo Wai San was lost in thought of the sea miles separating her from her own child.

Jeng Gei brought sweet cakes and a Western-style cake that she had proudly baked. Woo Sing cajoled Tong Pooi into tasting it.

'Come, Ah Pooi, try this Western cake, it is delicious.'

'You know I do not eat Western food,' he said, quite shocked as he inspected it.

'Oh?'

'A small piece only, Ah Gei,' he said reluctantly, and the tension eased.

Most of Woo Sing's questions were still unanswered, but now they did not seem so important. The child had been accepted, Wa Hing was safe, and she had made her peace with Woo Wai San. It was a good day, the best for a long time, and as her friends chattered and passed the child among them, she determined to try again in this city.

Tong Pooi and Jeng Gei strolled away and Woo Sing wondered what they were talking about. She must not let others ever decide anything for her, no matter how kind their intentions. Her decisions would be made for the two of them, for she had no illusions about how badly the city treated an unmarried mother and her child.

Little was said, no plans were made, and nothing serious was discussed to mar the day.

When Tong Pooi strolled back to the table, he turned his back to the others and secretly tried to cut a large slice of the strange cake with its peculiar fruits and delicious flavour. Jeng Gei watched and said nothing, but smiled broadly. Tong Pooi gave her a sheepish, guilty look and continued placidly eating the cake while watching junks in the bay.

Woo Wai San shifted her chair out of the sunlight and thought how strange it was. *No one here seems bothered and yet at home such a disaster would have been discussed in detail.* Marx or Lenin must have said something about such an issue, but Woo Wai San could not think of an appropriate quotation.

Her thoughts were broken by Woo Sing's laughter at Tong Pooi, who had written a single character in the old style and was holding the paper in front of the child.

'He can't even see properly yet,' said Wa Hing, grinning at the old man.

'Perhaps he can,' said Tong Pooi crossly. 'And if he can see, even a little, then the first thing he should see is his mother and next a letter from his own language.'

'Ah Pooi,' said Wa Hing, still laughing. 'If characters were babies, you would have the biggest family in the world.'

'I will start to save for a good ink block and brush,' said Tong Pooi.

'Of course, dear friend,' said Woo Sing. She smiled and touched his hand. 'I shall see he practises every day.'

Jeng Gei disappeared for a few moments and returned

with a selection of tasty dishes. They ate rapidly for soon they would have to leave for the bus stop.

Jeng Gei liked Woo Sing's friends. Even the slightly sullen Woo Wai San appeared to be a pleasant girl beneath her confusion. Wa Hing would look after her. Jeng Gei admired Wa Hing for he reminded her of her first husband—bold, good-humoured, and with that odd mixture of shrewdness and recklessness that had made her love him so dearly.

It had been a good day. Woo Sing and her son were looking well, the child thriving on his mother's milk. Once she began work, the child would need to be weaned. Jeng Gei found it hard not to compare him with some of her own babies, although she did not want to remember them or their fate. Even so, when she held the child, she felt the stirrings of an emotion that surprised her. She had thought that the past, like a searing iron, had burnt such feelings out of her forever.

As the friends began to depart, Jeng Gei took the baby while Woo Sing accompanied everyone down the path to the road. As they reached the end, she embraced Tong Pooi and Woo Wai San. She turned to embrace Wa Hing and the others looked away, but not before Woo Wai San briefly saw their faces. She felt no jealousy, for she did not love Wa Hing and it didn't matter if she never felt him between her legs again. Woo Sing had asked her to see her friend Chen Tien Wa and Woo Sing's friendship felt more important to her now than Wa Hing's thrusting body.

*

Woo Sing and Jeng Gei began to prepare the sweets and cakes for the following day's onslaught of children craving sweets to calm their nerves after a long morning of practising characters.

Jeng Gei asked Woo Sing why Woo Wai San had been so quiet. 'Most people who arrive here are happy and enthusiastic, at least for a few days.'

Woo Sing took a while to respond. 'I am not sure,' she said, nibbling at a broken cake. Her habit of eating broken sweets and biscuits annoyed Jeng Gei, as previously she had kept them in a special jar from which she sold them very cheaply. Woo Sing's appetite was somewhat alarming and her style of eating was hardly delicate, especially for such an attractive and intelligent girl. Jeng Gei decided she would take the matter in hand in future. Meanwhile, the girl spoke slowly and with hesitation.

'Ah San was an orthodox party member. I never heard her deviate from the standard line. She had a fine career open to her and it is hard to imagine what went wrong. Sometimes those who love the party most ardently begin to hate it, although that is very rare. Woo Wai San's husband should have corrected her.'

Woo Sing wondered about Woo Wai San's child. *The child must be dead or still in China for Woo Wai San said nothing about it. Perhaps her affair with Wa Hing had been discovered and she had been censored by the party.*

'It is too difficult to know, Jeng Gei. Perhaps there was a power struggle or trouble among party members. The party is made up of people and those not in the party tend to forget that.'

Jeng Gei sighed. 'I have never been interested in governments or leaders. Before I left the mainland our thoughts were confined to saving ourselves and our families. Not even friends could be considered when the Japanese were at their worst. I don't like to think of those times. I know that what was so bad for me has been good for China.'

'When a huge army marches there are many who fall by the wayside,' said Woo Sing. 'But one can still admire those who walk forward. Both of us love our home but neither of us can go there again. Let us not speak of it anymore.'

Jeng Gei nodded and they continued their food preparation in silence.

*

Woo Wai San knew Wa Hing would probably visit her cubicle on their return from Pak Tin. She had heard her neighbours on the other side of the cubicle walls quietly talking about her and was surprised to find she was more concerned about their views than she had been about those of her party comrades. She was answered by hearing her neighbours saying she was a cheap refugee from China and what could one expect. She was on the verge of shouting back that Hong Kong corrupted even good Chinese girls when Wa Hing entered.

Later, she realised she was fortunate that they were interrupted for Tong Pooi would have had to bear the disapproval of the nearby tenants. She tried to explain to Wa Hing that her desire had changed to revulsion. But he laughed and walked off.

Wa Hing came to her cubicle late that night as he been working on his maps, something that Woo Wai Sin admired. As they lay together, she brushed his hand away from her breast and whispered, 'Ah Hing, you knew all along that we did not love each other but I thought we might after a while. I still like you, even more than before, but I don't want any man again for a long time.'

He pushed his hand forward.

'Don't,' she said.

'Why not?'

'I still hear Lei screaming,' she said.

He realised he should have killed Lei at the moment of capture. *Back then he was still a dangerous stranger and he had died anyway. Woo Wai San would have forgotten about him. I liked Lei, a harmless but courageous boy, a real patriot. Such a pity that the party had so badly disillusioned him.*

Wa Hing set these thoughts aside, overcome by an increasing desire for Woo Wai San, and turned back to the immediate problem of relaxing and then exciting her.

'Lei asked to come and nearly got here,' he replied. 'His death was the result of his own choice, maybe the first choice he ever made, but it was his choice. He sought us out and asked to come with us.'

'And if we had refused?'

'He would have been caught and spent a few months in prison.'

'And he would still be alive,' said Woo Wai San triumphantly. 'He died because you came back for me.'

This conversation was not going as well as Wa Hing wanted it to. His excitement was gone, replaced by anger.

'Are you calling me a murderer?'

'No, not a murderer, Ah Hing,' said Woo Wai San softly.

'Better not. What would you have said and thought if I had refused to take him?'

He regretted it as soon as he said it and felt Woo Wai San's naked body stiffen beside him.

'You are right, Ah Hing. It is my fault, too.'

'I did not mean that. It is no one's fault and everyone's fault. Only the sharks are blameless.'

He waited, and in the half-light watched her turn towards him, desiring him. To his annoyance, he was no longer feeling excited, but her hands soon aroused his passion.

'Perhaps I really do love you, Ah Hing. You are much more thoughtful than most of us.'

But as their passion mounted, he barely heard her say, 'This is the last time for a while, or perhaps forever. I want to leave you for a while and find my own way. I won't have other men because I don't want them. Do you understand?'

'I think so.'

As her orgasm swept over her, she still heard Lei screaming, but the voice was fainter and no longer accusing.

Later, as he rose to slip away, Woo Wai San whispered, 'Ah Hing, if you ever love another, please tell me.'

He looked down on this enigma of a woman. Moments

ago, she was a female animal, all desire and no thoughts. Now she had changed into something else with emotions he failed to understand. She was not beautiful but the shadows falling across her face and breasts and mingling with her long hair momentarily transformed her into the likeness of those carved female figures he had seen in old temples, beautiful and sensuous. The light shifted, the spell was broken, and once more she became Woo Wai San.

'I will,' he said quietly, and left.

*

Woo Wai San took a while to find the little shack. She looked along the foetid path and thought, *I now understand why we had those campaigns to keep the streets clean.* She had always considered the party obsessive about the cleanliness of communal areas, but here she could see it was needed. She noticed a tiny portion of the tin wall shifting and realised that she was being inspected. A child's voice asked her name.

'I am Woo Wai San, a friend of Woo Sing.'

A door opened. 'Did she send any sweets?'

Woo Sing had forgotten to tell her about sweets. Woo Wai San thought quickly. 'It is my fault, I forgot them,' she said. 'I shall fetch them later.'

The interior was stuffy, damp and poorly lit. In the corner, a man lay on a bed breathing noisily. The children were waiting for their mother to return. One went to the man and Woo Wai San heard her whispering, 'It is not Mama, but a friend of Woo Sing.'

The man took no notice of her.

Jumbles of plastic pieces were piled into several bamboo baskets, but the children, who had been working at them, made no effort to return to their tasks. Woo Wai San noticed they were looking at her short dress and she felt herself blushing. Their watchful gaze irritated her.

'How long will your mother be?'

'Not long,' the oldest girl replied.

The girl knew what her mother was doing; she had once looked out over the yard when playing on top of some boxes. She had watched, curious but not shocked, for she thought she knew why her mother was doing what she did. She was about eight years old and very fond of her mother.

Woo Wai San could stand the inspection no longer. 'I will fetch the sweets and return in a while. What sweets would you like?'

The four children became animated. They crowded around her, giving their orders.

On her return, a thin, anxious woman introduced herself as Chen Tien Wa. 'Did Ah Sing send you with anything?' she asked abruptly.

'No, she simply asked me to find out how you were,' replied Woo Wai San. 'She was quite sick after she had her baby and has been unable to come.'

Remembering her manners, Chen Tien Wa asked her guest to enter. She warmed slightly when Woo Wai San delivered the sweets. Woo Wai San knew she had spent too much on the sweets but when she saw the children eating them like a meal, any regrets at her impulsive generosity soon vanished.

Chen Tien Wa gave her husband a small packet and he held her hand gratefully. He began coughing and wheezing, a relentless cycle of struggle and exhaustion.

'Come for a walk in the fresh air,' said Chen Tien Wa. 'Talk is too disturbing for my husband.'

They walked along a congested footpath bathed in belching fumes. A pungent stench from a small dyeworks filled the gap. *Fragrant Harbour indeed*, thought Woo Wai San, who was becoming used to it by now. This stretch of street had a particularly foul smell.

She listened to Chen Tien Wa pouring out her frustration. 'Tell Woo Sing my husband is nearly dead. I would take him to the hospital, but as he is an addict, they would not allow him any drugs, and that would kill him quicker. I am worried that he will infect the children, but they can't live anywhere else. We make enough from the plastic pieces to survive, but there is not enough for the children to go to school. I had to give a few dollars of emergency savings to an inspector, who came around asking after the children. If a typhoon comes and we are washed out, there'll be no money for another home.'

Woo Wai San let the woman talk for there was so little she could say. Chen Tien Wa wasn't really addressing her in particular but simply giving voice to her anger. She talked her problems around in circles until Woo Wai San felt utterly confused and depressed. *It would be nice to meet someone who was cheerful and successful in this city,* she thought. *But I suppose that part of being successful is to stay well away from the unsuccessful, and that is why we never meet them.*

In his own small way, Tong Pooi was successful. The city had never beaten him. He was lonely at times, but content with his job and lodgings. In the time she had been in Hong Kong, she had never heard him express a desire for anything better.

Woo Wai San could bear Chen Tien Wa's outburst no longer. She grasped her elbow and pulled her to a stop.

'I will walk back with you, but I must go soon. I will tell Woo Sing all you have told me. Although she has her own problems, I know she will try to help. I am new to the city and when I have a job, I shall try to help you too. I realise you have big problems, but you complain a lot—perhaps too much.'

Chen Tien San stared at her with tears in her eyes. 'It is only the children I think about. I complain not for myself, but for them.'

Woo Wai San felt embarrassed by her irritation at this woman who was so close to beaten. 'Why don't you ask for help from the government? Surely they won't let you starve?'

'Because they will take away my husband and any chance of returning to Indonesia would be lost if it was known that he has tuberculosis. I have not the money to pay the assistance official so my application would never be heard. Even if it was heard, there's bound to be a rule that claims the government does not have to pay us.'

It was too complicated for Woo Wai San. 'I shall see how we can help, at least until ...' She nearly said, 'Until your husband is dead', but finished her sentence with '… until your circumstances improve.'

They parted on the street. Woo Wai San could not bear to face that dreary lodging again. As she walked home, she realised it was a blessing that she and Wa Hing had not brought her child. Perhaps, someday, she could fetch her, but even if she never saw her again, she knew now that life could be far worse here than in Canton. She must talk about her future with Woo Sing, who had offered to help. Tomorrow, she would visit her.

Wa Hing listened when Woo Wai San told her about the visit. He gave her nearly forty dollars, which she realised must be most of what he had.

'Give the extra to Woo Sing. My pay day is only two days away.'

*

When Woo Wai San arrived at Pak Tin, the restaurant was overrun with noisy children. Neither of the women, intent on serving the crush of customers, noticed her. The school bell rang and the tables and chairs in front of the counter became visible. Only then did Jeng Gei spot Woo Wai San. She smiled at her and alerted Woo Sing with a tap on her arm.

The three women retired to the back of the shop where Woo Wai San helped with preparations for the next siege of children as they talked.

'If you have come to see me about something you can speak

to us both if you wish, as Jeng Gei is my friend,' Woo Sing said. 'Otherwise, we will have to wait until evening when it will be too late to go home.'

Jeng Gei said, 'I have no objection to Woo Wai San staying the night as long as she sleeps in your bed, Ah Sing, and not mine.'

They all laughed and Woo Wai San decided to tell her story—with a few omissions. She guessed Woo Sing knew of her relationship with Wa Hing, or at least suspected it. She found it surprisingly easy to speak of her serious misbehaviours in the commune and wondered if she was becoming a little shameless.

But to talk of Lei's death was agony. Ah Sing looked at her steadily without revealing her emotions.

It was also difficult for Woo Wai San to speak of her desire to live apart from Wa Hing, so she simply said, 'I must now work to support myself, even if this means separating from Wa Hing.'

'It is difficult,' said Woo Sing wearily. 'Every day here, one has to make decisions. If there was a problem at home everyone decided and everyone was responsible.'

'Everybody and nobody,' said Woo Wai San.

'One gets used to it here,' said Jeng Gei.

'Ah Hing has learnt to decide, and so shall I,' said Woo Wai San.

Woo Sing added, 'Ah Hing makes the best of things as they come along. He doesn't seem to need to decide much.'

'He decided to come and fetch me,' Woo Wai San retorted.

There was an uncomfortable silence before Woo Sing said, 'You are right.'

The two women looked at each other, smiling, for each wanted a female ally of the same age. But each wondered how Wa Hing would fit into such an alliance, and if it could last. Jeng Gei put a large pot of crystallised fruit on the table and announced, 'We will wrap these and that will do.'

They set to with speed, but only Jeng Gei enjoyed that pleasant tranquilly of mind that occurs when the activity of the hand overpowers the emotions of the heart.

The child, still unnamed, was bathed by Woo Wai San, and Woo Sing noted how carefully and gently she touched him. Jeng Gei was prone to pick him up whenever he cried; a practice that Woo Sing had been told was bad management.

The day at the restaurant ended shortly after dark and both women would be up again very early the next day. Woo Sing woke in the night to feed the child, and only drowsed a little as he suckled.

'I feel like an old can, full of holes leaking milk,' she told Woo Wai San, who was watching her.

Both were used to sleeping in a confined space, so sharing the narrow bed was not unusual. As they lay, they talked.

Woo Wai San asked, rather nervously, 'Do you think about clothes and men and such here?'

'When I first arrived, I was shocked by the dresses and close-fitting clothes and the way men look at you. Now I don't worry about it. The books in the pavement shops have dreadful photos, and with Chinese girls too.'

'Do you think I'm strange for what I did back home?'

'Do you think me bad for what I did here?' replied Woo Sing.

Woo Wai San said, 'When I came here, I thought I would feed my body with men, but now I don't want any. I think that was a childish dream. The men here fascinate me. Their clothes are well-cut and they look at you in that certain way. At home, if they look at you at all, they are wondering if you would be a good comrade in the paddy.'

'There was no time at home for me to ever feel that way,' Woo Sing said bitterly. 'I never felt it until I came here, and look what it has done to me.'

'It must be hard for Wa Hing and the other country boys when they come here.' Woo Wai San giggled.

'Yes, indeed,' said Woo Sing. 'A few times, I noticed him becoming uneasy when the lightly dressed European girls came past. Once or twice, I thought the lion might rush out and do his dance there and then.'

Woo Wai San laughed out loud and Jeng Gei, half-asleep next door, smiled. If only Wa Hing could somehow remain neutral.

'Do you think the men at home really didn't think about us, or were they shy?' Woo Sing asked.

'How am I to know for they never said anything.'

'Poor old Wa Hing,' giggled Woo Sing, and the pair of them grinned at the thought of Wa Hing resisting the temptations of the new city.

Jeng Gei was very tempted to talk over the future with

Woo Sing. But part of her warned against this. She felt she had brought enough disaster to all those she'd loved. She was sure there was a curse on her, the sole survivor of both her families, and somehow, she felt responsible. Woo Sing did not need any more problems.

Before the girl's arrival, Jeng Gei had been alone and content, helping no one nor ever hurting anyone. Woo Sing would have to do the asking and deciding, and she would remain passive and without responsibility. To remain apart was her decision.

To listen to the girls talking was to realise how little had changed. When she was a child, the family elders had made the decisions; now they had been replaced by the party chiefs. The ideas might be different, but the way those decisions were made was the same. Jeng Gei fell asleep, half-thinking and half-dreaming about the China of her childhood. *Some things have changed in China – in the old days both the girls next door would have finished up in a brothel or as the slaves of some family.*

*

The early afternoon was hot and the three women seated under the veranda did not notice the tiny figure carrying a large parcel and moving slowly up the path. Ng San Fong hated summer. It was the worst time of year for she had to wear thinner clothing that emphasised the irregular angularity of her twisted upper body.

Woo Sing saw her and ran easily and lightly down the path.

Ng San Fong watched her moving quickly towards her so she sat and waited, sweat trickling over her body. She brushed aside her old envy but still wondered if she had been wise to come. Woo Sing smiled, set the parcel aside and held out her hands.

'Welcome, sister. I have a friend to meet you. Have you thought of a name for my son yet?'

Ng San Fong was now sure she had been right to come, and smiling, could only shake her head. She led the way slowly, Woo Sing walking quietly behind.

Ng San Fong noticed a young woman seated at the table, not as pretty as Woo Sing, with her hair styled in the commune fashion.

'Woo Wai San, this is the plastic flower designer I told you of,' said Woo Sing.

Ng San Fong waited for signs of the usual shock of seeing her twisted shape, but the girl looked at her without any self-consciousness and smiled.

'I will fetch the baby,' she said. 'I will also bring tea. It is such a hot day.'

Ng San Fong noticed Woo Sing looking at the parcel. 'Unwrap it. There are some clothes and a small sleeping mat. I had to persuade Mama not to load me with too many things, as she is quite excited about the child.'

'You are both so kind, Ng San Fong. Most people would not want to know me in my disgrace,' said Woo Sing.

Ng San Fong did not quite know what to say. She simply replied, 'It is a bad city,' as though this was an explanation for all the unanswerable questions. 'I have not only come to see you, Woo Sing, but to talk business as well.'

'Business?' laughed Woo Sing. 'Jeng Gei is the business-woman. I know nothing of business except for a few hours selling cigarettes when I first came here.'

Ng San Fong was uncertain how to begin. For the next few minutes, she would need to be more tactful and careful than ever before.

She spoke slowly – hesitant, still unsure of herself. 'I want to start my own factory ... and I cannot do it without help from people I can trust.'

A long silence followed as the three other women studied her closely, each wondering how to politely say 'no'.

'None of us have any money,' said Woo Sing. 'And apart from my few weeks at the factory, none of us have any experience. Except for Jeng Gei, we do not know what business really means.'

Woo Wai San remained silent, and Jeng Gei said, 'I will never leave this place. What happens if the business fails and you all have a huge debt to pay?'

Ng San Fong's heart sank, but she was fighting for her independence as well as for friendship. 'I know all of these things. Listen to my proposition and then take a day or to decide. We can start in a small way with a single-room factory. My father will lend us the money and we will pay eight per cent. I have the technical knowledge and we can hire machines for a start. I can sell to some of the clients of the firms I used to design for, but I cannot supervise the factory staff. I have not the strength. What I need is help from people I can trust. I suggest we each take an equal share of the earnings and an equal share of the debt. We take only living expenses out of the business until the debt is repaid. If the business fails, I shall speak to my father, but I cannot promise anything.'

'Perhaps your father should have an equal share as well,' said Woo Sing.

Woo Wai San had heard all about usury and the way that capitalists trapped the poor into debt, much the same as the old landlords had back home. Once in debt, one was never free. Woo Wai San liked Ng San Fong, but also had a warped belief that deformed people were cunning and dangerous, and even perhaps skilful in deceiving others.

'What if we are unable to pay our share of the debt?'

'Then the lender has lost his money,' replied Ng San Fong. 'But if you repay the debt and the business is prosperous, then you will have a share of the business. That is the reward for taking the risk.'

'It is very exciting, but very dangerous,' said Woo Sing. 'There must be some other way. I am sure that the commune never took those risks, and many things were made in the factories.'

'But the state promised to buy everything you made,' said Ng San Fong. 'Here, nobody will buy unless the goods are right. My flowers sell well, which is why I am always being asked to design more. The debt will be about ten thousand dollars. If all goes well, we will pay it off in a few months. If we fail it will take several years of savings to pay it back.'

'Find some buyers then I will join,' said Woo Wai San.

'I'm not sure. I will ask Miss Campbell and Wa Hing, although I know he will say to do it,' said Woo Sing. 'He enjoys risks but I have the baby, so it is different.'

Woo Wai San remembered Chen Tien Wa and said, 'What if we could find one or two others to work if they did not want to share?'

'That's all right,' said Ng San Fong.

'Let us leave it for now and meet in a week,' said Woo Sing.

Ng San Fong hesitated. She would have liked an immediate decision but accepted she would have to be patient if she wanted to be successful. One of the things she admired about Westerners was that they made up their minds quickly and resolutely. She was afraid to go into business on her own but knew she must not show it. She needed the support of Woo Sing. Together they would make such a success of the factory that her father would no longer be able to ignore her because of her spine.

Chapter 11
Forecasting

After stating she would not join the factory venture, Jeng Gei decided not to interfere with the others. However, she listened with great interest as her two young friends debated the factory's prospects, their chance of wealth, and the threat of years of dragging debt. Woo Sing and Woo Wai San would sit at the table, fiercely chopping bean curd and talking angrily about capitalists and exploiters.

As the time for Ng San Fong's return approached, Jeng Gei noted the discussions became less political and more practical.

'We have so little to lose and no other prospects, so there is nothing else to do but agree,' said Woo Sing.

'If the business fails, Ng San Fong can soon repay her share and can still live with her parents,' said Woo Wai San. 'But we who have nothing will finish up with worse than nothing. Ng San Fong could start a factory without us if she really wanted to.'

Woo Sing interrupted her. 'In Hong Kong, we must trust each other more than we did at home, otherwise we will never progress. At home, we didn't need such trust, and there were no risks unless you argued with the party.'

'We trust each other and we will have to maintain that trust if we are to manage this factory,' said Woo Wai San. 'Let us agree that if we are suspicious of anything we will talk with each other.'

'Agreed,' said Woo Sing, although neither had said that they would join the factory.

Woo Sing wanted to ask Miss Campbell for her opinion but decided it might be interpreted as a request for financial help. It was useless to ask Wa Hing, who would suggest that she accept and probably offer to take some of the risk.

Woo Sing thought of the future when her son would need money for education. If she accepted a job with wages now, by the time she paid for his keep there would be little left for the future. In the factory, she could look after him herself or have him close by. If the factory failed, she would be in debt. But first she would educate her son and then pay it back.

The years ahead looked threatening and sometimes she felt afraid. The fears felt at home—invasions by foreign armies, the anger of party officials or the exhortations of street committees for better behaviour—seemed imaginary now. Here there was real uncertainty and no matter how much one repented or begged for mercy there was no one to help.

*

It was hot when Ng San Fong strolled up the path, sweat

running in sticky, itchy rivers through the unnatural folds and crevices of her body. She felt triumphant after a week of desperate persuasion, resulting in her father reluctantly agreeing to carry the bulk of the debt if the business failed. And they had agreed this should remain their secret unless such a situation occurred.

Now she had to convince her prospective partners of the factory's success. She had prepared a large folder of calculations and managed to gather a few orders. None were definite because even her best customers would not place an order until they had seen a sample. She had always thought her father made his money easily, but now she realised that the business world was tougher than she had expected.

With the school closed, the inhabitants of Pak Tin were enjoying the warmth and a silence broken only by the quacking of ducks in a nearby pond.

Ng San Fong found Pak Tin peaceful and dreamlike compared with the city only a few miles away over the coastal hills.

The three women were seated around a low table, half-empty tea mugs and the scraps of a meal strewn in front of them. They greeted Ng San Fong casually, almost indifferently, adding to her fear of failing and making her pulse race and her body tremble. She smiled and pulled a chair to the table, deciding she would also be casual.

'How is the baby, Woo Sing?'

'Very well, thanks,' said Woo Sing, sleepily. The baby had gorged himself and drifted off into a placid sleep.

Ng San Fong could not stop trembling. Here she was,

shaky, drenched in sweat and anxious to settle the most vital matter of her life, while her prospective partners lounged at ease, smiling placidly.

To conceal her irritation and rising temper, she bent low over her tea and made herself drink deeply. The tea was too hot and burnt her lips and mouth. She was so distracted by the pain that she barely heard Woo Sing say, 'We think the factory is a good idea, Ah Fong. Perhaps you could tell us more about it.'

She had won! She pretended to wipe her mouth while trying to flick the tears from her cheeks. She noticed Woo Wai San watching her closely but there was no antagonism on her face.

Ng San Fong gathered her wits. 'I realise it is a very hot day for business but I will show you my calculations and profit forecasts.'

From her folder she produced lengthy calculations of expenses and profits, details of the costs of the materials and the possible price of their product. Woo Wai San and Woo Sing stayed silent, impressed by such detailed calculations and profit forecasts.

'It's so complicated,' said Jeng Gei, attempting to stem a bout of hiccoughs. 'I'm so glad that my little shop does not need all that figuring out for I would never have time to sell anything. I started by selling products for a slightly more than I bought them for. Why can't you do the same?'

'Not with a factory, Jeng Gei,' said Ng San Fong.

'You will have to do all these calculations for a while, Ah

Fong,' said Woo Sing. 'But you must explain them to me and show me how to do them.'

'Of course.'

Woo Wai San was relieved, for she doubted she could master such a mass of figures. She would rely on Woo Sing to keep an eye on things and concentrate on doing whatever Ng San Fong wanted of her.

'I will draw up some papers,' said Ng San Fong. 'My father thinks it is best, but I don't really think it is necessary.'

'Will we have to sign them?' asked Woo Wai San anxiously.

'Of course,' replied Ng San Fong. 'That is what they are for.'

Woo Wai San and Woo Sing looked worried.

'It is a custom here,' said Ng San Fong and both women nodded their acceptance.

Ng San Fong had already prepared the papers and had them ready to be signed but decided it would be unwise to proceed there and then.

Jeng Gei cleared the table and Woo Wai San, without being asked, brought out a large bowl and several blocks of confectionary to be broken and wrapped.

The baby slept as the four women broke the blocks and wrapped the sticky products. Ng San Fong was not used to this manual work but she worked steadily, although it made her arms and body ache. When they heard crying in the other room, she was relieved that Woo Sing asked her to nurse the baby. When she picked him up somewhat clumsily, he sensed her awkwardness and cried even louder.

'Hold him tighter,' said Woo Sing.

'No, you take him and I will do the sweets,' said Ng San Fong.

'You will have to get used to him,' said Woo Sing, making no move to help.

When the crying stopped, Ng San Fong dared to look at the child. A strange emotion caused her to speak without thinking. 'Woo Sing, the factory must succeed, it must succeed for him. We cannot fail.'

Woo Sing looked at her then quickly turned away. Both knew their pact was sealed.

It was agreed that Woo Wai San would stay with Jeng Gei while Woo Sing and her son would live with Ng San Fong until the factory was producing. Then she would find her own place. Jeng Gei was sad to think of them leaving but said nothing apart from asking Woo Sing to come as often as she could.

After Ng San Fong departed, Woo Sing went to bed early, exhausted by the day of easy labour. She was excited at the thought of the new job and living within walking distance of Tong Pooi and Wa Hing. Although she loved Pak Tin, there was no future for her here and even Jeng Gei must know that. It was also time to help Chien Tin Wa, who was obviously on the brink of disaster. There were so many things to be done. It was with difficulty that she stopped thinking of them and composed herself for sleep.

*

The two rooms provided for Woo Sing were the most luxurious she had ever lived in. There was a long argument before she won the right to keep the baby in her room. Ng San Fong left with Woo Sing for the day, telling her mother not to interfere with her friend's arrangements of the furniture.

Ng Mei Yee was used to keeping her own counsel and was pleased at the thought of a baby in her home. She had never nursed Ng San Fong, as wealthy women were not supposed to breastfeed their own young. The baby amah had done everything, including infecting the healthy young child with the disease that had twisted their lives. How she had pleaded with her husband to get rid of the woman, but he could see nothing wrong. It was only years later that Ng Mei Yee realised that the baby amah was her husband's mistress. By then she no longer cared.

Her husband had been kind to their daughter, which she knew was a great effort for he disliked anything deformed or ugly. The baby amah had later died, a pretty young country girl eaten away by the disease. It was best forgotten, but the entry of another child into her home refreshed memories surprising in their intensity.

This time she would look after the child as Woo Sing would be busy in the factory. Ng Mei Yee had secretly determined that the factory would not fail. She would support it if necessary and without consulting her husband or her daughter.

The empty house would again have noise and people—such a change from the endless clatter of mah-jong tiles, which she found so tedious, and yet so exciting and exhausting when the betting fever rose in her blood. She was a good player but sometimes she lost and her husband replaced the money without comment or complaint. They realised this gesture was the last fragile link between them.

Ng Mei Yee knocked quietly on Woo Sing's door and smiled when she was invited to enter. The girl's Cantonese was rough. *I must try to groom her for better things.* She felt sure that with the right tools and training, Woo Sing would do well in the city.

'Can I help you, Woo Sing?' she asked, shyly moving towards the clothing trunk being used as a temporary cot.

'I have so few things that there is little to arrange, Ng Mei Yee, but it is kind of you to offer,' replied Woo Sing. 'I shall have to leave the baby here until the factory is ready and then I can take him with me.'

'He will be no trouble, Woo Sing. I would like to look after him if you do not mind.'

Woo Sing smiled broadly. 'Of course. I shall be pleased to have someone so experienced to look after him, but it is not really the job for a lady.'

'I will bathe him after you go to work and consult a doctor friend about modern baby feeding. There is no need to worry, Ah Sing,' she said, trying to appear supremely confident.

*

The journey to the factory took them through some of the most congested parts of Wong Tai Sin with its huge resettlement blocks. The only splashes of colour on the mustard-yellow buildings were the vast arrays of laundry suspended from balcony poles. These, along with the ceaselessly moving throngs of people, gave a false air of gaiety to the scene.

Woo Sing and Ng San Fong were too used to the passing scene to find it interesting. They knew all too well about the poverty behind almost every grilled door.

An office was situated by the door of a government factory building designed to house the businesses of hundreds of small entrepreneurs.

'The rent is very cheap here,' said Ng San Fong as they approached a bored-looking man seated in the office.

'There is some spare space,' the official said, smiling most pleasantly. 'The official rent is about one hundred a month but there is of course a settlement fee of two thousand and a watchman's fee of five hundred a month. You pay the official fee to the government at this address and the remainder to me at my flat.'

'I understood that the only money to be paid was for rent, electricity and water,' said Ng San Fong, trying to conceal her disappointment and anger at the blatant request for tea money. 'We shall see your superior officer,' she said angrily, not thinking of the consequences until the words had been blurted out.

'Indeed do,' replied the official. 'Please wait a minute. I must check my lists as I have just remembered I may have promised the rooms yesterday.' He returned a few minutes later with such an expression of false concern on his face that Woo Sing burst out laughing.

'I am sorry, there are no rooms in the building after all. One of my clerks must have made an error,' he said. 'But do go and see my superior, Mr Jones. Perhaps he will help. Here is his address.'

The two women left in a dejected state, their first attempt at a business deal having resulted in total disaster.

'No use going to see Mr Jones,' said Ng San Fong. 'He will be a European and they are even more greedy for tea money than the locals.'

Woo Sing was beginning to realise Ng San Fong knew a lot in theory but little in practice. The task they had given themselves was far greater than they had imagined.

'I think we will discuss it with Ah Hing,' said Woo Sing, without even asking Ng San Fong for her opinion. 'Ah Hing will help us. He's learnt something about business since working in the furniture trade. I think we should go and ask him now.'

Wa Hing was so pleased to see Woo Sing that he hugged her tight enough for her to feel milk expressed from her breasts. She hoped that it would not show on her blouse.

Tong Pooi was also delighted. Rushing into the corridor, he gave a passing boy a few cents to go and buy some cakes. He had not seen Woo Sing for some time and commented on how well she was looking. He almost asked if the child could talk yet but decided to not risk looking foolish again. He busied himself with making tea, all the while glancing at

Woo Sing and smiling. Even Wa Hing was surprised by the old man's animation and for the first time realised how lonely Tong Pooi must get during his hours in the cubicle.

Both men were pleased to hear that Woo Sing would once more be living close by. Tong Pooi immediately asked if he could see the baby from time to time.

'Of course,' replied Ng San Fong and Woo Sing, almost in unison. Woo Sing realised with a jolt that she really was a guest in her present home and needed to remember it.

Woo Sing and Ng San Fong wondered how they could broach the purpose of their visit without offending these two good friends. It was Wa Hing who eventually gave them an opening.

'What will you do for a living now, Woo Sing?'

Ng San Fong, although tempted to speak, decided to let Woo Sing tell their story. Wa Hing laughed loudly about the tea money. 'Wherever you go, you will have to pay extra,' he said.

'Of course,' said Tong Pooi, surprised that anyone should believe otherwise. 'But why not try the Walled City? Rents are cheaper there and although you have to pay a little each month to the triads there are no factory inspectors, no fire inspectors, and you can live in the same room and nobody cares.'

'You can employ children if you want to,' said Wa Hing.

'That is a very dangerous place,' said Ng San Fong. 'There are too many addicts and they would rob us.'

'Not if you pay the triads and, besides, Woo Sing can look after you,' said Wa Hing.

Ng San Fong looked doubtful.

'At least we could start there and if the business succeeds, we could then afford to pay tea money for a government factory,' Woo Sing suggested.

'I shall ask my boss. He knows quite a few people in the Walled City,' Wa Hing said.

*

Next day, they walked apprehensively along the narrow, dark slit between tall buildings that formed the Walled City's main road.

Woo Sing was puzzled. 'Where's the wall?'

'It was knocked down long ago,' Wa Hing replied.

Above their heads hung a lethal cobweb of dozens of illegal electric cables.

'Don't put up an umbrella if it rains or you will get electrocuted,' Wa Hing warned. 'The water is illegal, too, but it's all right. And you have to pay someone for the right to use it. There are no building regulations if you want to build something in the factory. You can build what you like as long as you pay the right people.'

The concrete path was four feet wide, slippery and damp. On all sides were small steps into dark, elevated alleys, and even narrower streets opened at sharp angles off those. Ng San Fong shuddered as a rat ran across their path.

Numerous small factories were squeezed in everywhere along the path with its angles, corners, ascents and sudden descents. Their occupants worked at a frantic pace, not stopping to cast a glance at anyone. Woo Sing remembered the photos from their commune town museum, showcasing exploited workers in old Shanghai. She decided that anyone who worked for her would receive good conditions.

The factory was a bare room, some twenty feet by twenty feet, with a high ceiling and a battered and filthy lavatory in one corner.

'The urban council drain is close by so we tapped into it,' said their guide, clearly proud of this infringement. 'Not many factories have a lavatory.'

The two women said nothing. They were not worried about the filthy room, but wondered if it would be big enough for their factory.

The price is right, if not the size, thought Ng San Fong. *Better to start with this than look for something grand.*

Ng San Fong looked at Woo Sing, who nodded gloomily.

'I will take you to my boss,' said the guide.

The boss was friendly and helpful. 'I can arrange for the carpentry and machinery to be installed,' he said. 'This is free but the usual arrangement is that I take ten per cent of the profit to ensure everything runs smoothly and that there are no fires or other breakdowns.'

The women agreed without hesitation. Wa Hing had told them that to argue was to cause more than ten per cent of trouble later.

'We must have an experienced machine man and I can entice one away from the firms I know,' said Ng San Fong. 'A little tea money will do it,' she laughed.

Woo Sing was shocked to hear her speak like this. Still, if they were to succeed, she would have to forget the rules of her past and learn a new set. She was coming to realise there would be no rules, only deals—some to be kept and some to be conveniently broken.

'Do you think we should paint the walls?' asked Ng San Fong.

'How Western you are at times, Ah Fong,' said Woo Sing. 'Lady Williams was always wanting to paint things and have everything clean. No, we will not paint the walls, it will be too expensive.'

Seeing Ng San Fong looking offended, Woo Sing tried to soften her remark. 'When the machinery is installed and everyone is working, we won't notice how dirty the walls are.'

Ng San Fong sighed and stumbled on the rough concrete steps they were climbing. Her friend's arm was immediately around her, saving her from a tumble on to the black and slimy concrete. She flashed Woo Sing a grateful look and they resumed their climb towards the streets of the very different city outside.

As they emerged into the daylight of modern Hong Kong, they turned and stared back into the narrow dark alleyway. They were going to work in that different world, a world of darkness, damp and danger. A frightening thought, but both were determined to press on.

*

The following weeks were desperately busy as Woo Sing assembled the chemicals and materials for the factory. Ng San Fong drew and painted designs and gradually got orders rolling in from reluctant customers. Most acknowledged the high standard and appeal of her designs and most agreed they would sell well. But when they learned the factory was to be run by only women, their eagerness to place orders cooled.

'If I give you an order, Ng San Fong, then I shall not order elsewhere, and if you fail to deliver, I'll be without flowers for some weeks. And no flowers for that time will mean all my customers will leave and not one will come back,' protested an old friend.

'Just give me a small order,' insisted Ng San Fong.

'But a small order will not be profitable to you and you will soon be out of business,' grinned her friend.

There is one advantage to being a hunchback, she thought. *I can always turn my face towards the ground to hide my feelings.*

Ng San Fong held this pose while she composed herself in front of her friend until she felt able to look up with a winning smile.

'If you take a small sample, I shall not make any money out of it. But if they sell well, I promise that only you will have that design of flower and you must promise to give me a big order next time.'

The customer looked surprised and then satisfied. He felt awkward, looking down with such superiority at this strange, twisted little woman and promptly sat down on a bale of clothes.

'That is a deal, Ng San Fong,' he said. 'I wish you and your partners success in your factory and I hope we can do business for a long time.'

Ng San Fong changed her pose again, but this time to hide a very different emotion. After thanking him briefly, she walked across the factory yard. As he looked at her receding figure with its crab-like gait, her new customer thought of his own daughter, so slender and straight. *They are a varied lot, our women*, he thought, *but I must remember that in business, they are ruthless. I will watch Ng San Fong and her bright smile carefully.*

Woo Sing also had problems. Some suppliers were incredulous that a young girl would want to buy an amount such as two hundred catties of plastic base, or twenty-five drums of solvent. Their amazement increased when it became obvious that she had cash.

A few tried quoting ridiculous prices but after one humiliatingly small purchase, Woo Sing asked Ng San Fong for a price list. Another merchant suggested slyly that he might have some cut-price material in his back room, but remembering the previous episode of the aged, horny hands on her breasts, she replied firmly, 'I will pay the ordinary price in the front room. I'm sure that your backroom stock is third rate and not of interest to me.'

The man looked surprised and then slightly ashamed. Finally, he roared with laughter. He gave her a good deal and a pinch on her bottom as she left.

Woo Sing turned in the doorway. 'I will come again, but only to the front room.'

'Fine, fine,' the merchant replied, and a long and profitable partnership began.

As Woo Sing walked along the crowded street, she thought with amusement that if she got much more brazen, she would be able to teach Woo Wai San a few tricks. Everything here, even business, was affected by the difference between men and women, and it took a time to learn how to exploit this subtle tension.

I will learn more powerful and cunning ways than showing off my body, Woo Sing thought, *but I will have to teach myself for nobody I know has this art*. Her relationship with Kim was still too painful to think about but now she recognised that if she learned to simulate some of the emotions she had shown, the power would be hers.

The large wad of notes pressing against her side in her secret pocket was a constant reminder to be careful in the street. It could soon be known that a young girl with large sums of money was frequenting suppliers of plastic materials. She therefore carried a purse containing only a few notes in case she was robbed. Ng San Fong hoped that later the firms would accept payment by cheque but for now they were too suspicious to take anything but cash.

The sums of money she was spending seemed immense. If she had been asked to handle them at home, she would have been hopeless. She was surprised by how quickly she had learned to deal with such amounts.

She never displayed any more cash than was required. Before entering a shop, she secretly counted out the money.

A few young men in the street made as if to move towards her. When she noticed them, she glared fiercely at them, holding her handbag close to her side and bringing her other arm up across her body with her fist clenched.

This was a feint to distract attention from her right foot, which was ready to kick an attacker. Woo Sing often wondered how such a tactic would succeed, but she was determined to defend the group's money at any cost.

It was now necessary to wean the child and Ng Mei Yee was becoming quite an expert in his care. She called him Little Boy in the absence of a given name. Woo Sing's friends were too polite to question her about the lack of a name and Woo Sing could not explain why she had not named the child. Tong Pooi had written a list of suggestions but was too tactful to put them to her.

'I suppose I shall think of a name soon,' she told Ng San Fong as she wrapped the child in a blanket and put him in the large trunk that was still his cot.

Woo Sing realised she would have to leave her son with Ng Mei Yee as the factory was too dangerous. The child might be attacked by the plague of rats that swarmed in the sewers and beneath the building's rotten foundations. She knew she was lucky to have Ng Mei Yee's help because most nurseries were poorly run and many babies fell sick or even died. At least she could work knowing that Ng Mei Yee was as devoted a mother as she was.

*

Chai Dung was near the end of his long and gasping journey. He spent his days dozing and his nights coughing and fighting desperately for the humid air that filled the little shack. The children avoided him as it was difficult for him to keep clean. The hut and everything in it smelled of the dead and dying tissues of his lungs.

Wa Hing arrived unexpectedly one evening. Chen Tien Wa had difficulty recognising him in the gloom of the hut. He said little, but after leaving a large bag of sweets by the sleeping children he slipped a bundle of notes into her hands. Grinning, he left before she could thank him. She carefully put most of the money aside for food. It would last at least two weeks with enough left for two packets of heroin for Chai Dung.

She was beyond feeling grateful or even relieved. She just accepted that they would be safe for another two weeks. Woo Sing arrived a day or two later and was shocked. Chen Tien Wa was about to rebuke her for not visiting when she realised that she had probably sent Wa Hing. But her friends seemed surprised when she mentioned it.

Woo Sing had come to offer Chen Tien Wa a job at the factory. 'The wages are four hundred dollars a month and you can live on the platform above the machinery for nothing. If the factory is a success the wages will soon go up and you will have enough to send the children to school in the Walled City.'

Chen Tien Wa's spirits rose on hearing the offer; to see the children back at school was her greatest ambition.

The problem was that Chai Dung could not spend the day with the machinery clattering beneath him and the smell of the factory would seriously irritate his lungs. When Woo Sing left, she told him of their good fortune.

He said, 'I have not the strength to live here alone. You must take me to a hospital where perhaps I will get better. You must go with the children.'

Chen Tien Wa knew he hated the thought of hospitals and separation from his family. This was the final sacrifice he was making for them. They sat silently for a long time, with only the restless sounds of the sleeping children scratching and stirring in the sticky heat.

Eventually, Chen Tien Wa quietly collected all the heroin she had and made a pipe for him. She boiled herbs from an apothecary—all of them, not only the lesser amount needed for each dose—and made the mixture into a warm drink over their tiny spirit lamp. Her husband watched, knowing what she was doing. Silently, he accepted the glass and drank it as quickly as his breathing would allow.

She sat quietly looking at him. As his face relaxed, he appeared in the shadows to change back into the handsome man she had once known. Something of the same must have happened to his perception of her for he smiled sleepily and murmured a childish name he had used for her when they were courting.

Soon he would fall deep asleep. She left his bedside and squeezed in alongside the cramped children. They stirred and complained sleepily, pushing at each other to claim a fraction more space. Chen Tien Wa fell into a deep sleep. When she woke with the dawn, Chai Dung was dead.

The district officer's clerk shouted at her. 'A dead body? I suppose you want us to pay to bury him. Why can't you squatters save money to bury your own bodies? I suppose you lost it all playing mah-jong,' he sneered.

It was far from being the first time Chen Tien Wa had endured the shouting and the threats. As she turned to walk away, the district officer emerged from an inner room and dismissed his clerk.

'Be seated and tell me what your problem is,' he said.

Chen Tien Wa told him. Although the situation now looked slightly more hopeful, she sat back prepared for a lecture about letting a man die in a squatter's shack.

Instead, the district officer said, 'I am very sorry. Someone will come and take the body away and the government will pay for your husband's burial. Here are some forms that you must fill in.'

Chen Tien Wa did not wish to sign.

'I cannot sign my name,' she lied, for she had a good grasp of many characters.

'Just put a cross,' said the district officer and to this Chen Tien Wa agreed.

She was not long home when the men came to recover Chai Dung. They nodded, placed him on a stretcher and covered him. The last she saw of her husband was his body being lugged down the narrow path.

The next day, a young woman called. Although very

pleasant, she insisted on knowing how they lived and where the children went to school.

Chen Tien Wa told her. 'I have been given a job in a factory and we can stay in a small room next door. The children will be able to go to a school in the Walled City.' She did not give the factory's address.

'The government will give you about three hundred dollars a month if you sign the papers I will bring,' the young woman said.

'I will not need help now,' said Chen Tien Wa. 'My friends will look after us for I can now work.'

The woman breathed out a weary sigh, as if this was the inevitable end to most of her interviews. 'If you need help come to the address on this card. Remember, the government will help you.'

Chen Tien Wa murmured her thanks but all the governments she had dealt with had made promises that later turned into orders, even into threats and violence.

The floor space built above the machinery was more spacious than their hut and the children could spread themselves out for sleep or play. Soon they didn't even notice the persistent strong smell of chemicals. There was a small cooking and eating area down the ladder and within a couple of hours the children had become accustomed to their new way of life.

One evening, when everyone had gone home, Chen Tien Wa inspected some of the complicated-looking machinery and wondered if she could ever learn to work it. She had met Taam Mo Jing, who was to supervise the running of the plant.

He was a knowledgeable young man and she felt her difficulties would soon be sorted out.

Until the plant opened, Chen Tien Wa had little to do and so worked at making their quarters as comfortable as possible. The children had to stay within the room for most of the day as the Walled City was no place to for them to play outside. Every now and then a child was savaged by one of the dogs of indeterminate breed but of undoubted ferocity that roamed the narrow streets. Next door was a much smaller space, almost filled with bales and sacks, where a middle-aged woman squatted among the tumbling mess methodically sewing hard sacking. All the time Chen Tien Wa lived in the factory she never saw the woman look up or give any recognition that there was any other living soul in her world.

Next door to the sacking room was a charcoal merchant whose main occupation was centred on the mah-jong table that formed the centrepiece of his shop. At all hours of the day and night the penetrating clatter of the shuffled ivory rang along the street. The owner was said to be an excellent player and he tended to become greatly irritated when anyone had the temerity to actually want to buy charcoal.

Woo Sing was prepared to move to the factory to live but Ng Mei Yee insisted she continue living with them. It was also agreed that Woo Wai San could live with Woo Sing.

Ng San Fong was surprised at the energy and determined persuasion of her normally sombre mother but was pleased as well. Now the main members of her work team were assembled and constantly under her watch, if not always under her control.

The day after Woo Wai San and her few belongings were established with Woo Sing, the three partners took an early taxi to the Walled City as Ng San Fong felt it would be dangerous to arrive in a chauffeured car. Ng San Fong shrank back from the tiny opening of the dark pathway but the others walked in briskly and so she followed.

It was a detestable place where some twenty-seven thousand lived on a mere six and a half acres. She decided they would move as soon as the factory became profitable.

Taam Mo Jing was already working and Chen Tien Wa was turning a fast-moving die-press, looking pale, frightened and determined all at the same time. A large pile of flower components lay beside the machines.

'They look good,' said Taam Mo Jing.

'But not good enough,' said Ng San Fong sharply.

'They are much better than in my old factory,' replied Taam Mo Jing.

'There will be no comparisons here,' said Ng San Fong. 'Only what I think is good enough will be good enough,' she said with a fierce look at Taam Mo Jing.

'Yes, Ng San Fong,' he replied, wondering what he had let himself in for. She had seemed a fragile and rather appealing little woman when he had agreed to take the job, but now he realised her twisted frame held a straight and steel-strong will.

By the time the day dragged to its close all the workers had been firmly corrected in their duties with the result that the final batch of flowers was the only one to meet Ng San Fong's standards. They drove home in silent exhaustion, two of them wondering whether they would have the strength and patience to cope through the following day. Ng San Fong was satisfied in her exhaustion. Now she knew all that mattered were time and ruthlessness and that they would succeed. As Woo Wai San fell asleep, she thought bitterly, *They are all the same, soft words and then stern words with hard work to be done. There is little difference between Ng San Fong and our party secretary at home. At least here the beds are more comfortable.*

Chapter 12
Deliveries

An argument developed among Wa Hing's work mates. At first, they jovially swapped opinions, but like small white clouds forming into a thunderhead, the banter grew until the high-pitched Cantonese echoed and rattled off the walls. The noise drew Lai Gwok Yuen from his office.

'Shut up or you will all lose your jobs.'

There was immediate silence.

Wa Hing had been adjusting the brakes, a delicate job on the ancient vehicle and one in which he took a personal interest. His optimism was not as strong as that of the others, who would cheerfully drive downhill with no brakes at all. The row had been about the quickest route to a small village beyond Shatin. The most knowledgeable driver had told Lai Gwok Yuen the best route and Wa Hing had agreed until the driver said, 'Turn into Boundary Street.'

'You can't go that way now,' said Wa Hing. When the others turned and looked at him, he explained, 'There's a new notice saying there's no access now.'

'Then how will you go?' snapped Lai Gwok Yuen, calmer but still annoyed. 'This way,' said Wa Hing, drawing a map on the side of an old carton.

'Then go that way,' ordered Lai Gwok Yuen and the old men clambered aboard among the rattan furniture. Wa Hing sat next to the driver and soon everyone was cheerful again.

On their return, Lai Gwok Yuen called Wa Hing into his office. 'You can draw maps?'

Wa Hing took a piece of paper from the desk and asked, 'Where to?'

'Hung Hom,' said Lai Gwok Yuen, picking a name at random.

Wa Hing quickly drew in the main streets, his accurate mental picture enabling him to keep a rough scale.

'Draw me the streets about Kowloon City,' Lai Gwok Yuen said.

Wa Hing responded without hesitation as he had reviewed that area a short time ago.

'Do you know which streets are one way and which are no entry?' quizzed Lai Gwok Yuen.

'Of course,' replied Wa Hing. 'I will mark them in if you like.'

'No matter,' said Lai Gwok Yuen. He glanced towards the slightly open door and Wa Hing realised that he was being watched. Lai Gwok Yuen did not see Wa Hing's quick glance and Wa Hing gave no sign that he had detected the watcher's presence. He felt his heart beat faster. A cool sweat formed in the palms of his hands.

'I think we can offer you a better job,' said Lau Gwok Yuen 'You will still be driving, but it demands a knowledge of backstreets and some night work. You will continue delivering furniture during the day. At other times you will collect a parcel from a junk anchored at one of the typhoon shelters and deliver it to an address in Kowloon City. You will never question your instructions or open the parcel. If you are stopped by the police, you will know nothing about the delivery address. As there will be other parcels on board you will not know how the important parcel came to be in your truck.'

'I understand,' said Wa Hing. 'And the pay?'

'It will be double,' said Lai Gwok Yuen.

'That's very satisfactory. Obviously, I will obey all your instructions,' said Wa Hing. He was thrilled by the new wage, far more than he had dreamed of ever earning as a driver.

'I will show you pictures of men you should avoid. If you notice them close by, you should not deliver anything but keep driving,' said Lai Gwok Yuen. He handed Wa Hing a book of photographs.

Although intent on studying the pictures, Wa Hing heard the door quietly close but gave no sign of being aware the secret observation had ended. As he turned the pages depicting Chinese and British men, he came upon a photograph of a very stern-looking European.

'Chief Superintendent George,' sighed Lai Gwok Yuen. 'A most difficult man.'

'I shall remember him,' said Wa Hing, idly turning the page. He hoped he had given no sign, but his hands trembled and he drew in a quick breath for the face smiling out at him was that of Inspector Campbell.

'All these European faces look alike,' said Wa Hing. 'I will look at the book a few times so that I can remember them.'

It must be drugs, he thought, as he walked back to the resettlement block. *I must never tell Tong Pooi or Woo Sing for they could be in danger if I am discovered.* He stopped himself from thinking too deeply about what his friends would say if he told them he was working for a drug syndicate. He would work there for a few years and get out—disappear one day with his money and maybe Woo Sing, or perhaps Woo Wai San.

He was pleased that his maps had won him the job. It would be dangerous and frightening, but he felt certain that he could manage. Thoughts of Chai Dung and his desperate wife and children briefly crossed his mind. *It was TB, not drugs, which had killed him,* Wa Hing decided. *And even if it was drugs, if I don't take this job someone else will.*

By the time he got home, he had thought the matter through and had decided he could adapt to the idea of being a drug runner. He knocked and entered Tong Pooi's cubicle. The old man smiled warmly at Wa Hing's cheerful grin and clapped his hands when Wa Hing produced from behind his back a fine fish, still alive in its plastic prison.

*

Inspector Campbell admired Chief Superintendent George for his aggressive efficiency, attention to detail, grasp of reports, and his precise instructions and management of the team. His promotion to the narcotics investigation team had been unexpected and he assumed it was his proficiency in Cantonese that had gained him the job.

The team had been trying for years to break into the Chui Chow families that controlled the drug trade. But family and clan ties were strong and sudden deaths tended to occur among clan members contemplating a chat with the police.

Somewhere in the background was a Mr Big who was always able to detect and avoid the traps set up by the tireless Chief Superintendent George.

'There must be a leak in our team,' George told Inspector Campbell, instructing him to watch his colleagues, and Campbell had no doubt his colleagues had likewise been instructed to watch him. The team had no trouble finding and arresting the small-time distributors but there seemed to be an endless supply of replacements. Within a few hours of an arrest, the shopfront or divan was operating again.

The only effective method to stop this hydra-headed activity was to destroy the site of the divan and surround it with high barbed wire. Even then, the fence had to be inspected daily otherwise it would vanish, replaced by a primitive shack soon full once more of addicts buying packets of number three heroin. Guards were always able to recognise plain-clothed narcotic agents. Despite these setbacks and hurdles, Chief Superintendent George never lost his urge to defeat the triads and he was known as an implacable and persistent foe of 'the trade'.

The drugs came in by trawler from Thailand or Vietnam and offloaded onto fishing junks in international waters. There was a continual movement of hundreds of junks sailing to and from the fishing grounds. It was a hopeless task to search all of them so only a few were examined. It was rumoured that the excise men became rich from tea money and certainly some of the English officers had retired in a state of great opulence.

Inspector Campbell found the work disheartening and futile. Accurate information was almost impossible to threaten or bribe out of anyone. His best contact had been found in the harbour with multiple chop wounds over his body. 'Caused by boat propellers,' the investigating officer said.

Campbell tried to make his voice sound as sarcastic as possible. 'So this poor man drowned accidentally?'

'Of course,' the officer replied, pleased that the case would quickly be closed.

'I noticed that the report said the deceased had two black eyes.'

'The water can be very hard here,' said the officer. 'Falling into it from a height can blacken the eye.'

'So you're telling me the water here is much harder than in Scotland?'

'It must be, how strange,' said the officer, closing the file. 'Shall we go to lunch?'

Why not, thought the inspector. *A good meal is more rewarding than a dead informer.* His lunch companion told him one of their colleagues had just bought a most expensive car, or rather his wife had.

'But of course, she gambles heavily in Macau and may have won a big bundle there,' his colleague said, carefully picking out a succulent piece of pork that the inspector had also had his eye on.

My Scottish mind is too slow, he thought. *My mind is as slow as my chopsticks. I might have been better off pounding the beat in Glasgow.*

As if sensing his thoughts, his host picked out a delicious piece of chicken and placed it on Campbell's plate. 'It is very difficult here, Inspector,' he said, feigning concern. 'But we need your persistence, for one day you will break the circle. Once one talks the others will squawk to try to save their skins.'

'As long as the five main syndicates keep to their own territory and do not inform on each other, I have little hope.'

'One day they will quarrel and you must wait patiently, perhaps for years, for that day,' said his host, expertly removing the finest meat from beneath the bone.

'Yes,' replied Campbell. Their meal neared its end. It had been a mournful affair.

*

Wa Hing had been receiving his increased wage for two weeks before Lai Gwok Yuen called him into his office.

'This evening you are to go to the Yau Ma Tei typhoon

shelter and find the junk *Chin Long*. You will receive five baskets of fish and several large bags of plastic flowers. There will also be ten drums of liquid, which sometimes smells sour, so make sure all the plugs are screwed in tight. Take the drums to Tam Kon Chau Road off Castle Peak Road. At the end of the road there'll be hand carts waiting for you.'

The other items were to be delivered to the address marked on them. Wa Hing nearly suggested it would be more convenient to deliver the fish first, but then remembered Lai Gwok Yuen's order to question nothing. Instead, he said, 'I understand.' He repeated his instructions and left to fill the truck with diesel.

Once he had located the *Chin Long*, he scanned the area for any of the police he had seen in the gallery of photographs but there were few people about. A few other junks were unloading but most boat people were eating on board. A boatman helped Wa Hing carry the drums up newly laid steps to his truck.

'These steps are very good,' he said. 'We must thank the government for them.'

Wa Hing laughed and said, 'Yes, and these drums are very heavy and smelly.'

The boatman chuckled. 'We have a good government. They pretend to be very interested in our welfare, but they leave us well alone.'

'The secret of a good government is to leave the people to get on with their own business,' responded Wa Hing.

'Well said,' the boatman replied.

With the last drum packed behind the bales of flowers and baskets of fish, Wa Hing drove off.

It was all so easy with little chance of discovery unless the police made a massive raid as the road ahead of him was full of trucks of similar appearance. To search even one in ten would require more men than were on duty in the whole of the city.

Wa Hing looked for signs he had been told to check to ensure the road was clear of police roadblocks. As he passed one corner, he saw the first sign—an old beggar standing by the kerb. Several miles further on a policeman sitting on a motorcycle at the side of the road raised his hand as if to stop the truck and then waved him on. That was the second sign.

On the northern outskirts of Tsuen Wan he pulled into a hawker's stand and asked for some oranges. The man gave him a bag containing five, the third and last sign that Castle Peak Road was clear.

The Tam Kon Chau Road wound for several miles over low countryside and Wa Hing was relieved when at last he saw several lights revealing men with small hand-carts. Although he had never seen them before, one called out, 'You are on time, Wa Hing. Was there any trouble?'

'No trouble,' he replied, clambering onto the truck and passing down the heavy drums.

'I have an extra job for you,' said an elderly man who appeared to be in charge.

Wa Hing sensed danger and tried to sound as casual as possible. 'My boss gave me instructions and told me never to depart from them. I'm going to finish the rest of my orders and if you want me to do something else you must ask my boss.'

The old man stepped closer and looked steadily at Wai Hing. 'This is urgent. You must do as I say.'

The others stopped working, quietly watching and waiting. Wa Hing guessed they probably had choppers concealed on them and could transform into a hacking, slashing mob within seconds. It would be risky to try to escape in the darkness; he had no idea which way to run and he could easily stumble into a drain or get trapped in the marshes. Perhaps he was just being tested.

'I am new to this job and must obey my boss completely. I do not even know who you are or whether I can take orders from you.'

There was a long silence while the old man continued to look steadily at Wa Hing. 'This could be the last night of your life, let alone your job. Others can drive trucks just as well as you,' he said.

'My life is lost anyway if I make a bad mistake on behalf of my boss. If this is a trap and I die, I won't be any worse off than if I refuse your instructions and die,' Wa Hing calmly reasoned, as if discussing some unimportant point in communist theory. But he knew that his voice had trembled, and he felt desperate and afraid.

'If I kill you, Lai Gwok Yuen might be a little annoyed,' said the old man. 'Come with me'

He turned and walked quickly down a narrow path. To Wa Hing's surprise, it led to a neat cottage built below the road, cleverly hidden by trees and a pile of old fishing baskets.

'Wait outside,' said the old man briskly.

Wa Hing adopted the pose of the other workers—hearing nothing, seeing nothing and certainly doing nothing for which he could be challenged. The door opened and he was roughly dragged inside. A telephone was thrust into his hand and he heard Lai Gwok Yuen's voice. 'You did right not to take orders but you are to obey the instructions you are given and complete my deliveries later.'

Lai Gwok Yuen sounded anxious and Wa Hing wondered if the old man was his boss.

'I shall follow my next instructions,' he said and handed the phone back to the old man.

'You are to do as he tells you,' the old man said. He pointed to one of the workers who had silently entered the room.

The truck was a welcome sight, and Wa Hing had to force himself to listen to the man, whose manner was much friendlier than that of his boss.

'I'm glad we did not have to kill you as we already have one body to dispose of,' he said. Wa Hing had noticed an unpleasant smell close to the truck, but the countryside was full of pungent and nauseating smells so had given it no more thought.

'Drive down the road and turn to the left,' said his guide after the workers had loaded the stinking bundle into the back of the truck.

'Not on the fish,' shouted Wa Hing.

Someone responded with a laugh, 'Too late. Anyway, the customers will never know.'

As they slowly wound down the track, his guide became surprisingly confidential.

'We have to leave them to rot a few days because the police and the doctors don't get too inquisitive then.' He chuckled.

'I certainly won't,' said Wa Hing. 'I only hope the fish is all right.'

'It will be sold mainly to *gweilo* restaurants and they don't know fresh fish from dead man fish,' said the guide. 'The police have been a little nosy of late, probably looking for extra money. This old chap visited them twice lately and as he had complained to us about noisy trucks at night, we were a bit suspicious. The boss decided to kill him and only later we learned he had been to see the police about a young grandson he thought was lost. The child hadn't visited him for a couple of weeks. So it was unnecessary work, but you can't be too careful.'

The guide touched Wa Hing's arm to alert him to a sharp turn off the track. It led to a stream where two workers removed the festering corpse and loaded it onto a skiff.

'The tide will carry it towards Lantau,' said the guide. 'Since the police already know the old man was agitated it won't take much to suggest suicide.'

Wa Hing fretted over the deliveries he still had to make. 'What will I tell the restaurant people?'

'You are a character,' said his guide and Wa Hing heard the other two laughing as they paddled the skiff towards the sea.

*

It was early morning when Wa Hing parked the truck in its usual place in the alley. An old watchman had received the fish and was so disinterested that Wa Hing believed he wouldn't have cared if he'd received the body instead.

The bales of flowers had been dropped off at the correct address where another watchman grumbled at the lateness of the hour. Wa Hing had helped him stack them in a corner. Despite the grumbles, the old fellow had gripped his arm and led him to a rickety table and a covered jar of hot tea. Wa Hing muttered his thanks but as he raised the tea to his lips, he could still smell the corpse on his hand.

A wave of nausea swept over him. He felt the vomit rising. A cold sweat broke out on his brow. He waited, pretending that the tea was too hot, and then managed to swallow a couple of mouthfuls. He nodded to the watchman, hurried to his truck and drove it around the corner. He managed to pull to the side before he was violently sick.

It was too late to go home and the back of the truck still smelled, or perhaps he imagined it. Either way, he curled his frame as comfortably as possible into the front seat and slept. His nightmare came to its climax as the body of the grandfather rose from the ground and walked towards him. He turned to run and a terrible panic overtook him. He found himself immobile as the murdered man moved closer. Sightless eyes stared at him. The corpse seized his arm and offered him a jar of tea and oranges mixed together.

Wa Hing woke, screaming, 'No! No!' and found a frightened Lai Gwok Yuen shaking his arm.

They stared at each other for a moment before Lai Gwok Yuen released his arm. Wa Hing clambered stiffly out of the cab.

It was still early, just after dawn, an unusual time for Lai Gwok Yuen to appear. They went into the office and filled a kettle for tea. Wa Hing grabbed a piece of grimy soap and went outside, jamming a cold-water hose into a gap in the truck frame to wash himself.

There was no one else in the alley except Lai Gwok Yuen, who looked on in amazement. He disappeared inside and returned with a rough sheet of packing cloth that Wa Hing used as a towel.

As they sat in the office drinking tea, Lai Gwok Yuen asked if everything had been all right after his phone call the previous night.

'I was very late but I followed the instructions given to me,' replied Wa Hing, still wondering how much Lai Gwok Yuen knew and who was really the boss.

'The old man was very angry at first but you did right and I think you have proved to him your loyalty and courage,' said Lai Gwok Yuen. He had answered Wa Hing's unspoken question and Wa Hing determined that from now on he would not be quite so afraid of Lai Gwok Yuen.

'I think we parted in understanding, if not friendliness,' replied Wa Hing, hoping he sounded unconcerned.

'Good, good,' said Lai Gwok Yuen. 'You can have the next two days off, but be sure to arrive early on the third day for we may have a big job to do the following night.'

Wa Hing thanked him several times and left for Tong Pooi's cubicle, which now appeared to be the most secure and peaceful refuge in the world.

He was woken much later by someone shaking his arm, but this time it was Tong Pooi and the terrible memory of his dream flashed only briefly through his mind. He felt refreshed and cheerful in Tong Pooi's presence for there was always something wonderfully calm and untainted about the old man. He had lived in the city for so long without losing a kind of completeness that Wa Hing found easy to admire.

'I'm very glad you are home, Wa Hing,' said Tong Pooi. 'We have been invited out to a meal.' His eyes were shining for as well as his friends and his writing, he loved good food.

There was only one person who would invite them to a meal and Wa Hing felt the last of his gloom evaporate at the thought of seeing Woo Sing. He barely heard Tong Pooi explaining that the factory had been running for only a month yet already had more orders than they could cope with.

'It's going to be a success, Ah Hing, and Woo Sing will be safe.'

The meal was in one of the better restaurants in Tsim Sha Tsui and neither Wa Hing nor Tong Pooi had ever been in such grand surroundings. They read the name of the factory, Morning Flower, on a board outside the main door and realised with surprise that they would eat in a separate side room.

'The factory must be doing very well,' said Wa Hing.

'This will be the greatest meal of my life. I am so glad I am very hungry,' replied Tong Pooi.

'I hope they have enough food for you,' laughed Wa Hing as the two friends walked through the imposing doors.

While walking up the stairs to the dining room, Wa Hing assumed Woo Wai San would also be there and was shocked at realising how he had forgotten her. The room was already buzzing – so many people, including Chen Tien Wa and her four children. Jeng Gei was there, happy to be with her friends again. As Wa Hing waved to her, he felt a surge of fear as he noticed Inspector Campbell behind her and sitting next to Miss Campbell. Wa Hing knew he would have to avoid them that evening and take care in future. If his bosses discovered that he knew the inspector he would be dead within hours, and perhaps Woo Sing and Tong Pooi as well.

But it was no use worrying now and he decided to enjoy his meal. The group was arranging itself around two tables and Wa Hing sat himself at the table away from the inspector. He was so worried that he did not notice two other guests watching every move, and it was only as he sat down that he found Woo Sing on one side and Woo Wai San on the other. Some of the other guests had noticed the rather odd shuffling of chairs and there were a few knowing smiles between the older women.

'You haven't said much, Ah Hing. I do miss you,' said Woo Sing.

'We live at Ah Fong's house and share the same room,' Woo Wai San giggled.

'Of course, I'm not always at home,' said Woo Sing.

'But I often am,' said Woo Wai San.

Wa Hing began to feel uncomfortably crowded. The women had obviously become good friends and he was not sure if it would be worse for them to be enemies. He didn't know how to cope and thought bitterly, *This has been a hell of a week.*

Woo Wai San put a piece of beef on his plate. 'The Westerners say that it gives you great strength,' she said, turning to him with innocent eyes.

'Perhaps he is strong enough,' said Woo Sing. Deciding the game had gone on long enough, she said, 'We miss you, Ah Hing. Try to come and see us now and then. We are working very hard at the factory—long hours, and it is still a strain to get everything right and to Ah Fong's liking.'

'I'm so tired most of the time,' said Woo Wai San. 'It is worth it, though, for already I have earned more money than in six months at home. It is strange to be working for oneself and not the commune. For a while, I wondered how I had become important enough to earn all that money for working hard; but that passed and now I'm looking forward to earning more as the factory gets bigger.'

'That's right,' said Woo Sing. 'You have to be your own person here, not just one of the masses. You can go where you want and not where you are sent. It is a Western idea and I like it.'

Wa Hing was not listening. He was studying Woo Wai San's face and detected in its subtle lines that her libido was returning. She sensed his interest and moved closer, turning her face to him and not bothering to conceal her desire.

Woo Sing understood the glance and felt herself blushing. For the first time, she felt jealous and wanted Wa Hing for herself. *But did I really?* Sometimes she dreamed of Kim and was angry with herself when she woke for he had tricked and ruined her for marriage for good. She had never wanted Wa Hing like Woo Wai San did, yet she loved to talk with him and have him nearby. He, too, enjoyed her company and perhaps wanted her body, but she had never noticed it. For now, at least, he was Woo Wai San's and Woo Sing decided she would ask Ng San Fong if she could share her room for the night.

'I will arrange to sleep somewhere else tonight, Ah Hing,' she said, in her usual direct manner.

Wa Hing did not know whether to feel pleased or crushed, but he knew he would accept the offer, although he pretended not to hear it. Woo Wai San also heard. With great pleasure, she decided to let her body wait for the night and in the meantime enjoy the food, Wa Hing, and the cheerful chatter.

Tong Pooi was disappointed that he had somehow become separated from his friends and was seated next to the four noisy children. He guessed that the solemn woman at the end of the table was Chen Tien Wa and, looking at the children, he felt she had a reason to be sombre. Jeng Gei sat on the other side of him so they chatted about places they had known in Canton. Another consolation was that the food was the best he had eaten since leaving his real home so long ago.

He helped the child next to him to reach the dishes further away and began to enjoy placing a portion on each of their plates while explaining the history of each dish: why it was so named, which ancient emperor had liked it, how it was made and what special flavour one could savour. As the evening progressed, the children came to admire him.

Other guests stopped to listen when he attacked a new dish, philosophically and morally. As the evening progressed, he began to enjoy his only real audience for many years. He became even more scholarly as he remembered facts and stories that he thought he'd forgotten years ago. Chen Tien Wa had never seen her children so quiet and attentive and even she forgot her problems for a while.

Mary Campbell was pleased when Ng San Fong telephoned to invite her and Ian, as she was worried about Woo Sing and knew her nephew had a soft spot for the girl. Neither of them had much of a chance to talk to her, but looking across to the other table she could see that Woo Sing appeared happy, if rather quiet. Meanwhile, Ian was alternately practising his Cantonese on Ng San Fong and patiently listening to Tong Pooi.

Mary enjoyed talking to Ng San Fong and found herself discussing the habits of the Williams family rather indiscreetly. But as her companion knew it all anyway, it did not matter. The laughter and food reminded her of her childhood in a large and boisterous Scottish Highlands family.

By the time the soup came, Tong Pooi took only one bowl and the children had gone to sleep. As the guests rose to leave, the Campbells made their way to Woo Sing, and Mary Campbell managed to say, 'I am so happy you are well, Woo Sing, and that you have a job.'

Woo Sing appeared embarrassed but happy. 'Thank you,' she said. 'I will come and see you when I have a free day and the factory is settled. Please tell your nephew that I'm very grateful to him for bringing a doctor for me when I was so ill. Perhaps one day I shall be able to repay you both.'

'There is no need, Woo Sing,' replied Miss Campbell.

Along with the other guests, they moved towards the door, following the custom of leaving quickly when the meal was finished.

Wa Hing put Tong Pooi into a taxi, telling the old man that he would not return with him that night. Tong Pooi was too content to care and had to be woken by the driver when the journey ended.

Chapter 13
Moving on

It was with some reluctance that Ng San Fong agreed to share her room with Woo Sing for a night.

'I have never shared a room with anyone,' she said. 'I doubt if my parents will like the idea much either.'

'Only this once,' pleaded Woo Sing. So the two found themselves undressing in Ng San Fong's richly appointed bedroom. Ng San Fong gave a bitter laugh. 'I am the only ugly thing in it.'

'You are not ugly to me,' Woo Sing assured her.

Ng San Fong felt a rush of pleasure ripple through her body and turned her head away to hide her feelings. She felt disturbed and restless as they lay together, not only at having someone so close for the first time but at the thought of what was happening in the adjacent room.

Eventually, Ng San Fong could bear it no longer.

'What is it like, Woo Sing?' she asked shyly.

'What's what like?'

'Being with a man.'

'How would I know? I was drugged at the time and can't remember anything,' said a sleepy Woo Sing.

Ng San Fong was surprised and shocked. 'Were you raped?'

'I don't know,' said Woo Sing, realising that she would have to settle her friend's curiosity if she was ever to get that warm and heavy sleep she craved. 'I was—or thought I was—in love with the *gweilo* boy. It was a strange feeling, Ng San Fong, the need to have him near, to see him and feel him close by. It is an unreasoning thing and a kind of illness which you know is not the usual and sensible you.'

'I understand,' whispered Ng San Fong, but both knew she had no idea and probably never would.

Woo Sing suddenly embraced her friend. 'Thank you for all you have done,' she said.

Ng San Fong was pleased that her friend was so close. 'You saved my life, I owe you that,' she replied. And for the first time she cried from neither bitterness nor anger. She fell asleep soon after.

*

By the time the taxi dropped them at Ng San Fong's home, Woo Wai San was in a turmoil of anxiety and desire. Relieved to find Woo Sing's bed was empty, she quickly returned to let Wa Hing in.

To her surprise, he displayed no loving signs towards her as they climbed into her bed. Instead, he lay quietly, thinking of something more absorbing than her body. She drew his hand to her breast and with her own explored those parts of him that had always gratified and intrigued her. He was unresponsive and she wondered if he was thinking of Woo Sing.

'This is a very dangerous city, Woo Wai San,' he said. 'We must all take great care. You and I and Woo Sing are living as if still in the commune in the way we think of people and problems.'

'That could become very complicated too, if you backed the wrong argument,' said Woo Wai San, desperately hoping she wouldn't have to engage in a political argument when she needed him in a far more basic way.

'Yes, but the penalties for being wrong were less and there was always a way out.'

She sensed a healthier tension in his body as if he had finally dismissed a horrible thought. She knew that whatever it was, the crisis was over. Now there was nothing but pleasure. There was no Lei Yuk Sin screaming in her head and the last remnants of the dying student had gone.

*

A continual gentle shaking woke Woo Sing; she found Wa Hing crouched by her bed with Ng San Fong still asleep. She put out her hand and stroked his face, thinking he wanted her. 'I am fond of you, Wa Hing, but no.'

He shook his head and whispered, 'For a while you must not see me, Woo Sing. I will stay away from all of you. There is a good reason but I cannot explain right now. Please trust me, Woo Sing.'

'Of course, but we like to see you and surely there is no harm in that.'

'There could be great danger.' Even in the faint early light of dawn she could see the anxiety on his face.

'I trust you,' she said quietly.

Wa Hing kissed her gently and was gone. Woo Sing wondered why the open and optimistic Wa Hing was so anxious. He was usually sensible but, as she knew, it was easy to become involved with Hong Kong's bad side. She hoped her friend was not venturing along a path towards disaster.

Sleep claimed Woo Sing again for a few restless moments before the alarm clock announced another day in the factory.

In the afternoon, she broke away from her machine work to begin her weekly rounds of their suppliers. The firm was still paying cash but she now knew the exact amounts to pay and carried nothing in excess.

She could always expect a pat on the shoulder or bottom when she visited the chemical supplier but it was given and received in such a jovial manner that neither party was offended or unduly excited.

'I have something special for you today,' said her merchant friend.

'Not another backroom special,' laughed Woo Sing.

'I will fetch it from the backroom,' replied the merchant, taking mock offence.

Woo Sing looked with interest at the two small drums he produced.

'This is a new plastic that holds its colour better and can be moulded into a very firm sheet. It is ideal for flower-making and is only slightly more expensive than your usual stock,' he said.

'I will have it,' said Woo Sing impulsively. She was a regular customer and they trusted each other. There were untrustworthy dealers but Woo Sing considered most of the traders to be honest. Some drove hard bargains but their word, when given, was kept.

'If Ng San Fong likes it, can we have more?'

'Supply may be difficult, but I think I could arrange it,' her friend replied. 'And no doubt there will soon be a Hong Kong copy on the market.

The drums were delivered in the late afternoon and by the following day Ng San Fong had agreed that the material was far better and that they needed more.

Woo Sing returned to the lecherous shopkeeper and bought a large quantity of the new product, which a very happy merchant agreed to have delivered the next day.

As the weeks passed, it became obvious that the overcrowded, stuffy room in the Walled City was not big enough. There was no air-conditioning and the mixture of chemical fumes, heat and stale sweat that substituted for air, drifted in through the open doorway. Yet it was not the smell, filth or danger of the close machines that persuaded the team they would have to move. They simply could not fit in the extra machinery needed to cope with demand. Also, the team had grown, with Seung Mei and her husband joining the staff.

Ng Laan Sang visited the factory with his daughter and returned impressed with the organisation and efficiency of this tight-knit team of determined women. The original plan to distract his daughter from her bitterness had succeeded and he decided to support her expansion and also make some money.

This helped the family prosper, settled a difficult domestic problem and put him in a favourable light with his family and friends. If only his friend, Sir William Williams, had the knack for such solutions, his business empire might not now be cracking at its heart.

The Ng family had no close relations in Hong Kong and lived an isolated life. Now, in a totally unexpected way, his wife and daughter were happier than they had been in years. The idea of a group of women with no business experience developing a factory had changed from a good joke among his friends to a commercial possibility.

Woo Sing was a stabilising influence on Ng San Fong and his wife had virtually adopted her baby. His two concubines, whom he suspected were rather bored with his attentions, had also been more responsive and affectionate, perhaps because his own temper had improved. For a short time, he wondered if he should take Woo Sing as a third concubine, for she had both spirit and a deliciously shaped body. However, he guessed that she was not for purchase, and harmony in his discordant household was even more important than his pleasure. The world of Ng Laan Sang was thus blooming with the wild abandon of an autumn flower.

A suitable space was found in a government factory

building and Ng Laan Sang secretly paid the allocating officer, a self-important *gweilo*, ten thousand dollars to find the name of Morning Flower at the top of his list. It was a high price to pay and one of the best the officer had ever received.

To cap it off, the old man had said he could ask another thousand from the factory manager when she called. 'If you ask no tea money, she may become suspicious,' Ng Laan Sang explained.

The officer was pleased to hear this as it would have appeared strange to obtain such a suitable space without tea money being paid. He did not want it known that he was no longer taking considerations for the allocation of units. *What would the people who had already paid him have to say?*

There was great excitement among the staff when Ng San Fong returned with the news the papers had been signed. Only Chen Tien Wa was worried – *will my family be without a house again?*

Ng San Fong, Woo Wai San and Woo Sing met that evening to discuss a more formal business structure. Decisions had been easy and Ng Laan Sang would shortly be repaid. The partners had also become used to profiting from borrowed money.

'Not an easy idea for a communist,' laughed Woo Sing.

Ng San Fong was shocked that Woo Sing still regarded herself as a communist. 'How can you call yourself a communist?'

'If I'm not a communist, then I'm nothing,' replied Woo Sing.

'Better be nothing then,' snapped Ng San Fong. 'And let's stop this silly argument and get down to business.'

'I think we should ask Chen Tien Wa, Seung Mei and Jaam Mo Jing to have a share in the factory,' Woo Sing said.

Ng San Fong was stunned. 'That's ridiculous. We are owners and they are workers.'

'But they've been good workers and we have prospered because they are loyal,' replied Woo Sing.

'Most of them could not find another job,' said Ng San Fong. Woo Sing remained silent.

'Ah Fong is right,' said Woo Wai San. 'We cannot have too many people controlling the business. Although we voted in the commune Woo Sing, it was only to confirm what the party decided.'

Woo Wai San understood the gulf separating her two partners. She did not care how the business was managed or who owned it as long as her share continued to increase. She needed to stop her two partners from destroying what they had built.

'If the business expands, we will need factory supervisors and perhaps our friends could have a share without a say in control,' she said.

'A bonus, you mean?' asked Ng San Fong.

'For us to work together, we should all have an equal share,' insisted Woo Sing. She did not fully understand her own reasoning but felt this was the right way to expand.

Ng San Fong knew she must stand firm or lose control. She could manage her father and her two friends but could be outvoted by a larger group. She wondered how Woo Sing could suggest the others be given shares when they were paid and uneducated. She could find dozens of workers like that, and ones without four young brats who occupied good storage space.

'We have to think clearly, as a business and friendship should not come into it,' she said.

'If friendship doesn't come into it, then I want no part of it,' said Woo Sing. 'I can sell my share.'

Ng San Fong feared being on her own again. She would still have the factory, but she would be alone. Her mother would be angry and she felt her father would quietly lose interest in her progress.

'Let us not quarrel, I must think about it,' she said.

Later, when preparing for bed and after Ng Mei Yee had put her son into his cot, Woo Sing wondered if she had acted rashly to say that she would sell her share. She would be selling her son's future as well. They could both survive but not nearly so easily. Their sacrifice would have been made for reasons she felt were right but hard to explain now, and even harder to explain to a grown-up son.

Ng San Fong did not understand her feelings, for Ng San Fong was Western, more Western than she knew herself, more Western even than Miss Campbell. It was no use trying to tell Ng San Fong of her feelings for she would just laugh and say something hard.

Ng San Fong entered without knocking—a bad sign, as if Woo Sing was now just a servant. The two women looked at each other for a few moments before Ng San Fong said quietly, 'Woo Sing, there must be a way.'

'The other three have a share but we three control it,' said Woo Sing.

Ng San Fong hesitated and then said, 'We each get ten per cent more than they ... for our extra work.'

'Agreed,' said Woo Sing.

'Agreed,' said Ng San Fong. Money was not that important to her. What she really wanted was control.

Woo Sing was pleased they had agreed. It meant she and Little Boy were safe. Chen Tien Wa and Seung Mei were also safe. After all, one had to bend with the wind a little in a Western city.

Chen Tien Wa, Seung Mei and Jaam Mo Jing received the news in bewildered silence. Woo Sing noted their suspicion and confusion, and guessed they were wondering why they were being offered a share.

'This is no trick. You will eventually get more money but you will work harder,' said Woo Sing.

'How big are your debts?' asked Seung Mei, the most business-like of the trio.

'About five thousand dollars,' said Woo Sing.

'Will they increase when we move?'

'We will soon pay them back if we all take only the wages we are getting now.'

'Can we just remain as workers?' asked Chen Tien Wa.

'If you wish,' said Ng San Fong quickly, and then regretted it for she saw that Chen Tien Wa and Seung Mei would immediately realise that it was Woo Sing's idea.

The two women looked at each other and nodded.

'I think I shall accept,' said Chen Tien Wa.

'So shall I,' said Seung Mei, noticing Jaam Mo Jing looking confused.

'I would like to think it over for a few days, but I'm very grateful for the offer,' was his reply. Ng San Fong looked irritated and this confirmed their impression that they had been right to accept the deal.

*

The merchant looked sad and Woo Sing sensed bad news. 'Has your backroom stock finally sold out?'

The merchant did not even acknowledge the crude joke.

'The special chemical has become unavailable,' he said.

After further questions and a few dollars, Woo Sing learned the materials had not been meant for general sale but a relative of a friend of the merchant had released them for consideration. The source was now blocked and even a larger consideration would not reopen the bolted doors.

'Who is the principal supplier?' she asked, but the merchant did not know. 'Fifty dollars to find out,' said Woo Sing. 'I will wait.'

Within the hour, he returned with a scrap of paper.

'It is an Englishman. Can you read it?'

Woo Sing was dismayed and angry when she saw the name on the paper—Williams Manufacturing—and then came a glimmer of hope.

Ng San Fong was in her most ruthless and arrogant mood when Woo Sing told her.

'You must see Miss Campbell and arrange a permanent supply for us. They owe you something,' she said brutally.

Woo Sing was so angry she could have hit her, but decided it was better she walk away. *Little Boy now has an innocent and passive role in building our factory,* she thought. If she was successful with the Williams family, the seed that Kim had planted in her would enable her each week to get a drum of plastic solvent. *Ng San Fong will not care if I have to lie with old Williams as long as the drum appears on time,* she thought.

Her anger faded. It was a sensible suggestion and she would ask Miss Campbell to help. She turned towards Ng San Fong, 'Don't ever speak to me like that again.'

*

Mary Campbell knew the best time to ask would be after Sir William had mellowed after his nightly tipple.

He stared at her, puzzled, as if one of the older pieces of furniture had suddenly become articulate. *A strange woman.* He vaguely remembered having seduced her at some time in the past. She had been useful in Kim's upbringing and certainly knew better than he how to manage his wife's moods.

With some effort, he brought his mind to focus on her slow and precise speech. It appeared that she had friends who wanted some sort of chemical that his company's supply section carried.

'Plastic solvent, did you say?' he heard himself asking, while desperately trying to remember whether he had ever been in her bed. 'Of course, of course. Just write it down, write down the name and give it to me.'

She passed the paper to him. He reached past her hand as if by accident to press her breasts. *Still firm*, he thought, as he slipped the paper into his pocket. Mary Campbell managed to smile, although it was really relief for his minimal and almost courtly sexual attention.

*

The factory had become so congested that there was barely room to crouch over the machines. Large bales of product were jammed to the ceiling in the area not taken up by the platform. The place was rapidly evolving into a potential massive firebomb.

Chen Tien Wa realised that if the cooking got out of hand or the children lit a match there would be no hope for any of them. She was pleased they were moving; the extra money from the partnership would mean they could hire at least one room for themselves.

Ng San Fong told her it was forbidden to live in government factories or to employ children. Once more, their future seemed brighter and the dragging sensation of tiredness left Chen Tien Wa's body.

The solvent arrived regularly for several weeks until one day the merchant appeared at their door, agitated and fearful. Not only had the supply been stopped, but he had suffered a visit from a shouting *gweilo* who had threatened him with gaol for theft. Woo Sing could understand the quiet fury in Mary Campbell's voice as Kim had perhaps unknowingly threatened the wellbeing of his son. The good Scotswoman promised to do her best.

'Circumstances have changed, Woo Sing. Sir William is now a figurehead and Kim has returned to the business. He is different from the boy we knew,' she said rather tactlessly.

Woo Sing remained silent, glad that this was a telephone conversation and Mary Campbell could not see her face. She knew Miss Campbell would be totally discreet, but she could not resist saying, 'Tell him nothing of me.'

'I had not intended to,' said Miss Campbell rather sharply. She again promised to act as quickly as discretion would allow.

Mary Campbell had suffered two agonising weeks since Kim's arrival as he spoke to her in the same manner as his father. The child, who she had imagined in other times as her own now, treated her with complete indifference. He rarely spoke to her and she changed her sequence of duties to avoid even the briefest of meetings with him.

Lady Williams barely noticed his return and what little interest she had rapidly transformed into annoyance.

Although his father protested in a long speech to his board, Kim became the new managing director.

A servant delivered a note asking Kim to grant an interview

to the housekeeper. As she entered, a little uneasy, he thought that perhaps she was shaken by the reversal of their roles. He could see her hands trembling.

'I think it best if I leave your service,' she said. 'But first, I have a favour to ask. Not for myself, but for some friends.'

She looked at him in the way that had once quelled many of his rebellious moods. He remained silent while she asked him for plastic solvent, of all things.

He replied, 'I cannot make a promise of a commercial matter without the full facts. As you know, my father's promises were easily given and forgotten. If it is possible to grant this unusual favour, I will see that the matter is drawn up in a formal agreement and that your friends will be secure. I will not accept your resignation until the matter has been resolved.'

Miss Campbell said nothing. She rose, nodded and left. She lay on her bed, reflecting on how arrogant and self-deceived she had been to believe she could rear him to be different from his parents.

The following day, an old friend from the office came to the Williams' home. Embarrassed, he handed her several papers. One was an agreement for the solvent, another the acceptance of her resignation, and the third a generous and permanent retirement pension.

'Please thank the managing director,' she said with dignity.

'And you should thank Sir William, too,' he replied. 'It was he who insisted on your pension.'

With great effort, Sir William had apparently remembered the pleasant evenings spent in Mary Campbell's bed. Stirred by this, he had given more thought to her work, and in an unusual, even unique, boost of generosity, had insisted on her pension.

Her thoughts were distracted by the noise of her ladyship arriving home with the dogs. *I am finally free from all this,* she thought with sudden exultation. *Free from this household that has dominated me as much as I dominated it. Free from short-tempered Shanghainese cooks and frightened servants. Free from fretfully watching for the next of her ladyship's strange attacks. At last, I can go home.*

With a great sense of elation, she opened the door to enter the long corridor. One of the Afghans was walking ahead of her. With a loud shout, she landed a perfect kick in the most sensitive area beneath its tail. The dog howled with surprise and fled to his mistress's room.

Mary Campbell sat on her bed and let her laughter wash the dreary years away.

Chapter 14
Matters of law

The new factory seemed huge compared with the over-packed matchbox in the Walled City. Seung Mei had recruited new workers and within a few days, the noise, fumes and congestion began to remind the partners of the conditions they had left behind.

'The workers never like things to be too neat for then it seems there is not enough work being done,' said Taam Mo Jing. Despite the crowding, he knew where the important materials and equipment were located and could find them quickly.

When an inspector called, Ng San Fong paid him off as soon as he was in the door. She hoped that Woo Sing would not see, but she did and turned away, hoping Ng San Fong had not noticed her.

The inspector was struck by that peculiar Hong Kong blindness that kept the wheels of industry turning and the English administration happy. He did not see the underage workers, the machines without safety guards, the fire hazards, or the overcrowding. His report was so reassuring that the Inspector of Factories felt that some progress was at last being made. If the Inspector of Factories himself had visited he might have made a fuss, and the whole system would have broken down. Fortunately, there was little risk of that and so the partners were happy, the workers were happy, the inspector was happy and the government was happy—an enviable situation for it was not so in many countries.

Ng San Fong obtained an option to manufacture under licence an American range of cosmetic containers. It was with relief that the factory stopped making endless bales of plastic flowers, whose phoney gaiety emphasised the drabness of the surroundings.

Woo Sing was delegated to arrange the legal matters for the American deal. After prodding from her partners, she bought some fashionable clothes before meeting Ng Laan Sang's lawyer and launching her career as a businesswoman.

The office was in an impressive building at a prestigious address in the Central District. Woo Sing wondered how she had found herself in such a place.

A superior, elderly Englishwoman showed her into an office of luxurious design. A man seated at an expansive desk stopped signing documents and rose quickly from his chair to usher her to a seat.

'Denys Lam, at your service, madam,' he announced, in an accent that Woo Sing could scarcely understand.

'A plastic *gweilo*,' Ng San Fong had jeeringly called him. Now Woo Sing could see and hear why. Although Chinese in appearance and Eurasian by birth, he was English by obsession. The rich, deep and fruity voice was truly legal in all its tones. He spoke to her in English and she was tempted to reply in Cantonese or Mandarin to show her displeasure, but she was here on business. He appeared taken aback by the Scottish tones of her English.

The interview was brief and he promised to promptly negotiate the arrangement. 'These matters are of a standard nature and should pose no insurmountable difficulty.'

Woo Sing felt that he was watching her to see if she understood the long word. She did not, but guessed the meaning and locked it into her memory for reference when she returned home.

'I would like a Chinese translation of any documents,' she said. He looked particularly cross. 'I am not sure of some of the English legal words,' she said.

'Indeed, you may also not be sure of some of the Chinese legal words,' he replied in a most superior manner.

Woo Sing flushed and replied, quite untruthfully, 'The Chinese legal system is not completely unknown to me.'

Due to her apparent Scottish background, Lam was uncertain of her legal knowledge. He noted there was nothing coquettish about her and wondered how that old lecher, Ng, had found her.

'You are a partner of Ng Laan Sang?'

'No, I am a partner of his daughter in the Morning Flower company,' replied Woo Sing quite sharply. 'We expect very rapid action in this matter.'

Denys Lam was irritated by this self-confident young girl.

'In Hong Kong, madam, lawyers are scarce and we do things in our own time.' His tone was one devised to make opposition witnesses shrivel.

'Well, I do not expect to be so served,' said Woo Sing, stepping close to him and staring at him fiercely. She was angry and somewhat frightened. This unusual creature was the first Eurasian she had met, and her first reference for what Little Boy could grow up to look like. *He won't be allowed to grow into this sort of man*, she thought, as they glared at each other.

Lam was becoming apprehensive; he did not want a scene in his chambers. He could already see the headlines and hear the chuckles in the Hong Kong Club.

'I will not be bullied but as it means so much to you, I will see it is done expeditiously,' he said, in his most haughty manner.

Woo Sing gave him a brilliant smile. After shaking his hand in a most affectionate manner, she gracefully left the office. *After that smile*, she thought, *I can certainly deceive even myself. If I ever go back to the commune with such duplicity, I will become a party delegate in no time.*

Returning to her room, she glanced up and saw Ng Laan Sang intently watching her.

'You look very beautiful today,' he said, smiling pleasantly.

Ah, another beautiful smiler, thought Woo Sing.

'I feel a little strange in these special clothes,' she said. Suddenly inspired to divert the conversation away from herself, she asked, 'Ng Laan Sang, what does "insurmountable" mean?' She carefully mimicked the lawyer's intonation. For a moment she thought Ng Laan Sang would collapse down the stairs with helpless laughter.

Finally, he slapped her on the back and roared, 'You have been talking to the plastic *gweilo*.' With that, he returned to his room where she could still hear him laughing.

With her question still unanswered, she gratefully reached her room to remove the constricting clothes and return to her loose blouse and trousers.

*

When Ng San Fong asked her to go to the local meeting of the Manufacturers' Association, Woo Sing wore her fashionable clothes and nervously edged quietly into the back of a crowded hall.

To her surprise, she saw Denys Lam. *Surely he's too grand to attend such a humble meeting,* she thought. The meeting could well have been that of the commune's farming or manufacturing group, and Woo Sing noted that these all-male meetings seemed the same. There was always a spontaneous speech that had been carefully rehearsed, and always an objector proving he was more enlightened than his fellow comrades, fellow citizens or fellow manufacturers. This one seemed no different.

The meeting broke up to vote on a completely mysterious issue. Woo Sing was wondering what to do next when Lam approached her from behind, catching her completely off-guard.

'What is it all about?' she asked.

'A complicated matter of tariffs,' he replied. 'Come and sit with me and I'll explain it as the meeting progresses. I am here to advise on the legal aspects.'

His manner was different from when they met at his office so Woo Sing settled next to him and listened carefully as the complex story unfolded. Lam could see she was listening, understanding and memorising. As he explained the meaning of a schedule, he realised that beneath the amateurishly applied cosmetics and uncomfortable clothes was a woman who had begun to interest him.

It is ridiculous, he thought as he drove her home. *She has no family, no money, no breeding, and probably little education. What can I possibly see in her? Yet she has wits and beauty.* He turned his attention back to her complicated question about import schedules. She also questioned him a great deal about political matters, but commented little herself.

She was shrewd but also disarmingly simple in the way that she asked the meaning of words and repeated them. A Chinese girl speaking Scottish and barrister's English; *what a horrifying combination I'm compounding.* But in that physically awkward moment of alighting from the car, as he held the door, he saw the springing, curving shape of a vital body and knew that as a slightly podgy, early-middle-age bachelor, he was deep in a struggle between desire and common sense.

A carefully thought-out, yet appearing to be a chance encounter with Ng Laan Sang enabled Lam to casually mention that he had met a charming representative of the Ng San

Fong company. The old man grinned, knowing that Lam was fishing for information about Woo Sing and was therefore determined to force Lam to declare his interest. He did not, and the topic was dropped. But towards the end of the conversation, the old man suddenly said, 'You mean Woo Sing, who lives with us?'

'Oh, yes,' faltered Lam, annoyed at being caught out so neatly.

'A very attractive girl,' Ng Laan Sang continued slyly, aware of the interest of the younger man. 'She was briefly the concubine of Kim Williams and has a child from him,' he continued, watching Lam.

Lam was obviously hurt. With his best courtroom manner, he murmured, 'Really? How disastrous.'

'No,' replied Ng Laan Sang. 'Unlucky perhaps, but somehow looking at her with her child enhances her attractiveness.'

'You like her, then?' asked Lam, dropping his guard in response to the old fellow's openness.

'Of course I like her, but she will never be any man's concubine again,' said Ng Laan Sang.

'There is an attractiveness that appeals to me,' said Denys, throwing himself open to the old man's sharp tongue.

'I know,' replied Ng Laan Sang. 'The women that an eligible man like yourself usually meets are either mercenary or complacent,' he grinned. 'If you win her, Lam, it will be a true and lasting victory.'

The conversation finished and they returned rather disconsolately to their offices.

Later, Woo Sing listening intently as Lam explained the complex arrangements of the licence to manufacture. He heard himself speaking clearly to her without a trace of courtroom airs, but at the same time he could not stop thinking of that supercilious Williams brat fondling her breasts and exploring her thighs. *How I really hate the English*, he thought, sick with rage. He became aware that the conversation had stopped and he was staring at Woo Sing's rather inelegantly arranged legs.

She noticed, flushed slightly, and rearranged herself. *These dreadful short clothes … I must remember*, she thought. To put him at ease, she smiled. 'Ng San Fong made me wear these clothes, but the habits of commune clothing remain.'

'We did not come here to discuss your clothes,' he replied quickly, only to regret it.

'But I was not the one who stopped talking,' she replied.

'I am sorry, Woo Sing, it is true that you distracted me, but let us now return to the papers.' As he turned back to the papers, he said, 'Perhaps we could get to know each other.'

Woo Sing thought for a while before giving him a very direct look. 'My last experience of getting to know a man better, Hong Kong fashion, ended very badly for me.'

'I know about that but it does not stop me from wishing to see more of you,' he said quietly.

'You are interesting and unlike the other men I know. You could teach me a great deal, but at what cost?'

Her tone sounded harsh and bitter.

'I will respect you,' he promised.

'Let us finish the contract,' she smiled.

It was with an easy and jubilant mind that he turned to the complex legal matters, so much easier to deal with than emotions.

Woo Sing was glad to return to looking after her machines, checking the workers' production, and seeing that there was always a ready supply of raw materials. She thought frequently of Denys Lam, his obvious intelligence, his peculiar variations in speech, and his interest in her.

She decided to ask Ng San Fong to help her with clothes, but Ng San Fong only looked at her through half-closed eyes, smiled, and said, 'I cannot help.'

Two days later, however, she brought an attractive young woman into Woo Sing's bedroom and introduced her as Alice Chen.

'You want help with clothes, I love clothes, and it will be a pleasure to help you,' she said.

Probably from Shanghai, thought Woo Sing, listening carefully to the slightly different intonations of her Cantonese.

'I would be very ...' began Woo Sing, but the woman cut her short.

'Put on your best clothes, walk about the room, sit down, stand up and stand still. In that order,' she commanded.

Woo Sing followed the instructions, self-consciously aware of the close scrutiny. She found herself walking stiffly knowing that Ng San Fong was also enjoying the scene, seated on the bed and watching with an expressionless face.

'Some things are good and some things are bad,' said Alice Chen.

'First walk with fewer steps and don't stride about like a man in a hurry. You should sit like this,' she said, demonstrating. 'Move your skirt down like this. Not only does it make you look demure and respectable, but it also makes a man look at your legs, and they are a good feature. You must not sit with your legs straight, for it looks common, distracts men, and can make some uncomfortable.'

And so, the lesson went on, with her posture, clothes, cosmetics, her movements and her gestures all criticised. Yet by the end of the long evening Woo Sing had learned a great deal about the average wealthy male in Hong Kong. She knew about his taste in women's dress, his taste in women's movements and behaviour, and a little about his taste in women. She learnt to arch her lower back forward, pull her shoulders down and backwards, and throw her breasts forward and upward.

'A useful approach, if not overdone,' said Alice. 'Men interpret it as desire, but you must not overdo it, or you will look silly.'

The sessions were repeated for several evenings. Woo Sing's clothes were modified and new ones bought, and one evening a tailor arrived to measure her for a suit. Ng San Fong watched, saying little, and revealing nothing in her face.

When Alice Chen felt that she'd finished, she said, 'The rest is up to you.'

Woo Sing asked how she could repay her.

'When the time is right, you can introduce me to Denys Lam,' she said.

Woo Sing heard Ng San Fong's gasp and the surprising nature of the request left her briefly speechless.

'I will do that. I think you will find him a very knowing man and a good judge of sincerity,' Woo Sing said.

Alice Chen smiled back. 'I certainly hope so,' she said.

There was a market some distance from the house where Woo Sing occasionally went to buy clothes for her son or small gifts for her friends. She walked through it, conscious of her fine appearance and pleased that the rather humiliating sessions with Alice Chen were over. She was carefully picking over some children's clothes when she glanced up at the hawker woman behind the stall. The woman appeared terrified, but before Woo Sing could turn, she was seized, her arms held, her mouth covered, and in a confusing rush she was carried down an alley and thrown into the back seat of a car.

'Keep still,' she was ordered as she struggled and kicked.

'You are very pretty. We would like you to work for us in a comfortable bar. We won't hurt you,' said a pleasant man of about twenty, leaning over from the front seat.

'Please let me go. I have a small child. I will pay you,' she begged.

'You will certainly pay us,' the man said sharply. 'Soon you might have another little baby,' he laughed. He leaned over and stroked her thigh.

It was no use struggling. She had to think of some other way to cope, so she relaxed and appeared completely cowed. The car sped along a main road and entered the Cross-Harbour Tunnel. The man holding her down relaxed his grip slightly. She waited only a couple of seconds before giving a sudden twist and throwing him sideways. She reached forward to grasp the wheel, wrenching it round. The car lurched across the double white line amid a blaring of horns and a screaming of brakes as other cars took evasive action.

The car corkscrewed back over the line, brushing the tunnel kerb. The four men in the car shouted and beat at her until she finally let go.

'You bitch,' screamed the other man in the back. 'You will have ten men through you by tonight.'

The car left the tunnel. It had been monitored on closed circuit television as it crossed the double line and an attendant moved out into the road to stop them.

The driver accelerated, knocking the man in a long curving arc over the bonnet. They saw the surprise and shock on his face as he carried towards the windscreen, missed it and struck the door pillar. Apart from the bump as he struck the pillar, there was no sound and he did not cry out.

'Well, I have had it before. If I'm going to have ten men, I might as well start now,' said Woo Sing, trying to slide under the man holding her and pushing her body against him. She rubbed herself against him and smiled as much as she could, hoping desperately for a response. 'I like it, I will be good,' she promised.

'Don't be a fool,' shouted the other man to her captor.

'Might as well start now. You always want them first, that is why you don't like me doing it,' he shouted back. He took his weight off her to open his fly and struggled with her skirt.

'There's a police car behind us,' shouted the man in the back as the car accelerated wildly.

Woo Sing lifted the lock door latch and eased the handle down, at the same time still smiling and wriggling.

'Stop, you fool, they're nearly on us,' his friend shouted.

The car lurched wildly around a sharp corner of the water-front road. Woo Sing slipped from under her would-be lover, thrust the door open, pushed her back against the other man blocking him, and kicked the surprised man out on to the road.

He screamed in terror and they heard the thud as he landed, heard it even above the noise of the engine and the screaming police siren. The police jeep swerved wildly, but it had already begun to overtake. Both left-side wheels passed over the screaming boy, who was instantly transformed into a silent and bruised heap.

The car swerved and crashed into the roadside railing.

As she ran from it, she heard the shouting man giving his final shout.

'You bitch, he was my brother.'

She heard them shouting to her to stop, but she ran into a side street, getting a last glimpse of the scene as she turned the corner. Two policemen were chasing after her, but she had a good start on them. There was a busy Wanchai street ahead where she could get lost in the crowd.

My red jacket, she thought. *It is so conspicuous!* She struggled out of it as she ran, flinging it into a rubbish bin. She turned the corner into the crowded street, smoothed her hair and clothes and walked briskly along the pavement.

She caught up with a young European boy ahead of her, and she walked alongside him, arch-backed, shoulders dropped and breasts up. She smiled at him.

'May I walk a little way with you?'

He had been looking for a girl for an hour or so. He was new in Hong Kong.

'I've been looking for you for ages,' was all he could say as he slipped his hand into hers.

Woo Sing walked close to him as policemen ran past, scarcely giving them a glance.

A police jeep pulled alongside the pavement ahead of them and several auxiliary police scrambled out.

Woo Sing continued to chat with the young sailor, saying, 'I like English boys, they usually give me a good time.'

'Where can we go?' the boy asked urgently.

'In a short while my flat will be clear and available,' she said. 'Perhaps we can wait in this restaurant.'

They walked into a crowded restaurant and found a table close to the wall. After a few minutes of chit-chat, she excused herself to visit the Ladies. Before she left, she turned back to the sailor. 'You are very kind to me,' she said. She slipped from her finger a quite expensive ring she had recently bought and gave it to him.

The *foki* on watchman duty at the back of the shop was understanding. The English sailors were too persistent with nice girls; for five dollars, of course, he would show her out the back.

A taxi took her to Denys Lam's office. He was puzzled to

hear his secretary announce Woo Sing was waiting outside. He hastily gave his client the remainder of his instructions and almost pushed the surprised man into an adjacent room.

When Woo Sing entered, he could see she was in trouble, barely in control of her emotions. She looked at him without expression. He took her hands and felt her trembling violently. Suddenly she was in his arms, sobbing, her body pressing hard against his.

This was no trick on her part. For once, someone wanted him not for his skill or his money, but for himself.

He calmed her enough to extract the basic facts and realised with horror what this entanglement meant. She had already compromised him. As a citizen, he should report her involvement in the night's events. It would go hard on him if it were discovered he had not. The only way out was to make her his client; her confession would then be privileged and he would be safe.

'If you are caught, you have nothing to fear,' he said. 'I will defend you. Is that all right?'

'Oh, yes,' said Woo Sing. 'But that is not why I came here. How can I live in this place that seems to want to destroy me and makes me destroy others?'

She continued gasping, sobbing.

Denys was sickened by violence. Even the thought of it disturbed him so much that he usually let other partners deal with it. His life had been carefully structured to avoid contact with those elements of the city that produced violence, or even had the potential for it.

Perhaps Woo Sing guessed this, and this is why she was attracted to him. He was well aware of his distinguished, though not handsome, appearance. He took his time to reply, unsure if she even expected an answer.

'The city doesn't want to destroy you,' he said. 'It is only stone. It is no monster. You have to find a way to live in it so that its people cannot hurt you.'

'How does an immigrant do that?'

'I do not know, but many people achieve it. Perhaps they are lucky. Woo Sing, you are beautiful. Why not use that to find a good husband?'

'I'm not sure what a good husband is.'

'Then find out by marrying me,' he replied, astonished at hearing his voice uttering the words.

The offer stunned her. In a day already full of desperate situations, she yet again had no idea what to do.

'I'm very fond of you Denys, but I am in such a tangle that now is not the time to say yes or no. Let us get to know each other better. I know you are Western in your outlook, so I will be your mistress if you want it, but there's still a lot of me that says no.'

She had unwittingly hurt him, but he let it pass. 'You are wrong. I am English because English means power here, but I am Chinese under the Western camouflage.'

She looked at him, kissed him, creating an inner urge such as he thought had left him with his boyhood years. The phone rang and they stepped apart.

His secretary sounded anxious and puzzled; her boss was

normally punctual. 'The director from Jardine's has been waiting here for some time for his appointment,' she said.

Woo Sing tidied her clothes and Denys showed her out through his private door.

The questioning look that was flashed at him by the *gweilo* from Jardine's made him even more flushed and flustered. His usually distant, almost regal, composure had come unstuck. Denys hastily ushered the man to a seat in his office and then he sat behind his desk to conceal a lower part of his person which had yet to regain its composure.

*

Woo Sing took the Star Ferry back to Tsim Sha Tsui, keen to avoid the tunnel. She had thought of trying to collect her red jacket but decided it was far too dangerous. She would also have to avoid the market where she had been kidnapped. Fortunately, nobody knew her there and the police would not get any information.

When Woo Sing arrived home, Ng Mei Yee had just bathed and dressed Little Boy. She took him firmly from Ng Mei Yee without saying a word and sat on the edge of her bed, nursing the child and looking intently at his face. *You nearly lost me, and I nearly lost you*, she thought, holding her son ever tighter.

Ng Mei Yee watched the pair, annoyed and anxious, for she felt that recently Woo Sing had neglected the child. She thought this was because of the immense effort required by the booming factory. Woo Sing had hardly thanked her for her care of him, although few words were required for her pleasure in the child was obvious. She sensed some crisis had happened to the young mother.

Woo Sing glanced at Ng Mei Yee and motioned to her to sit with her.

She rested her head on Ng Mei Yee's shoulder. 'You are a better mother to him than I am.'

'It is nothing,' murmured the older woman, noticing for the first time the bruising on Woo Sing's face. She now saw that she had been crying.

She put her arm around the girl. 'You are welcome here forever, Woo Sing.'

Woo Sing replied, 'Thank you ... please look after him for me. I must give him a name, for he is mine.'

*

The next day, the Chinese papers were full of the death of the tunnel attendant who had left a large young family, and of the girl in the red jacket who had completely disappeared. Ten youths had fought it out with the police and one had been gravely wounded.

Woo Sing read that they were from the 14K triad and wanted for previous abductions of young girls for the massage parlours.

The news was also read with great interest by Denys Lam, who estimated that the young thugs would be in Stanley Prison for at least five years.

Woo Sing suspected Ng San Fong might have guessed about her involvement when she casually asked her how she was liking her red jacket.

'It was too tight and impossible to have it altered, so I will wear something else.'

Woo Sing thought that Alice Chen might be dangerous as Woo Sing had shown her the jacket. That night, he could not resist telephoning Alice. However, she did not say anything about it and when asked by Woo Sing when she would meet Denys Lam, Alice replied, 'Not yet.'

When she put down the receiver, Woo Sing went out to the balcony and sat there among the expensive and luxurious plants. She sat still, letting the cool breeze pamper her skin while the lights of the city twinkled like a fairyland. The sound of the traffic was muted, but nothing could soften the noise of the giant jet planes descending into Kai Tak airport. Even so, she scarcely heard their engines, as she wondered how she and Little Boy could live in Hong Kong and still be safe.

*

The partners received a formal note from Lam asking them to appear at his office to settle the American franchise. The Americans were becoming impatient.

'Always wanting tomorrow's plans done today, and today's progress as statistics,' he told the partners. 'So, you had better be efficient.'

Ng San Fong was cross at having to come all the way to listen to the plastic *gweilo*.

'His body shape may be normal, but he is more twisted than I am,' she told Woo Sing.

'I think he has been efficient and helpful,' Woo Sing said. 'He has developed his manner so that he can move among the English.,

'Bah, you are soft on him,' Ng San Fong snapped.

Woo Sing blushed, to her annoyance, but replied, 'I am a simple country girl and he has been kind enough not to remind me of that.'

'You are as hard as I am,' said Ng San Fong. 'He is scared of you,' she added, not guessing that her statement was closer to the truth than she realised.

After the meeting, Lam asked Woo Sing to join him the following evening at a small reception given by some big industrialists.

'I would feel out of place,' she said quickly.

'They have a lot of money, but ...' He nearly said they were only peasants, but with a flick of his legal tongue continued with, '...they are only simple folk.'

'In that case, I will come with great pleasure,' Woo Sing said.

Ng San Fong was crotchety in the car back to the factory and Woo Sing made the driver stop so that she could buy some sugar cane juice, which she knew the little woman loved. The juice was freshly squeezed and Ng San Fong cheered up.

'I am rude to you, Ah Sing, but I don't mean to be,' she said.

'Dear Ah San, as long as you keep making us richer you can be as rude as you like.'

The others laughed and Woo Wai San hugged Ng San Fong. At last, she felt that she was among friends.

The mirror showed the success of Alice Chen's lessons as a perfectly groomed Woo Sing stood before it. They had been talking as she dressed and Ng San Fong tried bravely to restrain her contempt for Denys Lam.

'He is hollow,' she could not resist saying. 'Not because of his English ways, but because he is frightened to risk anything. Inspector Campbell, now, there is a real man for you, and so is Inspector George and even my father.'

'Ah Hing is a man, too,' protested Woo Wai San.

Woo Sing turned towards her with a start for she realised that she had not thought of Wa Hing for several days, yet obviously Woo Wai San had.

'Ah Hing has been a brother to me but I think he has yet to mature,' she said. Seeing Woo Wai San's expression, she added, 'But you love him and know him better than I.'

'Yes,' said Woo Wai San. 'I sometimes wake up wanting him more than anything in the whole world.'

'Yes, that's bad,' said Ng San Fong. The other women, surprised, turned to face her. Flushed, she went on the attack. 'Just because I am like I am, don't you think I feel desire? No man has touched me, and probably no man ever will, but that doesn't stop me from being a woman.'

'Of course, you are a woman and not a child,' said Woo Wai San softly.

This conversation was too intimate for Woo Sing. Even the commune had not dug this deeply into one's emotions, but she said, 'Ng San Fong, when you get richer, why don't you buy a man? Men buy woman all the time. If you want one, buy one, for other women often have to give much more money to get one.'

Ng San Fong had never known Woo Sing to be sarcastic so, although surprised at the insensitivity of her remarks, thought they must contain a gem of truth.

The reception was not one of the great social events of the year, nor were the elite of Hong Kong's industry present, but to Woo Sing it was exciting. There was an atmosphere of power and wealth. Lam was well known, and he introduced her to so many guests that it was hopeless to try and remember even the more important people. There were several short speeches full of technicalities that she could not understand and which Denys assured her were very dull. There was much guarded boasting although an industrial spy would have spent a futile evening for the Cantonese never gave even the slightest clue about their activities.

As Denys Lam drove her home, he asked, 'You have been to many commune meetings so what is the main difference between them and this one? People are the same everywhere, I suppose.'

'The question is easy to answer but hard to explain. People are the same everywhere if they are left to grow like grass in a field. In China, that is not so. The meeting tonight was full of people who were only full of themselves. At home, I have never been to such a meeting.'

'China is full of ambitious people,' he countered.

'Some are only ambitious for themselves and they are often found out, but many want only to help their commune and their country,' she replied.

'In the West, too, people follow causes greater than themselves. That is not confined to communists,' he said, warming to the argument.

'But they are individuals and must make themselves smaller than the cause,' said Woo Sing. 'In China, many of us never had to do that for it was hard to separate oneself completely from others. They have been with you since you were a child and without them there is no completeness, no full answers.'

'You mean the commune was like one huge person?'

'Not quite, but in some ways, yes. Some are always falling away from the mass and some are fused only from time to time.' Woo Sing was unable to find the Western word to describe that particular state of mind.

'Then why did you leave?'

'As I grew older, I felt pushed out. And when one feels pushed out, one begins to think of oneself as being separate, then different, and increasingly unimportant in terms of the commune, but important in terms of having then to develop an individual life path,' replied Woo Sing.

'If I did not know that you are an intelligent and very honest woman, I would say you're telling me a load of rubbish,' Lam said. He puzzled over how someone could feel that their desires, hopes and happiness were completely without point. 'In the West, they have a saying: "Embrace the chains that bind you".'

'That is wrong,' replied Woo Sing. 'It is only when you are pushed out that you find the chains, and then they are part of you. It is hopeless for you to understand for you are what Chairman Mao calls an *intellectual* and they have the hardest trouble cutting the "me" out of themselves.'

'Thanks,' replied Lam, his voice laced with sarcasm.

When they arrived at the Ng household, Woo Sing thanked Lam for the evening. They kissed. Their lips pressed hard together, their bodies apart, each trying to measure the quantity of the other's desire.

Woo Sing, trembling, slipped out of the car and ran quickly to the door. Silhouetted by the light, she waved and was gone.

As he drove home, Lam felt profoundly depressed by their conversation. He realised that between them lay such a gulf of incomprehension that he doubted even the outstretched arms of love could bridge it.

Chapter 15
Expansion

None of the partners worked at a machine now. As the business had grown, so had its complexity. It required paperwork and organisation to put the correct mould into the correct machine and with the correct colour at the correct time. The factory was becoming known for the high quality of its products and Ng San Fong had convinced her partners of the need for ruthless efficiency.

She confined herself to designing the products and to the hiring and dismissal of workers. Neither Woo Sing nor Woo Wai San, and certainly not Taam Mo Jing, could tell a worker to collect their pay because their work was not good enough. Ng San Fong, however, did this without a qualm and thus her presence on the factory floor was a great stimulus to efficiency. She knew the workers must hate her and joke about her figure, but this caused her not a moment of pain. She was in control and that was her compensation.

Chen Tien Wa supervised the packing of the finished articles and the workers regarded her as a silent woman, efficient and fair. Despite her newfound wealth, she remained sombre.

One day, when Ng San Fong was absent, Woo Sing urgently needed a new worker and engaged Tong Man Ho, a man with a large red birthmark covering much of his face and who seemed hardworking. When she returned, Ng San Fong called Woo Sing into her office. 'Why did you take him on?' she screamed at her.

'Because you were away and I think he will be a good worker,' Woo Sing replied.

'I do not like him,' shouted Ng San Fong, loud enough to be heard above the roar of the machines.

'I am sorry, I didn't realise you knew him,' said Woo Sing.

'I don't. I just don't like the look of him.'

'Then until he proves he is no good, he must stay,' said Woo Sing, her temper rising.

When Ng San Fong said nothing, Woo Sing departed, marvelling at how Ng San Fong could not bear to see deformity in others.

A working week in the factory ran from Monday to Saturday.

The incessant activity increased. The weeks passed so rapidly that Woo Sing, intent on her duties, only occasionally thought of Denys Lam or Wa Hing or Tong Pooi. The factory began shift work and took on new workers whom Woo Sing could not name. The family atmosphere of the cramped room in the Walled City disappeared in a forest of machines inhabited by workers who scarcely knew the name of the person three places away. There was no doubt that the business was an astonishing success.

Woo Sing, while enchanted by the rapidly increasing figures in her bank statement, wondered how long it could continue. The thought of even having a bank account had not occurred to her until a few months ago. Ng Laan Sang had spent a long, tiring evening convincing the partners that to store large sums of money in a house, particularly his house, was inviting trouble.

Chen Tien Wa grew more silent as her riches grew, but at least her children now went to school and there were two amahs to look after them. They had no problems adapting to their new life and were forever begging their mother to buy a car so that the driver could take them to the beach.

Of all the partners, Woo Wai San enjoyed her success most, for she was once more organising people and solving problems with rules, which she made up if necessary. This annoyed Ng San Fong when she discovered it. Woo Wai San gave talks to the slower workers to help motivate them and would persist with someone who wasn't quick enough until Ng San Fong stepped in angrily to dismiss them.

Ng San Fong and Woo Wai San finally clashed over a particularly slow worker whom Woo Wai San was patiently trying to encourage. Unable to stand it any longer, Ng San Fong dismissed the worker for holding up a long line of machines.

'That girl was getting better and in a few more weeks she could have been a model worker,' Woo Wai San said bitterly.

'We cannot wait a few weeks. This is not a commune rice

paddy,' Ng San Fong snapped. 'Nor is it a school for slow workers. It is a business.' She stomped off.

Woo Wai San moved into a comfortable apartment, and although some days she would come home more tired than usual, she remained very content. Woo Sing would guess Wa Hing had called in. Occasionally Denys Lam rang Woo Sing. A few times they lunched together but both knew that the brief passion was over although neither wanted to break their friendship totally. She told him much about the commune, a topic that fascinated him and which often led to questions Woo Sing found difficult to answer. Some were very personal, such as when he asked if she had been truly happy in the commune.

'I cannot say,' she replied. 'Sometimes I long for home, but sometimes I am reasonably happy here. We were not promised continual happiness at home. I don't think anyone ever mentioned happiness. Here, of course, no one promises anything.'

Alice Chen called to redeem Woo Sing's promise to introduce Denys Lam. She asked Woo Sing about her clothes and which parties she had been to lately. When Woo Sing replied, 'None,' Alice sat smiling and silent.

She has calculated very nicely just how long our passion would last, thought Woo Sing but without malice. Alice could not resist asking Woo Sing her opinion of Denys.

'I like him very much. Some people say he is a hollow man whose insides are filled with pages of books of law, but I did not find him so.'

Alice smiled and said, 'Most men are hollow somewhere

and if you can find the way to put your hand in, then you can move them to your will.'

'Men can move women, too,' said Woo Sing.

'Yes, some women.'

'I hope I'm still one of them,' said Woo Sing, looking firmly at her elegant tutor. Alice blushed and said nothing.

A lunch was arranged. Denys reluctantly accepted and no sooner were the three of them seated than Woo Sing was treated to a demonstration of Alice Chen searching deftly for her lawyer friend's weak spot, which she had claimed could lead her to the hollow place she needed. She was neither flattering nor coy, neither winsome nor cold, but exuded interest and attention. Her questions spurred Denys into his favourite topic, the administration of Hong Kong, and the right of the Chinese to control it within the boundaries set by China.

'Enlightened self-interest has never been in a resettlement block in its life,' sniffed Ng San Fong when Woo Sing mentioned this.

During their lunch, Woo Sing noted how well Alice and Denys demonstrated this art of advancing oneself with a good cause. With the new friends rapidly becoming immersed in deep conversation, Woo Sing politely excused herself. She smiled at Alice and winked, a bad habit she had picked up from Taam Mo Jing. Denys rose as she left and as they courteously bid each other goodbye, both knew the last link of desire had been gently broken.

Woo Sing did not want to return too early to the factory. Ng San Fong knew of her lunch appointment and would probably comment sarcastically if she returned too early. She felt free and relaxed, and on the spur of the moment decided to visit her merchant friend. She no longer needed to visit his shop as all arrangements were going smoothly.

The street was its usual dirty, noisy self. Acrid, sour smells continued to poison any whiffs of clean air that tried to intrude. The day was hot and the air full of the sweat of the Hong Kong summer. A few old people sat about the pavements, some holding out plastic cups. Woo Sing knew some were quite wealthy, but she could not sort the rich from the poor. She did know, however, never to give to those who had gold teeth. An occasional coin dropped into the cups, scarcely acknowledged by the beggars. The merchant looked surprised and then slightly worried as he saw Woo Sing enter his shop. Two apprentices paused their work to get a good look at the only beautifully dressed woman seen on the premises.

'How are you?' asked Woo Sing, cheerfully shaking his hand.

'Very well and prosperous, thanks to the large orders from your firm. I hope you haven't come to cancel them,' the old man replied.

'Of course not, old friend, I would never let them do that. We can make many things easily that others find hard.'

He looked relieved. 'Would you like some tea?'

'That would be fine,' said Woo Sing.

The goggle-eyed apprentices brought two cracked cups, for which the old man apologised profusely.

'No matter, the tea is as good from a cracked cup as from a gold cup,' said Woo Sing and for a while they sat drinking the refreshing, clear beverage. As she left, Woo Sing teased him. 'You have not pinched my bottom and you don't look at me like you used to. Have I gotten ugly?'

He looked embarrassed, then mumbled, 'Back then you were a good, cheeky city girl. But now you are a grand lady.'

'That was only a few months ago, old friend. I have not changed,' she said. She laid her hands on his shoulder and kissed him fully and warmly. She could hear the loud gasps of the apprentices as she walked from the shop. She turned to wave. He looked astonished and very happy.

The latest designs from Ng San Fong were beautiful but of such intricacy that Taam Mo Jing was driven to despair attempting to construct the mouldings. He felt she was challenging him, daring him to come to her and say it could not be done.

He had never asked for a single modification, although he spent many hours at home in the evenings moodily trying to resolve each problem. Tong Man Ho was a good worker and one evening Taam Mo Jing decided to ask him to be his assistant. He knew Ng San Fong disliked the boy but he would promote him regardless.

The boy accepted gladly. Instead of working repetitively at a machine he would now be in a small side room with only his boss alongside. A few days reassured Taam Mo Jing about his choice, for Tong Man Ho clearly had a natural aptitude. The two worked well together, encouraging each other to find solutions. Taam Mo Jing began to entrust the simpler mouldings to Ah Ho, as he called him.

To prove his point, he casually gave the boy something from Ng San Fong that was almost impossible to mould. *She knows it can't be done*, he thought, but a few days later he smugly gave the mouldings to Ng San Fong.

'They look all right,' she said.

'If you have any questions, ask Tong Man Ho. He made them and I think we should raise his wages.'

Ng San Fong carefully inspected the mouldings, turning them over and over with slightly trembling fingers. Rage, thought Taam Mo Jing, but he was wrong; it was delight. She had not thought they were capable of such complexity.

However, she was able to find a fault. There was a small curve on one aspect, different from her own design, and she pounced.

'This is wrong and it is not a difficult part. This is careless. We should wait before paying him more.'

Tong Man Ho was called. He explained, quietly and firmly. 'The change in the curve has been made to enhance the main feature of the design.' He produced a hand-carved model of the original design to compare with the moulding.

The little woman's pride was defeated. She admitted, 'Yes, the curve is better.'

At the next meeting, no comment was made about the generous increase in salary for Tong Man Ho and even Ng San Fong remained silent.

As the weeks passed, Ng San Fong began to work more

closely with Ah Ho, which was what she began to call him. This surprised everyone, for she was not given to familiarities. She noted that if she sat on his right side, the birthmark was not so prominent and she could almost bear to look at him.

He gave no indication of being aware of her shape as they sat together, planning and designing, she learning the limitations of the mould and he the limitless variations of true art. They argued fiercely, but only on technical matters and without malice.

Taam Mo Jing quietly withdrew to the more routine moulding, happy to be excused from the remorseless challenge of always having to do something better. Ng San Fong now scarcely noticed Ah Ho's face, instead admiring his short and powerful fingers, which were capable of such infinitely small and precise movements—shaving a little here, sparing a little there, or undercutting an arch to exactly the minimum thinness.

His hands fascinated her and one day she managed to accidentally run her hand across his. He looked surprised. Without thinking, she turned and looked at him, realising that the mask that had obscured her affection had slipped. He said nothing but let his hand remain while turning his face away. *He dare not look at me like that*, she thought. Rising quickly, she retired to her office.

They resumed work the next day as if nothing had happened, but more frequently their hands touched and their arguments, still as intense, were of a softer nature.

Late one evening, a rush order—difficult to produce

quickly—came into the office and Ng San Fong worked until the early hours, returning home exhausted.

The following day, she realised Ah Ho was at a family gathering to meet relatives from Canton. She removed her beloved rings, dressed plainly and arrived at the Tong flat where a surprised Ah Ho was brought to the door to speak to her.

She explained. 'Can you come back to help? Otherwise, we will not meet the order.'

'I will come in an hour or so,' he said.

Ng San Fong hesitated by the door, at a loss as to what to say.

'Come in and meet my family,' said Ah Ho.

'Only if you say that I am a worker friend.'

'Agreed,' said Ah Ho Hong.

Ng San Fong entered a room full of noisy people. She expected the usual silence and stares but few noticed her. Ah Ho introduced her to his father.

The old man was most gracious. He was pleased with his last son. Little money or time had been spent on him and yet he was now contributing a great deal to the household. He was the least smart of his boys and funds had run out long before his time for schooling had come. If he found pleasure in the twisted little woman, then he would not oppose it as long as the money kept coming in. The old man had done well by his children, or most of them, and now it was time for the children to keep their share of the bargain.

Ng San Fong saw a pregnant woman look away and walk to the back of the room. Usually such an act hurt her but she now thought that the woman was sensible. If the future mother really believed that the sight of her would harm the child, then she was wise to avoid looking at her. Of course, she could have easily been looking at Ah Ho, or perhaps both of them, and this thought made her move even closer to him.

The hour passed rapidly and Ng San Fong forgot Ah Ho's promise to return with her. She was surprised when he reminded her.

'No, let us stay a little longer,' she said. 'We shall soon fix it when we return.'

Tables were placed among the crowd. There was a rush for seats and food was carried in. Ng San Fong and Ah Ho moved to a table, but when she saw the pregnant woman about to sit, she steered them to another table.

If I spoil her happiness, then I shall spoil mine, thought Ng San Fong, and they found a place among a babble of noisy children.

'I have met so many people, Ah Ho. How many relatives have you?'

'I have never tried to count them, but I think I have about eighty cousins,' he replied.

'We have no family here,' said Ng San Fong sadly.

'Then you can have mine,' he said.

Ng San Fong smiled. 'Perhaps you have some cousins who would work in the factory? That's if you think they would be good workers.' Her business caution had not quite deserted her.

'Not now,' he said, and the matter lapsed.

They returned to the factory, arousing a few curious looks. The remainder of the day was devoted to the struggle to achieve.

Again, exhausted, she returned home to the hated bathroom, with its leering, taunting mirrors. This time she faced them squarely, inspecting her naked self as she would a moulding. Her legs were fine and straight and quite suitable for any male to see, and her breasts would be acceptable if they were not suspended awry on her twisted chest wall. Her face, too, was rather long, but could be made attractive. *But that scowl would have to go.* She would ask Woo Sing about her hair for she had always admired her style. *It was not an easy task but perhaps something could be done with it.*

She could look at Ah Ho without wincing and now she could look at herself in the same way. *Perhaps, with an even mightier effort, he would someday look at me and not be repulsed.*

Woo Wai San called the following evening. She and Woo Sing were lying on beds in Woo Sing's room and gossiping about the factory staff when Ng San Fong interrupted them. There was a brief silence as Ng San Fong grappled with what to say. She had expected Woo Sing to be alone and wanted to ask about hairstyles. The presence of Woo Wai San disconcerted her. She sat curled up into her usual angular heap and told them of her visit to Tong Man Ho's family.

'It sounds like my husband's family at home,' said Woo Wai San. 'They were always helping each other. A commune within a commune, you might say.'

Woo Sing and Ng San Fong laughed.

'I thought family ties were not allowed in the new China,' said Ng San Fong.

'Like many things that are not allowed, they become less obvious. With a strong party leadership, the families are weak, but with a weak party leadership, the families are strong,' said Woo Sing in the manner of a child repeating a lesson from school.

'The clans will die out in the end because there are so few children and because the relatives are sent to other parts of China,' Woo Wai San said.

'If you know what to look for, Ah Fong, you will see more of the old China here than we did at home,' said Woo Sing.

'There is plenty of the old China left in new China, only it is well hidden,' said Woo Wai San.

'Then there really is no difference between here and there,' said Ng San Fong with satisfaction, knowing she had paid tea money many times even in her short business career.

'There is a lot of difference, for here it is accepted as normal, while there it is bad and people know it is bad,' said Woo Sing hotly.

'You are always defending the place you ran away from,' replied Ng San Fong.

Woo Sing tried to think of a good answer but Woo Wai San replied for her, 'We thought we were misfits, and perhaps we were, but here there are worse problems for more people.'

'Often people do things against the rules but many try to improve at least some of the time. Here people are just trying to survive. Even those who study hard do it only for them-selves,' she said, suddenly thinking of the young and dead Lei Yuk Sin. In a strange way he had died for his country even when he was fleeing from it.

Woo Wai Sin decided to tell them the story and spoke calmly while the others listened. Only as she related the last few yards of that terrible sea journey did she begin to cry qui-etly. The two women were silent and motionless, mourning the gallant student. He, too, had been Chinese, and like them eager to enjoy life. Above all, he had been young.

*

The tempo of the factory increased. Each week the partners thought they had reached peak efficiency, but each week brought new ideas for saving time or material. Much of this was because Taam Mo Jing insisted on purchasing new equip-ment for new problems. Although the partners complained, they knew that this policy, although expensive, reaped greater profits. The workers, too, benefited, for Woo Sing and Woo Wai San had insisted on a bonus system to increase produc-tion. Ng San Fong had laughed and teased them mercilessly.

'You don't know how to appease your communist con-science,' she chided. 'I know bonuses are not given in China, but if you don't reward the workers, you will be exploiting them. What a dilemma,' she laughed.

'I just want to share my good fortune,' Woo Sing replied. 'The better the wages, the more loyal our workers will be.'

'The one thing that harmonises perfectly with communism is hypocrisy,' jibed Ng San Fong.

Woo Sing was silent but Woo Wai San replied, 'You know we are not hypocrites, Ah Fong. We live here with the simplest parts of Chairman Mao's teachings to help each other and be fair to others. The bonuses and other rules are technical parts of the great experiment and not what communists live by.'

Woo Sing asked, 'What rules do you live by Ah Fong? What are the rules here? I have not noticed any.'

Ng San Fong felt their replies did not answer her objection but she did not wish to offend her friends, 'I am sorry,' she said and another argument ended.

The workers got their extra pay, the factory received another boost in its earnings, and complicated political conundrums were soon forgotten in the turmoil of each day.

*

Woo Sing was surprised to receive a formal note from Denys Lam inviting her to lunch. She once more transformed herself into a well-dressed businesswoman for the occasion.

Denys, and a serene and confident Alice Chen, were already at the table when Woo Sing arrived. Denys came rapidly to the point of his invitation.

'I arranged a good deal for your factory and I was well paid for it, but perhaps you could repay me in another way,' he said. 'Alice, with my backing, wants to begin manufacturing jewellery. She will provide capital and manage the sales and distribution. Perhaps Ng San Fong could do some of the designing and the factory could make some of the settings.'

'I cannot reply for my partners,' said Woo Sing warily. 'We will discuss it carefully for it may be a good idea.' She wondered whether Alice had thought of this proposal before or after she'd met Denys.

'I think you should talk with Ng San Fong, Alice, because she would do most of the work,' Woo Sing added.

'I will be pleased to,' said Alice. The two women exchanged smiles and Denys shuffled his feet under the table, trying to rid himself of the feeling of being a rabbit caught between two lionesses circling for the strike. He decided to make an unplanned announcement.

'I have some rather secret important news,' he said.

Two heads turned towards him. 'The British are going to put a lot of money into the stock market,' he announced.

'Is that all?' said Alice.

'Is it important?' asked Woo Sing.

'The market will go high, perhaps even double in value. Anyone who buys shares now could make a great deal of money. I can give you the address of a good stockbroker, Foo Ji Cheung, but you must not tell him why you are buying.'

Alice was interested, but Woo Sing was not.

'I think I will stick to the factory.'

'A good idea,' said Alice. 'I think you would find it a very complicated business not suitable for a country girl.' She smiled indulgently.

'We shall see who makes the most money out of it then,' said Woo Sing. 'Could I have that address, Denys?'

Denys was relieved when the lunch ended and resolved never again to invite the two women together. He was annoyed he had revealed a valuable commercial secret and wondered if he was not better off locked in his office with his books.

Alice Chen visited Ng San Fong a couple of days later. The two women had known each other since childhood. For many years Ng San Fong had enviously watched the career of her friend—first a model, then a manager and owner of a dress shop patronised by the chicest Chinese women, and now probably the future wife of Denys Lam. First, she had watched with envy and later with admiration as her friend had moved steadily forward in the business world, never compromising herself. Unlike some of the other successful woman, she had never been known to use her body for the advance of business. Her personal life remained so private that even Ng San Fong knew little of its substance.

They sat quietly in two large chairs. Ng San Fong was so tiny that she looked like she was seated on a gigantic and powerful throne.

'I'm glad we are alone because it does not really concern your partners,' smiled Alice.

But Ng San Fong could not be lured from her friends.

'I am only here to find out the details and we will all discuss them later,' she said.

'But we need only a designer,' protested Alice.

'Then find a designer and not a plastics firm,' said Ng San

Fong, deciding that on no account would she mention the talented Tong Man Ho.

'I am sure you would like to design jewellery as a change from plastic goods for simple-minded American housewives,' said Alice.

'It would be a great challenge and I would enjoy it,' said Ng San Fong. Noting Alice's smile, she added, 'It would also be a great challenge and valuable for the factory to diversify. I would be prepared to employ silversmiths and goldsmiths, and perhaps try some combined settings in acrylic. This could provide a slightly cheaper line for large volume sales to the youth market.'

'I shall have to think about it,' said Alice thoughtfully. 'We would need a lawyer to draw up an agreement.'

'Not Denys, he is too involved with all parties,' said Ng San Fong quickly.

'Let us leave it, then,' said Alice. Her face was pink.

'Now I have something to ask you,' said Ng San Fong, herself blushing. 'I would like to change my hairstyle,' she said, and Alice wondered what had changed in her friend's life.

'Not difficult,' said Alice. 'I shall draw you a sketch of the style that would suit you most and give you the name of the salon that will manage it.'

'I do not wish to go to a salon,' said Ng San Fong quickly. 'I am too busy.'

'I can arrange for a man to come here,' said Alice. 'Next time we meet to settle the business details, I will let you know the arrangement.'

Alice departed, deciding to find out more about the factory and Ng San Fong; something somewhere might be turned to her advantage.

Stockbroker Foo Ji Cheung was not surprised to see a well-dressed young woman in his office asking about shares as he was beginning to see a type of client he had not encountered before. Woo Sing had decided to invest a quarter of her savings and a quarter of her future income into the market even though she knew nothing of the stock market beyond what Denys had told her.

'We only deal in good shares,' Foo Ji Cheung assured her. She left the details to him, confirming the amount she was prepared to spend. She did not consider the possibility she might lose it all. In any case, if the factory went into jewellery, as Ng San Fong was suggesting, there would probably be still more profits to invest. She was beginning to dream of owning a house. Not a grand one, like that of Ng Laan Sang, but a home for her and Little Boy. Ng Mei Yee would be angry, but she could perhaps find one close by as it was obvious that her son was becoming the family's adopted grandchild.

*

They had just finished inspecting a mould for a new design when Tong Man Ho broke the news. 'Ah Fong, I have a very good offer to work for another firm.'

Ng San Fong said nothing, but thought of Alice and her exit at their last meeting.

'Who is it?' she asked quietly, holding her rising fear and anger in check.

'I do not know. It was through a go-between,' he said.

'Aren't you just being very secretive?' she asked, barely able to contain her rage much longer.

'No, honestly, I hoped you knew me better, Ah Fong,' he replied.

She could already feel her back aching with tension. Her muscles restrained the worst of the stresses on her spine but when she was really angry or frightened, or both, they tightened into fiery straps that felt like steel rope slowly crushing her.

Tong Man Ho saw the expression on her face and said quickly, 'I did not accept it. I told them that ten times the offer would not separate me from you.'

Ng San Fong could not bear to speak. She began trembling violently and rested her head on the bench in front of them.

Taam Mo Jing entered and realised instantly something was wrong and called Woo Sing. She decided Ng San Fong should be taken home and was about to pick her up when Tong Man Ho brushed her aside.

'I will take her home,' he said. He picked up the pale, silent, trembling woman and carried her out to the car. Woo Sing began to climb in, but he snapped at her, 'No.' The two of them sat in the back as the chauffeur drove off as fast as the traffic would allow. Ng San Fong began crying violently but Tong Man Ho had grown up in a large family and seen many women in many moods and so he let her cry.

Ng Mei Yee was very distressed as she had never seen her daughter in such a state. Ng San Fong usually made clear what she felt was wrong. Her mother undressed her, put her to bed like a small child and was leaving to telephone their doctor when Ng San Fong called to her.

'Don't send him away, there is nothing for the doctor to treat.'

Tong Man Ho was waiting quietly downstairs. Ng Mei Yee called him up and pushed him through the doorway. She was relieved no illness had struck her daughter but the possibility that she might have adult emotions had never remotely occurred to her. She could foresee great problems and decided to speak to her husband, as despite all his indifference to her, he felt very strongly about his daughter.

'All right, Ah Fong?' asked Tong Man Ho.

'Come and sit by me,' Ng San Fong replied as approached her, bringing a comb and towel from the dresser. 'Do you think you could ever bear to look at me?'

'Can you bear to look at me?' he replied. 'There will be many difficulties other people don't have, Ah Fong, but we will have extra things that they don't often share, like our work.'

He kissed her for a long time until she gently pushed him away. 'Go now, for I feel very tired.' He left quietly, closing the door behind him.

Alice Chen called a day later, giving Ng San Fong great pleasure as she heard her decision. 'We will accept the terms for the design and manufacturing of the jewellery,' she confirmed.

Alice had learned long ago that to be a good loser was essential in Hong Kong business and it was important to turn defeat into victory. Ng San Fong said nothing about the offer to Tong Man Ho for Alice had broken a difficult barrier for her. To reveal it would have soured the start of a new business and silence would keep Alice wondering if she knew. Alice agreed to Denys Lam not drawing up the agreement, confirming Ng San Fong's suspicion that not even her friend's persuasive powers could convince him to get involved. The arrangements for the new hairstyle concluded the meeting, leaving both women happy with the outcome.

'Give us two months to produce the designs and find workers,' said Ng San Fong.

'No more, for I have to catch the Christmas trade,' said Alice. With that, the new deal began.

*

Ng San Fong was resting in bed and rather out of sorts, daydreaming about all manner of unlikely events and happenings when Woo Sing and Woo Wai San entered with a large sheet of accounts and wages for her to sign as a partner. This done, they sat around discussing the new deal, making plans, and at the same time quietly dissecting Alice—her clothes, manner and character.

'We must not talk about her like that anymore,' said Ng San Fong after a while. 'She is half-partner in our enterprise and we must work with her.'

The other two stopped, surprised and looking guilty at being caught gossiping.

Ng San Fong was also slightly embarrassed and felt compelled to break the uneasy silence. 'You must have guessed that I am foolishly trying to be a normal woman and have fallen in love,' she said, and slid down in her bed so that her eyes were all the other two could see.

Slightly unnerved, Woo Sing replied, 'What is more important, someone seems to be in love with you.'

'If he loves me, he will have to live the life of one of those Western priests. It is difficult to ask a man to do that,' said Ng San Fong.

'No, he will get used to you,' said Woo Sing.

'No, it is too risky,' said Woo Wai San, more practical in such matters and far more experienced. 'Let us discuss it as a problem.'

'It is a problem,' Ng San Fong said bitterly. 'It does not matter for me. I can always pretend, but he must have real pleasure.'

Woo Wai San said, 'Cushions, that's it!'

She left the room and returned with an armful of Ng Mei Yee's best silk cushions. With one flourish, she pulled the sheet from Ng San Fong who cowered sheepishly as Woo Wai San stared down at her.

'Here and here and here,' she said, placing the cushions about her friend. 'And then one here.' She placed the largest and longest across her chest. 'You will have to start with rules. The cushions will always have to be like this and he is not to remove them.'

'You have almost covered me up,' said Ng San Fong timidly.

Woo Sing looked down at her friend, a gnome-like creature peeping out through a cloud of exotic silk cushions. It looked crazy, but what could she say? Suddenly she was inspired, and said, 'I think the light should be out and that be another of the rules. That's because of his face, of course.'

'That's right. The cushions support me, so that I can lie straight and my back will not strain, and the darkness will solve the rest of it,' said Ng San Fong with great satisfaction.

Chapter 16
Taking stock

The impact of the stock market boom began to creep into the factory to the extent that Seung Mei and Woo Wai San banned the presence of transistor radios. Some workers left saying that they could make more on the market if they listened during the day. Eventually, agreement was reached that the market prices would be broadcast twice a day and workers would be given time to telephone instructions.

Only a few were involved, but the rest watched and listened, fascinated by this new and seemingly effortless way of making money. Woo Sing invested heavily and regardless of her broker's recommendations.

Share prices continued to rise. All the partners were now involved and Ng Mei Yee scarcely bothered to tell Woo Sing the daily doings of her son before she launched into her own daily activities on the market. Even before work in their car, the chauffeur had the radio turned to the market news. If two or three people were talking together the chances were that the market was the only topic worth discussing.

Woo Sing often wondered whether she should give all her money to the broker, but decided to stick with her plan of investing a quarter of her old savings but increased investment of her current earnings to half. The partners discussed whether they should float their own shares. Foo Ji Cheung was enthusiastic but Denys Lam warned them against it and the matter was dropped.

Even Wa Hing became interested and deeply offended his mistress by showing greater interest in her shareholdings than in her body. Woo Wai San eventually told him that if he mentioned the word shares again when his trousers were off, he could get out of bed. Sometimes, to tease her at her moment of pleasure, he would whisper slyly, 'How many Jardine shares have you got?'

The argument would dissolve into laughter, but sometimes they would spend several hours talking of shares and nothing else. Even he had bought shares from an old amah. The market rolled on and several of the better workers left the factory. They had always saved carefully but now, after long hesitation, they too plunged into the turmoil of the great money-making machine.

All manner of rumour swept the town, carrying with it a mass of believers who, the next day, pushed prices beyond the dreamed-of limits from the previous month.

Amahs left their masters of many years, concubines left their owners, and all who were lowly but brave enough to try, felt that the long years of waiting for luck were over. Soon they would be rich. And the market rolled on like a great wave, gathering even the last doubters, and it seemed like nothing could destroy it.

At first, Ng San Fong was another who succumbed to the market's allure, but later found it boring. Apart from having to give a few instructions, there were no problems to solve. Her broker always did as he was asked and there were no arguments to try to win. Besides, her mind was on other matters. She would return home from a day close to Ah Ho, knowing the situation must be solved and only she could solve it.

Meanwhile, Tong Man Ho bought a small car, took three lessons, and bought a driver's licence. As he explained to Woo Sing, the bribe for a licence was quite reasonable.

When Ng San Fong entered the street one evening after work looking for the family car, she saw another in its parking place. Tong Man Ho approached and proudly explained it was his and he had sent the family car home, the driver taking the message that Ah Fong would be out for dinner. Although tired and hot, Ng San Fong smiled and sat alongside him but asked him to go home first. She hated dining out but decided to allow him to make the decisions. A quick sideways glance at his determined face told her that sometimes she would not get her own way.

The restaurant was small, simple and one where he was known, but the food was equal to that of the grand houses of Kowloon. Driving home, Ng San Fong thought of the right thing to say or do to approach the delicate subject. She was distracted by her man's unnerving driving. Even the mini-buses began to avoid him, which she had never seen before.

With relief, she felt the car stop, for she had shut her eyes a mile or so from home She opened her eyes as he opened the door for her.

She told the *foki* who opened the outer gate that she would let her friend out later and decided to say nothing further. Holding hands, they walked quietly up the stairs into her room. She threw the cushions on the bed, and still without a word being spoken by either of them, Ah Ho turned out the light.

She felt a knife was splitting her in two. Through what seemed an eternity of pain, she thought, *Hell, I must be twisted inside as well, in which case it will just have to untwist.* When Ah Ho stopped, the relief was pure pleasure and she lay there gasping. 'I am sorry I was so brief,' he said.

'No matter, it is not an easy thing to learn. We will learn slowly.'

She gently pushed him away. Her chest was beginning to hurt. He lay alongside her and rubbed his face against hers, a face wet with tears. Although neither had truly believed it possible, they had begun a long and happy journey that would be with them all their lives.

*

The markets sped on and the factory lost more workers. Two old silversmiths were employed to work on the new project with Alice Chen. They were so old that other workers joked that Ah Fong was stealing from the cemeteries for staff.

They were the only ones available during the stock market boom and under the gentle guidance of Jaam Mo Jing and Tong Man Ho they performed miracles of intricacy and construction.

The factory, the market, the designs, the orders and wages, and managing the workers, left little time for emotions, and Woo Sing wondered how she had ever thought of Denys Lam as a lover.

Ah Ho infrequently visited Ng San Fong, and the next day she would look exhausted and a little frightened. The few that knew, detected a certain softness developing, not only in her features but also her character. Tong Man Ho became more outspoken and several times he and Woo Sing had a trial of wills over the management of staff.

One evening, Woo Sing paid a surprise visit to Woo Wai San, who admitted her with a smile and took her to the bedroom instead of into the kitchen where they usually sat. There she was greeted by an abashed and naked Wa Hing hastily pulling a sheet over himself.

'I am following the market, Woo Sing,' he said.

'Indeed. It is a strange way to follow the market—in bed with no clothes on, no radio and not even a newspaper close by.'

'Oh, I am his personal advisor,' said Woo Wai San, sitting close to his head and not bothering to adjust her gown. 'I'll get us some coffee.'

'I will make it,' said Woo Sing.

When she returned, they sat around for some time talking of all manner of things. Woo Sing was enjoying herself, but after a while noticed Wa Hing was becoming restless and realised it was time for her to go.

*

Woo Sing slept badly, and while dressing after such a restless night, decided to resume her English lessons. She telephoned a delighted Inspector Campbell, who quickly agreed to more lessons, although he now spoke Cantonese quite fluently during his duties and there was no real need for him to practise.

As he set out with a new set of English books for them to read, he was surprised to note the address was in the richer part of Kowloon Tong. He was even more surprised to be greeted by a beautifully dressed young woman, poised and with a new grace of movement. Her English was the same, however, and they agreed she needed more practise with English than he did with Cantonese.

An hour quickly passed. As he rose to leave, she moved close to him, standing still and silent. Their proximity required no questions. He put his arms around her and kissed her, at first briefly and then for much longer as he felt her arms embrace him. There was no doubting the passion in her face. She led him a few steps towards another room before she suddenly stopped.

'I have one *gweilo*'s child and I love him but I do not want another. Go and get something to stop babies and I will wait.'

'Is that what you want?' he asked, slightly shocked but very eager.

'Yes,' she said, and he quickly left.

The shops of Tsim Sha Tsui would be shut so he explained to the taxi driver his need. Not knowing the Cantonese term, he said, 'Stop baby medicine, quickly!'

The driver looked alarmed and drove rapidly to Kowloon City, stopping outside a herbal shop.

The herbalist did not understand the inspector's Cantonese either so the taxi driver explained and the herbalist rapidly concocted a mixture of ingredients unknown to the impatient Ian. He realised that whatever they were for, they would be useless. Nevertheless, he could not offend his anxious helpers and so he waited, paid the man and re-entered the taxi.

He was working out what to do next when he saw two officers he knew on patrol. Suppressing his embarrassment, he spoke to them in Cantonese about his requirement. They looked surprised, even alarmed, but could not help.

The taxi driver drew him back to the cab and called up the female taxi monitor, explaining in Cantonese there was a *gweilo* man with a problem about stopping or losing a baby. He asked that she fetch her friend, who spoke English well.

Squirming with a mixture of impatience and a grave loss of dignity, but protected by the anonymity of the radio, the inspector explained to a sweet and educated voice that he wished to buy contraceptives. There was a long silence, a burst of Cantonese, and a series of giggles clearly transmitted over the radio.

'I understand, sir. I will ask a man here to tell the driver,' the sweet voice replied.

The police patrolmen still listened intently, although the inspector tried to wave them away. The driver heard the reply first in Cantonese and then in English, as did the two police-men. The driver was still laughing as they rounded a corner. Glancing back, the inspector could see his two colleagues still enjoying the joke.

He paid the driver well. To his irritation, the man saluted as he drove away, grinning. The *foki* let him in, surprised that the *gweilo* had returned. Nowadays, however, he was letting all sorts of people in and he had even ceased to gossip about it with the amahs.

Ian climbed the stairs, hot and flustered and not at all his idea of the cool, confident lover. *If this does not go all right after all this, I will not be happy.'*

Woo Sing was sitting and reading when he entered but made no comment on his appearance nor the long time he had been away. He was disappointed that she was less respon-sive than he expected. Yet was also pleased, as he realised that she was not skilled in the art of love.

Afterwards, he told her of his shopping problems. When he felt her laughing body pressed against him, he decided he would love to have her as his wife. He didn't understand what had driven her to him, but was pleased to accept his good fortune and hoped it would remain forever.

Ng Mei Yee lost hope of ever understanding modern women. Woo Sing was such a nice girl and yet the servants hinted that the English lessons she was taking went on until the early hours of the morning. Ng Mei Yee had closed her eyes to her husband's roaming, at first in hatred, but later in relief. Now her own daughter was misbehaving, as was Woo Sing.

'Men are hard. It is better to close one's eyes and still one's heart,' her mother had told her. She had followed that advice throughout her lonely but dignified life. She would close her eyes to Woo Sing's behaviour and open them to her child, Little Boy, whom she adored, and she knew he adored her.

Woo Sing loved to lie close to her *gweilo* and ask him about his travels. He had been through much of Europe and America, but it was America that fascinated her most because of its wealth and power.

'We were always told that it was a paper tiger, but we were told so often that I used to wonder if it was really so weak,' she said. 'I even asked about it at a meeting but was reminded to think of it as a paper tiger.'

'Were you satisfied with the answer?' asked Ian.

'Yes,' she said hesitantly. 'Have you ever had an American woman?'

Ian was reluctant to discuss past conquests, but finally replied, 'Yes, why?'

'Because they say American women have all sorts of knowledge about love and strange ways to make it. Perhaps you could teach me some.'

'Most of them confuse acrobatics for passion,' he said. 'They cannot love anyone, not even themselves.'

'Without strong people, America is a paper tiger, then?'

'No, it is a real tiger but it makes paper love,' he said, a trace of bitterness in his voice.

He was almost asleep when Woo Sing startled him awake.

'How is your auntie?'

'She does not like Scotland much now.'

'Perhaps she could work for us,' Woo Sing said.

Nothing more was said until Woo Sing once more jolted him awake. 'About three years ago almost to this day, a Chinese boy was drowned off Sha Tau Kok. Perhaps his body was found on a beach. Could you find out where he is buried?'

'Many bodies are washed up but I will try,' he said dreamily, and as sleep claimed him, he felt her arms gently holding him.

*

Wa Hing bought more shares from the old woman who claimed she was an agent of a well-known broker. They seemed very simple pieces of paper to have such tremendous potential to make one rich, but if it was good enough for the *gweilos* then it was good enough for him.

His boss instructed him in a new duty, driving a car for another part of the firm's business. He was to practise driving for a day or so because it would be different to driving the truck. The car was responsive and he could take it around corners much faster than the truck. He marvelled at the design and construction. It was an American car, or so the boss told him. This did not surprise him, for only recently had he learned that Americans had flown to the moon.

He had lost money on that discovery. One of his work-mates had casually remarked that the Americans had driven a car on the moon. Wa Hing believed they were teasing him about his ignorance of the world and so with a great flourish had slapped down fifty dollars.

'The man who can prove that to me can take the fifty dollars,' he said.

Local newspaper and book vendors were puzzled when a line of men, not of the type generally given to lunar study, anxiously enquired about moon exploration literature.

The winner was the shrewdest and most illiterate of them all, for he simply asked his grandson, who produced beautifully kept newspaper clippings from a school project.

Wa Hing paid willingly, but his workmates knew how humbled he was and never teased him again. He read the first few papers mainly to convince himself of the truth but the complexity of it began to fascinate him. He read about machinery he would never have dreamed possible. The rocket he could understand, but the details about the spaceship were unbelievable and nobody in China would have dreamed of driving a car on the moon. He thought a great deal about the papers and one evening he called at the boy's home to return them.

'It was fifty dollars well spent,' he told the surprised youngster, who sensed Wa Hing was not as stupid as his gloating grandfather had said. Wa Hing looked at the boy's other books. 'You are a great scholar,' he said.

The schoolboy, an average student, replied, 'I wish my parents and teachers shared your opinion.'

Wa Hing remembered reading only a little about the world

outside China during his own schooldays. There had been no real world outside China and it had been hard for him to imagine even parts of his own country though they were shown plenty of photographs. He was now determined to learn more about the world, to save enough money to visit America and see for himself these strange technical people, who were such bitter enemies of his homeland, although even he knew that China must copy them to survive.

At home he found Tong Pooi cheerfully working on a colourful scroll for a special party. Admiring the old man's beautiful work, he thought of the young scholar and his diagrams of the moon rocket. The distance between these two devotees of the Chinese tradition of learning was so great that he could think of no way to measure it.

He was surprised to find the car he was to drive was not the one he had been using for practise. He was put with six cheerful and friendly young men about his own age.

They told him his boss had recommended him when their usual driver was unavailable. They drove across to Wanchai, talking noisily about all the usual racing, fighting, the lottery and girls. They stopped at a restaurant while one of the group checked inside. He returned to say they had time for a meal as their guests had not yet arrived at their eventual destination. The food was good, the *foki* much more attentive than usual and a few free dishes were sent out by the cook.

'You must be good customers,' said Wa Hing, finding room for one more piece of chicken. His new friends laughed and the *fokis* smiled. The phone at the reception desk rang and the team's leader, Ah Fung, was called to answer it. He returned to the table to inform them that they must leave in five minutes. Watching the playful scramble to select the remaining choice pieces, Wa Hing decided it was the most cheerful meal he had eaten since he, Woo Sing and Tong Pooi had eaten a long time ago in the old man's room.

Ah Fung guided Wa Hing to a busy Wanchai side street.

'Park here.'

'But there's nowhere to park.'

As he spoke, a car pulled away from the kerb and Wa Hing quickly claimed the space. The departing motorist did not look at them but he felt the matter had been arranged.

They were again parked outside a restaurant where Ah Fung said they would have to wait awhile. Like his companions, Wa Hing felt cheerful, full and sleepy. They said little, and two dozed off, bellies stuffed with good food.

Ah Fung left the car and opened the boot, taking out some short, thick bamboo poles, which he passed to those in the back seat.

Wa Hing took little notice as he was admiring an attractive girl who had stepped out from the restaurant with a man of about twenty.

The car doors were flung open. Wa Hing's companions jumped from their car, brushing aside the young girl to surround the man. Three chopped fiercely down with their bamboo poles as his hands rose above his head to protect himself while the other three drove their bamboos hard into his chest and stomach.

People in the street, mostly middle-aged or elderly, looked on helplessly, and aware that intervention could well lead to their own death together with that of the defenceless victim.

The girl screamed and rushed back into the restaurant to seize the receptionist's phone. The *foki* did not stop her, but neither did they help.

The blows rained down on her companion like drumming on an iron roof. With a tremendous effort he broke through the ring of attackers and staggered off down the street as fast as a fear of death could drive him. He could still feel the blows and the blood running down his back and chest. A bamboo thrust between his legs brought him down. Ah Fung bent his knees to give weight to the final blow that crushed his skull against the cobblestoned pavement. The girl had bravely returned to the street and began screaming again. The attackers ignored her and scampered back into the car where Ah Fung ordered Wa Hing to drive off at top speed.

'Turn left,' said Ah Fung.

A bus blocked their way. Ah Hing glanced back to see the girl kneeling by the battered corpse. Ahead, police lights were flashing.

'Turn left,' repeated Ah Fung.

'No, that street is one way and we will be blocked,' said Wa Hing. 'I can beat the police to the next left turn and then turn right. They will never catch us there.'

Wa Hing completed his turn, drove a hundred yards along a busy road and turned right into a narrow but empty access lane. They drove rapidly for two hundred yards before re-entering Hennessy Road where they were soon lost in the turmoil of traffic.

On Ah Fung's instructions, Wa Hing stopped periodically to set down a member of the gang, each parting cheerfully as though only the meal, not the murder, had happened.

Finally, Ah Fung said to Ah Hing, 'Leave the car here. Wipe the steering wheel and the door handle and anything else you may have touched.'

He did so and asked about the car.

'The owner will soon have it back,' said Ah Fung, and only then did Wa Hing realise it had been stolen.

Before they parted, each to find his own way back to Kowloon, Ah Fung said, 'I am satisfied with you, Ah Hing. Your knowledge of the streets helped us avoid the police and a nasty problem.'

The night's events overwhelmed Wa Hing and he tried to avoid thinking about them until he was home and having a final cup of tea with Tong Pooi. The old man was the centre of an oasis of calm.

Wa Hing began to wonder if the dead man was the husband, brother or lover of the young woman, or perhaps even a conspirator. Whhoever he was, one thing was clear: he had somehow offended or threatened the organisation in which Wa Hing was now involved.

He had seen people beaten during the Cultural Revolution, but never to death and never by people who did not hate or fear the victim. He was frightened, sickened and ashamed. He wondered if the usual driver had not really been sick and he had been sent to test what he would do if he broke the rules.

Perhaps the usual driver had broken the rules. Or the dead man was even the usual driver. To ask would be to reveal his fear. He decided it was no use worrying about it. If he were asked again, he would try to avoid the job but knew that also could be dangerous. His happy dinner companions, the friendliest he had known since his arrival, would cheerfully kill him before, or after, lunch.

It was with great relief that he began driving the truck again, but the freedom and pleasure of it was gone. He dreaded the next call to drive the car and although he had decided to accept his role as a driver, he could never forget the image of the young woman kneeling by the corpse.

Lai Gwok Yuen did not ask him about the night's adventure and Wa Hing assumed that either he knew or was wise enough not to want to know. Either way, he felt his boss's silence proved the importance of secrecy. Usually, he rarely thought much about his feelings but even he understood that the murder had affected him.

Woo Wai San noticed it too, and complained about his lack of interest in her. Wa Hing was not usually a morose or preoccupied man, nor likely to worry about the future, and yet here he was in her bed, silent and unresponsive.

'What's this?' she said sharply, pointing to his deflated member.

Disregarding all common sense, he told her the whole story, sparing nothing. He knew Woo Wai San was as hard as he was, and very realistic. She became watchful, guarded and silent, like the many times he had seen her at the commune meetings. She had often wondered what Wa Hing did, for he had always seemed to have enough money and yet he would never explain.

'Perhaps the man was somebody selected by chance,' she said. 'To show what would happen if you broke the rules. Perhaps he was killed as a warning for you.'

'No, that is not possible,' said Wa Hing, aware that she had placed a thought into his head that might not easily go away.

He realised Woo Wai San was fond of him and with her gentle encouragement managed to make love to her. Shortly after that he left in a far more cheerful mood.

*

Mary Campbell was relieved to receive the offer from Woo Sing, penned on her behalf by Inspector Campbell. She found her native Scottish village quiet and oppressive. Woo Sing explained that Ng San Fong had become more interested in jewellery design and the business needed a decisive manager. 'We're all getting richer but getting poorer at making decisions,' she explained.

The salary was generous. Along with her pension, she would be very comfortable. She bought her air ticket for Hong Kong the next day.

Woo Sing's letter also revealed she was taking lessons again from her nephew but did not elaborate on the nature of the tuition. Woo Sing had now learned to respond to his lovemaking and there were few pleasurable sensations her body had not only experienced, but also revelled in many times. She now understood what had driven Woo Wai San to other men. She realised Ah San's fanatical, tractor-minded husband must have also been a skilled lover. He had awakened something in his wife that meant she could not wait out the long years for him alone. She guessed that behind the public coolness of some of the men of the commune must have dwelt a private passion.

There was something else she was beginning to understand. As her passion for her lover began to leave her, a small and irritating sense of self-disgust added a rotten taste to her pleasure.

Woo Wai San now often invited Woo Sing to her flat where Wa Hing was becoming a much less frequent visitor. They would sit and talk about the factory, about the stock market, the commune, Alice Chen and a host of things, but they never spoke of their increasing loneliness.

*

The factory staff were talking excitedly when Woo Sing entered but she took no notice. Probably yet another upward turn in the share market. Then two old women came up to her and tearfully explained that Ah Cheung was dead.

The factory now had so many employees that for a few minutes she could not recall the victim. Then she remembered a tall and handsome girl, a reasonable worker, very cheerful and much liked by the others.

She had left some weeks before without explanation, which the two women now supplied. A triad member had seduced her. After a whirlwind courtship, a savage and crushing rape, and a threat against her parents' lives, she had become a massage parlour girl. Her family tracked her down and pleaded with her to return home. But now pregnant and hating her life, she had decided to protect her parents in the only way possible. She took a lift to the top floor of the resettlement block and calmly stepped out into oblivion.

Woo Wai San thought a great deal about the girl and her story, which she knew was not unique. Every estate housing block could tell a similar one. She made no move to undress when Wa Hing arrived that night, but offered him tea and gestured for him to sit in the kitchen. She spoke quietly and firmly. Her words had been well rehearsed.

'If you do not break with the triads now, Ah Hing, sooner or later you will die.'

He sat impassively drinking his tea, watching every flicker of expression in the face he knew so well.

'I have broken maybe most of the rules we were taught as children, Ah Hing, but I still don't believe in gangsters.'

'They would kill me,' he said. 'There is nowhere I can hide where I could not be found and they would also kill my friends.'

'At times I have loved you, Ah Hing, and perhaps I still love you, but if I regard this as your business and not mine you will drag me down too,' she said.

'There is no way out,' he replied.

'The door out is behind you,' she said briskly. 'And when you have finished with them you can return.'

'They would kill me,' was all he said as he shut the door.

She was still crying and wishing she had not ordered him out when Woo Sing arrived. No longer caring for the consequences, Woo Wai San told her the story. Woo Sing was not surprised, for she had expected Wa Hing's optimism would someday land him in trouble.

He could return to China and give himself up to the authorities, who were now said to be quite lenient. After a few months in gaol, he would be safe as the triads' power stopped at the border. He had been loyal and kind to her during her despair and now it was her turn to repay him. There was a saying that *owed favours are more urgent to repay than debts* and she would repay it.

She knew Tong Pooi must never be told. Few hated the triads as much as the old man.

'They belong to China's past and you are a traditionalist,' Wa Hing had once joked.

'They are part of the black side of the past. They are gangsters and it is a disgrace that they are Chinese,' Tong Pooi had snapped angrily back. 'We pay no tax to the English government because we don't get much in return. But we pay tax to the triads and get nothing but threats and fear in return. Which is worse?'

'Pay tax?' asked Wa Hing, puzzled.

'Of course, we all pay tax,' said Tong Pooi. 'The triads tax the hawkers, the shops and the taxis. All the little businesses are taxed by the triads. Those who are taxed, increase the prices of the things they sell and thus we're all taxed by the triads.'

'And the triads are taxed by the police,' said Wa Hing. 'I wonder who the police are taxed by.'

'No one knows what happens to the money when it gets to the top *gweilo* policemen,' said Tong Pooi.

Wa Hing said no more.

*

Woo Sing decided to visit Tong Pooi. It seemed a lifetime since she and Wa Hing had stayed together. So much had happened to them but if they could strengthen their bond, maybe she could save him. As there were enough funds available for him to leave Hong Kong, she decided that she and her son would go with him. *Canada was said to be a great country.* There the three of them could start again and she could ensure his careless optimism did not again trap him. Her son needed a father—a brave father, a Chinese father—and she needed a Chinese man.

She waited patiently for her lover to finish. Ian had suspected for some time that their affair would soon to be over. With great sadness, he knew she was quietly passing from his life.

'I looked up the records,' Ian Campbell said. 'There was no body of a young man found about that time. The sea takes them back sometimes and they are never found. However, the body of a local fisherman was found. He died of a heart attack but there was no boy.'

Woo Sing recalled the fisherman who she'd murdered in revenge for Ah Hon. She had never seriously thought about him until now.

'Thank you, Ian,' she said. 'The old people used to believe that if a body was not buried the soul could never rest, but I do not believe that. It pleases me to think that he was not buried in some pauper's grave along with a heap of other bodies. It was better that he was dissolved in the sea, a fitting grave for him. Please go now, Ian. I do not want any lessons for a while,' she said softly.

As he dressed, Ian could not stop himself from saying, 'I am always ready to marry you, but I suppose it will have to be a Chinese boy. I did love you.'

'Please go,' she said, and turned her head away, for she did not want him to see her tears.

Chapter 17

Loss and marriage

Superintendent George was much admired within the police force for being a fair and honest policeman. He had a challenging task in trying to destroy the Chiu Chow clans and had enjoyed a few of those lucky breaks, important in any career, which helped a professional push beyond his peers. A quietly spoken man, he lived modestly, unlike many of his colleagues.

'We can contain them, but not break them,' he'd once told Ian in a moment of despair.

Random searches in outlying villages and sudden road checks were largely fruitless. Ian had pushed him to develop informers and for a while they'd received information about small-time peddlers. It was merely the fringe, and whenever a trap was set for them, a large consignment was usually on the move elsewhere in the colony. They'd tried a combination of false traps, together with a widespread programme of stop and search along the usual routes, but nothing was found. Another informer later told Ian that the peddler had pretended to lay a trap for them but had really been carrying a large amount of heroin.

The two officers closely scrutinised the drug prevention team but finally agreed that if there was an informer in the ranks, he was well hidden.

'I think they are all clean,' said Ian's boss. 'If there had been a Chui Chow among them we would have watched him and I've always kept them out of the drug teams.' He added with a smile, 'I hear you have a Chinese girlfriend.'

'I tell her nothing,' replied Ian hotly. 'Anyway, it's finished.' He tried to look unconcerned but was aware of his visible disappointment.

'Sorry, Ian, I hear she is very beautiful and dangerously fertile,' grinned the other.

Ian blushed scarlet. 'It seems my little taxi ride is well known in the force.'

'My boy, we all had great sympathy for you in your hour of need.' They parted laughing.

Ian decided that the only way to succeed against the drug gangs was through intensified random checks with minimal information given to the team before they set out. Superintendent George agreed, and after a bout of intensive detailed planning, both felt optimistic that their luck would change.

*

Chen Tien Wa ran the packing room with great efficiency

and when the partners discussed anything concerning her domain, she spoke out firmly for her side of the business.

Many changes were being made to the packaging, and the firm had received compliments from America on the high standard maintained.

With her share of the money, Chen Tien Wa rented a three-room flat, an unbelievable luxury at which she daily marvelled. Two amahs cared for the children, who at last went to a school, however, as she had yet to find one to her liking. But it was a school and the children were slowly adapting to its discipline and dedication.

The packing room staff had become accustomed to her many hours of silence. She had become even thinner, and some felt that her combined responsibilities at work and home were too great a burden.

One day, she disappeared. She left home for work but never arrived. The police asked numerous questions that produced no idea of her whereabouts. They knew many people disappeared in Hong Kong. Some chose to lose themselves in Mong Kok or Macau, others cast themselves into the harbour and some retired to a quiet hillside with a bottle of insecticide. For others, their sudden removal from the city was the price paid for seriously offending the triads or drug syndicates.

It was eventually revealed that Chen Tien Wa had confessed to the amah that she had found a supply of her husband's heroin and started using this after his death.

Whatever had happened to Chen Tien Wa, she was never found.

Woo Sing consulted Denys Lam to arrange a trust for the children and after much hesitation decided she would be their guardian. It would make life with Wa Hing awkward, but she was determined they would manage. The children were not well disciplined but she could afford to pay for two old-fashioned and short-tempered amahs of whom even Tong Pooi would approve. Such women were hard to come by and their wages high, but money was the least of the problems for Chen Tien Wa's children.

Woo Sing spoke to Ng Mei Yee and the two women came close to a bitter row. Only the realisation that they both had too much to lose prevented them from saying the worst.

These last few months, Woo Sing has hardly touched the child, thought Ng Mei Yee. *She has been too busy rollicking in bed with that gweilo policeman.*

Ng Mei Yee has stolen my baby, and now cannot bear to see him taken away, thought Woo Sing, but she spoke slowly and quietly to Ng Mei Yee. 'I'm going to look after Chen Tien Wa's children. I will need a bigger house and Little Boy must come with me.'

Ng Mei Yee battled to control her feelings. 'Little Boy is used to me and I don't want to see him cared for by careless amahs.'

Her distress was so obvious that Woo Sing decided to postpone the final decision and allow Ng Mei Yee to find a solution. It was obvious that the determination and courage of Ah Fong owed much to this quiet and apparently timid woman who usually got her own way when she was really determined.

One evening a week later, Ng Mei Yee entered Woo Sing's room, all smiles. Woo Sing sensed a battle was about to commence.

'A very nice house across the street, suitable for children, has become available. It is well-guarded with a high wall capped with broken glass,' said Ah Yee. 'It is not a fashion-able house but a suitable one.'

'I didn't know they wanted to sell,' said Woo Sing.

'They didn't at first but they are old and looking for a grave site with really good fung shui.'

'Did you happen to have one?' asked Woo Sing.

'No, but we had some land near Shatin that a friend wanted very badly. We sold him the land for a grave site he had and the old couple have agreed to sell their house to you and buy the grave site from us.' Woo Sing noted satisfaction in her voice. 'Oh, and we made a good profit as well,' implying that the deal was already closed.

'What if I do not want the house?' Woo Sing was annoyed that these arrangements had been made without consulting her.

'A suitable house is very hard to find, and expensive. Besides, you are a good woman,' smiled Ng Mei Yee.

She has been a good friend, thought Woo Sing. *She took me in and never complained about my behaviour.*

'You are very good, Ah Yee,' she said, thinking also what a cunning fox she was.

'The children can stay where they are until the house is ready and then we shall all move,' said Woo Sing.

'I shall miss you, Ah Sing, even though you will be only a short way away,' said Ng Mei Yee, and peace was restored.

*

Woo Sing always checked her monthly bank statement with an air of unreality. Each month the factory produced a greater profit and her share totalled many times more than the life savings of a middle-grade cadre at home. There was no guilt or greed in her pleasure at the figures, nor was there much pride, for she knew that luck had played a major role. She had accumulated a large number of shares, although had no idea of their value. Several times, Ah Fong had been cross because Woo Sing had not added them up.

'How do you know how much profit you have made?' Ah Fong asked. 'I check mine every week and would check every day if I had time.'

'It is only paper,' replied Woo Sing.

'But paper that will buy you a house,' Ah Fong snapped back.

After one of these arguments, Woo Sing decided to see her broker and find out what her shares were worth. That same morning, she was surprised by a call from Denys Lam. He spoke tersely. 'Ah Sing, I told you to buy shares and now I'm telling you to sell. Sell everything, even Hong Kong and Shanghai Bank. Sell it all and sell it today.'

'But Ah Fong said that the market is still rising,' she replied, worried and confused.

'The market will rise tomorrow and maybe for another week, but it will turn, I promise you. The English are pulling out.'

'Denys, I am buying a house. Will you fix it, for a fee?' she asked, trying to get the conversation on to a ground she could understand.

'Only if you sell your shares.'

'I will ring Foo Ji Cheung today,' she said wearily. She began to thank him but he had already hung up. Instead of calling Foo Ji Cheung, she decided to ask Ng San Fong what to do.

Ah Fong replied, 'If you had sold this morning, you would have been at least two thousand dollars poorer by now.'

'But if the market drops tomorrow, I shall be poorer still,' said Woo Sing.

'Why should the market drop? It has been rising for months.'

Woo Sing could not reply. She spent a restless night, not worrying so much about the money but about whether she should offend Denys by asking some other lawyer to arrange their house deal.

She found herself thinking of home and how decisions were made there together. *Here, one decided alone. Here, one always seemed to be alone. At home, there was a rhythm to events. One idea became tremendously important and then faded to be replaced by something else. Perhaps the market had its rhythm, too, and Ah Fong was so blinded by wealth pouring in that she could not see it would not last forever.*

Woo Sing did not even understand what the share certificates stood for. All she knew was that one bought them and mysteriously they rapidly increased in value. In the darkness, she realised she had been buying pieces of paper alleged to be valuable but she had no proof of their worth. Early the next morning, she rang Foo Ji Cheung and told him to sell all her stocks that day and transfer the money to her bank.

'You must be crazy. Everyone is buying, I can't cope with their orders,' he said.

'Then you will have no trouble selling mine,' she replied.

That evening, he rang her to tell her everything had been sold. 'I can buy some more for you tomorrow.'

'I will tell you when to buy again,' replied Woo Sing.

Next day, the market spun another turn higher.

'Sold yet?' asked Ah Fong.

'Yes, everything,' replied Woo Sing firmly, determined not to be swayed. The market rose steadily during the week and she realised she had lost thousands in paper profits. She told Woo Wai San, who sold half of her shares without hesitating.

'Denys Lam knows what he is doing,' she said, as practical as ever.

Woo Sing told some of the workers in the factory. She knew the news would soon spread and she did not want to see them cheated. A few took her advice but most decided Hong Kong was such a boom town that the market would go on for years. The following week, Woo Wai San sold more and even Ng

San Fong parted with a few. 'Only the weaker ones,' she told them.

Woo Wai San sent Wa Hing a note telling him to sell, hoping he would return it to ask her why. He did not come and she spent an unhappy evening waiting. He already knew he had lost, as the papers were full of the news that forged certificates were everywhere. After checking his, he realised why the old amah always had a supply. She simply printed them and when he went to look for her the next day, she was nowhere to be found.

When the market climbed slightly higher, Ng San Fong took pleasure in calculating that Woo Sing had lost some twenty thousand dollars by selling two weeks earlier. Next day Woo Sing was so anxious that she could hardly take herself to work.

I will ring Denys Lam and ask him what to do. No, I will ring Foo Ji Cheung and buy to the hilt. No, I will use half of my money.

In the end she did nothing, deciding she was rich enough to stand her loss.

The following day, the market began dropping like a stone to depths no one had thought possible.

She watched, fascinated, as share prices fell faster than they had climbed. Within a few days, they were well below her selling point. Although she was triumphant, she kept it secret, as all around her friends were hopelessly trying to sell a product no one wanted to buy. The factory was quiet, the radios turned off. No one wanted to listen to a minute-by-minute account of the loss of their wealth.

Woo Sing wrote Denys a short note:

To remember a past love with kindness is to be a friend indeed. In repayment, I shall always be a true friend to you.

She signed it with her familiar name and sent a small, but expensive, jade ring, for she knew he loved jade.

The gloom in the factory lasted about three weeks. Then the optimism of the natural gambler returned to its normal level. There were jokes and laughter for they still had work, and what else could one do?

Ng San Fong tried to blame the British. 'They put their money in to start the market, blew it up like a big balloon, and quietly slipped their share out before it burst,' she said bitterly. 'You know the old joke? That if the Chinese can stand the taste and stink of the durian fruit, then they can live with the English? Yes, they are slimy dogs.'

Woo Sing remain silent and tried to look sympathetic, for she knew that if the British had exploited anything, it had been the Chinese passion to gamble. She began to understand why those who secretly gambled at home had been harshly punished. This passion made her people vulnerable and kept many of them poor. She was now a rich woman. Her friends in the factory, and others who were now poorer, had helped to make her so. On average, every man, woman and child in the city had given six hundred dollars to the English.

Woo Sing thought of the money she had made in Hong Kong through the capitalist system and the share market. She was not going to give her money away for she was a realist; she lived in Hong Kong now, not China, where a peasant at home earned less in a year than a high cadre earned in a month. If someone worked in a factory in China, she or he earned three times what a peasant earned in a commune. Here, Woo Sing worked for her living and the better she performed, the more money she made. That satisfied her conscience for the time being.

*

Mary Campbell had been working with them for about two months before the staff accepted her, but she was patient, did not shout, and treated them fairly.

It was slowly decided that she was a satisfactory *gweilo* as far as such creatures could be satisfactory. So she was regarded with the usual mixture of contempt, resignation and awe that is the lot of the satisfactory *gweilo*.

Mary suspected the relationship between her nephew and Woo Sing had changed but she never asked and soon thought no more about it.

She had met another satisfactory *gweilo*, but the satisfaction in this case was hers. Her evenings were no longer devoted to running a household for those who took no interest in it, but were spent solely on her own pleasure.

If she ever wondered how and why she had endured her previous employment for forty years, she decided it was due to her religious instruction as a child. She had been taught to 'know her place'. There was not much time left to her now and she did not want to play hard to get. It would be nice to be married but she would accept something less, as almost anything would be better than she had enjoyed before.

William Hunter had lived in Hong Kong since the end of the war. She knew that if all the Chinese girls who had laid down for him were set in a line, they would probably exceed the entire outline of Fragrant Harbour.

It was also probable that she could not quell his addiction for their narrow hips and snug genitals, but she would ensure her share before theirs. He wanted to exchange Cantonese giggles for a Scottish accent. He wanted to talk more and needed a listener. He was wealthy enough for them to travel and both hoped that time, affection and a mutual self-interest would weld them together.

When he offered her marriage she accepted, although both knew she would have lived with him anyway.

Their lovemaking had begun quite sedately, but within a few weeks his wife became determined to slake her thirst after all these parched years. At times, as he hung on tightly to the thrashing ex-spinster beneath him, he wondered who was really in charge.

All her friends had been delighted at her marriage, which they celebrated with an elaborate meal enjoyed by an unusually varied group. Jeng Gei and Tong Pooi had attended, along with members of Mr Hunter's club. The latter gentlemen, who had respected his reputation as insatiable, decided that their friend was showing signs of early senility. It is the Hong Kong equivalent of becoming a hippie, one of them mused mournfully, looking at the noisy crowd of Cantonese friends.

Woo Sing sat next to Tong Pooi to reassure the old man amid the unusual surroundings, but there was no need. He was totally immersed in assessing the quality of the dishes and, to her surprise, tasting some of the Western ones.

'One must not cling unnecessarily to the past,' he said somewhat pompously while chewing on a grilled steak and obviously enjoying it.

That night, as Woo Sing lay waiting for sleep, she thought of Tong Pooi and how even he, in a minor way, was adapting to the Western world. She was worried about her foster children, for when she compared their view of the world to hers or that of Tong Pooi's, they showed nothing but a loyalty to each other. They had no knowledge of Chinese history, only the memory of their parents' hatred for their Chinese homeland. Somehow, she must teach them about China, about Chairman Mao and how he had made the people of China stand up and walk on both legs.

She could see beyond the harshness and starkness of it now, for that great experiment, despite its many problems, was just. The few strands of barbed wire between Fragrant Harbour and China separated two vastly different worlds. Chairman Mao was teaching the people to respect each other even if they did not belong to the same family or clan. Some of the commune's plans could seem childishly naive when viewed through a Hong Kong lens.

The one thing that the simple commune had that this mighty city lacked was a will to work for the future, to work beyond its own desires for a China yet to be born. She suspected if the children did not have this ideal, they would not be regarded as Chinese later in their lives. Drowsily, she wondered what she should do, but there was no answer, and so she slept.

Ng San Fong arranged for them to meet Alice Chen for lunch and Woo Sing excused herself early from work to return home and change. Alice would be immaculate and she was not going to let her think that her grooming lessons had been forgotten. Inspecting herself with approval, she smiled at the memory of her baggy blue trousers and loose jacket. *I have become very vain*, she thought, *but it suits my present life.*

Alice was punctual and very calm, but both women sensed an inner anxiety, for she no displayed her customary disdainful look. Ng San Fong smiled and waited quietly to hear what would emerge from behind the polite chatter. When Woo Sing mentioned how grateful she was that Denys had warned her of the share market crash, Alice could no longer contain her emotion. Her expression told both women she had lost badly.

'I am consolidating my investments and wondered if you would be interested in buying my share of the partnership,' she announced, well aware a bluff would be wasted on Ng San Fong. Ng San Fong looked fierce but said nothing and simply passed a dish of pork towards Alice, who sat immobile and silent.

Ng San Fong knew she now had the power to badly damage or perhaps even destroy Alice Chen's castle of money. For money was a castle—no less effective than the landlords' towers of ancient China in which the wealthy took refuge in times of trouble. Alice had tried to lure Ah Ho away for commercial reasons and Ng San Fong could have lost him. However, the episode had begun their life together, so she could be even-handed with either vengeance or gratitude.

There was nobody to replace Alice in the sales side of the partnership. Woo Sing, although beautifully dressed, still looked like a dolled-up country girl, while Alice gave the appearance she had always walked on plush carpets and dined only in the grandest restaurants. She could sell their products and Woo Sing could not. Ng San Fong decided to extract a little revenge.

'We are not interested in buying,' she said, knowing it would be almost impossible to sell to anyone else. Alice took the blow calmly and said nothing, but Ng San Fong could sense that she had struck well.

As Alice made a move to leave, Woo Sing began to speak, but Ng San Fong interrupted her. 'I will lend you the money at eight per cent simple interest repayable out of your share of the profits.'

Alice barely hesitated. She grasped the hunchback's hand in hers to accept and quickly left.

'A good deal, Ah Sing, for she will work hard to pay the money and our business will increase,' said Ng San Fong cheerfully. It had been a good day. She too had lost money on the market but knew she would soon win it back.

*

The factory was becoming increasingly complex. More and more complicated machinery was being purchased for Ng San Fong's intricate designs. Seung Mei, who supervised much of the machinery, hated these new purchases, for her traditional Cantonese outlook was that anything new was troublesome. Ng San Fong always knew when a machine had gone wrong as Seung Mei would appear with a long list of excuses but few suggestions as to how to fix it. Ng San Fong preferred Woo Sing to tackle these breakdowns despite Woo Sing's irritating tendency to quote Chairman Mao. 'We must learn to stand on our own two feet and be independent of the repairman,' Woo Sing would say as she searched for the solution.

The demands of the factory, her son and her foster children gave Woo Sing scant time for other thoughts. She was totally occupied with each day's problems and if any man had asked for her favours, she would have rejected him. Desire had completely deserted her. Yet she was very happy, even though her foster children were difficult to control and her amahs hard to pacify.

She had started to read the children stories about the revolution. They were indifferent to their homeland and frequently reminded her that their parents had told them many bad things about it. So she tried another way by reading them ancient stories about magic foxes and poor scholars whose devotion to their parents earned them a rich reward from a generous emperor. The children enjoyed these and some she repeated several times.

Gradually, she introduced them to stories about the terrible years of the Japanese occupation and the fight against Chiang Kai Shek. To hold their interest, she told horrifying tales that incurred the wrath of the amahs. She told them of her own childhood, but the children were not interested. They clamoured for more magic foxes and so the cycle began again. The children were loyal to each other but Woo Sing felt that she remained an outsider.

Several times she visited Tong Pooi in the hope of meeting Wa Hing and finally she succeeded. He appeared cheerful but guarded, for he knew Woo Wai San would have told her of his new life.

'Ah Hing, please come and tell stories to my children sometimes,' she pleaded and he agreed.

The children loved his stories for he had a gift of making simple words shine. Woo Sing would enter the room and listen as his magic foxes and wicked emperors gently drew the children back to their homeland. She never told him why she wanted them to hear the stories for he would have gently scorned her. Stories are for telling and not for learning, he had once told her. *Perhaps he was right.*

She and Seung Mei went for an interview, or rather were *called* to an interview, by the principal of a well-regarded school. The women had optimistically entered their children's names, for there was tremendous competition for places. The children came with them. The smaller ones were placed in a room without supervision for an hour to see which ones would cry. Those who did were quietly removed and the parents told to try another school.

The smallest, as young as three, had to know their names in English and Chinese and be able to count to ten in both languages. Seung Mei had prepared her child but although Woo Sing's younger foster child easily passed the crying test she was excluded because of her lack of English.

'But this is a Chinese school,' Woo Sing protested. The principal was not interested and referred her elsewhere.

Seung Mei was luckier. Her children passed, but she found that more children were accepted than there were places. To guarantee admission she had to make a donation to the school fund. This ensured that her children had gained a foothold in the long, dreary and exhausting climb, which was the fate of the ambitious scholar in Fragrant Harbour.

Woo Sing decided to ask for help from Ah Yee who was delighted to be asked. She spent several happy mah-jong sessions finding out about school standards and costs, direct and indirect. They chose a school where pupils were taught Chinese and English, the uniforms cost as much as a socialite's ball gown, and where the books were worth the same as rare editions, in cost if not in value.

*

Mary Hunter found her days wonderfully full of running the business, managing a household, and each day learning a little more about the man she had married. One evening, she found him sitting before a small incinerator in their tiny patch of lawn and shrubs. He was burning the contents of several boxes arranged in front of him.

She walked up to him and examined the material due for the fire. It consisted of photographs of young women, almost all Chinese, most of them attractive and some very beautiful. The photographs were not obscene, the women were clothed and most were beautifully posed. He was startled by her quiet approach and began to say something. She shook her head and took the pictures from his hand.

'There is no need for this,' she said returning them to their box. 'They gave you pleasure once and someday the photos may give you pleasure again. You take very good portrait photos. Could you show me? I've always wanted to know more about cameras.'

They took the boxes upstairs and he took out his camera to explain the finer details. As she sat trying to concentrate on what he was saying, she kept thinking of the photos of the girls, comparing their lot with the exploited and dead women strewn about by Sir William Williams.

The couple was so immersed in the lesson that they almost forgot to go to a reception at one of William's clubs, arriving slightly late. To her annoyance, the first person they met was Kim Williams. He had assumed the vacuous amiability of his father, but she knew a determined and unpleasant man existed behind the smokescreen.

'What a sound bargain you drove for your friends at the plastic factory,' he said after congratulating her on her marriage, adding with false joviality, 'There is great pressure on us to let others have the compound.'

'It is preserving your own interests if you do not. It would be best to let it remain as it is,' she said, regretting the words as soon as she had uttered them.

'How is that?' he asked quickly.

'I cannot tell you now but in due time you will know,' she said.

'There is a local saying that you cannot wrap fire in paper, and so in due time I will know what you mean,' he replied.

For a while after they parted company she felt upset by his words. Her husband noticed but did not ask for they respected each other's pasts.

Even if Kim finds out about the child, Woo Sing will cope, Mary Hunter thought. *I have great faith in her.*

Chapter 18

Hot pursuit

Ng San Fong sensed Tong Man Ho was unhappy. Eventually, she wheedled out of him that his family was disturbed about their relationship.

'It would be simple if we were married,' he said, not wishing to directly ask her.

Ng San Fong drew in a sharp breath. Now was her chance, the only one ever likely to come her way.

'I would like that very much, Ah Ho, but it is what others would say about us that hurts me.'

'We could be married quietly,' he said. 'The only people who count are our parents and families, and they would agree. We must ignore what others think or say about us and cannot let them ruin our lives,' he said.

She remained silent. He gathered her gently in his arms, 'Only you and I know how brave we have to be to face every day among ordinary people. Your friends will admire you and the rest do not matter.'

'You might tire of me,' she said.

'Or you of me. That is a risk we have to take.'

She knew she could never be even faintly attractive. Even the plainest woman could lie straight for her man, and the plainest woman need not attract attention to herself as Ng San Fong always did.

Despite the pain of their lovemaking, she knew she desired Ah Ho. He was right, they should enjoy each day and each other, ignoring all else. Since the day of the fire and meeting Woo Sing, her life had changed beyond what she had ever dreamed possible. There was no need to stop that change now.

'Yes, yes, yes,' she said. 'We will be married.'

The marriage took place in private, for Ng San Fong could not bear the thought of the usual ceremonies, even among her friends. That was no reason, however, for the Tong family not to welcome the new woman into their household and a large banquet was held anyway. They were accustomed to her strange form and many admired her for the business aptitude that had made their relative a wealthy man.

He is not as smart as my other sons, thought Ah Ho's father, *and yet he is richer than them*. This paradox did not worry him. Ah Ho did not seem to care that little had been spent on his education and that he had been the least favoured son. He made it plain that he would observe his duty as a son and the old couple finally felt secure. There was loud talk, clattering of dishes and children shouting or laughing. Ng San Fong bathed in the sound like it was the climax of some great orchestra. At last she felt she belonged, for here was a family of suitable size for a Chinese girl.

Woo Sing and her five children were seated close by and once more Tong Pooi astounded all in his role as the small snake who eats an elephant. Whatever the turmoil and trouble of the outside world, Ng San Fong felt that inside this family was the strength to overcome it.

Woo Sing was busy with the children and Tong Pooi, but she also felt the pleasure of being among family. *This is a real family*, she thought. She decided to write to her own people at home even though there were many things she could tell them. She could say she was safe and well and that she had sufficient money and would send them some. She realised that most of her local friends had no family and were among the loneliest people in the city. *A family tends to stay within a family so it is difficult for an outcast to find a place here.*

Slowly she was being permitted to enter the closed circle of her foster children's lives. This kind of family was what she had wanted for herself and with Wa Hing's help she would make it happen. Perhaps the party was right about families blocking progress, but in the end, there would have to be a halfway solution for the family was the Chinese way.

Without any fuss or invitation, Wa Hing visited Woo Sing's house more and more often. Much of his time was spent with the children and he often talked to them about rocket ships and space travel. They understood little but sat quietly, knowing that when he had finished he would tell them a real story.

Woo Sing never asked about his work and he never discussed it. But they knew at some point they would have to.

He was no longer handsome, as the scars on his face, although fading, gave him a slightly sinister appearance.

Woo Sing became aware of the inner sensations she had dismissed along with her English lessons and occasionally felt tempted to ask him to stay. But a neutral topic of conversation was best and thus Canada and America were discussed at length.

He was so keen to visit both that she bought several books to check the truth of his glowing accounts of life there.

'There are many Chinese in Vancouver,' she told him one evening.

'That city is too quiet, I think New York would be better,' he replied.

'How will we get in?'

'Surely you can pay to get in, you can buy anything with enough money.'

'I'm not sure you can buy Americans. They are unusual,' she countered. But it was pointless talking about a new home until Wa Hing cut himself free from his present job.

The children were annoyed when Ah Hing told them that he had to leave soon.

'Why?' they chorused.

As Woo Sing entered the room unnoticed, he said, 'Because I must be at the Kwun Tong Wharf at eleven.'

He accepted tea and cakes from Woo Sing. 'Why hurry?' she asked.

'I have to go,' he replied.

'I know what you do,' she said, anger rising. 'Woo Wai San

told me. It is a crime against the Chinese people. Even the English don't run drugs.'

She had said more than she had intended. She hadn't meant to speak like this but now it was too late.

'You forget your history. It was the English who began it all,' he said quietly.

'I am looking after four victims of that dirty trade, Ah Hing.'

'I know and I admire you for it. You are rich, Woo Sing, and what you learnt in the commune lasts. You are Hong Kong's richest and most genuine communist,' he laughed.

'I don't want to discuss it,' she said.

'Ng San Fong says that you are a communist in spirit but a capitalist in the flesh. What do you think?'

'There is no other way to be in Hong Kong,' she replied. 'I belong to China and so do you. If it were the English you were destroying, it would not be so bad, but it's our own people.'

'It is a business, a business run for Chinese by Chinese. No one forces them to buy,' he replied.

'Once you have taken drugs, no one needs to force you,' she said bitterly.

'I must go now,' he said, but Woo Sing stood in front of him. 'Ah Hing, stay with me.'

She stepped close to him, her desire entwined with anger. She took his hands and placed them on her breasts.

'These have always been for you,' she said.

She studied his face, seeking any change of mood. She felt his hands exploring her swelling nipples.

'All of me has always been for you, Ah Hing, I know that now.' She thrust her body hard against his and felt him responding. He gently pushed her away.

'I must go.'

'Don't ever go again. Stop now,' she pleaded. but he was already walking to the door.

'Your kind killed these children's parents!' she screamed at him. 'Yet you can laugh with them and tell them stories. There are other children who have not yet lost their parents, Ah Hing. Stop now, please.'

Her voice faded away as she began to cry.

He stood at the bottom of the stairs, looking back up at her. 'Whether I stop or not it will go on. They will kill us both.'

She shouted for him never to visit her again, not caring who heard, choked by her emotions. As she rushed back to her room, she heard a car drive away. She would call Ian, call him to come and ravish her as he used to.

She hesitated when he answered. Without announcing herself ,she mumbled into the receiver, 'A drug gang at the Kwun Tong Wharf at eleven o'clock tonight.' She cut the call.

Because tips from women were so rare, they were usually regarded as genuine. There was little time, but as they were planning a raid later that night, Ian reckoned he could assemble his team to get there in time. He anxiously rang his boss for permission to proceed.

Superintendent George, relaxing with an old Chinese friend, at first sounded annoyed at being disturbed.

When Ian told him he was certain it was a genuine tip, he

said, 'Wait a minute, I have the operation plan here at home and will check the other information.'

As Ian waited, he thought about how the old man deserved a break. *He even takes the plan home just in case. At last, it may pay off.*

Superintendent George turned to his old friend, Ng Laan Sang, and asked, 'Is your firm running anything in Kwun Tong tonight?' Ah Sang shook his head and George said, 'It must be some new crowd, or the other side. I will tell Campbell to move quickly.'

'Thanks,' said Ah Sang.

George returned to the phone. 'Proceed, and the best of luck. Let me know what happens.'

Ian felt triumphant, sure of the tip. The caller's voice had sounded vaguely familiar but most Cantonese sounded the same over the phone.

'A damned enthusiastic idiot, that Campbell,' said Superintendent George. 'We could do with fewer of that type.'

'You are wrong, old friend,' said Ng Laan San, smiling. 'I wish there were more, for how could we run our business if the city was not lawful? I need my house and businesses protected and I do not wish to walk the streets surrounded by guards. Besides, Superintendent, if all policemen were as business-minded as you, the money would be shared among many. Have you thought of that?'

'Sometimes I wish I could go back to England. I find you Chinese too complicated,' George replied.

'My old friend, you are wrong. We sell things, buy property

and trade things, always trade,' grinned Ng Laan San.

'I wish some of your energy would rub off onto my son,' George said, seeking to change the topic, but Ng Saan Lan would not be deterred.

'Ah, yes,' he said. 'Wealth is inclined to drug the son of the *gweilo* but spur the Chinese boy. Perhaps I could find your son a job in one of my more respectable *gweilo* businesses.'

'I would be very pleased,' said George warily.

There was little time to plan an ambush. They needed to be in position by half past ten so that any early scouts would not detect them. Ian felt the tension growing as he collected his men and gave them brief instructions. This time they would succeed.

One of the cars was slow to start and he cursed the mechanic who serviced it, a sure hint to his men that this was an extraordinary job. Seldom did the even-tempered Scotsman raise his voice. The cars sped past the airport, sirens silent as they threaded through the heavy traffic.

Ian reviewed the sketchy plan and realised there was no water cover. There had been no time to call the marine police. *If they take to the water we've lost them*, he thought. But that was unlikely and they should still get a good haul if the tip was correct.

*

As Wa Hing drove, he watched Ah Fung and wondered why he had been sent as his guard instead of the usual old man. He must have guessed what Wa Hing was thinking, for he said, 'There will be a lot to unload this time.'

Wa Hing nodded. It was not really his concern. His job was to remain at the wheel for a quick escape in the unlikely event of an ambush.

They drove with the steady unobtrusive pace of a commercial vehicle on a harmless, if rather late, errand. He thought about Woo Sing and knew his time as a driver must soon come to an end.

They would have to plan their escape in great secrecy, but they would manage. He had joined the firm as a country boy and he would leave it as a man. They must go together, for the firm would soon find out where Woo Sing lived if they did not know already. He hated to think what Ah Fung would do to her. On second thoughts, maybe Woo Sing should go first, for she had her children and her wealth to shift while he had nothing. They would have to take Tong Pooi. That would be hard, but the firm knew that he lived with the old man.

He would leave Woo Sing alone for a few days, *to cool off and heat up*, he thought with a big grin.

'What's so funny?' asked Ah Fung sharply, rapidly bringing Wa Hing's daydreaming back to the present.

'Something a girl said to me,' he answered.

'Ah, girls,' said Ah Fung. 'I like the unwilling ones best.'

The junk was already alongside the wharf. Bales of rough cloth were stacked in two heaps. Ah Fung jumped from the cab and Wa Hing began backing to the nearest heap. After they lifted the first bale, Ah Fung began a rhythmic rapping of the metal bar on the vehicle's tailboard, the universal Hong

Kong sound of a reversing truck.

Wa Hing listened carefully. He must stop the truck as soon as the rhythm ceased. Rap, rap, rap, rap. Ah Fung banged a precise steady beat, judging the distance to the second bale.

Suddenly the rhythm changed, rap-rap-rap-rap. Fast and urgent. The message was clear. They had to get out quickly.

Wa Hing put the truck into gear and lurched away at high speed. A shout and cry of pain told him Ah Fung had been jolted off the back, but he did not stop. His instructions were to get the truck out in an emergency and that is what he would do.

He disliked Ah Fung intensely. Despite his cheerfulness, he was too cruel even by Wa Hing's standards. A car pulled alongside but he nudged it away with the truck's heavy bumper bar and caught a brief glimpse of it spinning into the opposite lane. It was a bad area to be for there were few roads or side streets to turn into.

He raced along a main road and turned into a side street. An old woman stepped out in front of him. He braked and swung over the wheel, almost stopping to avoid her. Ah Fung would have told him to run her over but he couldn't do that even though he lost valuable time.

He thought of abandoning the truck and disappearing into the resettlement blocks but he knew the firm would hunt him down and he and Woo Sing would be unable to flee. He had to stay with the truck, break the ambush and save the two of them.

*

The convoy of cars carrying the police team had been brought to a halt by a minor collision involving two broken headlights and a dented mudguard. The cars involved were angled across the road, holding up traffic for at least a mile. Neither owner would shift until the police came. Ian identified himself and ordered the cars be moved. His men pushed them to one side, ignoring the shouts of the owners.

The police team had arrived late at the wharf to find a truck already loading alongside. His men had swarmed across the road, some boarding the junk and others racing towards the truck but unable to stop it moving off. A man fell off the back and Ian drew his gun. Seeing no movement from the body on the road, Ian jumped back into the squad car with his team and drove off in pursuit. Others would cope with the junk. The truck was what he wanted.

When they tried to overtake, the driver bumped them off. For a few seconds he feared they were about to die as the lights of oncoming cars rushed towards them. Ian thought they had lost the truck but quick manoeuvres by his skilled driver quickly got them back in pursuit. He caught sight of the truck accelerating away down a side street that opened out into a broad road running close to the harbour. Ian knew he had it trapped and called the other cars to the chase.

Wa Hing knew he was cornered. All he could do was run to the harbour and swim for it. If he had time, he would burn the truck but the chase car was gaining.

He turned into a dead end where several old buildings offered good cover. He spun the truck into an alley, almost rolling it over as it screeched into an empty loading bay. For a few moments he thought he'd eluded his pursuers but then saw their lights approaching.

He lit a match and threw it onto some cotton waste in the truck, hoping it would catch. He scurried into another alley and worked his way along a wide footpath.

A shot rang out but the bullet went wide. Ian shrugged. He knew it was too dark for shooting with any accuracy but it would keep the pressure on. The lights of a turning car briefly lit up the alley. The beam illuminated their man trying to climb a wall. Ian drew on all his training and Scottish determination as he took aim. It was the best shot he would ever make. He heard the *thunk* as the bullet hit solidly into flesh and bone. Wa Hing did not even hear the shot being fired. An agonising pain seared into his back and his last conscious moment was one of pain and darkness.

'Got him,' cried Ian, almost under his breath. They had got the truck, the junk, the lot. Months of planning and waiting had at last paid off.

As they ran to the victim, Ian had a brief thought that the man had looked vaguely familiar when caught in the car's headlights. As they turned the man over it was clear he had been badly wounded. The police driver shone a light on the man's face and Ian knew immediately where he had seen him before: it was Wa Hing.

Ian walked a step or two away and was sick among some packing cases.

His driver, Ah Tung, ran back to the car to radio for an

ambulance and fire engine. The truck was alight and could set the whole street ablaze.

Ian returned to the junk to escape the hideous scene in the alley. He found everything in hand. His men had heard the news and congratulated him warmly but could see he was exhausted.

Ah Tung arrived. 'I will take you back to the station, sir,' he said.

As they drove, Ian gave Ah Tung a phone number. 'A woman will answer. Tell her Wa Hing is in the custodial ward at the Queen Elizabeth Hospital. Take her name and see that she is given admission.'

'I will see it is done and fetch the woman myself,' Ah Tung said.

A young doctor who examined Wa Hing in the custodial ward reported to Ian, 'He will need at least four pints of blood if he is to live.'

'Why aren't you giving it to him?' asked Ian.

'We are out of his blood group and someone needs to buy it.'

Without hesitation, Ah Tung said, 'I will send a man to buy supplies immediately.'

Ian handed him five hundred dollars, all the cash he had on him, and returned to the station in another car as Ah Tung went to buy blood and fetch Woo Sing.

She had spent the last few hours in an agony of reproach, anger, optimism and fear. Eventually she convinced herself nothing would happen as a result of her tip-off as the police were not good at catching drug gangs.

Maybe Ian had disregarded my tip or arrived at the scene too late. Perhaps the drug team had been paid by the gang and would not attack. Or maybe Ian was corrupt, although she decided that was unlikely.

She glanced into the children's bedroom and was on her way to her own when the doorbell sounded. Through the spyhole she could see a policeman. He gave his name and she opened the door.

'There is a man in hospital who needs you,' said Ah Tung.

Sick with fear, she climbed into the police jeep and took a few minutes before feeling able to speak.

'Is he a Chinese?' she asked.

'Yes.'

When she reached him, Wa Hing was unconscious, his face drawn. The stark light of the ward accentuated his scars but there seemed no pain in his features. Woo Sing sat as if in a dream, unbelieving. *Surely this is a hideous nightmare that will soon pass.* He was too strong to die. Since her life had begun in the city, he had been her one sure and safe oasis.

She watched numbly as nurses assembled technical apparatus and blood began to flow into his arm. His pallor improved. He stared blankly at her. One arm moved in small spasms and he grimaced.

After writing his report, Ian felt compelled to return to the hospital. Ah Tung told him he had asked the young woman if anyone else should be called. After some hesitation, she had given him the name of another woman who was now on her way.

'I'll not stay long,' said Ian, remaining in the shadows of the cubicle.

When Wa Hing stirred again, Woo Sing stretched forward to put her head against his side. They heard her sobbing. 'Forgive me, Ah Hing. I always loved you, sometimes as a brother and sometimes as a lover. You must forgive me for I shall join you soon.'

Ian recognised the muffled tones of the telephone informer. He knew now he had lost her forever. He looked at her, half stretched over the bed. Even in her grief, her vitality and grace seemed enhanced. Sick at heart, he knew his hopes for her playing a part in his future had passed.

She turned to Ah Tung, standing by her side. 'Do you think he heard?'

'Yes, I think he smiled a little.'

But the few lucid fragments of Ah Hing's dying brain were no longer listening. They gathered into one last act of life. As in a dream, he faintly saw the lights of his home winking through the drizzling rain in a rural village in Canton.

It was not Ah Tung's job to guard the prisoner, but he remained with the two women who sat silently, dumbly, by the bedside, watching Ah Hing's life ebb away. There were no tears or hysteria, only the grief and the dignity of what Ah Tung knew to be real love.

Towards dawn, he took them home, both so young that they could have been his daughters. They were obviously wealthy and professional. He decided this would need to be investigated, but for now his job was different. He instructed the amahs to watch the two women closely and to give them a large drink of wine or brandy if they had it.

The night had been a sad triumph. He hated the drug syndicates. He took no bribes and gave no mercy to those he caught. The death of a drug runner was no loss, even though two young women had grieved for him.

Ah Tung turned the jeep into the barracks wanting to tell his boss what he had done. But Ian Campbell was asleep and he did not disturb him. Whatever the news meant to him, there was nothing to be done now. But even he would have been surprised to learn that his tough and ruthless boss had gone to his dingy barrack rooms and cried himself to sleep like a child.

For Ah Tung, returning tired and with heavy limbs to his tiny family flat, the night remained a triumph, but a triumph without joy. Women would always grieve.

Chapter 19
Past and future

For a day or so, Woo Sing considered taking her child in her arms and jumping from the top of a factory building. She would not have been the first. Many such battered bodies had been collected off factory yards before. But somehow, she lacked the resolve and the extra amahs sent by Ng Mei Yee were very watchful.

Unknown to her, the food and drink she was given had been carefully mixed with some expensive herbs that blunted her sensations, her emotions and her will. Her children needed no such potions. They accepted Wa Hing's death with stoic grief which, in the way of childhood, did not last very long.

Somehow, Woo Wai San and a few others managed the simple funeral after going to a dingy mortuary to claim the body. Police sergeant Ah Tung attended the ceremony, mainly to see if anyone from the drug syndicate came to spy on the relatives. To everyone's relief, the syndicate was anxious to be as invisible as possible.

The two women paid for a grave site with good feng shui but wondered if Wa Hing would have cared. It was the children who saved Woo Sing, the children and the numbness that prevented her from suffering the sharpest emotions and remorse for her act of madness.

Woo Wai San said nothing, although Woo Sing suspected that she knew of the events leading to the death of her former lover. The practical Woo Wai San had long known it would end like this and someday she would say so to Woo Sing. Wa Hing had been brave and was nobody's fool, but he was also too kind to have been a successful triad member. He was a cheerful worker who had strayed into crime and the city had won.

The children admitted Woo Sing into the family circle in their own way. The six of them resumed patching together a daily routine to keep themselves distracted from the thoughts that doing nothing brings. The factory staff knew something had happened to two of the partners, for both were much quieter than usual. But while many guessed and gossiped, few knew the truth.

Tong Pooi attended the burial of the man who had become his only son. He said nothing and retreated to his street and tiny cubicle. It was Woo Wai San who arranged for his co-tenant to keep an eye on Tong Pooi's behaviour.

Woo Sing was preparing her accounts for a partners' meeting when Woo Wai San came to see her for the first time in many weeks. She said Tong Pooi was ill, breathless and coughing. His old street friends had found him and brought him back to his home.

'There is no time to waste with old medicines,' said Woo Sing, making her first real decision since Ah Hing's death.

Despite his protests, Tong Pooi was taken to a private hospital for Western medicine where his pneumonia was efficiently and promptly treated. His old street friends came to the hospital, each bringing a remedy from his own herbalist. They were collected without question or fuss by the nursing sister at the end of each visit and quietly thrown away.

When it was time for him to return home, Woo Sing decided to tempt him to live with her. He could help teach the children. He was not only kind and gentle but also brave, for he had the courage to stare eternal poverty in the face and never be afraid.

'I need help,' she told him. 'Help with the children as their learning is very poor. You can work each day if you wish but you will have enough money from teaching the children if you do not want to work in the street again.'

Woo Wai San also talked to him, and he reluctantly left his tiny room for a much grander one in Woo Sing's house.

'Why do you have such a large house?' he asked Woo Sing. 'We could live in a much smaller house and save the money you have spent on this one.'

Woo Sing shook her head but said nothing.

He tried again. 'Property and money can be taken away from you, but once you eat food no one can take it away from you,' he said crossly and rather irrationally.

'I have enough money for all the food we need and a big house as well,' replied Woo Sing as she unpacked his small box of possessions that required only a single drawer of a large cabinet.

'We all love you, Ah Pooi,' Woo Sing said.

The old man said nothing. He was thinking, *for me to be loved is a little strange, but to be old and useful is to be content.*

As the weeks passed, Woo Sing learned to accept that she, not Ian Campbell, had killed Wa Hing. She knew it was an act that would shape the rest of her life. Although she was only twenty, there would be no joy for a long time, perhaps never.

To seek happiness relentlessly, anxiously, was a Western custom. Although she had learned many Western ways, the persistent search for happiness was not one of them. She became content to work and to play with her children; to work with her partners and feel pleased when events ran routinely, smoothly and without surprise. Her body was so still it never troubled her, and the scenes of passion during her affair with Ian were remembered only with detachment.

She bore him no grudge and had briefly seen him several times. Woo Wai San had asked him to stop a triad gang of interior decorators who had terrorised their firm. They had demanded an exorbitant price and made threats to burn the house. Ah Tung had walked about the house, discussing a fair price loudly and repeatedly while mentioning he thought the police had seen the men elsewhere.

The gang left very quickly. Woo Sing felt reassured. To have money was good but to have powerful friends was even better.

Woo Sing began to read the children stories of the wider world. She did this in honour of Wa Hing's thirst to know more about countries outside China. She realised she had lived in two of the most different systems of human organisation that had ever existed. As she studied, it became obvious that the city was the last tattered remnant of a bygone age.

'Hong Kong, where everything goes and nobody cares,' a Chinese leader from another city state had once jibed, politely ignoring the fact that Hong Kong was run by *gweilos*.

She had seen the tremendous energy and ambition of her people when their actions were unfettered by the state—the businesses created from a few dollars, the optimism and tremendous hard work. To fail was no disgrace. One simply tried something else or the same thing in a different way.

It was the contrast between the people of Hong Kong and the people of her homeland that surprised her. There were plenty in the commune who could make a special sale or bargain in the town if they could. And here was the key to it all, for she could now see the miracle that Chairman Mao had performed. He had compressed this great power within her people and held it at bay, diverting it, releasing it, and always using it for China. There, they no longer worked for themselves or for their families, their ancestors or their clan, but for each other and for China.

She knew sometimes that the power nearly beat the giant who held it, that sometimes he pressed too hard. It was the only way and, looking at the city, Woo Sing knew that this was not the way.

There was a saying at home. It is easier to change the kingdom than the character of a man. There were eight hundred million of them to be changed somehow if China was to be saved.

Chairman Mao never professed to be more than a man, although some Chinese tried to make him so. Few of the gods of her fairy stories held such power. Few could move their hand and say a few words and have eight hundred million touched. They might be fearful, hopeful, pleased, angry or rebellious, but they would be moved.

In Fragrant Harbour, most people found that the only viable evidence of the state was the police. They were so closely linked with the triads and the drug smugglers that they could not be trusted at all. *It was so strange to think that at home, where things were so orderly, few police were seen. Yet here, where disorder was routine, there were police in every street.*

She knew the British were here because Chairman Mao wanted them to be. It would be easy for a Chinese army to sweep over the border, but she had never heard such an action discussed at home. It amused her to think that Sir William Williams, Denys Lam, the governor, all of them, herself too, the Chinese, the British, were all really working for Chairman Mao.

From Tong Pooi she had learnt how much her people had worshipped the past and why each family planned for the future. Without an assured future, the past would be forgotten. She realised the commune was a bigger family, but without blood ties, for they were still exhorted to save and work hard for the future, just like the old families.

It would be easy for her people to survive a war against the Westerners, but it would be more difficult to beat Western ideas. Machines brought wealth and wealth brought desire. So how were they to be hardworking, frugal and stable yet wealthy?

At home, it was the group that decided, yet they were also told to swim against the tide. Westerners were always swimming against the tide, and she thought this was why they had developed machines and were wealthy. *How did one maintain the group and yet be an American adventurer at the same time? That seemed impossible, but somehow, they must find an answer.*

To make China great, each of those eight hundred million Chinese could only have a little freedom.

She wondered if she would ever return to Canton. Maybe she would, but the Western life, if successful, was soft and difficult to leave. Looking at her people here, she could see that it would be generations before the personal ambition and desire for money could be extinguished.

Would they have to make a sacrifice almost as great as life itself? The sacrifice of one's ambition, intellect and natural abilities? There were too many sharp minds and too few strong hands, so who was to solve that?

When she tried to explain her thoughts to the children, they regarded such lessons as something to be endured for the sake of pleasing her. Their memories of home were fading and only the bitterness of their parents remained.

Wo Sing now refused to work on Sunday, another Western

idea. Instead, she took the children for picnics to the beach and countryside. Ah San had bought a car and their driver would take them and the children and Tong Pooi to have a barbecue, food that Tong Pooi persistently refused to eat.

'Western barbarism,' he would declare as he retired to some quieter place.

At times, their histories of China would clash and the children loved to annoy their two teachers with their contradictory statements.

'But Ah Pooi said … ' they would begin, watching for the look of resignation on their new mother's face.

One day, she was deeply shocked to realise her son still had no given name. And so Little Boy became Woo Man Chung, meaning 'swift and clever'. She had decided he would need both these qualities to survive in Fragrant Harbour.

Ng Mei Yee said nothing, but secretly rejoiced. She alone realised that the young mother had at last taken her part-*gweilo* boy for her own.

Tong Pooi was useful and content. Occasionally he took a trip to his old street. Another man had filled his place the day after he left, but looking at his Chinese characters, Tong Pooi did not think him suitable.

He still loved the street, and one day when rain poured down like water from a bucket, he stood beneath an awning alongside his laughing, joking countrymen to watch impatient Westernised walkers splash through the puddles and overflowing gutters. A wild beggar wandered past, oblivious to the water. Two schoolgirls, sisters, separated by the torrent in the street, shouted dares to each other to cross. An old street sweeper with her baskets sat thankfully as the rain gave her a rest no supervisor could deny. Only the men gambling on the fighting crickets took no notice, but they never noticed anything except the movements of the tiny creatures in the plastic bowl.

Sometimes in the emptiness of Woo Sing's big house, Tong Pooi longed for the sounds of his own people. Standing with them now as the rain poured down, he rejoiced.

One early summer day, Woo Sing took the children and Tong Pooi on a special journey. She had only told them they were going to a beach opposite the mainland.

She left the old man and the children and walked some distance before the landmarks became familiar. She had forgotten the exact date, but it had been about this time of year when she had first set foot here. Now, for no particular reason, she wanted to see it again.

There was a distant shout and she turned with annoyance to see the children racing after her. She would rather have been alone for a few minutes.

'Ah Pooi sent these,' the children shouted. They were waving small bundles of incense sticks in the air.

Tong Pooi no longer talked of Ah Hon and perhaps this was his way of saying he understood the fate of the boy he had so long desired to meet. She took the sticks and the box of matches but was at a loss of how to explain them to the children so chose to say nothing.

This secluded beach, which had once seemed the brightest

haven, was only a patch of coarse sand littered with stones. It was here she had landed with the man she had later loved and killed. Here she had seen the body of her closest childhood friend. Now she was here, she wondered why she had wanted to see it again. The children waited to walk back to the car, watching and trusting.

She was glad they would never have to make that terrible swim, braved at a time when she thought one needed only to swim four miles to be free. Now she understood how much greater that barrier was.

One could write to people on the other side as she had done, and she hoped her parents would answer soon. One could cross the barrier physically as she had done, but to cross it psychologically and ideologically might take a lifetime, if it ever happened at all.

She gazed at the distant shore, then stared down at the incense sticks in her hand as though wondering what they were for. All of a sudden, she bent down, scraped together a mound of sand, set the sticks upright and lit them.

As the smoke from the incense sticks drifted out to sea, she wondered who it was for. For Ah Hon? Or Ah Hing? Or the young student she had never met? Or was it for all of them? And for China, her beloved China? For all the power, sacrifices and the suffering that had yet to be endured to make her country great again.

In front of the silent wondering children, the country girl from Canton knelt on the sand and wept.

www.ingramcontent.com/pod-product-compliance
Lightning Source LLC
Chambersburg PA
CBHW060729190726
48285CB00001B/127